PRAISE F[illegible]WIFE

"*The Midwife* has the feel and complexity of a big novel . . . Amid impossible circumstances an impossible love story is born, the telling of which is flavored with a pinch of magical realism and fistfuls of harsh realities. The fate of women in the prison camps of World War II was cruel, and Kettu depicts the era with an agonizing precision. The sentences are juicy, earthy, meaty. To resort to a culinary comparison: as an author, Kettu has not satisfied herself with tenderloin and sirloin alone, rather she also understands the straightforward delicacy of liver, kidneys, sweetbreads, and gizzards. It is a helping of innards served piping hot: frightening but fascinating."

—The Statement of the Runeberg Prize Jury in awarding *The Midwife* the 2012 Runeberg Prize

"Astonishingly wonderful . . . An exceptional reading experience."

—*Turun Sanomat*, Finland

"Katja Kettu's storytelling abilities have been compared to those of Karen Blixen [aka Isak Dinesen]. I associate her with Jeanette Winterson. They both share an astonishing imagery and a fruitful relationship with the grotesque, with its raw vulgarity, exaggeration and carnevalistic shifts in equilibrium . . . *The Midwife* is an astonishing novel with a raw soul, brimming with liberating energy. It wouldn't surprise me if it ended up on a shelf with the classics."

—Cecilia Nelson, *Göteborgs-Posten*, Finland

"Katja Kettu demonstrates strikingly how there is only a breath between caring and birthing, and violence and killing. Both the victim and the executioner co-exist in the same person. The reader will be both fascinated and repulsed by *The Midwife*, which glows from its first page to the last."

—*Aftonbladet*, Finland

"*The Midwife* is not a book you read, it is a book you live through to the very last breath. It is impossible to get through it without it devouring you."

—*Dagens Nyheter*, Finland

"The depiction of this magical love story makes the novel heartbreakingly intensive and almost explosive . . . Katja Kettu's narrative is full-bodied, poetic and impudent."

—*Arbetarbladet*, Finland

"Kettu's narrative has power, natural talent, ferocity that's almost unreal."

—*Dagbladet*, Norway

"A naked, raw description of what war can do to a man and where love can take you."

—*Adresseavisen*, Norway

"Tremors on the Richter scale of love."

—*Jyllands-Posten*, Denmark

"Although the language—alive, intelligent, coarsely poetic—is the first thing the reader notices, it by no means hampers the other merits of the novel . . . The author carries the story line stylishly by using different perspectives and points in time, revealing details gradually and only exposing the full picture at the end. Nothing redundant."

—*Latvju Teksti*, Latvia

THE MIDWIFE

THE MIDWIFE

KATJA KETTU

Translated by David Hackston

This is a work of fiction. Names, characters, organizations, places, events, and incidents are either products of the author's imagination or are used fictitiously.

First published by Werner Söderström Ltd in 2011 with the Finnish title *Kätilö*. Translated from Finnish by David Hackston. First published in English by AmazonCrossing in 2016.

Published by arrangement with Bonnier Rights Finland, Helsinki.

Published by AmazonCrossing, Seattle

www.apub.com

ISBN-13: 9781503938434
ISBN-10: 1503938433

Cover design by David Drummond

Printed in the United States of America

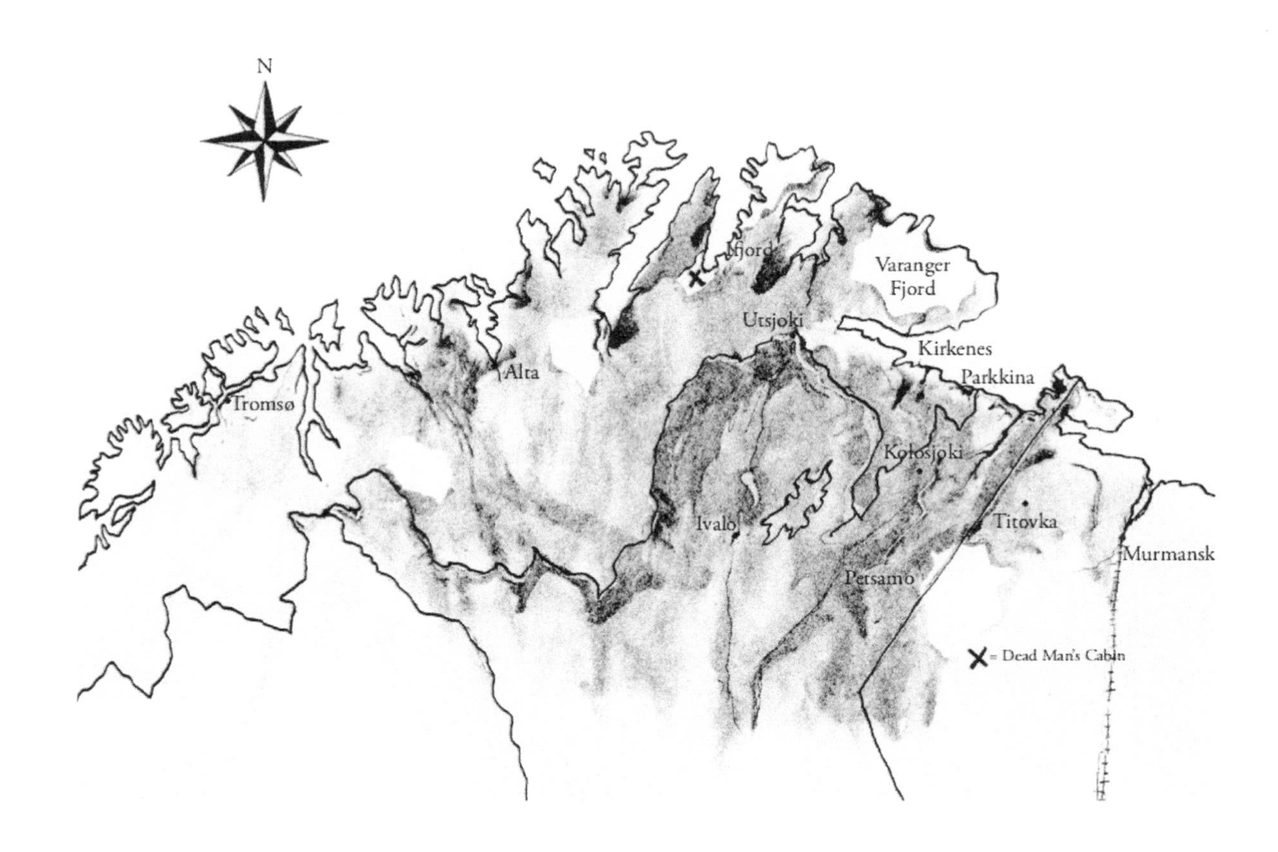
N
Tromsø
Alta
Ifjord
Varanger
Fjord
Utsjoki
Kirkenes
Parkkina
Kolosjoki
Ivalo
Titovka
Murmansk
Petsamo
= Dead Man's Cabin

THE LAPLAND WAR

JUNE 1944

President Risto Ryti assures German foreign minister von Ribbentrop that Finland will not negotiate a separate peace with the Soviet Union. The Germans have controlled the Lapland Front since 1941.

Locals dub the period the "summer of fear," as the Vammelsuu-Taipale line is broken during a large-scale Soviet offensive and the Salla regiments, which had been operating under the Germans, are moved farther south.

The civilian population of Lapland is left unprotected. Atrocities committed by Russian partisans escalate. Entire villages in the provinces of Salla and Ivalo are destroyed.

Residents of Petsamo feel increasingly vulnerable because the local harbor has lost its strategic significance. The Allies have governed the Arctic Ocean coast since the sinking of the *Tirpitz*.

JULY 1944

Victory at the Battle of Tali-Ihantala forces Stalin to desist and interrupt his offensive. On July 12 the civilian population receives no news from the front.

Commandant Eduard Dietl, a German officer sent to oversee operations in Lapland, is killed in a plane crash in Austria. The heavy-handed Lothar Rendulic is named as his replacement.

The Germans speed up the construction of their fortifications. The code name of the Karesuvanto station, running across western Lapland, is Sturmbock, and the Ivalo station is known as Schutzwall (the "protective rampart").

Suspicion toward the Germans increases.

The Germans plan the implementation of Operation Birke. The operation, first outlined in 1942, involved the torching of Lapland. Protecting retreating troops and securing nickel reserves from Petsamo are of the utmost importance.

AUGUST 1944

The Ryti-Ribbentrop Agreement is dissolved as Ryti resigns the presidency. On August 4 the Finnish parliament unanimously elects Mannerheim as Ryti's successor.

German defeats on all fronts encourage Finland to enter into a separate peace with the Soviet Union. Rumors of mines and the construction of fortifications rapidly spread through communities in the north of Finland. The Germans begin to destroy evidence of the existence of prison camps.

The Germans begin to seek out resistance fighters from the Allies and the NKVD, notably in the area around Petsamo and Kirkenes. In the final years of the war, several hundred civilians are executed and villages destroyed, partly in retaliation for sabotage strikes.

People in Lapland are worried that Finland will hand over the territory to the Soviet Union as part of any cease-fire agreement. Military leaders in the south begin planning the large-scale hiding of weapons in preparation for a future guerilla war.

SEPTEMBER 1944

A cease-fire is agreed. Finland ceases its military operations on September 4 and the Soviet Union on September 5. The terms of the cease-fire agreement include the removal of all German troops from Finnish territory by September 15. At the time, there are around 200,000 German soldiers in Finland.

At first German troops begin moving peacefully, as agreed, in what came to be known as the "autumn maneuvers." Infrastructure is destroyed and bridges blown up, but civilian settlements are left untouched. No battles take place.

The Control Commission demands that Finland enter into direct combat with the departing troops.

Around 168,000 people and 51,000 animals are evacuated from northern Finland to Sweden and Northern and Central Ostrobothnia.

Hundreds of Finnish women leave with the German soldiers. Some are taken with the troops, others left behind.

On September 15 the Germans initiate Operation Tanne Ost, an attempt to occupy the island of Suursaari in the Baltic Sea. This gives Finnish military leaders the moral justification necessary to engage in battle with the Germans.

On September 19 Finland signs an interim peace agreement with the Soviet Union. The terms of the agreement include the surrender of Petsamo and the return of regions lost during the peace agreement of 1940.

Rovaniemi Liaison headquarters, which had previously collaborated with the Germans, is relieved of its duties. Lieutenant General Hjalmar Siilasvuo is appointed head of the III Corps in northern Finland.

OCTOBER 1944

Finnish troops attack German strongholds in Tornio on October 1. Lieutenant General Hjalmar Siilasvuo acts without the official jurisdiction of the defense command. The battle lasts one week and claims the lives of 376 Finns. The Lapland War begins.

In retaliation, German troops take 262 civilian prisoners. They threaten to execute the hostages unless German prisoners of war are released. These demands are not met, but the Finnish prisoners are eventually released.

Finnish troops begin chasing the Germans out of the country. The orders of the Control Commission are to surround and destroy the retreating German troops.

The first Finnish troops arrive in Rovaniemi on October 14, but they are forced to watch from the shore as the heart of Lapland is destroyed. In the space of two days, the city is in ruins and the Germans have gone.

Because of the devastation to roads and bridges, it is impossible to catch up with the retreating German troops. Siilasvuo's army lacks air cover and heavy artillery. Meanwhile older generations are rehoused in accordance with the stipulations of the Moscow Armistice. The Lapland War was often referred to as the Lapland Crusade, because only younger reservists took part in it.

As they retreat, the German troops destroy their prison camps and any evidence thereof. Zweiglager 322 at Titovka was one such camp.

Most of the Finnish women who had left on the arms of German soldiers are abandoned in camps in northern Norway. Only a fraction of them ever made it to Germany.

An extensive political purge is initiated in southern Finland, and many SS officers who served under the Germans either flee or try to hide their tracks.

A major Soviet offensive against Petsamo on October 7 hounds the German Alpine Jaegers' operations out of northern Finland.

Hitler agrees to the initiation of Operation Nordlicht, whereby fortifications built in Lapland are no longer to be manned permanently. Everything is to be destroyed.

Petsamo, badly damaged by Finnish troops during the Winter War, is burned to the ground again, this time by German troops.

NOVEMBER 1944

Active warfare ends in Finland. In Kilpisjärvi, a small group of exhausted reservists can only look on as the Germans retreat, making use of the Sturmbock station.

The Lotta Svärd and Academic Karelia Society are disbanded. Criticism of the women who worked for the Lotta Svärd is stern, as it is for the approximately 1,000 Finnish women in the employ of the Third Reich.

The status of the 700 or so children born as a result of liaisons with German soldiers is not acknowledged in the new social order. In northern Norway, the number of such children exceeds 11,000. Around 1,100 children are believed to have been born as the result of liaisons between Russian prisoners and Finnish women.

APRIL 1945

The Lapland War ends on April 27 as the last remaining German troops leave Finnish territory via northwestern Lapland. Only a battalion of around 600 riflemen is still engaged in trench warfare. From the German perspective, Operation Nordlicht was a success. Retreating troops were protected until the very end. Finnish Lapland and the Norwegian province of Ruija have been cleared of civilian population and all buildings burned to the ground.

The Soviet Union continues to occupy the eastern regions of Lapland until September 1945. For the residents of Petsamo, there is no chance of returning home.

An extensive haul of hidden weapons is uncovered in southern Finland, leading to the largest legal case in the Nordic countries. To the Soviet Union, however, the hidden weapons are evidence that Finland is ready to defend itself even in the most desperate of situations. It also gives people in the north of Finland renewed hope that Lapland will not be relinquished.

MAY 1945 ONWARD

Germany surrenders unconditionally on May 8. On that same day, the final German troops leave northern Norway.

Total Finnish casualties sustained during the Lapland War: 774 dead, 264 missing, and 2,904 injured. One-third of those who died were killed by land mines. German casualties: around 1,000 dead, over 2,000 injured, and 1,300 taken as prisoners. Prisoners were turned over to the Soviet Union.

The majority of those evacuated return to Lapland despite official advice to the contrary. Hundreds of civilians and mine-clearing personnel are killed by German land mines. Reconstruction is extensive. Over 22,000 new buildings are erected in only a few years.

In the following decades, approximately 800,000 explosives, 70,000 mines, and 400,000 other incendiary devices are removed from Lapland. Some civilians were killed by land mines as late as the 1970s.

FOREWORD

Contemporary witnesses compiled all the diaries and annotations presented in this work. In 1985, the undersigned acquired a wooden chest, ornately decorated in the Kurbits style, which contained these writings. For the sake of clarity, it must be stressed that the messages sent from Dead Man's Fjord fall into two categories. Messages from the agent operating under the code name Redhead were sent to the liaison officer of the Main Security Office (the RSHA) of the Gestapo and the Third Reich, whereas signals from Whale Catcher were sent by the Special Operations Executive (the SOE), the Allies' intelligence organization. Lines of communication appear to have been established with at least two mutually hostile informants. However, no messages sent to the Soviet Commissariat for Internal Affairs (the NKVD) have been preserved.

There is some doubt as to the precise location of Dead Man's Fjord, which features prominently in the transcripts. Some of the coordinates seem to indicate a location to the west of Ifjord, and some the location of Varanger Fjord or the area around Kirkenes. The discrepancy appears to result from the phenomenon known as Struve's Paradox, which first came to light during the land-surveying project conducted by Herr

Friedrich Georg Wilhelm Struve, stretching from the Black Sea to the Arctic Ocean. Struve's entourage arrived at the Arctic Ocean in 1855. The aim of his mission was to establish the precise size of the earth and to demonstrate that the planet is concave at its poles. The Struve Arc comprises 258 main triangles and 265 geodetic vertices extending across the territories of Norway, Sweden, Russia, the Baltic, Moldova, and the Ukraine. Due to exceptionally strong magnetic fields, Struve miscalculated the measurements around eastern Lapland and the Finnmark fjords by several dozen degrees. "There, at the farthest reaches of the world, I fear there is a tract not marked on any map. At that spot, the edge of the world is bare and white, and now every man strives toward the white."

HELENA ANGELHURST
Sammatti, Finland
May 8, 2011

PART ONE

DEAD MAN'S DIARY

September 6, 1944

My dear daughter,

I hope you will forgive me. I stand on the cliffs and stare out to sea, at the same straits where I first saw the whales. That was now four years, two months, and five days ago. They glided into the fjord like great, playful islands. In the evenings they sang me to sleep, lulled me into dreams that were more real than the gauze of mist that hangs in the sky for days at a time. In my dreams, your mother, the only woman I have ever loved, is waiting for me, her neck white.

I load my Mauser. Now there is nothing else I can do. I have prepared everything for the new arrivals. In the Kurbits chest there are twenty notebooks, each containing information and coordinates.

As I light my first smoke and inhale the world's potent spirit, I am not sad.

If only I knew whom they were sending. A man from the SOE, the Merchant, or Hyyryläinen? A spy from the NKVD? Redhead or another one of the Gestapo's men? For now I know with certainty what I've suspected for some time. They started calling this place Dead Man's Fjord for good reason. It must be one of the Allies' security measures against the Laplanders. Now I realize that the Dead Man will be me.

DEAD MAN'S FJORD

October 1944

I am a midwife by the grace of God, and I'm writing these simple lines for you, Johannes. In his wisdom, the Lord Almighty has granted me, of all the people on this earth, the ability to give life and to take it away. In the course of my own life, swept away in bloodshed, I have given both, life and death, in equal measure, and I don't know whether the path my life has taken was guided by the turmoil of our times or because the Lord decided that it shall be so. My skill is my cross and salvation, my burden and my damnation, and it has forged a crooked path for me through this life, one taking me far from home and far from you, my love. I scribble these memories in a small bay to the west of Ifjord. Winter hasn't yet reached the shores of the Arctic Ocean, though it's already October. Still, the air is numb and icy, the earth a bluish black, and the sky bears the furrows of God's brow.

As you know, I am nothing but an uneducated midwife, worthless, and coarse by nature. Everything I know I learned the hard way during the final months of the war, pricks and the blood-spattered earth as my instructors. I already knew that at the moment of birth, we all let out a small, gooch-tasting cry. Now I know that in the course of our lives, we shed many a tear, weep many woes, many laments, and that folks sob just as much in the trenches as they do in the ranks of the Wehrmacht or in the Motti bunkers at Kuolajärvi. It's all one. Sometimes we weep for joy, sometimes for sorrow, sometimes with a speck of grit in our eye or the barrel of a gun pressed against our foreheads, but in the measure of a single tear, every last one of us, we mortals eking out an existence in the Lord's unerring presence, is worthy of life. I weep too, though I'm not sure why. For my own sake, or because I'm uncertain as to which side of this conflict I find myself on? For now the Finns, against their mousey nature, have attacked the German wolf, driving it back while the Russian bear embarks on foul attacks from Varanger and Petsamo, and the whole of Lapland fills with a sense of disquiet. Everyone in these regions weeps—the White Guard for their broken dreams, the Jaegers for the switchboard Lottas, whose thighs were only yesterday still lolling with puppy fat, and the cherry-cheeked kitchen girl for the mobile spinning in the window of the soldiers' canteen. Only the Communists rejoice as they pull themselves up from the fetid earth, as if from the womb of Mother Russia herself, but even they will soon wail and cry out, for in the whole of my life I have met only one person who was truly incapable of tears—our friend Hermann Gödel, a man whose grubby hands gathered gold and glory like the black flank of a turbot hauled up from the groundwater and brought to the shore to breathe in the Lord's air. I'll tell you all about him, but later. Now I haven't the strength. Clouds of bluish ash hang above the fjord this evening, and my war hound, Hilma, is whining at my feet, looking for comfort. I've made up my mind: I must tell you everything, come clean about everything. I have left my position in the employ of the Third Reich and forsaken my life of the flesh in order to make amends with myself and with the Lord my God. Now finally I will pick up the bullet-crested ink pen that has lain beside my wax-covered jotter for days.

I know you're here somewhere, Johannes. For all I know, you could be lying in a truck, taken prisoner by the Russians, your eyes dug out of their sockets, or limping through a gorge, starving, your ankle gnawed away by a fox. But you're alive. That much I can tell. In a world of imperfect, sinful creatures, I am guilty of many things, but not a lack of love. And I hope these words will help reveal to me too just how the daughter of a devious Red Guardist and the village idiot's wench became the Angel of the Third Reich and the feared bedfellow of the SS-Obersturmsführer, and how I ended up clipping bulls' balls and carrying out the work of the Angel of Death at Titovka Zweiglager 322.

DEAD MAN'S FJORD

October 1944

I arrived at the cabin in Dead Man's Fjord exactly ten days ago. As the bloodshed in which I've been caught up draws to an end, everyone—those spared from the artillery fire of Stalin's Organs and those whom the bitter hounds of death haven't yet gnawed to the bone in the frozen hell of Petsamo—should thank their Maker. The Fritz threw me and my dog overboard the SS *Donau*, less than two weeks after leaving Kirkenes when the English almost sank the armored ship. After the little English tea party, there was no functioning navigational system on board; the radio and sonar anti-submarine equipment were broken. We rode the choppy seas. The officer corps was lying in the hold, stiff with nickel poisoning, while seasick Alpine Jaegers and a motley crew of home reservists roamed around on deck. After that, many things happened on board, things I'd rather not talk about, but it all resulted in my being thrown to the mercy of the sea. The worst of it was that they took away my map and compass.

A storm had been raging all week, and the latrines stank of gangrene and vomit. That morning, to our surprise, everything was calm.

The clammy, foggy weather tickled my face as little Alexei Ignatenko approached me. The Russian lad was the only one left on board who knew how to steer the ship, and that's why he was allowed to wander undisturbed around the deck in brand-new leather boots. Under his arm he clasped an ancient chessboard. I remember you laughing once, saying the only thing we'd remember about that kid was his ears. You guessed wrong. Instead of badgering me to join him in a game, Alexei said, "*Medizinitsa!* Time to go."

After that, for the very first time, Alexei called me by my real name. At that moment I realized I was essentially a prisoner of war, or worse. I felt woozy. I'd been dreading this moment. I ran my tongue across my new set of whalebone teeth (I'll tell you about that later, dear Johannes!) and asked, "What about the map?"

Alexei shook his head. We looked out at the sea as it sloped gently into the fog.

"The weather's fine now."

It was a lie. We both knew that even the whalers feared this kind of weather far more than they did the battleships. In weather like this, currents beneath the surface could snatch the ship and carry it hundreds of miles across the water without the crew noticing any movement. But I won't reproach my young friend for deceit. Without Alexei Ignatenko, I would have been hurled into the sea headfirst. The Alpine Jaegers lying on deck were exhausted from war, hunger, faulty supplies, rotten preserves from Sweden and Argentina, missing woolen socks, bedpans with holes, the howling of the amputees, and the incessant wind and snow. But more than anything, they were tired of me, their *Fräulein Schwester*.

I clambered into the dinghy without a struggle. Alexei handed me a Mauser. I gripped its cold surface when I saw who would be rowing. The one wearing a duffle coat with bone buttons was called Montya, a trusted prisoner from the Titovka camp. I imagined he would kill me the minute we were out of sight of the ship. I took a breath and stepped into the boat.

"Is the Mauser loaded?" I hollered to Alexei.

"Nyet."

Before I could even set myself on the thwart, something sticky hit me on the cheek. It began to trickle down under the collar of my uniform. I did not turn my head. At the last minute a small creature burst over the gunwale and nimbly climbed into my arms. Masha, the Skolt girl.

"*Parmuska*, don't go!"

These were the first words the girl had uttered in weeks, but it didn't cheer me. Now the scrawny lass wanted to come along, wanted to die with me, after all that had happened. I tried to shove her out of the dinghy, but the little thing grabbed the side of my wolf-skin coat the way a louse clings to a lumberjack, and so the two of us were lowered down to the mercy of the waves.

"I give you your life," shouted Alexei, craning his frail neck over the gunwale. "Now you give the world your laughter!"

It sounded so Slavic, so bleak and idiotic, that I had to catch my breath, and I would have shouted back something like *It's hard to laugh with the wrong teeth in your mouth,* but it would have been drowned out by the German soldiers' vulgarities. They gathered around Alexei and brawled, bellowing as though a whole war's worth of rage and grudge were suddenly bubbling overboard.

"*Finnenlümmel!* Traitor!"

Hocks of saliva dotted with chewing tobacco struck my face. Montya stared at me and groped his groin. I closed my eyes, and, my eyelids firmly shut, I shouted a final farewell. "To hell with you!"

The ring of the Germans' obscenities quickly died down once the boat was released from the side of the ship. The dark mountain of steel disappeared into the fog. I felt the languid, long-rolling sighs of the waters beneath us. I didn't look up at the Hilfswilligers, and especially not at Montya. I clenched my fist around the Mauser in my pocket. My heart was thrashing against my chest. What did Montya have in mind? A wooden truncheon dangled from the twined belt he'd stolen from one of the Skolt prisoners. His gun must have been in the pocket of his silver-buckled overcoat. Upon leaving the camp, Montya had become a rich man, and his eyes betrayed contempt as he stared at us swaying there on the thwart. Two cardboard suitcases tied to a yoke; a threadbare wolf-skin coat; the fingerless gloves Lisbet had given me, so beautifully knitted and purled; my nervous, war-weary dog, Hilma; and Masha, the silent Skolt girl. There was nothing left of my previous life. Masha edged closer and started sucking my thumbnail. She does this all the time now, big girl. And it was this that made the Hilfswilligers gawp at us, and probably what gave them the idea of taking away my beautifully embroidered gloves.

The Hilfswilligers left us at the first skerry. Oh, Montya, Montya, that Balkan-smelling bastard, the kind of gentleman who believed he could cure gonorrhea by screwing seals or stuffing his prick into some young trout's twotch. Even after trying it, he wouldn't accept that a fish doesn't have such a thing. He snatched my gloves and ran his fingers across his throat, then forced me to look him in the eye so I'd know he wouldn't forget. Now he's going to kill me.

I groped the pocket of my ripped wolf-skin coat and felt the Mauser. Montya raised his truncheon. The ship's foghorn sounded.

Montya didn't have time to strike me.

"Enough! Let's go!"

Montya clambered into the boat with a hiss. They left me the wolf-skin coat and the Skolt girl, and set off paddling into the fog. I watched them and wondered at how they suddenly looked like nothing but strange, lost hares. I almost pitied them as they crashed against the surface ice and rowed out to sea, going the wrong way around the skerry, which was shaped like a reindeer's head. Farewell, Montya-Pontya. I won't miss you.

The three of us stood there, Masha fumbling for my thumb with her icy lips and I grieving for my lost gloves.

In my world there have always been sounds. The sounds of the village, the whining of Big Lamberg's bairns, the wailing of the Kyrgyz prisoners at the camp, and the wheeze of the midges' incessant tormenting. Now I heard silence for the first time, and it frightened me like death. Long-nailed fingers of mist curled through the air, excruciatingly tickling my neck and shoulders. We hunkered there, each sniffing the air in different directions, listening, but there was nothing—no shapes, no sounds, no smells. Half an instant passed, perhaps longer. Hilma made a few halfhearted attempts to lie down; she wanted to lick the ice packed around her paws but almost slipped into the green slush below. The sea panted slowly, lazily. For a moment I thought I heard the sputtering of a motorboat through the fog, but then everything fell silent again.

Suddenly I felt Masha pinching my side. The girl was pointing at my feet. One of my suitcases was floating on the crest of a small wave, just out of reach. I had placed the suitcase at least two feet from the edge of the water, but now it was drifting away. It took a moment before I realized. High tide!

"We're in bother now."

I crouched down to lift my remaining suitcase farther up onto the rocks in front of us. I pushed Masha ahead and edged my way after her. It didn't work well. It didn't work at all. The ice beneath my hands was as slippery as a dragon's back. If either of us slipped, we would both be killed. The old mongrel thrashed beside me and farted into the brightening Arctic evening. I guessed the height of the cliff at about ten feet, but perhaps that was an underestimate. I recalled the fifteen-foot poles at the quayside in Pummanki and the fishermen's desire to get home before six o'clock. There was nothing else to do but climb. Crunching pack ice ground into my kneecaps.

We had to try.

Finally I managed to haul myself over the cliff edge.

Bewilderment.

I'd hoped to find myself at the end of a peninsula leading to a larger island, somewhere we could find shelter for the night. But on the other side of the cliff, another soupy moat of melting ice stretched ahead of us. There was nothing to do but sit down and howl with sorrow. The rising tide would soon carry us away, snatching me and Masha into its underwater currents. Our bodies would end up rattling against each other somewhere on the other side of Varanger Fjord, then drift all the way around the Korsnes Peninsula or farther still, to the place where the sea spits out her shipwrecks. The water level rose in lethargic sighs. Soon it was tickling our toes.

We couldn't climb any higher.

My hands were blue. I found myself caressing the Skolt girl's cheeks, and suddenly I felt an indescribable bitterness. I remembered only too well everything that had happened because of Masha.

Not Montya, not Hermann Gödel, not you. But Masha.

How much easier it would have been to die with warm hands, I thought. I'd cherished the gloves the Hilfswilligers had taken from me. They were a present from Lisbet. With those gloves on my hands, I could give a camphor injection in temperatures well below freezing. What's more, they were cozy and comfortable for the simple reason that they were my own, and not a smutty trophy pinched from the Russians. Collecting leather mitts and fur coats from the mound behind Operation Cattlehouse always left me feeling grubby. It was a pity that something Lisbet had knitted should be the Hilfswilligers' final piece of loot, their final reminder of a life in which people lived in fear of the Lord, lowered their heads in prayer, buttoned their trench coats right up to the top, and took off their hats upon stepping indoors, a life in which nobody spat in corners or pissed in the car's combustion engine, a life in which they gave pots of homemade jam as gifts and gurgled their morning hymns with a full set of teeth, their mouths parsley fresh. A life in which they knelt in the sauna, their joints scrubbed. In that world there was at least some rhyme and reason.

I felt the life flowing out of me like steam through my nostrils. I wouldn't be able to tell you everything I'd wanted to.

PETSAMO

June 1944

It was a June night the first time I saw you. We'd heard there was nothing coming back from the Karelian Isthmus but body bags. There were rumors of a major Russian offensive, and some folks said the lines had been breached. There wasn't a word about it on the wireless, but there was a hunched fear in people's posture. An unprecedented heat wave was caressing the shores of the Arctic Ocean. Blood pulsed in our veins, the turbots gasped for breath in the muddy waters of the Kolosjoki, the hares seemed exhausted, and the reindeer stags trudged across the fells beneath the silvery-yellow sun. Everyone was at it, sex and sensation aplenty. Only I was pedaling back from a job at the Salmijärvi Shanghai. The patient's medical card read:

> *Precipitate delivery. Child born prematurely, weight 3 lb 4 oz, height 13½ in. Life expectancy bad. Bleeding into vagina. Pumped blood into mother's veins with ½ in tube.*

What I didn't write down was that the child was the Pöykkö woman's eighth and that her gooch was so loose, I'd had to be quick with the shears to clip her knickers out of the child's way, or that I'd pumped away the excess fluids, sucked plasma from the needle, and spat it out. I'd been working without a break for twelve hours. I'd taken responsibility for the area around Parkkina and Liinahamari after things had gone so downhill for Aune Näkkälä that she'd locked herself in the woodshed behind the barn and refused to come out. What's more, I had to go everywhere by bicycle because all our oil coupons went toward repairing district doctor Etelän-Hulkko's coal carburetor. And there was plenty of work too because, as Aune Näkkälä had said when the Fritz first arrived, "Two hundred thousand fellows roaming the hillside will do nobody any good. Fewer cattle we'll have, and fewer pretty lassies too."

The Pöykkö woman had never been a pretty lassie, neither at the outbreak of war nor before, when the church's poor relief had assigned her a trusted Russian prisoner to help in the granary. Right up until the end of the pregnancy, she'd traipsed through the scrub with the Russian farmhand, gathering bundles of horsehair lichen that she boiled into feed for the cattle, and it was on those excursions that she'd ended up with the child in her belly. She'd come to visit me during the Northern Light season the previous autumn and asked if I could help her. I told her to go and see Aune. The Pöykkö woman implored me, saying she'd nothing to pay us with. I told her simply that children are a gift from God.

The Pöykkö woman's old man had been killed in the Isthmus the week before, sparing him the shame of becoming the local cuckold. My stomach ached from a meal of bread baked with bark and lichen flour. I thought of the Pöykkö woman's pallid body, her dimly lit cottage, the scuttling of cockroaches behind the wallpaper. The farmhand had run away and got himself shot. Children crawled across the floor, pale as turnip shoots. Every last one of the poor things had scurvy, maybe even rickets. Their lips cracked, their palates blistered, children as young as ten were losing their teeth. It's butter and milk they need. Ovomaltine. I resolved to send a recommendation to the medical authorities the following day, though I doubted they would approve it as they had nothing left to give.

I had to stop at the Parkkina crossroads. The Germans had blocked the road, as usual, though, to be fair, by this point there were fewer green-bereted Jaegers, trucks, and cattle convoys flowing eastward than before. Now they generally arrived at night. The last exodus had passed through the day before last, and I'd been counting on this night being a quiet one. It was not.

Old Keskimölsä stood by the side of the road, muttering that the quality of the newcomers was slipping, young whippersnappers barely out of diapers and decrepit old men who would soon need diapers again. Three years earlier crotchety Old Keskimölsä made a point of calling them an occupying force, just to be different from everybody else, but by now something had changed in people's perception of the Fritz, and the old man didn't know whether to bow or spit at them. Gone were the days when the old-timers at the fisheries stood at the roadside, praising the masculine prowess of the AK20 machine guns and extolling the Führer's wisdom in sending Alpine Jaegers, boys born and bred in the mountains.

"They'll not freeze to death come the first frost."

Back then the sight of an army of Alpine Jaegers in their green uniforms had seemed overwhelming. Now things were different. The girls from the Lotta Brigade no longer rushed up to the soldiers with bunches of flowers, though a few girls at the Salmijärvi Shanghai still showed a bit of ankle through the fence at the inn, and Old Keskimölsä's girl, Anette, stood as ever, flaunting herself in her summer dress. And then of course there was Jaakkima, the Alakunnas boy, whose brother had fallen in the Ukraine in 1942 while serving as a voluntary soldier with the SS Wiking Battalion and who for that reason considered himself an SS man too. He stood by the roadside, directing the traffic with his arms raised at an angle, and upon seeing me he shouted, "Red b-b-bastards, make way when the men of the Wehrmacht are m-m-marching."

He'd clearly gotten his hands on some of Jouni Näkkälä's moonshine.

"Don't you st-st-start with me, Jaakkima. I've whacked your backside before, and I'll do it again," I whispered to myself, then regretted it. After all, I'd been the one to drop poor Jaakkima and let him fall on his head in the first place.

"Weird-Eye," Jaakkima bawled after me, and this time he didn't stumble over his words.

Jaakkima Alakunnas, my very first delivery, the one whose life I'd saved when I first became a midwife by the grace of God in 1929. Jaakkima, the reason I've borne that cross ever since. First he had gastric problems. Then he developed a speech impediment, and nothing seemed to help, no matter how much they stretched his tongue with tongs or stuffed round stones into his mouth. The stammer was there to stay. Then fifteen years later the Fritz arrived in town. Now here he stood, yelling by the roadside.

I continued on my way and tried to dispel my irritation by admiring the rows of German soldiers. Young, innocent, boyish faces, the mouths of their cannons glinting in the midnight sunshine, eagle insignias on their berets, the black leather, the swastika flags. All this helped calm my mind. There was something comforting about the knowledge that Lapland was now full of thousands upon thousands of unfamiliar men who knew nothing of my shame. Yet still it made me livid, my dearest Johannes. Do you understand me? The fact that the locals still have the spirit to rile me, their Red bastard child, after thirty-six years. The Red bastard, the Weird-Eye. At the Big Lamberg house, my foster family never let me forget that I was a poor, orphaned creature to be kept in the closet, a child to whom nobody ever bid God's greetings in the street, and all because of my father. I didn't even make fifteenth reserve place for the Parkkina Lotta Brigade, though they took Lisbet Näkkälä, a sliver of a girl who to this day cavorted around the village in her Lotta uniform despite no longer having the right to do so, not after what happened at Marshal Mannerheim's birthday celebration a couple of years earlier.

Before I could wallow in self-pity any longer, two things happened.

First off, I heard the sputtering and rumbling of a wood-burning car behind me. I turned and looked. Jouni, chortling along in his Destroyer Ford, shouted at me to join him.

"Put your bike in the truck and hop in! Lisbet's having her bairn!"

"Why don't you phone for Etelän-Hulkko?"

As the district doctor, Etelän-Hulkko usually took on all the houses requiring more demanding procedures, or the houses that wanted nothing to do with me. The Näkkälä croft was one such place. Jouni was wrenching the crank of his Ford's combustion engine and cramming woodchips into the burner, muttering something about the damned phone not working. The bow-legged man from the operator's office had resigned the week before because his wages hadn't been paid for as long as anyone could remember. Now he'd gone to work for a more generous employer, the Fritz.

His news made me catch my breath: Aune's girl was having a child out of wedlock. Aune Näkkälä, a woman who could tell from a girl's tongue if she was with child. Aune, who had taught me the secrets of herbs and carbolines. Aune, the woman who was never wrong, who could tell the sex of the baby from its position in the belly, and who could command Northern Lights across the sky whenever she pleased. Jouni started to explain before I had time to look surprised.

"Mother's not up to it. Another bad spell. She's resting in the woodshed behind the barn."

Now I understood where Aune's troubles stemmed from. She'd crawled behind the barn out of shame for not having noticed in good time that her own pride and joy was expecting. She didn't dare show her face around the village.

Lisbet had always been Aune's weak spot. Her steely eyes loved that girl so much that she was as blind to her as a hawk moth brought out into the light. Of course, the whole tract knew about the beautiful Lisbet Näkkälä, and lasses like that end up having little accidents all too easily. Lisbet's demeanor and skills as an actress had been lauded in the pages of *Lappland-Kurier* when she'd performed in the student amateur-dramatics society's production of *A Midsummer Night's Dream*. Earlier that spring she'd started swelling and began eating clay and sand under the jetties in the harbor. Aune Näkkälä clenched her eyes shut and claimed the girl had constipation and tooth decay, and decided to treat her ergotism with bearberries and gargling-water boiled with sorrel.

Jouni's lips twitched to the rhythm of silent curses. I hesitated. I'd been forbidden from ever setting foot in the Näkkälä croft. Up there they lived by the crooked cross. Big Lamberg wouldn't like it, and Uuno even less so. He believed Aune's healing powers came from the Devil and had nothing to do with God.

I cannot say why I agreed to go. Perhaps I wanted to prove to Aune that I could carry on God's work where she could not. Besides, at the Näkkälä croft they still ate soft, moist cake instead of chaff bread; they dipped pancakes in their milky coffee while the rest of the country had already switched to a coffee substitute ground from roasted dandelion roots. But the real reason I acquiesced was, of course, because I saw you.

At first all I noticed was a young lad hopping from the back of a German truck and onto the road. Spotless boots despite the dust, a camera slung over his shoulder. Some sort of officer, I thought, judging by the insignias, though I didn't understand their significance back then. A Gestapo cape and SS lightning bolts on his shoulder. From his neck dangled a peaked cap with the emblem of a skull that was both frightening and exciting.

You turned the camera's crank and pointed it at us. I was taken aback. This can't be good, I thought. There were rumors that the Fritz sometimes pushed any combustion engines they found into the nearest ravine. You raised your hand in a salute and cried, "*Heil Hitler*, Bruder Rumrunner!"

I realized that you and Jouni must have known each other. Then you turned to me.

"Everything all right?" you asked.

I was surprised to hear you speak Finnish. And right from the start, your voice seemed to me like amber and the heady smell of smoked, burned spruce tar, almost too dark and too deep for such a slender frame.

"*Heil Hickler*, and the lass is fine too," said Jouni, and rambled that he'd better be getting home because his sister had gone into labor. "This here's the midwife."

"That's no problem!" You waved your hand. *"Halt!"*

And everybody stopped.

You carried on snapping photographs, as though the enormous convoy behind us were parading along Russenstraße for you and no one else. There was some confusion, as the mules didn't understand that the command applied to them too; the trucks braked and men bumped into one another.

Then you turned and looked at me, and you didn't recoil at the sight of my crooked eye, the way most men did. You opened your mouth to say something, but Jouni reminded us of the imminent birth. Was it possible to hitch a lift to Näkkälä on the Wehrmacht truck?

Yes, it was.

PARKKINA

June 1944

We could hear Lisbet's screams from the yard. I'd spent the journey sitting on the back of a green Tatra truck, my thighs caressed by the wind. Initially I tried to force my way into the cab beside you, Johannes, but Jouni forbade me. I didn't protest. There's no arguing with the greatest rumrunner in Lapland.

I didn't wait for Jouni to haul his stout body down from the passenger seat. I barged through a sea of head scarves into Näkkälä's rose-patterned bedroom. The air smelled of incense and blood. A candle flickered on the altar, and next to an icon, Greta Garbo gave a divine, papery smile. I gripped the white lintel decorated with lace, because the sight of Lisbet shocked me. She was still beautiful, but distress and pain were pushing forth from beneath the beauty. Her milky-white thighs were caked in blood and mucus, her hair stuck across her eyes, now wide with the fear of death. Without ceremony I slid my hand between Lisbet's thighs. I recalled my very first delivery, at the Alakunnas household, just as I did every time I midwifed.

To this day I can't say what spurred me into action the first time I helped bring a life into this world. The unfamiliar flesh. The smooth, open thighs, the pubic hair and the soft, strange wetness between her thighs, fingers slipping between the folds of flesh. The pungent odor of camphor and vagina. Something had compelled me to examine that unknown woman's insides, and I soon realized that the baby was in the breech position and was about to come out the wrong way. Until then I hadn't known the powers of the Lord, but that evening the spirit moved within me. That night a song rang within me, a song that lent me the expertise to flip the child around in the womb, and before long he was born as angry and healthy as a Stallo cub. When news of the miracle delivery reached folks' ears, such a clamor of joy and emotion ran through the village that it sent the waterfowl into early migration, and the whole of Parkkina went without seagull stew that autumn. It didn't seem to matter that the bairn slipped while I was washing him and fell on his head, leaving him with a persistent stammer. Nobody blamed me, and besides, damage like that is only diagnosed years later.

"The peace of God be with you," the womenfolk muttered at me for the first time in their lives.

"It's Big Lamberg's Weird-Eye. The Red bastard."

"God bless you, girl. You've a great gift."

That was the local midwife, Aune Näkkälä. She squeezed me in her arms the way no one had done before.

"You're Pietari's lass, all right. I mind your father. From now on I'll treat you like my own."

Aune's voice rasped like soft flesh beneath a slowly twisting, red-hot, cast-iron poker.

"You've a great gift and a great sorrow. We'll see what kind of crooked path the Lord has in store for you."

Quite. That's how Aune became a mother to me.

And now she lay moaning in the woodshed behind the barn. She was a tough woman. But it was because of Aune that I knew how to act. *Roll up your sleeves. Brush your nails with lard soap. Ask for carboline from the instrument case, and rinse your arms up to the armpit. Feel the vulva and sniff for infections.*

I pressed my fingers inside Lisbet. At least the baby's head was in the right place, but the cervix was only dilated about an inch and a half and the child was stuck. The cervix ran diagonally to the right, and the fontanel was on the left. Lisbet panted, gasping and sweaty.

"I've never been with anybody, Mammy . . . I never."

"Well somebody's got the lassie up the duff," muttered Old Keskimölsä's wife. "And I'll tell you one thing, it wasn't the Holy Spirit."

I told her to fill the samovar and boil some water. She stood there, wagging a loose-jointed finger at the sinner.

"Hold your trap when Aune Näkkälä's daughter's lambing," I snapped. "And will you hurry with that water."

Keskimölsä's wife did as she was told.

"Aye, it was God that knocked me up," Lisbet whispered, her eyeballs gleaming white.

Just as before, certainty came to me straight from the Almighty, flowed into my mind the way water bubbles up to the bottom of a bog hole. I saw immediately that I'd have to use the forceps. As I inserted the tip, sweat ran down my back. The German officer was outside somewhere, the one who'd looked at me without flinching. The one whose voice was like amber, who made the Wehrmacht stop in their tracks. I didn't want the bairn going up to heaven right there in front of him. I began to hum.

"At our time of need, we pray unto the Lord, and he shall aid all those who cry for help . . ."

Aune's moans carried in through the open window.

"My only daughter turned a trollop for the Fritz. An actress, that's what she was supposed to be. The new Greta Garbo, they said. Now look what you've done! They can both die for all I care, mother and bairn."

Neither of them died.

The boy was healthy and covered from head to toe in fine fluff. I slapped his backside, and straight away a merry bawling pealed out into the yard and behind the barn. Even Aune lumbered in to inspect the newborn.

"Well. You're back." She glowered at me. "Hairy little runt. Doubt it'll live till morning. Throw it in the swamp."

"Looks lively enough to me."

"The boy mustn't be left with Lisbet. She can't get too attached—he'll soon die all the same. And she can't sleep with a sickly child, she'll only end up with bags under her eyes and tits suckled to ruin. You'd better find a wet nurse just in case. Our Lisbet's too sensitive for a bairn like this."

I tried to stand my ground. He was a fine-looking creature, though he was hairy, and the smell was that of a healthy baby. I reminded her that such fur was normal for newly born children and that it would molt before long.

Aune wanted to see for herself what I'd scribbled on the patient card.

First-born child, mother 23 yrs. Contractions for four days. Forceps birth. Patient received six stitches. No complications. Child healthy and hairy.

Aune scoffed, slipped the card into her pocket, and that's where it stayed.

But an almost churchlike murmur ran through the congregation gathered there when you stepped inside. I recognized you instantly. The womenfolk made way, as they would for the Messiah. Jouni must have come in too, but I can't remember for the life of me. At most, a male shadow flickered behind you. No. From the very outset I saw only you, for your shadow engulfed even the greatest rumrunner in Lapland.

"Gute Nacht," you greeted us as you hunched under the doorjamb. You were almost a head taller than all those present.

"God's greetings, God's greetings," folks muttered along the walls and in the shadows cast by the lantern. It seemed the zealots and Bible-thumpers were happy to give you their God's greetings.

"Damn you, man, did you have to bring a photographer here to witness our shame?"

"Quiet, woman," Jouni barked at her. "He speaks Finnish."

Nobody seemed at all surprised at the presence of a reporter from *Lappland-Kurier* or by the fact that you took off your boots in the doorway. In an instant I realized that everyone in the room knew who you were. Nobody batted an eyelid as in slow, pleasurable movements you mounted a wide-lens camera to your tripod. LUDO 231, it read on the side. Those gathered held their breath as you set up the shot, focused the camera. Keskimölsä's wife carried lanterns over to the bed without anyone asking. Apparently people knew that good photographs needed light. You glanced up at Lisbet, your look a mix of distant acceptance and nausea. The hairy child was swaddled and tucked deep into her armpit.

Your eyes flitted across the women in the room, lighting on plaits, scarves, and skirts, caressing every face, and each of them seemed to flinch, even Aune Näkkälä. All of a sudden I understood the imperfection of my own womanhood, that and the fact that I was covered from head to toe in blood and membranes and that the umbilical cord I'd ripped with my teeth was still dangling from the side of my mouth. I spat it to the floor and prayed: Don't look at me now. Please God, please don't let that man see me now.

You did, of course.

Before I could disappear, your eyes were on me, your pupils zooming in and your brow furrowing like that of a botanist upon discovering an unknown species of forest fungus. Then, for a split second, I sensed something change, and for a moment they were the eyes of a reindeer stag, a male that had caught the scent of a female. That gaze was gone in a flash, but I had already melted, dissolved, sunk to the bottom of an ancient ocean where sea monsters lick your heels and a burning star sears the flesh. It felt as though you were looking at me in a way that I'd never been looked at before.

"Well, well, Fräulein Schwester. We've met."

You could see the female in me through all the dirt and filth, I imagined, just as you saw the female in all women. Somebody gave me a spiteful shunt in the back, and I staggered against the bed.

"Over there. He wants you in the picture too."

You took the photograph. As the camera gave a magnesium puff, everyone stood stock-still, as this was the right thing to do. Everyone except me.

"Can't even stand for a picture," Old Keskimölsä whispered, loud enough. "Somebody hold her up straight."

From where you stood, you strode right over and grabbed me. You were in your stocking feet, but I was still only as tall as your chest. I could smell you through the stench of blood, guts, and urine. Through all that, I sniffed the odor you gave off.

You let Jouni use the manual trigger. As we waited for the flash, I inhaled your scent. You smelled so achingly good, Johannes, of angel's milk smeared on a reindeer's coat, of rough-cut Virginia tobacco and cheap cigarettes, of children's fingers rubbed in marsh tea, of God's shirt. Of pure prick and of nothing at all.

You must have noticed my involuntary gestures, as you smiled and leaned over to say something to Jouni. He muttered something and tutted.

"This is our Johannes," he snapped disparagingly. "Johannes Angelhurst, a real reporter he is. Wants to interview you for the paper."

"Why's that?" Lisbet piped up.

Somewhat puzzled, Jouni turned to you. Again you whispered in his ear and looked at me surreptitiously.

"This midwife is a strong, modern woman. Germany needs women like this, and so does Finland."

Jouni's expression betrayed that he couldn't agree less.

"And what about our Lisbet? Will he write about her too?" Aune asked impatiently. "You tell him our Lisbet is Lapland's very own Greta Garbo. Even said so in the paper."

"I'm a Lotta girl too, you know!"

That wasn't strictly true, but I held my tongue. Again the two of you leaned over and whispered like the grocery lads at Schörner's, and it amused me. You shrugged your shoulders. Jouni interpreted, embarrassed.

"Some other time."

You pulled on your boots. Then you left. The women crowded in to count the newborn boy's toes, but I followed you through the lace curtains and held your scent in my nostrils.

"Johannes. That's a name for saints and mule foals, for the innocent and the blessed. The name of John the Baptist."

I watched your strong, upright back through the rippled windowpane. I gave a sigh as the two of you disappeared into the height of summer and a receding cloud of midges.

"Forget it, lass. You're too old for that kind of sport."

Only then did I notice Aune standing next to me. She gave her nose a canny tap.

"You've got Uuno. You mind that."

"I wanted some air, that's all."

I groped the window frame. The hook wouldn't open. Uuno. I hadn't heard a peep about him since April, when he was sent to Syväri. He was reported missing at the end of May. I had the feeling the swine might have deserted, but in the villages nobody talked about things like that.

"Uuno's dead."

Aune grabbed me by the scruff of the neck and hauled me around.

"You don't know that. They could've taken him prisoner."

But Aune didn't care about Uuno.

"You've got restless blood, lass. Don't be foolish, you'll regret it. Uuno'll come back."

I wasn't listening. The war would soon be over; Uuno would soon be home. And from out of nowhere a prayer reared up within me, more powerful than any prayer before it. I looked at the gap you'd left in the summer evening, pressed my forehead against the cool windowpane, and begged: Lord, I want that man.

If I can have that man, Lord, I'll wish for no other.

PARKKINA

June 1944

I don't wish to hide anything from you, my dearest Johannes. There was Uuno, the only man who would look at me, if you don't count the grifter from Turku who died at the Parkkina infirmary and who had been arrested in 1939 in connection with the Petsamo espionage affair. He was a marked man. He wanted to marry me before the Security Police got to him. He died before daybreak. He left me his lead-ridden body, a lock of clipped hair, and his patent certificates:

> *Product: Hornless reindeer, genotype. Acquires two-thirds of its nutritional needs directly from ground on which the moon shines but where lichen does not grow. Fed on a diet of chopped hay and lumpfish. Unfortunately, the specimen escaped into the pastures and must be reconstructed from remains, now located in 20 lb manure sacks at the casino stables.*

I first met Uuno when he turned up to investigate the espionage affair. They arrested more than a hundred Petsamo locals on suspicion of spying for the Communists, and all kinds of strange things started to happen. Weapons went off accidentally during the interrogations, and illiterate Skolts produced lengthy statements about how they had deciphered messages in secret Russian code. Uuno worked himself into the ground as the left little finger of Hillilä, the governor of Lapland, and because of his bowed legs, he was ordered to stay in Petsamo when the others left. A bone-dry, religious busybody, that's what he was, from a long line of tosspots. At first he was almost endearing. He gathered plants and dried their petals in folders of silk paper, and didn't believe me when I told him you wouldn't find cinquefoil or dewdrops on the shores of the Arctic Ocean. He got on well with Big Lamberg, being a member both of the Laestadian Church and the deeply patriotic IKL movement, and hailed from somewhere in Ostrobothnia. He had an unpleasant accent too, but folks were afraid of him because he had the power to accuse any petty reindeer thief of being a spy. He never fully understood that the Skolts simply followed their reindeer herds about the tundra and didn't care a hoot for the southerners' border formalities.

He was officious and somehow insidious in his dual ideologies. He had the IKL's *Tide of the Times* magazine delivered to the governor's office, while from Big Lamberg he borrowed copies of religious pamphlets, including *The Olive Branch*, *Word of Mercy*, and the *Zionist Mission*. At first he didn't much care for the Fritz. When they started flowing into town three years ago, he'd stand at the Arctic Street crossroads in his uniform cap and mock them, with nothing but his brass buttons trying to push back the Wehrmacht as they spilled out of their tanks. It wasn't until he received a call from headquarters ordering him not to ask to see their passports that he really believed it was happening. He was sickened at the sight of the Lotta girls clamoring to hand the soldiers bunches of mountain avens.

"Strawberry sweethearts," said Uuno. "Harlots, that's what they are. But you, lass, I can save you."

By "save," Uuno didn't mean from the Fritz, but from myself. My father had been killed in 1918 during the Civil War, in the Lainaanranta district of Rovaniemi. He and my mother had been living in sin at a tavern in the notorious area of Sahanperä because her family wouldn't give the couple its blessing. What's more, it was general knowledge that I could never bear children. Nobody really knew why. According to Big Lamberg, I'd come down the hill at Pelastusvuori in a toboggan and hit a branch, which had sunk into me like a stag into a deer, rupturing something essential within me. I don't remember the incident. The more general assumption for my infertility was my bad blood and the sinful circumstances of my conception, and nothing could be done about that. Nothing at all, though in Big Lamberg's house we lived in fear of the Lord. There were no curtains in the windows, and instead of sweeping, we strewed juniper branches across the floor to keep away the vermin. Once a week Big Lamberg blessed the corners of the cottage with his bitter, resinous urine.

Big Lamberg's wife saw Uuno as a way of getting rid of me.

She promised that Uuno could follow me home after church, and whispered from Big Lamberg's arms, "We'll not need to worry about the lass anymore."

At the first bend in the road, I told Uuno I'd never bear children. He didn't seem to care.

"Once this war's over, I'll build you a house with a fence right around it. The Lord will bless us with a bairn, sure he will. You'll calm down like the other womenfolk. And you'll stop running about with all that midwifery nonsense."

I nodded, though it felt as though a great fist had clasped my throat, choking water out of my eyes and nostrils.

"No tears now, lass."

Uuno thought I was upset because I couldn't have children. He tried to comfort me, assuring me that though I was coarse and carefree by nature and descended from the Devil, he could save me. By the grace of God, I would bear him a child. The church folk in Parkkina appealed to God to forgive my father's sins. It was a rigorous ceremony. Old Keskimölsä's wife was moved by the spirit; she started speaking in ancient tongues and dancing up and down the aisles, her hollow bones whistling. The congregation wept, and the pastor proclaimed, "In the name of Jesus Christ our Lord, and in his blood, may these sins be forgiven!"

It didn't help.

Uuno never understood how I loathed his scuffed boots.

"You pray to God, lass, and everything will turn out just fine."

Then he quoted from the sermons of Laestadius: "'For though we have here a worldly paradise, there exists in our midst the very stench from the jaws of the old Dragon.'"

Uuno didn't understand. Nobody understood before you. I didn't want to settle down, didn't want to stop, not after Aune had taken me under her wing and taught me her secrets. I loved that world of herbs, the scent of marsh tea, the bog into which Aune immersed me and forced me to swallow. Thanks to Aune, I had something the other women didn't. I had knowledge, and with that came the freedom to come and go as I pleased. I managed to escape Big Lamberg's roach-eyed boots, and I was something more than just a barren, abandoned, Red bastard child. I loved the magic of blood-stopping, the old spells that Aune whispered in my ear. Because Aune had given me far more than merely scientific instruction. Besides knowing all about vaccinations, enemas, and the art of pumping blood, I knew how to cure stomach cramps by gargling salt water mixed with soot. I learned to seal wounds with an ointment of lard and wood resin. I learned to gather wild oregano, valerian, sage, angelica, and to mix a draft from honey and bishop's wort to alleviate lovesickness and melancholy. I learned to soothe the misery of grieving war widows with an infusion of nettles and bromine, and to add webcap mushrooms to the cows' troughs to make their dreams peaceful and to make them bellow in their stalls for the calves the Fritz had commandeered.

Uuno thought Aune's remedies were the work of the Devil.

"You can collect plants for other things."

Uuno showed me his herbarium. Dead pistils between sheets of silk paper, pressed flat with bricks and heavy tiles. Uuno didn't understand that my skill was a potent, dark current heaving within me, the voice of God pulsing and chattering in my veins, that ultimately it was God who gave me these orders, not the Devil.

Uuno wasn't a bad man. He was mediocre. He visited Big Lamberg and asked him to forbid me from gallivanting with the Germans. I assured him that I never traveled alone; I was always with Aune. But Big Lamberg answered curtly.

"Enough."

And I hadn't seen Aune since.

Please forgive me, Johannes, for ever even looking at Uuno. But back then I didn't know anything of you, and I suppose my blood must have started simmering, though I tried to cool it with an infusion made of beaver musk and wolf's balls. But when one day Uuno and I had been out cycling and it had started to rain and we'd found shelter in a barn, and his little organ stood tall, I no longer had the strength to resist. But Uuno wasn't man enough to take me. He twitched and cursed and tossed off on my thigh. Then he wept and prayed for the forgiveness of his sins.

"Seduced me on purpose, you did. Bride of Satan, that's what you are."

I wiped my soiled frock against the sweaty hay and glanced at Uuno's scuffed boots.

Uuno's demise began once he got too close to the Norwegians and the Fritz. He sometimes tried to explain away the situation, saying that as far as Germany was concerned, Petsamo wasn't part of Finland but was illegally controlled by the Norwegian intelligence services. He wanted to play with the big boys of the Third Reich, but he didn't know how. And while he was busying himself up near Alta, the inevitable happened. A large warship was damaged at sea, and poor Uuno granted the spies all the documentation they required. He stood on deck, waving at them as they carried out measurements and checked their torpedo nets, shouted hurrah as a spy pretended to lift a salmon out of the water, and gave his word about things he should not.

That was Uuno. I felt sorry for him.

"They all blame me now."

Uuno had already been told to keep his nose out of police matters; the Gestapo wanted to check his background. As if he had anything to hide besides his pollen-smelling leather folders. Then came a phone call from the Rovaniemi Liaison headquarters to inform him that he'd been called up for the home reserve, despite his bowed legs.

I didn't accompany him to Rovaniemi to wave him off, though I might even have caught sight of a train there.

PARKKINA

June 1944

That day the White Guard was carrying out weapon practice on the shores of Parkkina and Liinahamari, and volunteers could sign up. I had plenty to do in the Red Cross tent that stood at the edge of the field. The atmosphere was charged. There had been no news from the front, and nobody was granted leave. The mud in the giant's cauldrons had dried up; the air was heavy with the smell of Mother Earth's dusty, sinewy bosom and the barns reeked of veiny, German prick. There were Russian bombing raids almost every night, and now they were even sending fifteen-year-old volunteers to the front. Administering vaccinations, weighing patients, falsifying milk recommendations. Old Keskimölsä was lumbering around the field, drunk as a coot and bellowing that the German *Blutsbruder* had started to stink like an infected wound in a crippled cow's twotch. He'd sent his daughter to a factory in Oulu to assemble Molotov cocktails.

"We'll soon need them against the Fritz," he said. "They're building garrisons at Salla and Kilpisjärvi. I've seen them, I have."

"What do you think?" asked Lisbet.

She had propped herself on the edge of the table to flash her thighs. She was wearing a baby-skin-colored frilly hat and a cretonne frock. She hadn't brought the bairn with her. I managed to stick the final vaccination needle into her bony Skolt skin and started packing up my syringes and plungers.

"About what?"

"The garrisons, of course."

"Nonsense. Idle coachmen's prattle."

I glanced out into the yard. Scrawny little lads whose balls hadn't yet dropped were waddling about with wooden sticks and elk rifles at the ready. Most weren't in uniform. At least Jaakkima Alakunnas had his dead brother's SS Wiking insignia on his sleeve and a *Totenkopf* helmet. He seemed to be conducting a marching song.

"Let D-d-Deutschland strike the Russian threat, and F-f-Finland fill their hearts with dread . . ."

Every now and then a German convoy passed, and Jaakkima raised his hand in a salute.

"H-h-Heil Hickler!"

The other lads looked embarrassed. Were we supposed to send this lot to the front? Forget Hitler salutes. These lads should be force-fed a diet of whey milk and brawn sausage. In the distance came the boom of cannon fire.

Lisbet sipped a lemon soda sweetened with saccharine. Lemonade, she called it. A look of pain flickered across her face with each sip. She had a sore tooth, and Aune refused to help her. The old crone was still upset about the baby. Lisbet sighed.

"Imagine. My little one turned out to be a darkie."

It was true. The bairn's skin had started to darken, and it didn't matter how much they scrubbed it with lemon soda, how much they tried to keep him cool in the sawdust behind the barn. Nobody had seen any darkies or Jews in the village since an American ship had docked to pick up the last of them in 1940. One of the local scoundrels had been going around saying that the kid's father was none other than the infamous Sulo of Kiikala, a well-endowed bull that ran around terrorizing the heifers at Alaluostari croft.

"I couldn't keep the bairn. Too sensitive, I was. Didn't make a drop of milk."

And with that, all of Lisbet's worries disappeared. Her tooth no longer bothered her.

"Look at that. I'm going to have that Fritz for myself."

I turned to look. My syringe plunger fell to the floor, and I cursed out loud.

Lisbet squealed with shock. I explained that now I'd have to boil the syringe and disinfect it again. But that's not why I cursed. The man Lisbet was pointing at was you. You and Jouni were walking toward the edge of the meadow. Jouni was carrying your tripod.

My voice hoarse, I forced myself to ask who on earth that was.

"Have you not read his articles in the Fritz newspaper?"

I had not read them, and neither had she, but for different reasons. The only thing she read was *Filmiaitta*, a magazine about stars of the silver screen, and even then she only read articles about Greta Garbo. I, on the other hand, didn't care for traditional information sources. The only book we ever read at Big Lamberg's house was the Catechism, old copies of *The Olive Branch*, a religious tract discontinued in the nineteenth century, and other Laestadian publications. I sometimes flicked through copies of the illustrated monthly magazine *Suomen Kuvalehti* in the neighbor's outhouse when I needed to wipe my backside.

Everybody loved you, Lisbet informed me. You'd endeared yourself first to the local mothers and grandmothers by hanging out washing and fetching runaway cattle from the pastures, then to the landowners by not getting their daughters into bother. You'd become the young lads' hero by log running down the rapids and whistling for clear weather. I hadn't known about any of this. All I knew was that your boots were in a league of their own, that you took them off before stepping indoors, and that your scent made my blood roar.

As if to taunt me, Lisbet told me that your scent was in fact a common topic of conversation among the local lasses. Henriikka Autti decided you must have caught the smell of a rutting bull in heat. Men couldn't smell it, but the reindeer and other animals certainly could, and folks were worried that during the autumn mating season you'd be in a terrible pickle out in the woodlands, being chased by both the bulls and the spring chickens.

"I says to him, for the love of God don't you go out there."

I watched you across the yard. You looked so immensely accomplished and yet somewhat vulnerable without your cap and SS uniform. There was no dung on your boots, and the cows had licked your fringe into a tuft on your forehead. The camera was on the tripod, ready.

"What's he taking pictures of now?"

"He photographs everything. And he makes garlands for the lasses."

"Does he want to take your picture too?" I managed to ask, my head turned away.

"Aye."

"Did he write about you in the paper?"

"No."

I sighed with relief. But then Lisbet cocked her pretty head and casually flicked one leg over the other.

"He made me a garland, though."

All at once I hated her. Garlands of marigolds and glinting golden globeflowers, of daisies, marsh rosemary, spotted moorland orchids, parsley ferns, wheat flower, chervil, and dogwood—these you braided for all the girls and took their picture. I gripped the syringe plunger in my fist and envisaged every floozy along the coast begging you for a garland of their own—and getting one. And you took their pictures. I imagined the local sweethearts, their skin like buttermilk, their legs open and ready, undressing for you, straddling a chair in front of you, raising their thighs a little, coaxing the whiff of their flesh toward the camera and gently pressing their breasts, oozing with whey, against the rattan chairs in the officers' barracks. *Where are these thoughts coming from? Help me, Lord, help me!*

"He'd have to have a crooked thingy not to want me."

Lisbet arched her spine and tilted her head backward. The hat slipped from her head, and at once the sun played upon her forehead, her loins pulsed like those of a mare on a summer's night. I glanced at you across the yard, and there you were, standing and looking at us. Lisbet nudged me in the side, as if to taunt me.

"He's eyeing you."

"Don't be soft. It's you he's looking at."

Lisbet smiled at this statement of the obvious. Then her expression clouded over.

"He'll be gone soon. The Titovka camp, apparently. He told Jouni yesterday."

I gave a quiet yelp, and Lisbet peered at me. But she didn't understand. Nobody understood that inside me there lived a true woman. Nobody but you.

"Look what I found behind the barracks!"

Lisbet pressed something into my hand.

"I'll not be needing it, for I've just had my bairn."

I blushed. It was a rubber made of pig's guts. Uuno never would have accepted such a thing. During the Interim Peace, Aune suggested we establish a horse-drawn chastity carriage that would travel through the villages, handing out prevention devices to women whose husbands were working at the garrisons in the Karelian Isthmus. After a meeting of the local council, Big Lamberg clipped me round the ear and told me I was to have nothing to do with Aune Näkkälä. Uuno agreed. They threw her out of the house the next time she came to fetch me for a vaccination run. Called her a quack and a charlatan.

Now Uuno was missing, perhaps killed in action. Big Lamberg had his work cut out looking after his own loose-legged wife. I fingered the rubber. My heart started throbbing as I imagined how two people had placed this between them while inside each other. Lisbet snatched it from my hand.

"Well, you'll not be needing it neither. You know what?"

Lisbet croaked with laughter, all the while staring at you across the yard.

"I reckon our Johannes has the same problem as Old Hickler. Only one ball left."

I looked, and there was nothing wrong with you. You had a beautiful back, an altogether handsome frame. I knew I'd have to see you again. You were supposed to write an article about me, the strong, modern woman with the ability to give life and to take it away.

"Ouch," Lisbet hissed, touching her swollen cheek.

"Why don't I help you with that tooth?"

The next day I marched up to the Näkkälä house. I wrenched Lisbet's tooth out behind the granary with a pair of tongs, lying that I didn't have any anesthetic with me, then told the bogus Lotta girl to fetch yarrow root for the bandages.

There are different kinds of houses. There are houses where folks live by the word of God and fear the Lord's punishment if a wooden spoon falls on the floor. You shouldn't barge into houses like that if you want to have your way. Then there are places like Näkkälä's croft standing at the foot of the fells at Neitotunturi. There, behind the tin-lined windowpanes, lived Jouni Näkkälä, the greatest rumrunner in Lapland. A stern, unrelenting man to those who tried to double-cross him. But I knew a different side of him, the fellow who swallowed trout whole, who wept when folks drowned their kittens in the brook, and who cranked the laundry for his mother in a hand-operated washing barrel.

Jouni had power.

He'd inherited the business from his father, Aslak Näkkälä, who had kept Lapland's moonshine stores open even through the dry years of prohibition in the 1930s. Jouni had accompanied his father all the way to Oulu, from post to post, making sure that liquor still flowed up to the Arctic coastline and didn't disappear down the gullets of thirsty southerners. It was in Rovaniemi that Aslak had found Aune, while she was working as a maid in a hostelry. Aune fell in love and ran away with him, though it was with some sadness that she left the life of the big city behind her. Aune still wistfully recalled the Rovaniemi fair, and she rued the fact that the Näkkäläs no longer had any business showing their faces down that way, not after what happened at Mannerheim's seventy-fifth birthday. Only a few people knew what actually took place that day, and even fewer dared speak about it.

"Aye, life's been fine here too," Aune assured us.

It certainly had. Aslak built his young bride the finest house in Petsamo. He did to his own people what the southern townsfolk had done before—plied the Skolts with moonshine and made a quick buck by swapping liquor for their valuable animal skins. But affluence was to be the undoing of Jouni's father, and it wasn't long before he got his comeuppance. From a group of English seamen he bought the first orange ever seen in Parkkina, had an allergic reaction, and died. At first it was a terrible setback for the Näkkälä household, particularly because prohibition laws were revoked at around the same time; after all, they had a reputation to uphold. Once the province of Lapland banned liquor again in 1942, business started to pick up. Jouni and Aune began distilling moonshine themselves. By now Jouni had only the best cars and good contacts with the Germans. The Näkkäläs' was the kind of household people visited when they needed to get things done.

It almost looked as though Aune was pleased to see me. Wheat buns were laid out on the table and real ground coffee served in decorative, cherry-patterned porcelain cups. I breathed in the scent of the coffee and licked the butter dripping from the bun as I assessed the situation. Whom should I appeal to? Jouni or Aune? I had at least one advantage: I had come to ask for something Big Lamberg never would have agreed to. Both of them loathed Big Lamberg and Uuno from the bottom of their hearts. It was Aune who broke the silence.

"So, Pietari's lass?"

During a forceps delivery a while back, I'd once asked Aune how she knew my father's name. Had they known each other back in Rovaniemi? But you could never get an answer out of Aune when she didn't want to give one. She simply stroked my hair with a bone comb and asked me to sing for her.

"You've a fine voice, lass. You can sing folks to sleep, bairns and grown men. I've only known one soul that could sing like that, and that was my sister, Annikki. Poor Annikki, ran off with the Fritz back in 1919."

So Annikki's gift was her voice, Aune's her ability to cure and to destroy. I swallowed a mouthful of delicious bun and licked a grain of sugar from my lips.

"I need to work in the camps. I want to go to Titovka."

Aune and Jouni's cups stopped and hung in the air. Aune muttered, a sugar cube between her teeth.

"Don't talk nonsense, Weird-Eye."

"What are you asking us for?" Jouni joined in. "Go and talk to one of their henchmen. Go to Rovaniemi. That's where they make all the decisions." But we all knew nobody in Rovaniemi would give me a second look. They'd check my background and they'd find out. About my father and everything else.

Something lit up in Aune's eyes. Jouni had blabbed to her that you were on your way to that camp.

"Oh, poor lassie, is it that Jerryman you're after? Forget him. I'll make you a dressing of wolf's balls so the lust won't keep you up at night."

But Aune looked satisfied. It was Uuno and Big Lamberg's fault that I no longer traveled the countryside with her. Jouni was sitting at the end of the bench, scraping beneath his nails with a knife. I turned to him.

"I'll give you gas coupons."

"Don't need 'em. We get gas from the Fritz."

"Help me."

"I can't."

"Aye, you can. Pull some strings."

"I won't do it. The camp's no place for a lass like you."

"I can look after myself."

"I'm sure you can," Jouni spat, and promised he'd think about it.

I knew he wouldn't help me.

"The bombs out here not enough for you, girl?"

I'd have to visit Jaakkima Alakunnas or talk to the Fritz directly. But they'd look into my background and find out, and my life would carry on as before. Uuno would come back with his muddy boots and would miraculously father a child with me. I'd turn into one of those housewives slumped over the kitchen table while cockroaches nested in the bark flour. Lonely evenings at the cottage while the menfolk spent the night at the Salmijärvi Shanghai; a kid with deficiency and anemia, colic, inflammation of the nipples, a pestilence preying on the children. No.

Then I remembered. Jouni would be wise to help me get to the camp. For a long while he'd been cavorting with a married woman. She was from Varanger, and she'd disappeared when the Fritz had started burning houses and killing anyone suspected of working for the resistance movement. Operation Wild Duck, he'd called it. Jouni knew plenty of things that other folks didn't. For instance, his lady friend hadn't been killed; she'd been taken to a camp.

"I could look for Hedda, check she's not being kept at Titovka."

That made him sit up for a moment. But the scrawny rat just shook his head and continued scraping his nails. I was growing desperate.

I know, my dear Johannes. What I did next was beneath me. I waited for Aune to go outside to sprinkle the coffee grounds across the herb garden. I gripped Jouni's arm and hissed at him.

"I know what happened to Lisbet's bairn."

Jouni was so startled that the knife fell from his hand.

"What do you know? An eagle snatched it."

Last year an eagle had snatched a baby somewhere near Inari. Ever since, this had become a popular explanation whenever newborn children mysteriously disappeared.

"I know where you buried it."

It was a lie, but it did the trick.

"Hold your trap, Weird-Eye," Jouni snapped. He thought about it for a moment. "Are you really that soft in the head that you want to get to the camp?"

"Aye."

Jouni spat into the palm of his hand.

"I'll sort it out. I'm going outside for a piss. You'd better be gone when I get back."

Jouni stormed out to the yard, slamming the door behind him. Aune came back inside and closed the latch. She glanced at the empty cot, then at me. Aune isn't stupid. She crept up close to me and whispered so that I could smell the moonshine on her breath.

"Careful what you wish for, lass. You might have it after all. Your father was a good man. Don't you forget it."

I didn't listen. I started packing in secret. I didn't care for the howling of the air-raid sirens, didn't listen to all the folks saying that come autumn they'd be leaving for Sweden, for Ostrobothnia, anywhere they could. Other people fled the war and headed for safety. I wanted to follow you to the place where the air smelled of gunpowder and the ground was bowed from the constant clamor of Stalin's Organs. I could still smell the stinking nightshade, and midges rose from the ground like a living cloud. Before the month was out and the bishop's wort on Aune's window ledge had come into flower, I was called up for work at the Titovka camp.

PETSAMO

Johannes Angelhurst

June 12, 1944

I should be finishing the front page of the latest edition of *Lappland-Kurier*. Instead, I'm sitting by the window, looking at the photograph I took at the Rumrunner's house. It's hard to concentrate. I must.

I've been transferred. Titovka Zweiglager 322. It's a former transit camp that's been made more permanent. I don't know anything else, only that something is happening there.

One Eduard Dietl, the Kriegsgefangenen-Bezirkskommandant of Lapland himself, also known as Arctic Fox, called me up to the headquarters at Kursunkijärvi. I tried to persuade the Rumrunner to accompany me to Rovaniemi for a little fun, but he refused. He seemed positively startled at the suggestion. Didn't he want to see the trains, I asked, or fly in an aircraft? (That normally got the locals excited, particularly the women.) He'd seen trains before and quite enough bombers, he replied, and explained that he'd lost his appetite for city life when he'd seen a crocodile and a Negro at the Rovaniemi fair in the same year.

"When there's a crocodile and a darkie in the Alakunnas meadow at the same time, then you know at least the crocodile is in the wrong place."

I laughed and asked why such a wise man wasn't involved in the war effort.

"Shot myself in the foot."

I pondered this as I sat with Dietl eating Greek lamb shanks, a dish with a name that made me think of infanticide. Some people can shun their responsibility to the fatherland and not even feel ashamed of themselves. How is it possible? My idol, Horst Wessel, wouldn't have hesitated. MY HONOR IS LOYALTY, read the words above Colonel Oiva Willamo's door at the Rovaniemi Liaison headquarters.

"Meine Ehre heißt Treue," I interpreted flippantly.

The Arctic Fox laughed. He laid his hand on my shoulder.

"You're a good photographer and documentarian, Angelhurst. But even the *Finnenlümmels* can aim a camera if need be."

I knew this. Whereas we staged battle scenes for the camera, Finnish reconnaissance troops were pushing toward the front, bareheaded and without tanks.

"First and foremost you are an SS officer in the employ of the Security Bureau of the Reichssicherheitshauptamt—not of the Finns."

I stressed that my job was not only to photograph and document events but to gauge the mood of the people. I'm well aware that I work for the Security Bureau. I'd received specific instructions to get to know the locals, to build good contacts, to observe. I was to produce articles about collaboration between sister nations. And that's what I had done. Dietl sighed. The directors of the RSHA had expressed dissatisfaction with the sister nation. The Finns' system of censorship was weak, and the black list we received from the Liaison headquarters was a joke.

"The North is leaking like a sieve. Any Soviet spy can befriend them."

I observed the meager figure of the Arctic Fox as I lit my pipe. Had he heard rumors about my photographing activities? My companionship with the Rumrunner? Did he doubt my loyalty? SS officers shouldn't jolly around with people like the Rumrunner. But the commander had other matters on his mind.

"You are an SS officer. A superior lieutenant."

I drew in the smoke. That at least was true.

"Why, you were in the Ukraine in 1941."

The air in the Cabinet suddenly felt heavy. Fireflies stung my eyes, and I had to steady myself against Willamo's crest of tree gnarl. The smoke from Dietl's pipe must have gone to my head.

"Excuse me, Herr Commander."

The Ukraine, 1941. At that point there's a gap in my memory.

I cannot remember anything that happened in the Ukraine, no matter how hard I try. Whenever I try and think back to it, I feel woozy and my mind becomes blurred.

All I know is that I woke up in an infirmary in the Ukraine. My uncle and a Gestapo officer were standing next to my bed. Apparently I'd been struck by a stray bullet from the rifle of a drunken SS soldier in Babi Yar. A cold bandage throbbed against my forehead. I asked, "Where is Babi Yar?"

"It's in the Ukraine. Near Kiev."

"What was I doing there?"

My uncle gave a chuckle.

"You were digging pits, my boy!"

I didn't have the strength to inquire further. Later I was told that I slept solidly for three months, and when I finally woke up, I was transferred to Finland, to Suomi, the land of my father's dreams.

I have been happy here.

But this photograph in my hand, the one taken at the Rumrunner's house when his sister was in labor. Snapped with the manual trigger. I can't take my eyes off it. That nurse, the midwife, she's caught my attention. Wild-Eye. Utterly different from the other women I've met here. She wanders around Petsamo by herself, unaccompanied by men, and doesn't seem afraid of anything. There's something about her that reminds me of my mother, Annikki. With someone like that, I'd have no need to worry about losing my way in the fells. A woman like that could sniff out a ptarmigan's egg on a tussock of grass, pluck a sandpiper out of the air with her bare hands. I really should do an interview with her, especially now that I've promised her one. Of course, I won't. Promises like that are only given to help raise the locals' morale. What's more, I don't have time. I've been transferred to Titovka, and I'll never see her again.

It sounded distinctly ill-omened when Eduard Dietl said that soon we wouldn't need staged battle photographs. What's more, I'm at a loss as to why they want me of all people sent to Zweiglager 322—and why now? Why does the RSHA want to send a reporter to a place where there's nothing to report? No photographs, no news bulletins. Dietl assured me that I'd simply have to take his word for it and be like Horst Wessel, the national-socialist martyr who took to the streets to fight the Bolsheviks and was killed in action. That's what I want to be. Unless this is a matter of something that needs to be hidden, quickly. If I remember correctly, that too is something I am good at.

TITOVKA

June 1944

Jouni and I rattled into the camp unannounced in the early evening. We were exhausted. I'd crept out of Big Lamberg's house with my suitcases at four in the morning, before Big Lamberg's wife kicked me out of bed to milk the cows. Jouni was roaring drunk after the day's drive. He'd taken a delivery of saltpeter to the Finnish garrison and toiled away while I counted the number of twotches scrawled on the privy wall. Two hundred and thirty-one. Now he had to steer the car through the camp gates edged with swastikas fluttering in the wind. Oh, Johannes, your camp made an impression on me straight away! A barbed-wire fence ten feet high surrounded the barracks compound. A sign decorated with skulls had been erected for the benefit of the Finns: HALT! DO NOT FEED THE PRISNERS.

We were welcomed by a high-ranking officer. I was taken aback by his beautiful face. A curved, aristocratic nose and long eyelashes. The evening wind caught the man's britches, ruffling them into two rippling sails. The corners of the barracks smelled of dropwort.

"SS-Obersturmführer Hermann Gödel," the officer introduced himself, bending down to kiss my hand. "We've been expecting you, Fräulein Schwester."

I took an instant liking to him.

Gödel began to show me around the camp like a respected guest. From his words I tried to establish what belonged where. I'd never visited a prison camp before, though the majority of folks in Petsamo probably had. I knew that Jouni had fabricated a fake background for me in which I'd worked at numerous infirmaries along the Karelian Isthmus. I concentrated hard, so as not to seem ignorant. I could see for myself that all four corners of the camp had searchlights and watchtowers raised on stakes.

"From up there we can see if Fräulein tries to run away," Gödel teased me, and I blushed.

All in all the modernity and cleanliness of the camp felt comforting. Over there were a telephone switchboard and electricity grid, then the washrooms with their notched log walls, the food and munitions stores, and a large building with a sign above its whitewashed door reading OPERATION KUHSTALL. The building was cordoned off behind another barbed-wire fence. The infirmary, presumably. Everything was neat and peaceful, not at all intimidating as I had imagined. The midges sang in the long grass. At the corner of the infirmary, a dragonfly was chasing a horsefly. There were no flocks of starving Russians roaming between the barracks with their tongues drooping from the side of their mouths. Instead, a few trusted prisoners were dragging a goulash cannon toward a building with separate hatches in the walls for soldiers and prisoners.

Reindeer soup and flatbread for supper.

"Bruder Rumrunner!"

I smelled rather than heard you appear next to me.

Be still my heart!

I lowered my eyes and ran my tongue across my teeth. I had scoured them with soot water until they gleamed. At the same time I saw once again your insolently clean boots and raised my head. You must not think me a coward.

You bowed respectfully to Jouni. Then you flinched.

"Fräulein Schwester, *willkommen*!"

Again Gödel hurried to kiss my hand.

"Sieg Heil!" you growled.

I didn't answer, and with a wave of his hand Jouni walked off to unload his cargo.

We walked into the barracks that you called the Cabinet. You asked everyone to take off their shoes at the door. Gödel obeyed, albeit reluctantly. I wondered which of you was supposed to be in charge of this camp, Hermann Gödel or you. EIN VOLK, EIN REICH, EIN FÜHRER, read the banner fluttering above the oak table. One people, one nation, one leader. I looked at the slate fireplace built at the end of the room and the row of framed photographs on the table.

"We start work tomorrow. But tonight we shall celebrate your arrival!"

Gödel rang a small silver bell, and a prisoner as thin as a twig shuffled into the room with a tray. A war hound had been tied to the prisoner's ankle. The dog bared its teeth, then slunk into hiding beneath the table.

"The interpreter," Gödel explained. "He speaks German, Finnish, Russian, and a few unfathomable Uralic languages."

That was the first time I laid eyes on Alexei Ignatenko, though of course at the time I didn't know his name. Wrinkled, childlike toes in a pair of worn slippers. A long chain made it possible to walk despite the mongrel tied to his ankle.

"A poet once said there's as much chance of taming a Russian through education as there is of turning a pig into a noble steed," said Gödel. "The same rainfall brings up roses in a garden and thistles on the marshland. Isn't that right, *Russe*?"

The boy nodded obligingly and continued pouring us drinks. The strain of a violin could be heard outside. A distinctly Slavic rendition of "Lili Marleen."

"Ah, the Moscow Philharmonic!"

We sat down in green armchairs, and the Russian lad lit the hearth. The war hound whimpered contentedly beneath the table. Gödel assured me that I would enjoy my time at the camp, particularly now that most of the other nurses had left. There was only one Finn left at the camp, the head nurse. It was a shame, he said. Finns were good workers.

"We must make the Finns stay on longer. That's why we consider you more a guest of the Third Reich than an employee."

Then he showed me two gold-plated goblins that he had acquired from monks fleeing a monastery.

"You see, we're not animals. After all, we didn't destroy Paris as we did Warsaw."

Gödel slipped a drop of cognac into my hand. I tasted the Devil's piss with my tongue. It was bitter. Uuno would have disapproved. Big Lamberg would have denounced me as one of Beelzebub's whores. I took a good swig. Jouni sat down next to the door to rest, while you and Gödel began filling your pipes. I relaxed. Pipes always make me feel at home; they remind me of my childhood in Rovaniemi and the moonshine taverns of Sahanperä. The homemade tobacco, cut with moss, that my father used to smoke in the pipe my mother had given him, and his delicate Sunday *latakia* tobacco, its aroma with a hint of rum. *Forgive Our Sins*—those were the words engraved on my father's pipe. I looked around. Framed photographs were propped on the lace tablecloth and along the mantelpiece. Generations of stately, trustworthy men adorned with medallions and homburg hats stared at us from the frames. No spy would snatch me away from here. The two of you blew smoke rings toward the red-domed lamp drawing crackling light from a generator at the dam.

"Johannes and I are old brothers-in-arms. Childhood friends, actually."

"That's right, Fräulein Schwester. Our mothers used the same butcher shop."

This made me like Hermann Gödel even more. You had been in the same brigade of the Hitler Jugend, fought together in Einsatzgruppe C in the Ukraine. It sounded grand. I'd read about the Ukraine in *Suomen Kuvalehti*, about the mythical land of Cossacks and horse chestnut trees. I'd read other things too, in an 1870 copy of *The Olive Branch* at Big Lamberg's house. I asked whether what it said about heathens was true. That in the Ukraine the infidel women carried children for eighteen months, and all that time the child hung from the mother's groin and grew. Eventually it gnawed through its own umbilical cord and crawled off and out the door, cursing, denied its family, and never came back. Gödel laughed and nodded toward you.

"If you want to know about the women, you should ask Johannes!"

So a woman had lain beneath you somewhere far away, licked the dust stuck to your sweaty neck, and whispered to you about things that I would never know.

"I could tell you all sorts of things about this young rascal's adventures in the Ukraine," Gödel said with a laugh, whacking you on the back.

More liquid appeared at the concave bottom of our glasses.

"Oh, Kiev and the Ukrainian steppes!"

Your childhood friend was becoming nostalgic. Back there things had been much grander and the operations far more extensive. Back there they had used more-advanced chemical compounds, and the best doctors in the world had worked alongside the best scientists. All this made a great impression on me. Gödel examined his curved gnarl pipe.

"It's curious that even primitive peoples can fashion a pipe from which to inhale the smoke of peace. Some races learned this noble skill long before they knew how to grind grain into flour. But those peoples had too great a penchant for recreation and gratification. Unlike the German people. Or the Finns, mind. Germans and Finns. We're one and the same."

Jouni was dozing by the door; a droplet of spittle had soaked neatly into the sackcloth of his jacket. The Cabinet smelled of musk and pipe embers. Gödel bragged that you had received this tobacco blend from your uncle, who in turn had received it from Rommel himself, a gift from Africa.

"But this is all degeneration; it's in the past now. Let us enjoy the moment! The Russians are the only race that understands nothing whatsoever of the joys of a good pipe. Isn't that so, *Russe*?"

The Russian boy nodded politely and concentrated on staring at the volumes of *Der Stürmer* and other such magazines collected on the bookshelf. The shackled dog's legs twitched rhythmically in time with its dreams.

"Johannes Angelhurst, my brother! Let's take a photograph!"

You brought out your camera and nudged Jouni awake to take the photograph with the manual trigger. Gödel shouted so vigorously that cognac splashed from his glass.

"*Die Arktis ist nichts!* Johannes, my boy! Why, he's going to dig us a pit!"

With the exposure meter in your hand, you stood stock-still in the middle of the room. Jouni muttered to himself on the bench near the door. The cognac in my stomach warmed me, and you were so close. I could have pressed my head into your groin and given you a gentle bite.

"What pit is that?" I asked.

TITOVKA

Johannes Angelhurst

June 25, 1944

My worst nightmare has come true. Hermann Gödel is here, talking about things I cannot remember, and he doesn't believe there's a gap in my memory concerning the Ukraine and Babi Yar. That being said, Gödel himself I remember only too well. Before the war he earned a living as an antiques dealer. In his hands bedpans and catheters could turn into angelic drinking vessels, and similarly Gödel could make the truth contort into a grotesque caricature of itself. I've hated him ever since we moved onto the same street. They shoved my good mother, Annikki, around in the queue at the butcher's, tormented us long before they found out about my uncle.

My father used to call my uncle *"die Alte Sau,"* but he should have been grateful to him instead. My uncle arranged a job for his Jaeger brother as a typesetter at Franz Eher Verlag, the first house to publish *Mein Kampf.* I respect my uncle. A decorated fighter pilot in the Great

War, Tegel Angelhurst joined the National Socialist German Workers' Party as member number twenty-four, the Führer being number one. From its inception, he belonged to the Brownshirts. My uncle is so influential that he visits the Führer's Eagle's Nest and sleeps in Göring's guest room. He calls Goebbels *"Komischer Heini"* and mimics him at the dinner table by puffing out his cheeks and tapping his foot. He raises toasts to Horst Wessel, the martyr I so strive to emulate. Because of my uncle, we were left in peace. A Party vehicle parked outside works wonders.

Yet I am afraid of Gödel. I've feared him since the days of the gravel pit at Babi Yar (precisely what happened at that pit, I really cannot remember). And here we were, sitting by the fireplace, eating reindeer stew cobbled together by the trusted prisoners, and drinking from our pipes a smoke that takes away the tedium and envelops the smoker in a sweet-smelling, bitter-soothing fog of oblivion. I remembered once meeting a Finnish informant, sitting in that chair and smoking a pipe, his face badly burned and scarred. Along his pipe were the words *Forgive Our Sins*.

I looked at Wild-Eye and thought, Why not? I would take our picture and see whether her spirit stuck to the magnetic surface of the film. Everything was set up and ready. The 35 mm cinematic camera, the 105 mm objective, blender 5.6, exposure time half a second. I showed the Rumrunner how to use the manual trigger and demonstrated how it could be used to take a self-portrait. He was irritable when I woke him up.

"Forgotten what you look like?"

"Sometimes a man can forget," I answered. It was the truth.

Then it happened.

"Our Johannes, he certainly knows how to dig a pit!"

That's what Eduard Dietl had told me. That's what I was here to do.

Wild-Eye caught up with me before I'd fetched the spade. She sat on the steps, blew the midges from her forehead.

"How come you've a local accent?"

I lied, of course, just as I'd lied to the Arctic Fox. I told her I'd learned the language from the *Soldatenwörterbuch* handed out to all reconnaissance troops. An old lie. I was called up for the SS because of my pure lineage, my flawless reputation, my health and heritage. How else would I know the language? As Dietl put it when he presented the report from the Gestapo and the RSHA, because my mother was of an inferior race. She was Finnish.

I could have explained that my father, Fritz Angelhurst, arrived in Lapland with the first division of Bomber Jaegers in 1916 and enjoyed it there so much that it was four years before he returned to Berlin, that something happened during that time, something that rendered him a pacifist for the rest of his life. I didn't say that. I didn't say that when he arrived back in Berlin, he sowed his seed in the young Sámi girl who had joined him, and that this woman was to become my mother. The dark-haired pariah of the butcher shop, a descendant of the blood-stoppers. Because of my mother, I could never become a national hero the likes of Horst Wessel, the embodiment of the pure Aryan.

My blood is impure. And it's my father's fault.

My father never cared for the Cause. He was eventually fired from the publishing house, and it was only thanks to my uncle that he managed to get a job at a newspaper that, though suitably anti-Semitic, had few literary merits. The NSDAP took a dislike to my father after he refused to publish a slanderous essay about the Viennese quack in association with an article entitled *"Juden Unerwünscht."* After this incident we were forced out of Berlin and into a house with shabby roughcast and where the kitchen walls were papered with old banknotes devalued in 1923. The dishcloths smelled of mold, and as you fumbled for the bedpan in the night, you could feel the cockroaches brushing against your fingers. My mother never complained, but I know she suffered. I only once heard her scream. On that occasion she cried that the floors were so terrible that they rotted our shoes. Father didn't reply, but after that, we started wearing slippers indoors.

"Your father was a good man, but I don't understand the fuss about Horst Wessel. Who is he?" asked Wild-Eye.

I saw red. Didn't this damned *Finnenlümmel* understand anything? Horst Wessel is one of Nazi Germany's greatest martyrs, an ideological hero who gave everything for our sakes and who was murdered by the Communists. Father called Horst Wessel a hooligan. He was no such thing. Horst Wessel was a battering ram of a man. My father, on the other hand, was a pitiable creature. Without my uncle's intervention, he would have been sent to Sachsenhausen to test marching boots after he tried to sell the medal of honor he'd been awarded by the Party Writers' Association to the Gypsies.

I imagine Father had secretly hoped that I too might become a writer.

I remember one day in particular. Father called me into his office and handed me an ink pen. He claimed that a man called Bertolt Brecht had once used it to sign his name, then to pick his ear. The nib was splotched with ink, the water in the goldfish bowl tainted. I turned the pen in my hands and pointed out that the nib was broken. My father, Bomber Jaeger and sabotage-battalion commander Fritz Angelhurst, shrugged his shoulders and lost forever any interest he'd once held for me.

"Well then, you might as well start peeling potatoes for a living."

I did not become a potato peeler.

I became a photographer instead.

Taking photographs is the only thing I have ever wanted, ever since I saw the works of Leni Riefenstahl at the Berlin Olympics. My uncle got me a 35 mm Leica. At my father's editorial office, I learned to use the magnifying lens and to calculate development times, to understand the secrets of gelatin, to record the world on a magnesium surface. The upside-down world seen through the camera lens is more real to me than one governed by the laws of gravity. The image of a woman's thigh, burned onto paper with development fluid, arouses me far more than real, moving flesh.

Until now, that is. I sensed the woman next to me edging closer. All of a sudden I felt the urge to brush her hair to one side, stick my fingers into her mouth one by one, and let her suck away the dirt and blood.

Then I remembered what the Rumrunner's sister had told me about this woman. She'd come to bid me good-bye. Sat straight in my lap, her breasts bobbing against my shooting jacket.

"I'll miss you, so I will. But I could come and pose for you again. Would you like that?"

I nodded. I remembered the words Mother had once said: "What's beautiful on the outside is often empty on the inside." And then, on the spur of the moment, I asked the name of the midwife who had helped when she gave birth to the darkie child. Instantly I realized that I'd committed one of those errors that occur only in the world of women, those little transgressions that men cannot understand. The girl's entire body seemed to cloud over. At first she pretended not to remember the woman at all, though I'd seen them chatting together in broad daylight on the green in Parkkina.

"Don't you worry about her. She's barren," said the Rumrunner's sister, eventually. "She's got bad blood."

I didn't know what that meant.

"It means lying with that kind of broad is as much use as buggering a barrel of herring. It'll hurt, and it'll all come to nothing."

I still didn't understand.

"Weird-Eye, that's what she is. Don't you touch her."

The Rumrunner's sister tapped her finger against my forehead.

"She makes folks do funny things. She can read men's minds. She'll give you the evil eye. *Verrückt.* You'll go mad, so you will."

That's a language I understood. I didn't dare become any madder.

Now I sensed Wild-Eye next to me, and I was startled at how powerful my desire was to touch her.

I couldn't be weak. I had a task to complete.

I escaped from the camp the very next morning.

TITOVKA

June 1944

After that first evening, you were nowhere to be seen. Apparently you'd gone to Parkkina to take part in some kind of documentation exercise. The head nurse at the camp was called the Resurrectionist, and from what she said, I gathered that your departure was frowned upon but that there was little anyone could do about it. From this I concluded that Hermann Gödel must be the person truly in charge, because a commander couldn't just swan off like that. So I waited, lay on my bunk in the empty barracks, and crushed hawk moths between my thighs, protecting the midges that let your blood, wherever you happened to be. The sheets dried beneath me; the air reeked of resin. My whole body quivered as I touched my forehead at the spot where you had brushed my hair to the side. I caressed my hips and prayed to God to take away the unclean desire to pleasure myself. I drank tea brewed from castoreum and the leaves of bishop's wort. I prayed to God, chanted Big Lamberg's words.

"Your twotch is twisted like a hare's muzzle."

You're bad, bad, bad. A harlot. Filthy is she who covets her own brother. But longing had consumed me. Now, instead of Big Lamberg's, it was Aune Näkkälä's words that thrust their way into my mind.

"You've hair strong as a horse's mane, lass, and thighs like a young foal."

I began to prepare myself for the interview you were going to do with me. The Russian lad took the shears and cut me a neat fringe for the photograph, and coached me by asking the kinds of questions we imagined reporters asked. They wanted to know everything, right from the beginning. I geared myself up to tell you.

"I was born in 1908 as balls of fire flew through the Siberian night."

"*Medizinitsa*, don't talk nonsense."

The Russian lad read extracts from real interviews published in *Tide of the Times*. Subjects had to be clear and concise in their answers and not witter on about events from time immemorial.

Again. How did you end up in this profession? How do you do your job? But these questions were all wrong. I couldn't answer them truthfully. That my sides burn day and night, that I want you to defile me right here, right now.

The Resurrectionist was a Finnish spinster who read German medical publications and who believed in eugenics as fervently as she did in the resurrection. She rinsed her equipment in carboline and scrubbed her knuckles in an enamel bowl to wash off the Russian stink. Legend has it she got her name at an infirmary in Petsamo after she managed to bring a Red Guardist back to life. The story goes that the whiskered Russian had skied north from Rovaniemi in February 1918. The Resurrectionist had already started plugging all his orifices with resin so that pus wouldn't leak through the boards of the coffin, when all of a sudden the corpse had come back to life.

"By Lenin's flaming backside, woman, stop poking around!" cried the Communist.

He clambered down from the gurney, picked up his pipe, and fled across the border to join the legion in Murmansk. That lit the Resurrectionist's undying hatred toward all things Red and Russian.

When I asked about you, the Resurrectionist simply shrugged her bony shoulders.

"The commander's been sent on a mission. Haven't seen him around here."

I went directly to Hermann Gödel.

"Just do as Fräulein Vaataja says."

So the Resurrectionist had a name after all.

A light caress on the cheek, the suggestion to get to work, for the camp would soon fill up. And that's what happened. It turned out that there were around three hundred prisoners in total. Until now they'd been laboring around the clock at the roadworks on Russenstraße.

"There is plenty of light up here," Gödel consoled me when I expressed shock at the working conditions. "You are like a well-preserved vase from the tomb of Alaric, Fräulein Schwester."

He bent over to kiss my hand, and again I blushed. He explained that he'd previously worked for the Ahnenerbe, Himmler's historical–scientific organization that aimed to research the illustrious ancestors of the Teutonic peoples. It had been Gödel's dream to travel to Italy and uncover the tomb of Alaric, king of the Visigoths. My lips moved in time with the commander's words. Goodness, how well an SS officer schooled in classical antiquity treated me!

"Nothing to get on your high horse about."

The Resurrectionist had appeared on some errand or other.

"You're a simple cockscomb just like the rest of us," she muttered as soon as Hermann Gödel was out of earshot.

Then she hurried toward the barracks with the words Operation Kuhstall above the door. I followed her, but she wouldn't let me inside. She pointed to another barracks and told me to concentrate on cutting away the prisoners' gangrene.

"Can't let you do the important jobs, can we? Best if you just keep yourself to yourself."

I decided to show her that it wasn't for nothing I'd been brought into the employ of the Third Reich, so I established a louse sauna at the camp. The Russian lad struggled to read aloud from *Tide of the Times*:

"'Des–pite their race, even Russians can be made tol . . . tolerable by scr . . . scrubbing them with soap, sweating them in tem–pe–ra–tures over 140°F and by not letting them relieve themselves in the bar–racks.'"

The Russian lad seemed entertained by the idea of prisoners relieving themselves in the barracks, but I didn't think it was remotely amusing. The Russians are animals. Only animals shit on the floor. The fact that the constant stench of ammonia hung around your nostrils as soon as the northern wind died down was proof enough.

The Russian lad helped me select prisoners for the cleaning troop. Otherwise he was lazy, like most of his compatriots, loitering on the steps, carving wooden figurines, horses, towers, that kind of thing. Out of sheer spite, the war hound, which the Hilfswilligers had tied to his ankle, was particularly afraid of bombs. On top of that, the thing was now expecting puppies and whimpered incessantly. I tried to treat the lad the way I did everyone else, especially because he spoke Finnish. He was a queer creature; he didn't consider himself Russian at all but a Mari, a people related to the Finns.

The prisoners had their hair shorn off, and their rags were laundered in an enormous pot that used up a gallon of soap with each wash. I soon realized that we'd need more of everything. If there's one thing I've learned from my years as a midwife, it's that disease spreads, sows will die, and their offspring develop infections and tooth decay unless we tackle the root of the filth.

I handed the list to Montya, the Serbian Hilfswilliger that Gödel seemed to trust. Detergent, lye, soap, sulfate, petroleum, vinegar, pure alcohol. Behind the last row of barracks was a flimsy plywood tent, and to that tent I marched the human wrecks that we called prisoners of war. They were scrawny, but Gödel said that's just because they're too lazy to earn their meals. I could believe that. At first the guards spluttered and frowned at the idea of the prisoners bathing and joked about the kindheartedness of the *Finnenlümmels*, but they relented before long. At a camp like this, people were more afraid of a typhoid epidemic than they were of an attack by the Russians, though the cannons boomed in Litsa all day long, and sometimes in the evenings I caught the whiff of gunpowder, which mingled with Gödel's scent of Ukrainian cypress.

It was eighteen days, three minutes, and a very long moment before you returned. And you didn't come alone. Jouni and Lisbet Näkkälä slouched along behind you, Lisbet in a red frilly hat and a cretonne frock.

"Don't let the *Finnenlümmels* fraternize with the prisoners!" Gödel shouted just as I walked into the yard in my bug-eaten cotton dress.

A new shipment of prisoners had arrived. I'd been given the task of listening to their lungs and documenting any cases of tuberculosis and pneumonia. On top of that, I was to note down any chilblains and assess the condition of the cocks and pricks, measure them, and catalog any cases of syphilis or the clap, and to pay particular attention to any that were circumcised. Such cases were to be reported immediately. The Resurrectionist had already found two. Without hesitation Montya dragged them outside and left them to shiver naked in the cold. I complained that their disinfection process wasn't complete.

"Don't fret about that, Fräulein Schwester," Gödel replied. "These *verjüdelte Russen* will be taken to another camp."

But where?

Gödel shrugged his handsome shoulders and hinted that I shouldn't ask about such things. It uses up air. Unlike in the rest of Europe, there were no decent *Schutzhaftlager* this far north.

"The Einsatzgruppe will take care of things."

In addition, there were some prisoners whose gunshot wounds needed urgent attention, some whose limbs had to be amputated without anesthetic. It was this commotion to which you and the Näkkäläs arrived. Jouni was blind drunk again and wanted to inspect the camp. I managed to intervene; I knew what Jouni had in mind. He was running around looking for his Norwegian sweetheart. Apparently her husband had been sent to the Sydspissen prison in Tromsø, and there were rumors that the Fritz had sent his wife to a camp in the east.

"Your fancy woman's not here. There are no women here."

"You sure about that? Ginger curls and a twotch like a mare's muzzle."

"Hold your trap or they'll shoot you."

But Jouni started calling out.

"Hedda! Are you here?"

I hurriedly dragged him into the barracks to sleep it off.

"I've so much to tell you," Lisbet shouted, waving from the truck when I came back into the forecourt.

Her mouth was pretty and pink, and she was wearing a pair of Löfsko ankle boots that Aune had ordered for her all the way from

Stockholm. The armholes of her sleeveless dress offered a view as lascivious as the gates of hell. You grabbed her waist and lifted her from the back of the Destroyer Ford. Lisbet flew toward me, smelling of sperm and lily of the valley.

"It's our wee Weird-Eye." She giggled, wrapping her arm around my neck. "That new hair makes your eyes look right devious."

I gripped the silky down at the back of her neck and felt the delicate vertebrae beneath her skin. So brittle and fragile.

"But you're busy," she said. "We're off to lie down."

"I could stop now."

Lisbet rolled her eyes and grabbed you by the arm. I prayed to God: Give Johannes the power to say no. Let him ask me to join them.

But the Lord's face did not shine on me.

"Want to go to the Cabinet? I'll tell you about the time I bathed Hickler."

"How about that?"

And with that you gripped the little strumpet's waist, a beanstalk who'd barely survived giving birth, a nest of filth soiled by a stinkhorn. No, my Johannes. Lisbet turned and waved. That victorious look of hers. I am a strong woman. I can topple a reindeer stag in the marsh anytime I want. With a snip of a girl like Lisbet, I could wring her neck in an instant. I returned to the infirmary, the hiss of midges ringing in my ears, and hacked the bone saw hard into the next patient.

"*Medizinitsa. Vot*, you have guest." Montya's voice came singing from the door.

Lisbet tiptoed in to see what I was up to.

"Ugh, it stinks of the plague round here."

I didn't respond. I was delicately trying to cut a piece of gangrene from a mustachioed Belarusian as he sobbed, insistently showing me photographs of his wife and two children. The wife had a dacha-scented garland of flowers on her head. The little girl was wearing lace frills and a pearl brooch; the boy had a pair of thick glasses and a Bible bearing the crooked cross pressed against his chest. They were a handsome family. I hummed comfortingly and tried to sterilize his leg as best I could. It wasn't easy. I'd used up most of the disinfectant in cleaning the sauna tent. The Resurrectionist had whispered that this patient was suspected of being a commissioner of the people, and advised me to saw off his lower leg without anesthetic. I told Lisbet to draw up a list of the prisoner's belongings so that everything could be duly returned after the war. She didn't obey me but instead stood throughout the operation, slowly reading through the list of medicines attached to the wall. Blood made her queasy.

"You know, I've worked out how to get through this war," Lisbet rambled as I washed my hands in an enamel basin. "I'll give that Johannes a bairn. That's what he wants."

"You'll not become pregnant all that quickly."

"Aye, I will. Johannes said I smell fruitful."

The roof beams seemed suddenly so fragile.

"You'll never believe what happened yesterday during the air raids. There's nothing wrong with him after all, down there. He's wild, pushed inside me, there in the dark—with my own brother lying right next to us."

Back and forth, back and forth, your prick in an unfamiliar twotch, there amid the earthy smell of the bomb shelter beneath the officers' club. The bogus Lotta lass with her legs open, the panting, the glow of Jouni's pipe right next to them. The Russian bombs had missed a golden opportunity.

"I'm going to have him," Lisbet said.

There came a boom somewhere out in the tundra. The war hound tied to the Russian lad howled and scarpered beneath the gurney. Lisbet's brow furrowed. Most people had headed south to escape the bombing.

"Hickler's not winning this, is he? Only one ball left, sitting at home chewing the carpet."

I was offended at how little she believed in our Cause.

"We've to think of the future."

But as Lisbet wisely said, it was unwise to pal around with anyone and everyone. We'd to be careful with the Fritz.

"Turns out Oili Jaatima's man, Holger, found himself a German strumpet in Aachen."

Oili had been killed during a bombing raid on a train station, Lisbet couldn't remember exactly where. I could have told her it was at Elisenvaara. Jouni knew all the news you never heard on the wireless. But I didn't say anything because I doubted Jouni would be pleased.

"Good job our Johannes is a different kettle of fish."

I looked up at the rafters, and again they seemed fragile. They could come tumbling down on her at any moment, split open that head of flowing locks. That damned bogus Lotta, that simpleton, that garrulous Greta Garbo, that counterfeit and trollop. Why did she have to take you, of all people? She'd have no bother. After the war she could marry a wealthy heir with a good upbringing or the owner of the Kemi Forestry Company, a man who hadn't knocked up any Svetlanas along the White Sea coast and come back with syphilis. Lisbet could have anyone she wanted. But what about me?

"You know what? I could keep a bairn with that Johannes. Will you help me? Tell me how to run a good bath?"

Lisbet's gaze washed over my eyes; her ochre, girly fingers stroked the back of my hand. Her hat was the size of a cart's wheel, dark, bloodred velvet, and its faded felt like a child's sunburned skin.

"I'll make you a potion strong enough to waken any man's desires and make a hay pole fertile," I answered. "But I want that hat and frock in return."

Lisbet shrugged her shoulders.

"Suit yourself. Not that they'll do you much good, mind."

TITOVKA

July 1944

The Russian lad and I scoured the Communist sweat from the sauna boards. My hands were trembling as I stirred honey, rowanberries, and kiss-me-quick into the bucket of water. I told him to lay juniper branches on the floor and around the door frame. From time to time I crouched down and scratched the war hound's neck. I was out of breath. I'd been out of breath since the moment you stood in the doorway and said, "Fräulein Schwester, would you run me a bath?"

You looked perturbed. Lisbet Näkkälä was lying in bed, moaning. Overnight her blood had turned to mud, and her groin smelled of rotten herring. I tried to calm her down. The Resurrectionist would take care of her with bismuth injections and valerian.

"Women's problems. It'll all go away by itself once she's rested."

I patted talcum powder on my armpits, which I'd shaved with chlorine water. I rubbed my face with dew and gargled with catmint. The Russian lad trimmed my fringe, and the war hound licked the calendula ointment I'd rubbed on my ankles.

"*Izvinitye.* She's a good dog."

I canceled all other bathing for the evening and didn't care a jot for the protestations of the Resurrectionist. The Kyrgyz prisoners could cry themselves to sleep; let them drink swill and feed on flies' eggs. They could all hang, for all I cared. For you we prepared a bath of pure nectar, and inside its balmy, marsh-tea steam, the mind could rest and drift into a bluish, resinous sleep for hours afterward. We carried in a copper-edged bucket, and I slowly filled it with bathing water as velvety as milk. I whisked the water into an aromatic, herby froth and hummed to myself. You could soak in there to your heart's content. I placed the cupping equipment on a stool within easy reach. With those implements I would work the evil out of your back muscles. I threw an initial ladle of water on the stove to release the carbon and let the smoke clear.

You appeared in the doorway like a dark silhouette. You undressed slowly, and I didn't dare look. Candles flickered in the steam, casting fluttering shadows on the walls. You remained standing by the bathtub, almost helpless.

"Fräulein Schwester, should I step in now?"

Outside came the melancholy Slavic tones of the Moscow Philharmonic. Your foot touched the edge of the steaming-hot tub, your toes tensed. Then you slipped into the water with a groan. I poured dark, fragrant herbal water over your shoulders. Warmth pulsed down to my groin.

"I must ask you something," you said.

"Anything, anything at all."

My dearest Johannes.

All of a sudden your hand gripped my wrist.

"Wild-Eye."

It was the first time you'd called me by that name.

"Wild-Eye, I have bad dreams."

"What kind of dreams?"

For a moment you hesitated.

"I can't remember them."

I placed a warm lavender cloth on your forehead, worked up a lather, and started rubbing in slow, slow movements. You moaned with pleasure and slid deeper into the steam.

You told me you wake up at night to the sound of women laughing across the fells.

"Can you hear it?"

"Aye," I answered, though I'd never heard a thing.

"I know fine well what it is. The Communists are belting women's laughter through enormous loudspeakers to make the enemy lose his mind."

Women's laughter? Why? I didn't dare ask. I promised to brew you a nightcap and sing to you if you wanted.

"My mother, Annikki, was a fine singer."

I began to hum. I felt your finger drawing a line along an artery pulsing through my forearm.

"Danke schön," you sighed, closing your eyes.

That's when the noise started. Such a terrible din carried in from the forecourt that at first I thought we were all done for. A moment later I heard a volley of cackling and the Russian lad's distressed screams. I realized that Montya and the other trusted prisoners were tormenting him and amusing themselves by pulling the puppies from the womb of the war hound tied to his leg. I hesitated a moment. If only they'd kill the Russian lad one day, either accidentally or deliberately. There was something about him that annoyed the other prisoners. It was none of my business. I was here with you, here to touch your body, to experience it. My Lord, do I really have to go out there? Now? In hindsight, I shouldn't have done so. But at that moment, as if driven by divine command, I staggered through the steam and out into the forecourt.

It wasn't my trusted Russian they were tormenting.

A convoy of new prisoners had arrived at the camp. They were cowering at the edge of the forecourt, not bothering to swipe at the midges swarming around them. But there was a commotion going on too. In the middle of a ring of SS officers was a slender creature, hissing and writhing. The squadron said they'd found the girl in the village of Vartiolahti, washing her underwear in the river that formed the border. I asked the exact location of the village. In the Kalastajasaarento Peninsula, very near the front.

"There's nobody there but spies," whispered the Russian lad. "Kill her."

And with that he returned to the steps and continued carving his wooden figurines as if the matter didn't affect him in the least.

If only I'd turned back. If only I'd left the Skolt girl to her fate and returned to you. There you were, soaking in my misty steam, and I hadn't finished washing you. I wanted to soap you, make you slippery, lick you clean. I wanted to lather your skin, pour water between your nipples, let it run to your belly button, and farther still. But something forced me to intervene. Poor slip of a girl. This was a spy? She wasn't smart, that much was clear, kicking and screaming when she should have kept quiet and prayed. She was so pitiable that nobody dared put her out of her misery. Or as I've come to think, the girl had an unflinching aptitude for lies, a skill with which she managed to deceive us all.

She was perhaps thirteen years old, but she was already pretty as a peony. Dirty, yes, but dirty from the woods, not the war. With her scarf half-knocked from her head, she was entrancing. I'd never seen a lass like her. Raven-black hair, high cheekbones, soft lips that hollered curses, sending an inappropriate rage across the forecourt and into the war. On her arm was a strange vaccination scar the shape of a wolf's head. The SS officers shoved her from side to side, laughing idly as she spluttered.

"She's a spy," declared Hermann Gödel, flicking his hand toward the barracks named Operation Kuhstall. I glanced at the sauna, but you were out of sight. I panicked. The oldest of the guards, Holger Heider, was about to grab the girl.

"Nein!"

I'd shouted out loud. I instantly regretted it. I was supposed to return to you. What was I thinking, doing something like this in the middle of everything? Everyone fell silent, and Gödel wrinkled his brow.

"She's nothing but a lass," I garbled. "I'll take her on. She can help me gather moss and mushrooms. This one's not a spy."

I don't know what would have happened if you hadn't walked out of the sauna hut. Steaming beneath your overcoat, you approached us, as languid as if you were on an evening stroll. The marsh tea I'd mixed into the bathwater had done the trick, and again I regretted not running back inside straight away. Marsh tea makes all those who inhale it uninhibited and susceptible. But the moment had passed. I knew it. A look of understanding returned to your eyes. I touched your hand and let the words flow out of me.

"Let me keep the girl."

You gave her an absentminded glance and waved your hand in affirmation. What of it? Keep her, as long as she's no trouble. I nodded. Gödel nodded. You spoke so that everybody heard.

"The girl will be Fräulein Schwester's trusted prisoner."

Fräulein Schwester. I was no longer Wild-Eye. You made me promise that the girl would be tied either to me or the war hound at all times, and that I would be held personally responsible for her. She mustn't run willy-nilly around the camp or talk to the other prisoners. I hurriedly agreed. What's more, I'd make sure the girl had as little to do with the soldiers as possible.

"And keep her away from the Cattlehouse."

It took a moment before I understood. Operation Kuhstall. The Resurrectionist still wouldn't let me in there. I felt the nectar steam rising from your body and evaporating into the summer night.

"Shall we carry on your bath? I could sing for you."

You plucked off the juniper needles that had stuck to your skin. "We've other things to do now."

The new prisoners awoke a fresh sense of enthusiasm in Montya and his gang. To me they looked the same as all the other Russians. Each was cataloged and assigned to a workstation, each assessed on physical condition. Their possessions were confiscated until further notice.

I carried their belongings to a hut behind Operation Cattlehouse. Among the piles of photographs, I saw the one belonging to the mustachioed Belarusian man whose leg I'd sawn off. I looked at the photograph, in which the daughter was dressed so prettily and the son in thick spectacles stood holding his Bible, and sent out a prayer to the infidels far away: Daddy won't be coming home. Godspeed, little ones.

This newest collection of personal effects puzzled me for the amount of jewelry and other feminine wares this fresh consignment of prisoners had been carrying. Of course, soldiers had a tendency to cherish mementos of their sweethearts—a name embroidered on a handkerchief, a bodice with buttons of bone, a half-used tub of calendula ointment. I could understand that. But a drawstring bandage used during menstruation? A willow pessary to stop a Skolt woman's womb tumbling into the road after her eighth pregnancy? A sports card for the Odessa Women Comrades' Association and a flimsy woolen sock on a set of wooden needles?

Only once I saw the prisoners naked did I understand that some of them were women. Naturally, I'd heard of desperate, fearless Russian womenfolk being called up for the Red Army. I'd thought this was the same kind of tall tale as the stories about a new race of humans bred by Stalin, half man and half Siberian wolfhound. Legend had it that these dog-men could smell the enemy in the forest and gallop for leagues at a time on a diet of waterless borscht and dried meat.

The female prisoners were sent to Operation Cattlehouse.

"Why?" I asked you.

You hesitated, as if you couldn't remember. Then your expression cleared. The women were being taken there to weave their hair into sacks and stocking thread for submarine crews in the Barents Sea. Women were better at that sort of thing. No point taking them to a Motti bunker.

"We'll not let them waste away," you said, and once again I fell in love with the way you spoke the local dialect. So wrong and so right.

That evening the Hilfswilligers and the guards celebrated well into the night. Jouni had given them some of his moonshine, and at around midnight Holger Heider started blaring "Lili Marleen" through the camp's loudspeakers. The Moscow Philharmonic was wrenched out of bed and told to scratch out marching songs and dance the German polka. At two in the morning, I knocked on the door of the Cabinet, but nobody answered. I wasn't worried, because pretty little Lisbet Näkkälä was tucked up in her camp bed and vomiting. The Resurrectionist had taken a phial of veronal and was sleeping soundly, far away from this world.

I stood in the forecourt and listened. A godwit was cooing somewhere nearby. The air smelled of a stern, uncompromising summer evening, of the frost slowly encroaching from the Arctic Ocean. Autumn could wait a while yet; there were still no ravens in the sky. I gazed around. For a moment I thought I saw a figure lying asleep on the roof of the barracks. A sheet of mist had moved in from the fells and descended upon the camp, so I couldn't be sure whether my eyes were deceiving me.

I went to check on the Skolt girl. Masha was her name. Now she was huddled by herself in the forecourt and looked like what she really was: a lost, helpless little fledgling. I could only guess what life at the camp would do to such an innocent thing. A few weeks were all it would take. She wouldn't be much help. But she wasn't a spy. That much was clear.

"Chin up. It'll all be just fine," I comforted her, though I knew it wasn't true.

I couldn't help feeling sorry for her. She looked the same as I had when I'd first arrived at Big Lamberg's house. I took the girl to the sauna and scrubbed her in your now-lukewarm bath. Then I asked Holger Heider to open the canteen door. He was the only guard I could find, and by now even he was steadying himself against the barracks wall with his fly open. I told him to bring me flour, saccharine, and a cast-iron griddle. One of the cows was ready for milking, and with a little egg flour we whipped up some pancake batter. I taught the Skolt girl to toss pancakes in the air, though one of them ended up stuck to the canteen's log floor. It made her laugh.

"*Parmuska,* will you make me a kite?"

I was so taken aback that the bowl of batter almost slipped from my hands. I wouldn't have thought the Lappish Skolts knew what a kite was.

"Da, da," Masha eagerly assured me, and told me her *Babushka* used to make her a kite every year at around this time.

"Why?"

"*Dyen razdeniya.* Birthday," she told me, her face serious.

She didn't know the precise date. Masha's mother had run off to Murmansk to become a telegrapher and left the girl in her grandmother's care.

"The sorrel was in blossom when they found me in the woods. *Miehcest von tam kavnim,* my *Babushka* used to say."

I took the girl in my arms, hugged her.

"Aye, I'll make you a kite."

I sniffed her childlike head and kissed the wolf's-head scar on her arm. You and I would have children just like this one day, I thought, *rein und unschuldig*. We would make them kites. They would have medallions, curly hair, and lace collars like the Belarusian's daughter. If we had boys, we wouldn't need to sit them on an anthill every time they wet the bed. Meringue and sweet, aromatic bread for breakfast every morning, pockets strong enough to hold birds' eggs, and round spectacles to make them smart. At that moment a thought entered my mind, so dazzlingly clear that I was surprised it hadn't occurred to me earlier. None of this would happen if we remained at the camp until the war was over. There would always be something in our way. Lisbet would inevitably recover; then someone else would come along. I handed Masha the bowl of batter and let her lick the sides. I stroked her head and walked her to my camp bed to sleep. Back then she smelled of marsh herbs and angel's piddle.

Now the stink she gives off makes me want to wretch.

PART TWO

DEAD MAN'S DIARY

Scarface to Whale Catcher (SOE), September 9, 1942:

Battleship Tirpitz*: sabotage unsuccessful. Torpedoes mistakenly deployed after English frogmen took the helm.*

PS: *Permission to relocate. Current location partly out of signal.*

Whale Catcher:

Relocation denied. Location strategically important. Germans cannot intercept transmitter.

Scarface to Redhead, September 10, 1942:

Foiled sabotage on Tirpitz. *Numerous communications intercepted. Decryption methods already attempted: Diplomatic Code 26, Pobeda Code, and GRU codes. One message decrypted, sender unknown: "False calculations added to Fritz maps. Cable car along Russenstraße down. Imagine what German colleagues capable of, erecting contraptions like that during wartime.* Tirpitz *to be targeted again soon."*

Suspected informant: Commissioner Uuno R of Parkkina.

Redhead:

Bulletin received. Payment 300 kronor. Revenge action to be implemented. Initiate Operations Wild Duck and Midnight Sun.

September 10, 1942

My dear daughter,

I write to you because there is no one else. Of course, I know who really sent that message. But I'll not inform on Aune's boy, for I owe that woman my life. She helped me escape from Rovaniemi when the White butchers came down to Lainaanranta and rounded up the Red Guardists at the Workers' Theatre in February 1918.

Instead, I informed on the police commissioner who was bumbling around during the Petsamo espionage affair and who had his claws into you. That scoundrel with his crooked, goat-assed eyes left an unpleasant taste, and now he's running around these parts all the while. Collects flowers, a botanist, apparently. A queer customer, I'll tell you. A Laestadian, to boot, and I can't abide those zealots. It was because of them that your mother was forced to live in sin and had to knock around in bars and taverns with me. That's when she caught the tuberculosis.

And that's why I'd like to see this Uuno swinging from the gallows, but Rovaniemi Liaison headquarters got there first and sent him to the front. Let him die for all I care, him and the whole heretical bunch.

Your mother was a good woman, far too meek and mild for this world. She thought well of everyone; it was only because she asked me that I tanned the Bible-thumpers' shoes for years without any recompense. At the annual church meeting in Rovaniemi, I looked after the preachers' worn-out Lappish boots. They thanked the Lord for their shoes, but nobody thanked me. All that wailing, shouting, longing, rattling, and pounding the floor with their feet wore away the soles of their shoes. More than anything, it meant plenty of work for your father. They were traitors to their class, every last one of them, refusing to join the popular front.

"Calm now, lass," I told you. "Sharpening their knives for their own hide, so they are."

I was wrong. It was my hide they were sharpening their knives for. The moment of truth finally came on February 20, 1918, when in the south the war of brother against brother was only just getting started, but up in Lapland all had long since been lost. Nobody in your mother's family lifted so much as a finger to help me, no matter how often I'd mended their shoes. The White butchers followed the Kemijoki riverbank at night and dragged your father out to Konttinen's field in his underwear and bare feet. I told you to hide under the blankets, quiet as a mouse.

"Daddy'll be back soon," I lied when I saw who was coming for me. They arrested eleven Red Guardists that night. Only one managed to escape; the other ten were

sentenced at a court-martial, and their bodies were sunk in the quayside at Lainaanranta during a hard frost. They say the ice was dyed the color of rust for two weeks. It was Aune who helped me escape, strapped the skis to my feet, and told me to ski over the border and into the Soviet land. When I arrived in Parkkina, I was already dead, but there was a nurse who cured me, and as if by a miracle I woke up there on the gurney and continued on my way. Aune's sister, Annikki, met me in the borough of Moscow, and it was there that the Englishman signed me up for the Murmansk legion—me, a Red Guardist, serving under a White lord fighting against God knows whom. I've had numerous such lords since then.

Now I'm here on the coast of the Arctic Ocean, alone. There is nobody I can trust. Hyyryläinen and the Merchant have just brought me more provisions. They've both got nationalist tendencies and collaborate with the SOE. The Merchant: dishonest in business, honest for the Cause. Hyyryläinen: a grifter, close-cropped hair, speaks with a thick Turku accent. He brought me here after the Petsamo espionage affair in 1939. Jaarikki Peltonen, his name was. Another of your suitors. But, my dear child, I couldn't give him to you. You deserve far better. He's the kind of man that can't take life up here in the north. Men like that end up shepherding reindeer around the fells and living in fear of birds and colorful wallpaper. There's something not right about him, but I'm only a father speaking on behalf of his daughter. He's too interested in my notebooks, shudders at my wretched appearance, and can't hide his discomfort. Because of him, I've decided to use invisible ink in these diaries.

I have just deciphered a message sent by the Gestapo using the Schiffer A2 table: "Contact from Kalastajasaarento Peninsula arrives Wed. Code name Redhead." My dear girl, you cannot imagine what this is like. I know him. The man's a figure from my past. The moron has red hair.

DEAD MAN'S FJORD

October 1944

We didn't die on the skerry after all. It was a miracle, Johannes. You must believe me that it was a genuine miracle, brought to us by fate, for, when I had lost all hope, a long, narrow Nordland boat glided out of the fog. The kind of ancient boat that the Vikings used for marauding along inland water channels or fishing for cod. Inside the apparition sat a haggard old man, probably not the driver of the motorboat whose engine I'd heard previously in the mists. No. The screech of the rowlocks and the whoosh of oars as the raw-wood boat sliced through the fog. For a moment I thought this was the same apparition I'd once seen in Parkkina when three angels had appeared playing their trumpets, or that it was the same red-haired Jerker we'd seen traipsing round Dead Man's Fjord last summer. Do you remember? But this apparition was different. You could smell the tarred boat and the ingrained whiff of male sweat a league away.

"*God kveld!* Evening all!"

Two pitch-black tern eyes peered out from behind the man's frosted beard, his nose like a bridge across the Neva. The bird's-eyed boatman scratched behind his ear.

"*Hej hej!* You folks deaf and dumb?"

"Evening," I whispered.

"Right then. My mate here warned there'd be guests coming in. Quite a place you lasses have found."

I pulled my thumb from Masha's mouth and bowed politely. Hilma didn't bark once.

"Drowned afore long, so you would. Folks don't go out in weather like this."

I told him I'd heard a motorboat earlier. At that, the old man seemed graven and serious.

"You watch yourself, now," he said, and glanced knowingly at the back of the boat.

"By Lenin's flaming backside!"

Only now did I notice that what looked like a bundle of netting on the aft thwart was in fact another man. I was startled. He was grotesque, his face so badly burned that you couldn't make out his features, though somehow he looked oddly familiar. Perhaps it was a smell, a stench stretching across the intervening years, something I couldn't place. He stared at me from behind his mangled features as though I were one of those strange sea creatures with the face of a human and the body of a seal, a creature that sometimes washes up on the shores in Parkkina and that the children poke with sticks and tickle to death. I didn't like it. I didn't want anyone to see me in this state.

The disfigured man cleared his throat.

"The mice squealing for you yet?"

A sense of relief. I realized that, though he was Finnish, the man was utterly insane.

"Don't worry your head about him. He's only asking what side of the war you're on. But we don't care about sides now, do we, Jaarikki?"

Fear rushed again into the palms of my hands. These two were Communists. Resistance men, Soviet spies, or what have you. They'll doubtless report me to their comrades the minute they're back to the *kolkhoz*; then they'll come back to skin the lonely woman in the fjord, to strip the flesh while they're at it and sell it at the markets in Leningrad. Out of nowhere, an old saying popped into my mind and slipped out of my mouth before I could do anything to stop it.

"Somebody once told me, if the Communist Cause really comes from the Lord himself, there's precious little we can do about his kingdom."

Scarface scoffed on the aft thwart.

"And if it's from the Devil, it'll die when the time comes."

With that he began to cough, and I couldn't tell whether he was laughing or choking, and only then did I see that his lips too were almost charred to nothing.

"Bjørne," Birdseye shouted, reaching out his hand.

I gripped the unloaded Mauser in my pocket and gave my name, but I didn't shake hands. "How much for a ride?" I asked.

"We'll take you for free."

I had to take a gamble. Bjørne helped us into the rickety boat, loaded to the brim, growled at Masha to get herself out of the way, and began to row. Someone handed me a bottle. It was impossible to see anything. The fog whirled around us, up and down, and suddenly I was afraid of what might appear from within it. The wrong landscape? An unfamiliar fjord? I held the bottle up to my eyes and tried to decipher the tattered label: *Captain Morgan, Scotland, 1940.*

Devil's piss. Uuno would never have let me drink the stuff. I took such a gulp that it burned my stomach, and I made Masha take some too. Things felt instantly better.

And the mist dispersed.

If there was ever a time in my life that left me speechless, this was one of them. A mainland appearing behind the fog, blown up out of the water, a landscape deepening into ravines, waterfalls, dark blue shadows, and light. I recognized the cliffs at Seitakallio, the skerries of Valaskari, and before long our cottage. A warmth rippled through me: I have been here before.

Dead Man's Cabin looked like a ragged scab on the landscape. I pulled Hermann Gödel's wolf-skin coat tighter around my body and thanked fate for sending three angels to lead me here.

"Spot of luck, eh, fishing for cod in the fog?"

I know a thing or two about the gulf streams that keep the shores up here ice-free. I know you don't catch cod in a wooden Nordland boat, particularly with neither a hook nor a line in sight. But I was pleased all the same. Birdseye either didn't know where I had come from or was pretending he didn't know. But when I told him I wanted to go ashore, he changed his tune and said he would take us to his store five miles to the south.

"There's nothing up here," he assured me.

"No, no, can't set ashore there, lass!" Scarface protested.

But I could plainly see we had arrived.

Bjørne shrugged his shoulders in resignation, but the swine behind him shook his head. No. Bjørne's comrade didn't like the idea of taking us to Dead Man's Cabin one bit. Bjørne looked on helplessly as the man scratched his head with his stumpy fingers, hunched his shoulders, glared helplessly at the cabin, then at us, muttering something about the bloodthirsty Arctic fox, eagle owls, and what have you, but eventually he grunted that we might as well shelter there as long as we kept our heads down.

We landed. Hilma jumped ashore and ran off after a crab numbed by the cold. I lost my footing, and the coat slipped from my shoulders. I noticed Jaarikki the Scarface staring at my stolen Lotta uniform, my leather brogues, and weapon jacket from which I'd torn off the Third Reich insignias and matching cotton collar. I'd thrown the blue Lotta swastika in the sea long ago.

"Wouldn't stay here if I were you. Back of beyond, this is," Jaarikki grumbled, perplexed.

I noticed Birdseye staring at my sheared hair, now revealed beneath my cap.

"Pretty lass you've got there. But there's no good two women pottering out here all alone."

"My man's out . . . fishing."

Bjørne scoffed and lit his pipe.

"Wouldn't move around much if I was you. The gorges are full of bombers and saboteurs. The Russians have taken Tana, and the Jerry troops are already up as far as Alta. They're torching the villages quick as anything."

I found myself involuntarily staring at the face of the demon on the thwart. There was something mesmerizing about his monstrousness, his features so badly burned that the nostrils barely parted from the nasal bone. All the while Bjørne raved about the Germans' new commander, Lothar Rendulic, who'd taken up his position after the Arctic Fox had been killed in an aviation accident, listing all the terrible things that had followed or that would have followed. That they'd burn Lapland to the ground, slaughter anyone found rambling about these fjords. Half-baked lies and claptrap, it was. Meaningless prattle, fishermen's gossip.

That being said, Bjørne's presence wasn't entirely meaningless. He gave me some dried meat, British tinned meat from the boat, a wineskin the size of a lamb's womb full of rum, and a knife.

"Take some corned beef so you don't freeze to death."

I offered Bjørne my wolf-skin coat in return, but Jaarikki butted in.

"Can't give away your only coat, lass."

Bjørne growled at him.

"What's the matter with you, man? Gift for a gift, rides and all."

Jaarikki shook his head sternly, and I thought it was odd the way Birdseye gave an ear to the local lunatic. He looked longingly at the coat, but eventually gave up the idea and told me to pop by his shop sometime. And with that they paddled out into the dusk in their crammed Nordland boat. Jaarikki sat on the aft thwart and stared at the shore until they disappeared behind the Valaskari skerries. With my new set of teeth I tore off half the dried meat and admitted to myself that, though the old pair had fed me a meal of greasy lies about the burning of Lapland and the rest of it, I couldn't really rebuke them for it. As folks like to say in wartime, there's nothing as certain as uncertainty. And that much is true. Only the Almighty knows where our journey will take us.

Once Bjørne and Scarface had left, I walked Masha down to the shore to wash her. Rum swirled in my veins. I began to undress the girl in the fractured, glimmering light. Rocks smoothed by the tide, covered in slush. I couldn't bring myself to look at the thrashing little girl. Instead, I watched as our visitors hurried back into the fog, and ran my tongue across my whalebone teeth. They still felt strange against my gums, and I'd always been so proud of my teeth. Bitterly I wondered which of us you would look at now, Johannes. An ugly old hag or this slip of a girl who, despite her battered appearance, still managed to retain a modicum of innocence? There was no doubt in my mind.

"*Parmuska*, I don't want to."

Teetering there on the rocks, Masha looked so pathetic that I almost relented. Then I remembered everything I'd gone through because of her. I waved away the wind as it blew the cap from my shaved head and started yanking down the girl's underpants.

"Don't you start. We've to wash you, else you'll rot away. We'll soon get inside into the warm."

"Don't want to."

The stench of the girl was horrific.

I rinsed the bandages I'd placed between her legs and scrubbed the filth clinging to her white thighs. I slapped the wet bandages across her shoulders, perhaps a little too forcefully.

"Why did you have to follow me out here?" I whispered.

The girl stared at me as though I'd leathered her with a belt. She waded out of the water, laced up her pointed Lappish boots, and skulked off. I didn't go after her, Johannes, because she had come to torment me, to torment us, to remind us of the war and Operation Cattlehouse. Hermann Gödel said they weren't really human, these Skolts. Wild creatures from the woods, oblivious to everything but Mammon. Or worse still, *rein und natürlich,* as you would have put it.

For you did look at her. What man wouldn't look at a lass like that? Little tits like a fox cub's snout, a mouth just big enough to accommodate a larger member, and eyes to look up trustingly at her violator.

I wanted to shout obscenities after her, to scream that it was all her fault, and that without her everything would have been different. You would be beside me right here and now. Instead, I lost my footing, slipped into the icy water, and struck my elbow in a tangle of seaweed. I staggered to my feet, my lips numbed. I opened my mouth, felt the urge to howl at my broken plans and all the evil in the universe, to rip from my soul a God that could permit the existence of such evil. Instead, a slow, salty apology slid the length of my tongue.

"Forgive me, Masha."

DEAD MAN'S FJORD

October 1944

There's no food left. This morning I left the remains of the dried meat on the hoarfrosted cliff top. I don't know if the girl ate it or whether one of the wild creatures gobbled it up. There's not a soul here. I've carried out a few cautious exploratory hikes into the surrounding terrain within half a league's radius. My heels are blistered from my leather brogues. Masha is nowhere to be seen, and we've heard nothing of you. War booms in the distance. Last night I woke at the witching hour to the sound of footsteps in the attic. Hilma started to growl and hid beneath the camp bed. I was startled, thinking the Russians were on my trail.

"Who's there?" I called out.

No answer.

Then I calmed down. The Russians would come barging through the front door, not tiptoe about in the attic. It's Masha, for sure. I clambered upstairs with a lantern and a moth-eaten reindeer skin. I'd thought I might tuck the stubborn lassie in as a show of reconciliation, twirl my fingers through the hairs on her neck, and let her sniff my armpit. But there was nobody there. Not a footstep on the frozen floorboards, nothing to suggest a living creature had ever been up there.

I'm hungry.

At the Titovka camp I learned that one thousand three hundred calories is the measure of humanity. That is the trusted prisoners' daily ration. The instinct to acquire that amount of food turns a Georgian, a Belarusian, a Serb, a Croat, or a Kazak into an animal in a manner so profound that there can be no return to normality. One thousand three hundred calories measured out on an iron children's scale: one pint of tea, three pieces of sugar beet, a pound of *liebuska* bread, and a packet of rutabaga soup, which, if they were lucky, contained a chunk or two of Greek donkey meat.

There's now only one item in the cabin that I haven't turned upside down looking for food: that strange decorated Russian chest, locked fast with iron clasps, beautiful. It is beautiful because you said so. Because your father had made a chest just like this with his own bare hands, and that's why it would make a suitable souvenir from Lapland when the war finally ends. We could paint it again and display it on the veranda, decorating it every morning with a fresh bunch of lilacs. But now all I can think about is that there might be something delicious hidden inside it. Tins of preserved meat. A great hunk of dried meat. Honey. Pots of jam.

Forgive me, Johannes. Hunger turns us into animals.

In a moment of raging madness, I broke the only beautiful item that we could have taken home. I hacked open the decorative lock with an ax, taking care not to damage the surface of the wood, just for you. But what was there inside? No food. No. Only a broken wireless or some kind of transmitter. I would have laughed, if only the wax candle I'd just eaten weren't rumbling in my stomach. There was also a collection of blue-covered jotters, some kind of logbooks, full of entries and measurements. Strange messages, the Fritz's secret code. I've tucked them back into the chest, because the pages stick together and the ink smudges when I try to flick through them. But be that as it may, the Dead Man that gave this place its name wasn't your average fisherman.

When we came out here in the summer, I'd asked Jouni if it had been *Selbstmord*, whether the Dead Man had died by his own hand.

"He's dead all the same, I'm telling you. Dead and buried."

Old Lappish men dead in their cottages are two a penny. Nobody cares who his family was or where he came from. The natural decline of a degenerate people. *Natürliche Todesfälle*, logged as 14 F 1 in Operation Cattlehouse, which meant anything but a natural death, as did 14 F 2, *Freitod oder Tod durch Unglücksfall.* Maybe that was it, Jouni rambled on.

"But in that case he was quite the magician."

For though I don't know much about firearms, on this matter I agree with Jouni. It would be quite a trick for an old fellow stiffened out here by the Arctic coast to shoot himself in the back of the head with a Mauser, an m/38 short rifle, or any other firearm.

No photographs, no family portraits, nothing to indicate a family left behind missing him. The ginger-haired fisherman they called the Jerker had found the old man at the table with the back of his head blown off. A *gákti* headdress, decorated in gold and red, hanging at the door, his reindeer-skin shoes by the fireplace, hay strewn across the sleeping berth.

"Tragic," you'd said. "It's tragic when a man's left to die by himself."

Everybody should have pictures of their family, the same kind of family portraits as Gödel had on display in the Cabinet, reminders of a happier time, a time when the sea was fragrant and the salmon sniffed their way back along the rivers to their breeding grounds upstream. A time when the dead bodies of soldiers didn't wash up on the shore and when the lighthouse keepers had time to fly kites.

I'm becoming afraid that I might not have time to put up a single framed photograph on my dressing table before I die.

At least there's one thing that comforts me. Bjørne and Jaarikki haven't turned me in. I've spent endless hours counting the number of people who know I'm still alive. The answer: nobody. I hurled my temporary passport and visa into the sea as we left Petsamo, and Alexei Ignatenko helped me burn all my documentation from the prison camp before I left. There's nobody in sight. At low tide, I wade out into the fjord to wash myself, scrubbing, scouring the past from my skin—all for you. Thank God there are no mirrors in Dead Man's Cabin, because I don't want to see my monstrous reflection. Yesterday I made the mistake of leaning over the still waters in the fjord, and caught a glimpse of my battered face.

My hair still won't grow.

DEAD MAN'S FJORD

October 1944

Salvation lies on the table. When I look at it, it seems like a divine miracle. But it isn't. British tinned preserves, dried meat, pipe tobacco, reindeer milk, and a sheepskin canteen filled with Captain Morgan. The reindeer milk stinks of pork, but I don't care. I can't remember ever pouring anything more sumptuous down my throat.

It happened in the morning. I was scrubbing myself in the Arctic waters when I noticed something glinting on my thigh. A beam of light coming from the wrong direction, traveling up along my thigh and stopping around my stomach. I gave a start. In peacetime people were used to seeing flashes of light like this, bairns playing with mirrors, trying to ignite a bale of hay. In wartime it was a different matter. All I knew was that flickering lights like that didn't belong in this fjord. I quickly waded back to the shore and wrapped a scarf around my shorn head.

"Who's there?" I shouted, though straight away I knew it would have been safer to keep quiet.

"Only me! Bjørne!"

Hilma, my war hound, didn't so much as raise her snout as Birdseye stood up. He had a rifle slung over his shoulder and a pair of binoculars. I hurriedly fastened my tights.

"Came to check you're all right."

I was relieved. Just then I noticed the familiar Nordland boat out in the fjord. Jaarikki was rowing toward the shore as fast as he could. When he reached land, he hauled the boat up by the rocks and leapt into the receding water with surprising agility.

"I'm almost late," he panted.

Jaarikki pulled a satchel out of the boat and waded ashore. There were pieces of fish guts and strands of tobacco caught in his beard. On his head he had the same old fur cap that covered part of his charred face.

"Fair mild for this time of year, eh?" Bjørne commented.

For a moment the men took stock of each other. Bjørne raised his rifle.

"Just missed a nice couple of hares."

There we stood for a moment, staring out at the autumnal sea. Only a few days ago, there were still blocks of ice floating across the surface, but the glowing eye in the sky had thawed them for now. The lower cliff edge at Seitakallio was still ablaze with autumnal splendor, while the upper ridge was frosted over. A reindeer bell clanged somewhere across the fell. I was puzzled by the men's arrival; it was as though they'd turned up without knowledge of each other, and yet at precisely the same time. Still, it was a relief. They weren't spies or Russians, or malevolent Germans for that matter. I caught Jaarikki's whiff, a blend of freshly cut tobacco, shoe polish, willow bark, and sweaty reindeer-skin trousers. It felt strangely comforting. Bjørne meanwhile stank of fresh liquor and nothing else.

The men stomped inside, rattling the window above the door. I hurried in after them. They sat down at the table without my permission and cracked open the bottle of Captain Morgan. Bjørne piped up.

"How's your lassie?"

Haven't seen her for days. Every day I trudge around the ridges, hoping Hilma will catch her scent. She's gone and she'll stay gone. I tried to think why Masha had wandered off. There were no berries to be found at this time of year, only a cranberry or two if you were lucky. Thankfully I didn't have to answer.

"So, the mice squealing for you yet?"

Bjørne clapped his mate on the leg.

"Don't you worry your head about him—he's not the full shilling. How's it been up here? Your man still out fishing, is he?"

I nodded curtly. Bjørne scanned the cabin, his brow furrowed. Jaarikki stared at me and slurped his rum, making the skin beneath his chin wobble. The disfigured old boy looked oddly familiar. But where had I seen him? In the infirmary at Petsamo? Long before that? Could he have been one of my father's drinking mates from Sahanperä? No, I'd have remembered such a mangled face. His ink-stained tongue licked the corner of his mouth as he noticed the Russian chest, now smashed open with an ax.

"Looks like you've been through the wars here too, lass."

"I was looking for food," I said, feeling embarrassed as we glanced at the splintered lock. "Nothing important in there, though."

I opened the lid. Bjørne snatched up one of the jotters and started leafing through it.

"I'll be damned, there's plenty here."

"Told you," Jaarikki retorted.

"You hold your trap. You can't read these, can you lass?"

I told him the truth: I could not read them. Strange mumbo jumbo, columns of numbers.

Bjørne scoffed. Some poor hermit must have lived up here at the beginning of the century, lost his mind in the winter darkness, and scribbled this nonsense.

I didn't say anything, though we could both see that some of the entries were far more recent than that.

"You lasses should come and live at the store."

Bjørne described all the wonderful things that awaited us at his store. Cod and coalfish heaped in silver mountains by the counter, tinned meat from Argentina. The mere thought of a real wheat loaf made with Canadian flour brought tears to my eyes. Danish milk powder and tins of ground Brazilian coffee. Hot water to bathe in—and soap! Large clumps of seal-fat soap, none of the standard leathery rubbish. With that I could scour myself, wash away all the dirt and the filth, and make myself clean for you again. Up in Bjørne's attic I would cleanse my mouth with salt water and spit out the window onto the quayside below. My bloodied gums would stop bleeding, and the roots of my teeth would stop aching. If I washed myself enough, I would become beautiful again. If I washed myself enough, you would come back.

But I couldn't leave. You might arrive back at the fjord at any moment. Reluctantly I shook my head.

"We're staying put."

Bjørne didn't like my answer.

"Can't have you wandering about by yourselves at a time like this, eh? The Einsatzgruppe will turn up and shoot you dead on the spot. They hunt for folks up here, just like the ospreys hunt for young salmon."

I looked at the pair of binoculars hanging round Bjørne's neck and didn't answer. Jaarikki began stacking groceries on the table. Battered tins of canned meat and a bag of peas, dried meat, and salted fish. More Captain Morgan and a wineskin of reindeer milk. Saliva flooded into my mouth.

"How can I pay you?"

"We could take that chest off your hands," Bjørne said. "A collectible souvenir, that is. The Fritz'll pay good money for it."

I panicked. Thank God Jaarikki butted in.

"It'll not fit in the boat."

"We can fetch it later."

I hesitated. You liked this chest so much. We're going to put that chest on our veranda with lilacs on top of it. There's pollen hanging in the air, and the crickets are singing in the rushes. Our legs intertwine beneath the white wrought-iron table, cherry-patterned glasses in our hands. We have two children too, a son whose spectacles steam up because a practical joke they played at school makes him laugh so much. Our daughter is already asleep; she's had a tiring violin lesson. Her teacher proceeds slowly and methodically, and he might be Jewish, but that doesn't matter—he's a good teacher. He has bad heartburn; sometimes I make him a pot of sage tea, and that helps him instantly. None of us ever has toothache. My apron is always spotless, and I climb along your sweet voice to find happiness.

"I can't give you the chest. You can have the papers."

"It's up to you, lass."

Bjørne glared at Jaarikki.

"You'd better be right about this."

Birdseye snatched up three of the jotters, stuffed them into his satchel.

"Seen any movement out on the fjord?" he asked. "There's a Casanova running about up this way, some skirt chaser that speaks German and Finnish."

I let out an involuntary peep. My dear Johannes! If ever there was a time to be quiet, it was now. Say nothing, nothing at all! But I could already feel my cheeks starting to burn, my heart hammering so powerfully inside its bony cage that they'd doubtless hear the drumming across the fjord. I turned away to pour water into the pot, and Jaarikki's gaze bored into my shoulder blades.

"Haven't seen a soul."

I began prattling about the winter that might or might not be coming, about a fungus that might or might not be eating the leaves of the dwarf birches around Varanger or wherever it was.

"Winter will come, sure enough, don't you worry your head," Bjørne promised me. "You lasses won't survive it by yourselves. You've not even a pair of skis."

I poured the tea into tin mugs and peered at Bjørne out of the corner of my eye as he fingered the Dead Man's jotters. Jaarikki didn't care for them but sat gently prodding Hilma with his leather boots.

"Probably best if we take that wireless too. Can't have folks hearing you listening to that out here."

The men left as evening drew in. With one foot in his Nordland boat, Bjørne hollered to me.

"Just you mind not to go sticking your nose into other folks' business, eh. It'll come to no good."

I watched their departure against the sunset.

All evening I'd had the feeling someone was breathing down my neck. Hilma jumped to her feet every now and then and started growling at the sighs of the sea. At some point I resolved to light a beacon, in case it was you wandering around in the gorge. I climbed up on the cliffs with the bottle of Captain Morgan. All the while I felt the urge to sneak a look over my shoulder, to see if there was someone lurking in the rocky terrain. Only a few white birds swooped over the sea as though they had been cut out of the sky with scissors. As I climbed, I went over and over what I had let slip to them. Nothing about you, at any rate. Yet something deeply disturbing had happened that day; I just couldn't make sense of it. I took a swig of Devil's piss and wondered where I'd seen Jaarikki before. Where did Bjørne get his hands on all that food? There was a shortage of everything from medicine to ethanol. Things didn't seem to add up. Then it occurred to me how much Lisbet Näkkälä would have loved being caught up in a farce like this, everyone wearing the wrong clothes, bearing the wrong name, peddling the wrong currency. Me with a set of false teeth and lines I didn't know by heart. I suddenly felt such longing for Lisbet and Lisbet's endlessly generous arms and the fingerless gloves she'd knitted, without which my hands are so numb, I can barely hold my pen.

TITOVKA

July 1944

Lisbet's condition didn't improve. On July 3 you decided she would have to be taken to the infirmary in Parkkina. You thought she might be pregnant. Jouni kick-started his Destroyer with impure German petroleum and cursed that the gearing had been damaged in Saariselkä. Some amateur driver had run the Ford up a hill while it was still in gear, and all the while the motor was about to stall. He muttered something about the wood burner and the crank, but I wasn't listening. What if Lisbet really was with child again?

"Seems your medicine doesn't work," she said.

"Don't say that. Keep taking it no matter how sickly you feel. At the infirmary they'll give you something stronger, sulfates if you're expecting. I promise you."

I straightened my stockings, pulled on the pair of lavender-colored lace knickers I'd found in Lisbet's bag, and packed my medical bag full of good, healthy herbs.

I was eager to leave the camp early because I didn't want to see Masha's face when I wasn't there to make her a kite. I soothed my conscience with the thought that Hermann Gödel had given Montya, the Hilfswilliger, the task of looking after the girl.

"Don't worry, Fräulein Schwester, everything will be fine. You'll be back tomorrow."

But there was another reason too that I wanted out of the camp as soon as possible. The Russian lad had run off and taken Hilma, the war hound, with him. It was my fault. The previous evening I'd found him behind Operation Cattlehouse, burying something that looked like a hare's corpse mauled by a fox. The war hound tied to his leg stood howling next to him and went for my leg. The Russian lad explained that she'd eaten her own puppy.

"She's not a bad dog. She's frightened."

"Frightened of what?"

"The war."

I rubbed the bite mark between my shin and the top of my boot. It didn't hurt, but it had startled me. The Russian lad started praying. I didn't listen.

"Thing needs putting down."

So he ran away, taking the dog with him. I knew that the gold diggers and reindeer herds would raise the alarm by evening at the latest and send out a search party. I felt sorry at the thought of them chasing the boy across the tundra, pursued by a crowd of haggard, stony faces marked with soot and gunpowder, folks who in the 1930s hunted the Skolts the way they did any other game. Lappish men like that can smell prey like wolverines, and often play with it before going in for the kill. And what would happen if they brought him back to the camp? He'd be made to dig his own grave before they shot him in the head at close range. The lad had no chance.

"We'll lynch him yet."

So said Old Keskimölsä, who'd galloped off at dawn on a bone-white mare in the hope of blood money.

All this I forgot as I saw you striding toward the car in full SS regalia. It pained me that you wanted to accompany Lisbet to the hospital, but at the same time I had the sneaking suspicion that you too simply wanted to get away from the camp, to take pictures, to breathe, anything at all. In your uniform you looked like one of the Lord's troops, shining boots on your feet and the Gestapo skull insignia on your forehead. You were carrying your camera bag and a black leather satchel with an eagle cockade on the buckle. How handsome you looked, and in the car mirror I tried to snatch glimpses of the two of us as we sat there, my fringe curled with tongs, the cretonne frock that kissed my thighs. A sense of contentment filled me. Someone could have snapped a family portrait of us just like the one the dead Belarusian had been carrying. If a degenerate like that could make his way into a photograph, why shouldn't we? An SS officer of the Third Reich and his young bride setting off on their honeymoon. To the Ukraine, perhaps.

There was a roadblock at the end of Russenstraße. A fence of wooden stakes and a checkpoint had been erected. The prisoners of war were busy hauling fresh timber brought in from the fells at Salla. Jaakkima Alakunnas was pottering around too. It was strange that a stammerer like that could wheedle his way into everyone's business, I thought, and wondered whether he was now officially employed by the Fritz.

"N-n-nobody through without permission!"

"Give it a rest, will you?"

You jumped out and peered inside the checkpoint. Jaakkima poked his bayonet inside the car and rambled on.

"We must see your p-p-papers."

"Quit your whinging," Jouni quipped, and accelerated through the gate.

As if to taunt the boy, he stopped for a moment to smoke his pipe and relieve himself against the other side of the fence. You came back just as Gretel, the kitchen girl, had chased her cat up a tree and come out carrying a pitcher of floury strawberry cordial. You stepped back, your camera bag swinging on your shoulder, your back straight, and I envisaged your nose and my set of teeth cutting a far finer figurehead for the Third Reich. You jumped into the cab and asked whether everything was loaded. Yes, it was. Only your satchel with the eagle cockade was missing.

"What're they building?" I plucked up the courage to ask once we'd crossed the bridge at Alaluostari.

"Eine Schutzstellung," you replied off the cuff, staring at the sky, lost in your own thoughts.

I tried to remember what that word meant. A rampart of some sort? I looked up at the horizon.

"Donner."

"What does that mean? A storm?"

Jouni didn't answer but carried on driving right down the middle of the road, listening to the engine's hoarse wheezing.

"Whole thing's going to fall apart one day. The cylinder can't cope. You don't run the motor while it's still in gear."

I was in a good mood. I sniffed your scent, now mixed with the fug of carbon fumes from the wood burner and the smell of marsh tea that hung in the air around us. I was wearing my cretonne frock and frilly hat. The hat was as wide as a cart's wheel, and Jouni swiped it to one side with a curse. You were examining your binoculars and wiping the lenses. Lisbet was lying on the planks in the back, whimpering, swaddled in a kaftan taken from one of the Kyrgyz prisoners.

We dropped Lisbet in the yard outside the infirmary, then drove through the German military cemetery to the officers' club. You were worried and wanted to stay behind to look after Lisbet. I assured you she'd be back on her feet in a few days. I didn't tell you how I was so sure of this, how I had fetched castor oil from the medicine cabinet, mixed a tincture of frog spawn and tar with some moonshine and poured the lot into a little glass bottle, given it a shake, and glued a label to the front with the instructions: *To be taken morning and night. Swallow no matter how bitter the taste.*

That put an end to her cooing and hip-swinging for a while.

Now I could keep you to myself for a moment, whether at Titovka or not.

But then there came a change of plan.

"We're going to swing by Alta first," Jouni said breezily as he strode out of the officers' club.

He'd heard that they were keeping his lady friend in a camp near Alta.

Jouni asked us whether we wanted to join him or wait for a cab back to the camp.

"A ride," I explained to you.

You hesitated, looked at me. I shrugged my shoulders, though I wanted to scream and shout, *Come, come with me to the ends of the earth.* I forced myself to mutter something.

"Maybe we should join him? It's easier to breathe out here, and it'll give you a rest from digging that pit."

Suddenly you had nothing against accompanying Jouni.

The horizon glowed red, and there came the sound of distant rumbling as we crossed the Norwegian border. Once they saw you, nobody asked for our papers. The hairs on my skin stood on end as the border guards saluted us.

"If only we were there already," Jouni murmured, stamping on the twin pedals.

I could feel that you were enjoying it, that there was electricity running through you. I touched your arm with my finger and immediately felt a shock. Let the road continue, the journey run longer, the bog stretch out. Let lightning strike down and set the sky ablaze. Please, journey, never stop.

The accident occurred somewhere near Ifjord. We had just seen the ocean, and a bolt of lightning reached like a fist from the sky and struck the water. At that moment a white-painted VW Kübelwagen spattered with dead midges swerved around the bend ahead, with a German officer in an SS cap bobbing in the front seat. I saw that there was a Finnish border guard behind the wheel. I recognized him because, unlike the others, he only had the Finnish lion crest on the front of his gray army shirt. Mud spattered, grit flew up, Jouni's Destroyer careered off the road and hit a row of trees. Crash. Nothing too serious—I cracked my head against the dashboard and Jouni chipped a tooth. We stumbled out of the car before the roll of thunder from the next flash of lightning carried across the sky. You staggered against the back of the truck and waved your skull-insignia cap at the VW so that they knew whom they were dealing with.

I approached the Finnish border guard, who had frantically jumped out of his vehicle.

"Didn't hit anybody, did I? I can tow you to the officers' depot in Kirkenes if you like."

The sound of giggling came from within the Kübelwagen, and a girl's stockinged ankle stuck out the window. I didn't need any of that on this journey. I glanced at Jouni and at you. You were on the other side of the road, out of earshot.

"Nobody's hurt. On you go, now," I said.

"Shouldn't we haul you out of the ditch at least? I'll call the switchboard and let them know. There will be someone out to help you before morning."

I looked over at you again. You'd turned to the verge to answer the call of nature, and Jouni was banging the hubcaps with a wrench.

"Absolutely not. Unless you want to get yourself in even more trouble. If you tell anyone about this, they'll have you up at the court-martial before you know it."

The Finnish border guard turned pale, ran back to his car, and started the engine.

Jouni didn't notice them leaving until the Kübelwagen disappeared around the next bend.

"Where they off to?" he snapped.

"Probably in a hurry to get to the dance," I quipped.

You both looked bewildered. Then the cursing started. We'd be making an official complaint as soon as we arrived, you shouted, haul them up before the court-martial, and have them charged with the maximum penalty. You don't leave an SS officer at the side of the road just like that.

Jouni pulled on the crank and cursed again.

"No, suit yourself. We don't need your help," he said, waving his hand in disgust. "To hell with you, you rotters."

You removed a plank of plywood from behind the driver's seat. "Fräulein Schwester," you said quietly, "shall we sit down for a moment?"

"This might take a fair while," said Jouni.

He kicked the fender and walked back and forth, furiously pressing the ignition button. I delicately crossed my legs and tried to shuffle along the plywood plank, as close to you as possible. You filled your lungs with air.

"Feels good to breathe out here. You run out of air at the camp, have you noticed?"

I nodded, though the air in my lungs felt heavy because of the coming storm.

"Do you want to interview me?" I asked, trying to sound playful.

"What?"

"Are you going to interview me now? We've got plenty of time to kill. If not, I'll interview you."

You nodded, and I hurriedly tried to remember the things the Russian lad and I had read in *Tide of the Times*. One had to give a refined, professional impression; one mustn't be sloppy. But before we could even get under way, Jouni started ranting.

"Right, you two, push!"

"I can sit up front," I suggested.

"I'm not letting a skirt behind the wheel. You're not that much of a lady that you can't come and push this thing."

I bit my tongue and pushed. The earth had turned to a slurry of mud, and my cretonne frock became glued to my back. I didn't care.

Jouni eventually gave up. The journey wasn't going to continue by car. The wood burner had struck the trees, ripping a hole the shape of a twotch in the edge of the burner's stove. The burner was taking on air, and the motor wasn't getting enough carbon monoxide. Trying to fix it would be pointless.

"Did you have anyone to look after you back in Germany?"

You didn't get a chance to answer. Jouni grabbed the radio handset and a weapon from behind the driver's seat.

"Enough of the chitchat," he bellowed. "We're off to look for shelter."

Jouni stared at the sky as though he feared an attack from some enormous, skeletal beast. You winked at me and lit your pipe. Right then the storm broke. Rain lashed down from the clouds and hid the landscape from view.

"I quite like being on a trip with you," I yelled over the noise.

Either you couldn't hear me, or you weren't listening.

DEAD MAN'S FJORD

July 1944

We arrived at Dead Man's Fjord one sprained ankle and ten arduous fells later. Jouni was hobbling and cussing; you were worn out, exhausted, and you smelled of earth and male sweat. The heavy rain abated just as we were walking down the last promontory and heading toward the shore. The seaweed was steaming, a two-ridged mountain poked through the fog. The passing scent of cloudberry blossom and heather. From farther up the ridge came the rushing sound of cascading water, as though the world were wetting itself. Then I saw it.

"A cabin! Over there!"

"I'll be damned. Surely not," Jouni muttered, squinting at the landscape and hacking up the iced phlegm from his throat. "Nonsense. There's nothing there."

"Over there. Look!"

We might never have noticed it if we hadn't wandered so close. There beneath the promontory was a low-lying shack built of driftwood, with iron hinges and a bone latch on the door. Slightly farther down the ridge was a boat shed with a peat roof, and from up the hill came the stench of forgotten cod trimmings. Steps the color of bone cut from a long-dead birch tree, roof rafters carved from tree roots. The walls had been stuffed with newspaper, lichen, and bark. Fishnets and glass floats hung from the corner timber. Reindeer skulls and bones rattled in the grass.

Jouni cursed and said, "I'm not going in there."

"Why not? Don't start that."

"A dead man's cabin, that is. It's not on any map."

"Don't talk soft, man."

"A man was killed out here."

"How do you know that?"

"Either that or he soon will be. A dead man's cabin. I know it," Jouni persisted.

With that Jouni hurled the wireless to the ground and limped off to sleep among the rocks, still damp from the downpour.

I didn't give Jouni's nonsense a second thought. An otherworldly light hung above the fjord. It seemed to be coming from nowhere, yet shone from all directions at once. A few hundred yards west of the cabin, water broke free of the Arctic ice, and thawed streams rippled down the ridge like a glistening veil. A quarry and the fields of hay formed a strip of blue-and-yellow fell, behind which another similar creek seemed to open up. If not for the cabin, it would have been easy to imagine that not a single living creature had stepped foot here before us. But even that, with its peat roof, was like a small mountain crag pulled from Mother Earth's womb.

We climbed in through the window. You pulled off your sodden moleskin trousers, and I hung them in front of the hearth to dry. For the first time there was mud on your boots, and I felt a shudder. Then I took comfort; I would scrub them until they shone again. Very soon, but not now. I felt your whole body shivering with the chill, and I knew what had to be done. I took your left foot between my palms and squeezed, letting your shivers flow into me. I bent down and pressed your big toe into my mouth.

"Fräulein Schwester, what are you doing?"

"Don't worry, I know what to do."

I sucked until the blood started to build up behind your nail and you were howling in pain. I didn't stop. I moved on to lick the soles of your feet and your ankles, which smelled of salt, flint, newly discovered corners of the earth, and disinfectant. I continued until your swollen skin began to throb. Then I wrapped you in a reindeer skin, like a parcel, and told you to lie still while I made a fire.

I found an old firesteel by the stove and struck sparks into the pile of damp roots. They wouldn't catch. I stuffed birch bark into the fireplace and opened the flues. You started spluttering as smoke came billowing into the cabin. At that, I pulled Laestadius's sermon book from my breast pocket and tore off a few pages to use as kindling.

"No, Wild-Eye. That's important to you."

"I know it all by heart," I said, and continued lighting the fire.

Forgive me, Lord, I prayed. But I have to save my darling little starling from freezing to death out here on the shores of the Arctic Ocean. He's from the south, made of weaker stuff. He wouldn't survive up here by himself, you understand.

For once, the Lord heard my prayer and forgave me. Flames greedily licked across the yellowed sermons. But though the Lord forgave me, Laestadius did not. I could hear Big Lamberg's damning words from among the flames:

"For the sinner shall not enter the Kingdom of Heaven through repentance and the acknowledgment of his sins alone . . . Though the sinner knows his sins and though he should experience profound repentance, pain, and spiritual anxiety, he shall not be saved from damnation until the Holy Spirit teaches him a lesson."

Verily I was a sinful harlot for seducing a strange man and taking him out to the fjord with me. For sucking his toes like a calf suckling at the udder of a strange heifer. But I was not ashamed, Lord, not one bit. For the first time, I felt no shame. Still, I couldn't bear hearing Big Lamberg's words. I banged Jouni's wireless on the table. It was a black, cheap model the size of a hatbox, meant only for listening to marching music. The text on its side read *KdF—Kraft durch Freude*, strength through joy. It didn't work. I hit it with one of the fishing sinkers. The corner cracked. I twisted the dials, but the contraption remained silent.

"Johannes, why won't you make me one of those?"

"*Meine Mutter* used to wrap me up like this when I was little," you whispered drowsily from beneath the blankets.

"Why won't you make me a garland? You've made one for all the other lasses."

"What?"

Again, Big Lamberg's accusatory voice boomed from the chimney.

"Those who doubt will be cast into sin and lie there like cattle, and they will not lift a foot until they are duly whipped."

"A garland?"

"Aye, will you make me one?"

"I could make you one," you promised, looking around the room, your eyes bleary with sleep. "We had a chest like that back home too."

I glanced at the Kurbits chest, an item that seemed all too refined for this cabin. I was going to ask you something, but when I looked back, you had fallen asleep.

Oh Lord. Oh, Johannes, my love, my cluttercake. You, my redeemer, rising like a true barbarian from the murky swamp of my earthly wandering. You, a trailsman to tread my path. You, my stalwart seedsman. I should have been whipped, just as it said in the sermons. But at the same time I knew that it would have been futile. No whip would ever change me; neither glowing branding iron nor devils raining down from the sky would change me. You had promised to make me a garland. I wrapped myself in a pelt next to the camp bed and lay there awake, keeping watch over your sleep. I chased goblins from the end of your bed and thanked God. And long before the hearth began to warm us and the cabin filled with the sweet smell of tar, I knew that I would do anything at all so as not to return to Titovka. I wanted to stay here.

DEAD MAN'S FJORD

Johannes Angelhurst

July 12, 1944

I knew I shouldn't have gone to Parkkina in the Rumrunner's car. But the sun refuses to set now, the air in the forecourt is stagnant, and I cannot sleep. I lie on the roof of the barracks and wait for the stars. Hermann Gödel's friendliness makes me suspicious. He gave me some newfangled medicine called Adolfin. Apparently it doesn't have the same side effects as the Pervitin they gave us in the Ukraine.

I must own up: I did escape from the camp. Anyone could have taken the maps and documents to the Schutzwall. It's all one. Now Wild-Eye and the Rumrunner need no longer wonder what this garrison and others like it are for. As Eduard Dietl, the Arctic Fox, said on a recent visit, the less the *Finnenlümmels* understand of what's going on, the better. He hoped we wouldn't have to initiate Operation Birch Tree until the first snowfall.

Now Eduard Dietl is dead. It makes me frightened, scared of what will happen now that Dietl can no longer take responsibility for me. I'm afraid of Gödel's revenge.

"I know your loyalty to the Third Reich will never falter," the Arctic Fox had said as he'd shown me the report the Security Services had drawn up on me. He confided in me that they were wholly satisfied with my work in the Ukraine. I thanked him, though I wasn't sure what for. I cannot remember anything. I asked whether I would be allowed to continue as a reporter for *Lappland-Kurier*.

"Now, this is your chance to show us you are a more valiant soldier than your father! Hermann Gödel tells me that you understand the situation. Operation 1005 requires that we complete the work begun in 1941 and 1942. We've already done so along the Eastern Front from the Ukraine to Tallinn, and we'll do so here too." The Arctic Fox laughed, telling me he'd heard that I'd inherited from my father such a hatred for the Bolsheviks that my first encounter with a Russian had left me with a permanent squint.

"In the right eye," Gödel added convivially.

It isn't true. It's the left eye. Gödel knew it perfectly well. And it wasn't the Bolsheviks either, but a badly aimed arrow fired by Gödel at a Hitler Jugend summer camp long ago.

I'm neither a coward nor a wretch. My father was. There is a crumbling photograph in the breast pocket of my officer's coat. In the photograph a weather-beaten man with angular features poses for the camera. In the background is a snow-covered marshland; there's scrap metal on the ground. The text on the back of the print reads *Pelastusvuori, Petsamo 1919. Blown-up ammunition store.* I keep this photograph separate from the others held in a velvet-covered cardboard folder in the side pocket of my leather satchel.

I don't know what Father would say about those other photographs. My mother would surely find them demeaning, but my mother lost any right to judge me after the trick she played on us.

It's true: Father loathed the Bolsheviks. In contrast, he had a fascination for the quiet, proud Finnish people. He had first met some Finns on a Scout course at Lokstedt in Germany in 1914. These were activities disguised as Scout events, where Father trained groups of naval cadets and turned them into spies and saboteurs. It was with these cadets that he had first come to Finland and met my mother, who continued to love him long after it turned out that Angelhurst didn't mean "angel wing"—quite the opposite—and when she learned that Father would never become a writer, let alone be called up for another war.

I should have stayed at the camp to complete the task I'd been given. But I couldn't take the sleepless sunlight or the boom of Russian harlots laughing at me from behind the fell night and day. At times my head buzzes with the sound of thoughts left there by agents of an enemy country. The copper eagle on the wall of the Cabinet has been polished so much that I can see my reflection in it, a reflection that has faded since the evening I sat there smoking with Gödel and the Arctic Fox. Between these two warmongers sat a novice, his back straight, his face ruddy from the warmth of the fireplace. Then they brought in the Skolt girl, like something straight out of a nightmare, the same head scarf as those fluttering in the wind by the edge of the pit, the curses, and a gaze that bored right into the barrel of a gun and pressed itself into the lead surface of the bullet in the fraction of a moment before it was fired. That night I lay on the roof of the barracks, willing the stars to arrive and cool my mind. Gödel gave me a bottle of medicine and told me to take some whenever I felt unwell.

Now I'm stuck here with Wild-Eye. She's no normal woman. She's a force of nature. The rage of the age-old mountains runs in her arms; her feet grope the rocky ground as if guided by a third eye. She didn't stumble once—even the Rumrunner sprained his ankle hopping into the thicket from a rock in the rapids. It was clear he had no idea where we were going.

When we arrived at the cabin, I was convinced it was booby-trapped, an ammunition store perhaps. The familiar skull emblem had been seared into a sliver of rock farther up the ridge, but neither of them noticed it. Perhaps the Rumrunner noticed, for he hobbled into the rocks and wished us luck. But Wild-Eye was unfazed. She admired the light hanging above the fjord, walked back and forth, kicking the corners of the cabin. I'd lost the sensation in my toes long ago. I knew we would die if we stayed here to be swept away by the northern winds.

"We all have a chance, even those God has abandoned."

"But don't you have any . . ." I couldn't think of the word in Finnish. *"Ehrfurcht, Angst, Phobie?"*

"No. You're the one that's bait for the bogeyman out here."

With that, this rugged woman, this simple midwife, showed me, the son of Jaeger Captain Fritz Angelhurst, how to break into an ammunition bunker. All you need is a knife and the willpower to break down the wall timbers, eaten away by the wind. She loosened the bolts holding the window frame. And, as Wild-Eye explained, once the bolts on the other side start to rattle, you're practically already inside. I should write down what she said.

"The window frame is like the daughter of a large family: if she succumbs to one, she'll soon succumb to another."

I got the impression she was talking about the Rumrunner's sister.

"You pick up these things," Wild-Eye continued. "The landlords have lost their minds because of you lot, and they keep their wives under lock and key. Still, folks always need a midwife."

We used a cod-fishing pallet to climb in through the window. With one hand I gripped the window frame and with the other I held on to the roof timbers. I sensed that Wild-Eye and I were here alone. I watched her pottering in the glow of the hearth and wondered her age. The Rumrunner's sister calls her ancient, but it's hard to say. Unlike many people around here, she has a good set of teeth. The raised cheekbones of a lesser race, but a handsome, Aryan posture. The dignified hands of a mature woman. Her eyes and gait are innocent like those of a little girl. Has any man ever taken her? If not, why not? She's an old maid. She's got bad blood, or so the Rumrunner's sister says. I try to gauge from Wild-Eye's movements whether she knows I've lain with the Rumrunner's sister. At any rate, she doesn't seem to disapprove. Gentle and ravenous, she sucked the blood back to my chilled toes, wrapped me in a blanket the way my mother used to, and made me drink a bitter, fiery herbal infusion. She asked me to make her a garland. I had no choice but to promise I would.

Once Wild-Eye was out of sight, I got up and took a sip of Gödel's medicine. I don't dare go without it.

DEAD MAN'S FJORD

July 1944

The next morning there was a garland of crowberry sprigs, heather, and Lappish poppies waiting for me on the chair. I placed it on my head and went to fetch some water, humming to myself. My good mood disappeared when I saw who had turned up to dry his shirt in the garden. Jouni.

"Fine time to start cavorting with the Fritz."

He was angrily carving a lucky charm in the shape of a bird from a piece of driftwood. He spat an accusatory glob of mucus at me; half of it landed on his own boots. My blood boiled.

"You keep your nose out of this!"

"You're an old crone, lass!" he shouted.

I didn't listen. I stomped inside, slammed the door shut, and put down the latch.

A moment later I looked out through the rippled windowpane. You and Jouni were arguing, and then you plucked a roll of fishing line from the edge of a timber and headed off toward Seitakallio. I was startled. Surely Jouni hadn't scared you away? I rushed outside, stubbing my toe on the doorjamb, which sent sparks up to my eyes. Jouni sat on a rock, muttering to himself, smoking his pipe, and gazing at the sky.

"There goes your man. *Avot.* We should be going too."

"I'm going nowhere."

"Listen, you. I worked hard to get you that job at Titovka. I'd to bribe the old girl at the Red Cross with eight coffee coupons just to get her to listen. You're a *Schwester* for the Fritz now, and don't you forget it. They're testy these days; they'll have you up at the next court-martial."

"They wouldn't do that to a Finn."

"You promised to look after that Skolt lassie."

That hurt me. Somewhere in the camp little Masha was waiting for me, the girl I'd promised to look after, for whom I'd promised to make a kite. But Hermann Gödel had sworn he would take good care of the girl.

"What's the rush? Let's wait around, see if someone turns up."

"Don't you understand? There's other folks' lives at stake here too!"

That damned Rumrunner, why did he have to come back? Couldn't he just limp off into the rocks and complain to the lichen?

"I'll make some tea."

Once inside I leaned against one of the wall timbers and allowed my breathing to steady. I didn't want to leave this place, not now that I had you, a camp bed to sleep on, and a stool where I'd placed my bone comb next to your bird's-eye briar pipe. I opened the stove and chucked in more pages of Laestadius's sermons. I watched as the flames curled around the yellowed papers. I knew the words dancing in the fire without even looking at them. I hummed to myself so as not to hear Big Lamberg's condemnation from among the green flames. Once the water was boiling, I went out to fetch Jouni. He still refused to step inside the cabin.

"You just don't understand, Weird-Eye. We need to leave. This minute."

"What about Johannes? We can't just abandon him."

"He'll be fine. The smart ones are always fine."

"You go."

"You're a fool if you stay here. I'll not leave you."

He mounted the rock and took out his knife. Ten good-luck birds stood in a row next to him. I knew he wouldn't leave until I said something nasty.

"I'll not believe the word of a drunkard. Cut back on the moonshine, man. You'd have fewer premonitions. And maybe you'd stop running around after that piece of married tail."

"Don't you talk ill of Hedda!"

"You know fine well what kind of hussy she is if she breaks the seventh commandment."

"Stupid lass! Damn it, I'll not listen to this a minute longer."

Jouni lumbered to the ground, shrieked with pain. I could tell that his ankle was sore. But he wouldn't give in. He brushed the worst of the tobacco crumbs from his trousers, tied his wooden mug to his belt, and marched off up the hill, sending peat flying with each step.

"Where you going?"

"I'll kill the lot of you!" he screamed before turning back to face me. "Well, don't know about that, but I'm not coming back!"

Jouni disappeared behind the bluish-gray cliff edge before I could think how to insult him further. And with that, I was alone, utterly alone. I took in the empty landscape, not a single tree to hide behind. There was no way of escaping an air raid. All of a sudden I felt jittery. Silence. I'm used to it now, but it was the same sensation I experienced standing on the skerry with Masha, only not quite as powerful. I've learned that silence is death. In Big Lamberg's house we were always surrounded by people. There was always someone dying or being born, moaning about their chilblains or a urinary-tract problem, and though at times I loathed all those small-minded mediocrities for looking down on me, there was nonetheless something safe and comforting about the moth-eaten menagerie. Somewhere there was always noise, always life. Once you disappeared, Johannes, there wasn't even the song of the midges out here, and even the dragonflies had gone to ground. I wondered whether I should have run after Jouni after all, but commanded myself to calm down. You would have to come back. If for no other reason than to fetch your camera bag and your pipe lying beside the camp bed. What's more, you'd made me a garland.

I sat down on a rock to wait.

You loped back as evening drew in, trout speared on a branch slung over your shoulder and a catch of mushrooms rolled into your SS jacket. You brought the sounds back with you. The moment I saw you, the Arctic current began to roar, the sea to rush, the bumblebees to buzz. The silence was gone. You strode down the hill as carefree as young lads who have been out enjoying the sunshine and their freedom, lads whose mothers' embrace is always waiting back home. The world was filled with a warm hum, an echo. I wanted to fly up the hill and take your moving body in my arms. Still, I forced myself to remain where I was and admire your leisurely gait from afar. How handsomely you lilted against the light. Without a word you laid your catch on the steps at my feet, but there was a look of pride in your eyes. From inside I fetched a bowl, a knife, and your pipe. We sat down on the tree-root steps and gazed out at the water, the sky, the fells. The wind sang once again in the hay; your breath was hoarse. For a long while I didn't dare utter a word in case you became angry, took offense, and walked off again. I gutted the fish and chopped the mushrooms, sneaking glances at you from the corner of my eye. A couple of blue-winged butterflies were fluttering by the steps. Eventually you pointed at the horizon. There were aircraft flying overhead; you squinted to try and see if they were ours or the enemy's. I turned my head back to the butterflies, because I didn't want to see aircraft. I wanted to shut the war out of my soul and remain here alone with you.

"It's going to be a cold night."

"Where did Jouni go?"

"Went to look for help. Don't worry about him."

Though I realized we should be worried about Jouni. I should've been worried about the Skolt girl. Without you and the protection of the Third Reich, they would be defenseless. Jouni would doubtless roam the Fritz's pastures, searching for his lady friend until someone came along and shot him. I didn't want to think of that now. I brushed the lousy Rumrunner from this fjord and the next, brushed everyone in the world beyond the force of gravity, casting them away to float far out in the Milky Way. For I was jealous of anything that might wrench you from my side. I was envious of the war and the camp, of Lisbet lying in the infirmary and the scrawny cat I'd seen you stroking in the canteen. For the first time in my life, I quietly thanked the Russians, because without the wretched enemy, I wouldn't have ended up huddling next to you, here at Dead Man's Fjord.

We sat there throughout that heavenly evening. There were two skerries jutting out of the crashing waves, and we decided to call them Valaskari. You seemed amazed that there was still snow running down the sides of the fells at hay-harvesting time. But the most magical sight of all was Seitakallio, you said. At the top of the cliff was a Stallo stone the shape of a skull, and farther along the ridge the gaping mouth of a cave. As the wind pounded down across the fell, the cave's mouth turned into a dull kettledrum. The boom reminded me of the cannon fire at the Kalastajasaarento Peninsula, and for a moment I thought I saw an angel standing at the top of the fell and blowing into a trumpet. But there was nothing there, of course. It was just the wind driving air through the rooms and sweeping the heavens. We're lucky the Dead Man's cabin is so tucked away, you mused. I agreed. We were lucky.

Here between two cliff faces, the heaving of the seas subsides into a series of slow breaths; the fjord stands on the wild shoreline like God's own spittoon, naked and placid compared to the churning convulsions in the bosom of the open sea. The earth is covered in a dark red blanket of crowberries, the permanent snow on the northern face of the fell untouched by living paws.

Late into the night we watched as lightning sparked across the sea and the sky swirled in a dark, ominous mass. God had wisely drawn a thin silver line to mark the point where the water and the air met. It bodes ill when even God cannot remember where the boundaries of the heavens stand. I knew this, but I didn't care.

DEAD MAN'S FJORD

Johannes Angelhurst

July 19, 1944

Wild-Eye is a fierce woman. She's frightening because she's not afraid of me, though I have a weapon and an organ with which to defile her. Oh yes. She doesn't seem to appreciate that. She trusts me, polishes my boots, and combs my coat like a normal woman, yet she speaks to me like an equal. She approached me just now, propped one foot on the wooden chest.

"Why won't you take one of me?" she demanded.

I just looked at the chest. It's exactly the same as the one Father used to have, a beautifully decorated Russian-style traveling chest, the kind that sailors used in the past. Before family funerals we moved it out to the veranda, and Mother would gather apple blossoms and lilac branches in a little bowl placed on top of it. This chest has the same small image of a storm petrel as there was on the one Father made. It's almost as though it were the same chest.

"A photograph, a picture," said Wild-Eye, and pointed sharply at the camera bag. "Seeing as you made me a garland."

I thought she wanted to be photographed for her interview—which I'm never going to conduct, though she won't believe it. Very well, I resigned myself. We had plenty of time. I began attaching the camera to the tripod, and wondered which lens to use for the portrait. I'd left my exposure meter in the Rumrunner's car and the nightless night can be treacherously dim when it comes to Kino film rolls like this. A 1/8 lens, perhaps, exposure around half a second. I was so focused on setting up the camera that I didn't notice what Wild-Eye was up to. When I looked up at her, I took such a fright that the lens almost fell from my hand.

She had let her hair down and was loosening the laces of her dress.

"This is what you wanted. You've paid for this."

It wasn't a question.

Wild-Eye undressed for me.

This was a different kind of undressing than the Rumrunner's sister swinging her hips, different from any woman's undressing that I'd ever seen. The others were nothing but film material. I've never been interested in living flesh beyond what it takes to satisfy my needs. Without the flare of magnesium and the contours of a hip imprinted on the negative, they were nothing but seductresses showing me their suspender belts and tormenting me. Some of them looked like young salmon thrashing on the shore. This woman removed her skirt matter-of-factly and showed me her hips. She had a white, unscarred stomach and dark skin around her nipples. Then she removed her knickers. I felt an ache in my groin when I saw it: this woman was hairless. I caught my breath. The last time I'd seen a twotch as smooth as this was in 1933 when, at a Hitler Jugend summer camp, the girls of the Bund Deutscher Mädel had stripped off their bathing suits in among the scrub willows while I sat high up in an elm tree photographing them. It was a fine porcelain, so bare and white, as downy as gooseberry jam. And the smell that wafted up from those smooth twotches, at once innocent and yet like lewd chain letters, kisses blown into the ether. Mother caught me red-handed while I was developing the images and burst into tears.

"Don't you have any respect for those lasses?"

At the time I was more ashamed that my mother had muttered this in Finnish so that Father wouldn't understand. My mother, salt of the earth, just like Wild-Eye.

Now Wild-Eye moved closer. I was consumed by an indescribable shyness. I wanted to knock back some of Gödel's medicine, but there wasn't the time. I've never met a woman who *yearns* so explicitly. And though I was still fully clothed, it felt as though her gaze were all over me. I was bare naked, my every movement clumsy as that of a newly born fledgling. She lifted my hand to her hip. I ran a trembling finger along her delicate skin. I touched her thigh, then her groin. How could a grown woman's crotch be as downy as that of a young maid? What would it feel like to bury my face in that groin? So bare, so vulnerable and tight? Blood came rushing to my head, and I could no longer think clearly. I pressed my thumb inside her, into the soft and warm, and it only just fitted. Wild-Eye's nostrils quivered like those of a young mare.

"My twotch is the right way round, isn't it?" she whispered.

I flinched. What did she mean, the right way round? Did she really have bad blood like the Rumrunner's sister had said?

"It's just fine."

"You're the first man to touch me."

All of a sudden I was frightened. I couldn't carry on, not after she'd said that. I stormed down to the shore and started skipping stones across the water. I couldn't fathom what was holding me back. I could take her, of course I could. From the front, from behind, on our sides, indoors, outdoors, upstairs, outside on the cliff, at the bottom of the boat, on top of the chest. I wanted to lick her all over until she was moist and quivering, press myself inside her again and again. A stone bounced three times across the surface of the water.

"You're too good for that," I whispered to the seaweed, and I meant it.

Wild-Eye wasn't the kind of woman they called an easy ride, a strawberry sweetheart, or a Jerryman's glory. She wasn't the kind that loitered around the Salmijärvi Shanghai and let you have them for a block of chocolate, or the kind that cadged liquor at the barn dances and then boasted in the villages that they'd bagged a German officer. She wasn't the kind that huffed and puffed with the Bavarian boys beneath the bridge or bit their knuckles at the foot of Pelastusvuori or wherever it was their skiing trips took them. She wasn't the kind to sell her twotch for a dram of moonshine.

Four bounces across the water.

Wild-Eye had followed me. She walked along the shore, the midges following like a veil behind her, and she still hadn't dressed.

"I will be all yours, if only you'll have me."

"Please. You are so . . . *unschuldig*. I can't touch you."

Five bounces.

"You think my God can see us out here."

I asked her to stop. I told her I was a bad man.

"You're not. You're a poor man, a man of peace."

Another stone skipped across the water. Six bounces.

Wild-Eye asked where I'd learned to skip stones so well. In the Hitler Jugend, on the shores of the Wannsee. Every summer we took a ride out into the lake in a white sailboat. We learned marching songs and competed with one another. I was good at athletics and the shot put. In floor gymnastics I took second prize in my age group at the Berlin regional championships. The memory of moist strudel and warm apple lemonade in green bottles.

"Why are you really at the Titovka camp? Seeing as you're always trying to escape."

I thought about this for a moment. I said I originally wanted to be a pilot like my uncle. I wanted to fly and photograph the world from the air. Before the war, I was accepted to the Luftwaffe's Bavarian training corps near Munich, and that's when they uncovered the problem.

"Anxiety. Degeneration. Vertigo."

"There's nothing wrong with you."

A stone plunged straight to the bottom.

Now I didn't dare look her in the eyes. I was so ashamed, I wished I could've died. I'd gone and told her about my weakness. At the same time I felt wild and curious. I watched her walk away. I'll either have to kill her or love her. I still don't know which.

Now I've cleaned my lenses and magnifying glasses with an old rag, placed them on the table, and wrapped them one by one in fabric, put them away, safe from the mist blowing in from the Arctic Ocean. I put a set of 16 mm negatives in the Ludo. I've checked that the bottle of developer fluid is firmly shut and kept separate from the other liquids. You have to be careful with these things. If even a single drop of fixative gets into the developer, it'll ruin the expensive photographic paper and chemicals. If the developer fluid is contaminated, the prints become blurred and shaky. What would Father do now? Or rather, what would my uncle do? Or Horst Wessel? How on earth am I going to deal with this woman? Why hasn't anyone come to rescue us?

DEAD MAN'S FJORD

July 1944

The measure of your goodness is endless, your balls are like crisp red apples, and you have the peace-loving soul of a mushroom picker. I can say nothing bad about you. That evening you lit candles, placed the reindeer skin across the footstool and a floral embroidered quilt on the chest. The wind caressed the corners of the room, hummed its ancient songs in the gorge. The hay swayed like a monster's mane. The sea withdrew from the cabin, restless. You asked me to sit down. Your boots stood by the door.

"Tell me something, Wild-Eye. I want to do your interview now."

"I'll tell you everything if you tell me."

I laced our tea with a tincture of ground reindeer antlers, true-lover's-knot berries, honeydew, and the aphrodisiac drops that I was supposed to give Lisbet.

"What do you want to know?"

I was afraid this was all because of what I'd asked you earlier. I longed to explain it to you, all of it, to explain how a midwife, who had peered between hundreds of women's legs, doesn't know what her own womanhood looks like. How at Big Lamberg's house I used to sit up, wide-awake, every time I heard footsteps in the cottage. How I felt a sense of relief once I heard the slapping of Big Lamberg's wife's fleshy thighs on her way to come in and rock my eighth stepsister to sleep. It was thanks to her I could change the nappies on a Tasmanian devil with my right hand tied behind my back.

Still, Big Lamberg's footsteps frightened me the most. His boots reminded me of how I was forced from my childhood home at the age of nine. My mother was the love of my father's life, she was one of a kind, and it's a pity that her alabaster throat turned out to be the first symptom of consumption. Mother was already coughing up blood when they moved under the same roof. She died in childbirth, and for that my father never forgave me. When they came for my father in 1918, hauled him down to Lainaanranta, and executed him, all I could remember were the boots. I remember the black, shining boots and the silver fish scales stuck to them.

After my father's death I was sent to Petsamo to be looked after by my mother's relatives. I'd been living at the Lamberg household barely three months when, on a moonlit night, I awoke to the sound of panting. Big Lamberg was standing next to my foldout bed and staring at me.

"Your father's original sins and your mother's lewdness live inside you, lass, and it'll come out as blood between your legs. Have you started bleeding yet?"

I remember the dirty boots covered in pearly, silver scales. I stared at them through the threadbare blankets and began praying that I would never bleed. And I didn't. I learned to remove the downy hair on my groin with candle wax. In the summers I moved into the attic to live with the mice.

I didn't dare talk about any of that. I asked you a question instead.

"Do you think I've got bad blood?"

"*Nein.* You're pure. *Unschuldig.*"

You rubbed a bruise that had appeared behind my knee.

"Have you ever had a . . . *Geliebte* . . . a lover?"

I shook my head and blushed. But it's true, my dear Johannes. No man had ever touched me. The frock that Uuno soiled I'd burned in the Midsummer bonfire.

That evening you did something that is surely wrong according to Laestadius's sermons and singled out for special mention in the word of God as blasphemous or obscene. You turned, knelt down before me, and gently opened my legs.

"I'm going to give you something good. Tell me if it hurts."

You took hold of my thumb and cautiously put it in your mouth. You sucked it between your teeth, stained with honey and tea, until it was moist. I caressed the top of your head and felt the scar of that stray bullet on your left temple.

"Stick it inside."

It wasn't an order; you asked me gently.

I softly pressed my finger into the unfamiliar space inside me.

"There's nothing the matter with you."

I straddled the chest and felt that there was nothing wrong with me.

"Tell me more. Surely something must have felt nice when you were a child? *Kindheit?*"

Childhood? What had that been like? I fumbled to remember. Horses siring the mares out in Alakunnas's pastures; the monks' thick honey and the taste of prick between women's breasts as I sucked on their nipples until they expressed milk; the smell wafting from between Lisbet's thighs after the village dance. All this caused a strange knot in my gut.

But this sensation was a hundred times better. For the first time I sensed what it felt like to make a child and not to bring someone else's child into the world.

"You're an intimidating woman, Wild-Eye."

What would it feel like when you pressed yourself inside me?

"What do you want?"

"I want you to come inside me."

I let out a moan. All around us shadows danced and licked our skin, lightning streaked across the sky, and the landscape held its breath as if before a downpour. But the rain didn't come. Lightning struck an Arctic birch standing by the cabin, and the cable attached to it snapped with a boom. You gripped my hand, and I felt an electric shock from your fingertips.

"Slowly. You're tight."

"Does it hurt?" I asked.

"No. I'm just sensitive."

You laughed, and I knew that the moonshine and the tincture had worked.

"Have you been eating fruit?"

"Why?"

"You smell so fruitful."

"Is that what you say to all the girls?"

"Only to you."

You'd said the same thing to Lisbet Näkkälä when you took her, but I didn't care. I closed my eyes and let my fingers run up and down your chest, where wisps of velvety ball-lichen grew across the terrain of your skin. I wandered across the sternum and spread across to your nipples, which were rock hard, cracked, salty little South Sea islets, the metal knobs on the back of a jammed Bolex camera. I wandered down to the thick skin of your stomach, and across the body that breathed so excellently on the route that all pilgrims must undertake to the narrow-edged oasis of your belly button. I stuck my finger into the sweaty spring and felt the human life pulsating beneath it.

I allowed my hand to meander downward, tentative and hesitant. Your body jerked when I struck something hard. I gripped it, and it fitted in my hand as snugly as a knife in a sheath. Its tip was soft like a horse's muzzle, and blood pulsed at its hilt.

I too felt the urge to laugh.

DEAD MAN'S FJORD

Johannes Angelhurst

July 22, 1944

It happened today. I couldn't help it. May Wild-Eye's God have mercy on me! I wanted to tell you about it, Wild-Eye. The way you walked in, wearing that gray cotton frock of yours. It's a fine frock; it doesn't scare me like the other one, the red one. You'd taken off that ridiculous frilly hat, the size of a cart's wheel. I was relieved. Nobody should have to wear a thing like that on their head, particularly not since the wind and the rain had battered it out of shape the night you arrived.

I asked you to tell me about yourself. You took a green bottle out of your bag. A liquid glinted inside, a drink that smelled bitter yet somehow enticing.

"What's that?"

"Don't ask."

You measured out a spoonful and gave it to me the way you'd give medicine to a child. You told me to swallow it and knock it back with tea and plenty of water.

"Otherwise you'll feel poorly."

"Wild-Eye, what will happen now?"

You had the same expression as when we'd first met, that predatory wolf's gaze.

"Now I'm going to mark you."

"What?"

"Come."

You pushed me back, laid me down on the footstool, took off my sweaty military coat, undid my buckle with the eagle insignia. You said it was a good thing I didn't wear my boots indoors. You placed my clothes on the camp bed with a sense of routine, as though you'd skinned a hare. Your movements were slow and precise, and you were my Wild-Eye, now suddenly unfamiliar, far from the God-fearing country lass I'd mistakenly thought you at first, far from that invisible creature who pedaled from house to house on a rickety bicycle from the military warehouse, who brought children into the world, who blew snotty noses, who crawled on all fours, keeping the mothers' tobacco fields free of weeds. Far from the strange woman who only a week ago demanded to be photographed. And though in your figure I could still make out that selfless benefactor, pure and untouched, all the while I saw her dwindling, disappearing into the shadows, replaced now by something else, a frightening creature with shoulders of fire. The creature grew and grew and soon filled the room, smoke billowed from its eyes, and where there should have been skin, there was now only raw flesh. The creature climbed on top of me and whispered into my ear.

"Take me, Johannes. Take me now."

PART THREE

DEAD MAN'S DIARY

Scarface to Redhead, July 5, 1943:

Operations Wild Duck and Midnight Sun completed. Strike successful, 26 resistance operatives arrested, 16 executed at edge of grave. Almost all resistance operatives apprehended. Houses burned, cattle destroyed. Information extracted from interrogations: Oswald, a wing of the German–Communist Wallberg division, now collaborating with the nationalists. Nats being trained in Sweden as "police reinforcements." No information on names of local operatives.

July 12, 1943

My dear daughter,

I don't know whether you will ever forgive me. I am an evil man. I do not have a single friend; the ashes of the only friend I ever had, I scattered in the Titovka River long ago. I am at war on two fronts. I work both for the Allies and the Third Reich. I remain in the employ of the Gestapo as much out of fear as for the monthly payments of three hundred crowns. The number of people killed in these operations is just as big. And I am partly responsible. In my dreams I see images of burning rams, glimpses of women's backsides amid the hay, their flesh whipped raw. The excruciatingly slow final prayers of men standing at the edge of pits they have dug themselves. For the Germans are a cruel and paranoid people. They're afraid of the nationalists and the Communists going into league with each other here in the north, though they've nothing to worry about. Such a collaboration would never work.

In many ways I think of my task as I would think of any form of work. War has its own laws. But now I am plagued by a guilty conscience. Redhead visited—an uncivilized, brutish man. An ass scratcher who visits the sailors' quarters in every town and brings his wife far more exotic gifts than mere seal fat. He said something strange today when we were talking about Operation Wild Duck and the fact that he would have to spend a little time in the Sydspissen prison in Tromsø so as not to arouse suspicion. Apparently his wife has been sent to a camp somewhere. I asked if he was worried. Redhead scoffed.

"That whore will get what's coming to her. That'll teach her to go off with the Rumrunner."

I broke out in a cold sweat. I've just informed the Gestapo about a village full of nationalists. We all know what's going to happen to them. They'll be murdered, every last one of them. Why? Because that good-for-nothing prick wants to take revenge on his wife for doing the same thing he brags about all the time. I feel ill. To get my own back, I've been teaching him an incorrect method of using the encryption disc, though I doubt he'd ever learn the correct method if I showed him. He hasn't the slightest sense of rhythm. Instructions: twenty-six randomly selected alphabetical characters, with secret characters on the fifth ring. To decipher the code, the disc is placed back at its starting position. I'll not tell him the starting code. I'm trying to think of a way of getting rid of the wretch of a man. Men like that should have their families taken away. That and far more besides.

Only once in my life have I met someone to whom wickedness would not stick. It was in 1919, under odd circumstances, when I met Fritz Angelhurst, a German Jaeger who was to become my only friend. I had been instructed to plant ammunition along a bridge dangling precariously across the Titovka River. At first glance, I thought the wolves must have driven a young reindeer into the swamp, but it seems that my fellow Red Guardists had tied up a German soldier and left him there. His upper body bare, he was up to his hips in the mire. Midges and clegs were attacking him; ants were eating his flesh. When he saw me, he raised his hand as much as the ropes shackling him would allow.

"Nasty weather," I said, pulling the poor wretch to the surface. I applied tar and elk-antler oil to the bite marks. We sat beneath the bridge. The drumming of heavy rain. A malitsa *draped over his shoulders. A bonfire of resinous wood. A gnarl pipe with a thick chamber. I had my very own calabash:* Forgive Our Sins.

The bonfire crackled, the rain eased, eventually stopped.

"Why are we here?" asked the German.

I told him about you and your mother's family, about how I'd tanned the local zealots' shoes for free, and instead of thanking me, they thanked the Lord. Bitterness probably made me believe life with the Communists would be cozier. It wasn't.

Dostoyevsky said it's only really cold when the mice start to squeal.

"No. I mean, what are we doing here, slaughtering complete strangers? They're someone's children too."

Angelhurst became my friend, the only friend I've ever had. He told me he could never again raise a weapon against another man, and that it's always from the little things you can tell that the enemy is still human. Their ability to blush, to hiccup, to love. These are things we all do.

I set off toward Murmansk and ended up swearing allegiance to the NKVD, enjoyed nostalgic evenings at the kolkhoz *and a longing that reeked of makhorka tobacco. Fritz Angelhurst left warfare behind him and became a pacifist. Later on I heard he'd taken Aune Näkkälä's sister, Annikki, with him back to Germany. In 1938 I received a final letter from him:* "The insanity afflicting this country will be the end of me. If I die, collect my ashes and scatter them in the Titovka River. Annikki will understand."

I tell you this now because I want you to know that your father carried out at least one good deed in his life. I have let one man live, and through this deed life continues, for I've seen Fritz's son. I was once sent to a German camp to decipher coded messages sent by the Russians. The place was called Zweiglager 322, a transit camp established to meet the needs of Operation Todt. I couldn't say where the messages had come from. Somewhere in Maatti Fjord, sent on a worn-out transistor apparatus. The messages eventually opened up using the Pobeda Code. But what stayed with me was the information that a young officer had just arrived at the camp. At first I thought Fritz Angelhurst must have risen from the dead. Of course, it couldn't be him as his ashes were at the bottom of the Titovka River. But it was his son, of that I was most certain. And he was frightened too, nothing but a skittish little pup, and in a single glance you could see right into his downy little soul. I didn't care to look.

The boy has often been in my thoughts since then. There was something about him. It must have been 1941 or 1942. He'd just returned from the Ukraine, where he'd taken a stray bullet in the head. Fritz Angelhurst's son didn't want to stay at the camp under any circumstances; that much I understood. By that time there was already talk of eliminating the undesirable elements of local society. Upon hearing that, a stork-shaped scar appeared across his brow, and he didn't enjoy a smoke that evening like the rest of us. He gripped his balls when he thought nobody was watching. I was watching. How he squeezed and squeezed, squeezed and fainted. That takes willpower, lass, but in wartime it's called cowardice. The camp director would have had him executed. Eduard Dietl told the guards to leave him. Later on, I heard he'd gone to Parkkina and become a reporter for Lappland-Kurier.

DEAD MAN'S FJORD

October 1944

I'm lying on the camp bed, listening to the autumn winds pummeling the corners of the cabin. The petroleum lamp has almost burned out. A blizzard of white ice whips up from the sea. Summer now seems an eternity ago. When you pressed your way inside me, my former life flowed out of my body like water from a broken pail. Johannes Angelhurst, my angel sent by God. How your prick forged a channel into my black soul and let the brightness stream in. Now I wait, reminiscing about you, longing for you. The Dead Man is making a racket. Every morning the diary lies open at a different page, and the corners of the room creak.

Something happened today. I was crouching on the rocks, watching as the rising tide slowly caressed the seaweed, snatched it up, creeping ever closer. I haven't slept for many nights now, and I must have slipped into some kind of stupor. In my daydreams I saw a Russian platoon setting up camp on the shore. The camp's commander had the face of Alexei Ignatenko, and I could hear the melancholy strains of the Moscow Philharmonic and the clang of the canteen bell. The purr of a motorboat brought me back to reality.

I leapt to my feet.

Johannes!

The same back, curved against the light, the same self-assured gait, the same slender body as you. The way you sat out in the fjord, leisurely fishing without any bait, the motor raised out of the water. Everything was as calm as it had been back then. You looked as if you and your square-rig sails were floating in the air. I remember how a warm wave washed over me. You pretended to be busy with the job at hand; you sailed too close to the shore. You didn't fool me.

I dove across the autumn-red thicket, ablaze like a swift dipped in petrol. Only then did I recognize him. The scraggly red hair, the beady eyes, the pocked skin of one who had doubtless been the object of taunts and scorn as a child. It wasn't you, but a man I remembered from earlier in the summer. We called him the Jerker. I backed off, and suddenly longed for the Mauser, safely hidden in a drawer inside the cabin.

Back in the summer I hadn't much cared for the Jerker. What room could there possibly be in my world for anyone but you, Johannes? A snipe cawed somewhere on the fell. The possibility of love rendered me restless, fearless, insatiable. The thought of your flesh had made me forsake God.

On one occasion you came bounding into the cabin and said you'd seen a fisherman out on the cliff with his trousers down.

"There's someone out in the gorge watching us."

I was busy crushing crowberries and starch into a sweet *kissel.*

"Don't be daft. There's nobody there."

If only you were here now, Johannes! The Jerker must have seen smoke coming from the cabin chimney. He knows there's someone here. Besides, I yearn for news of you, for the company of another living person. Since the Dead Man's visit, I've felt jittery and on edge. The corners of the room watch me, alert; the walls give way to the touch. At around six o'clock the sea seems to heave toward me, the fell to press down on the back of my head. What if you never come back?

I step closer and wave, saying, "So, you're back?"

The Jerker empties the burned charcoal from his engine and explains that he's on his way north. He's managed to escape his cell in the Gestapo prison at Sydspissen. Again I think of the Mauser in the desk drawer. If I run quickly enough, I'll get inside before he does. Hilma is wagging her tail and crouching down in front of the fisherman to play. She's certainly got a knack for sniffing out the enemy.

"Come inside. I'll make some tea."

The man doesn't take off his boots when he crosses the threshold. I pour a good dram of Captain Morgan into his wooden mug.

"Saw that lass of yours wandering around the hills."

Masha! I haven't heard anything of her in a long while.

"Aye well, *tyvärr*, that's too bad. Have yourself some of these."

He holds out a bucket full of flounderlike fish dangling upside down. Virgin Mary fish, he calls them, says he'll show me how to make a trap to catch anglerfish, mollusks, and other creatures.

The ginger-haired man eyes the Dead Man's diaries on the table, then me.

"I was watching you back in the summer when you were cavorting with one of the Fritz."

The Jerker holds out his hand and strokes my shorn head. I close my eyes and let him stroke, let him stroke me for a long time.

"You've no man up here with you—that's plain as day. You've no teeth neither. But I can help you out, sure enough."

The Jerker pulls my hand and pushes it down on the buckle of his belt.

"If you help me first. Now take out those teeth."

I place my whalebone teeth on the table next to me. Midges swarm inside my head.

"Take him in your mouth. John Thomas'll think it's Christmas."

I shake my head.

"At least give him a stroke then."

I feel sick. I know I'm good at stroking. Just as God is good to his universe and a few creatures are good to others of God's creation. I know how to use my hands. I can sing bairns to sleep and women into a slumber; I can make grown men quiet and lustful. How you enjoyed it when I touched the inside of your thighs, how you giggled, how in an instant you turned serious and contemplative.

"Shall I stroke you some more?"

I remember the first time you entered me back in the summer. A storm was howling across the sea, and you were strange and yet so thoroughly familiar. I cannot lie: it hurt me; Jesus, how it hurt me. As though I'd been cleft in two and a huge, glowing rod thrust right through me, but I wasn't afraid. On the contrary. For at the moment the pain struck, an indescribable joy filled my purged skin, a sense of calm, and I was happy and full of love and the certainty that you felt the same, because you moved inside me slowly, beads of sweat dropped from your forehead onto my neck, and your breath warmed my ears as you whispered meaningless, unrecognizable words—is this love?—all the while ramming back and forth inside me was a strange creature that had suddenly claimed me for itself.

"Can I come inside you?"

"Yes."

At that I felt your body stiffen, you gave a short cry, and a rush of warmth filled me. Semen, the sheets stained with your seed, and I lay beneath you, taken and spent. I lay there, the sense of joy twitching in my limbs. It was a summer night, and with that my fatigued body was reborn. You were young and at the same time warm and strange, but a moment later you were smiling, bashfully licking my armpits and my groin like a puppy, and before the sun raised its head above the hillside, you tore through my every orifice once again. You whimpered with pleasure as I tousled your hair, asked me to touch you with my mouth, and you came again as soon as I touched the tip of your penis with my tongue.

My heart was full of tenderness, overflowing with emotion. I lay there amid the itchy hay pillows as a storm gusted out at sea and the world drowned, and I prayed: My Lord, let me keep him. I want for nothing else, I'll never ask you for another man. I am your little fledgling. I am your Chosen One.

God didn't answer me, and perhaps God demands more of his chosen ones and in different ways. For if you are but one of God's cruel games, a yardstick sent to test humanity, then what am I? Why have I been given the gift of healing, and why have I been forced to work against that gift? Why should I, of all beings on this earth, have to sit here in the bosom of the Arctic Ocean waiting for the Reaper to come and cut us down with his frosty scythe? What am I, other than a sinner who wandered from her path? A young elk that strayed from the herd, a lamb with a hoof wedged among the rocks, a blindworm whipping across the sun-seared cliffs, or a marsh-tea blossom that should have been plucked by a young girl but that has instead withered and sunk into the swamp? I swore that if God let me have that man, I would never pray for anything else.

But no. That's not what happened. I didn't ask God for permission. I'm taking him. I won't ask for another.

Now I know. You can't make deals like that with God. For you should never try to take something by force that God in his infinite goodness has not deigned to share with others. At most he might lend it, but even that comes at a price, and the price is a life of suffering. Even now as I lie here in Dead Man's Fjord, alone and abandoned, my womanhood chafed from the ravaging of countless members, now that I've been driven away from home and the children chase me and the landlords set their dogs upon me, even now I ask why. Why didn't God, in all his wisdom, recognize my weakness? Why couldn't he let me be born the youngest child of a simple country family along the banks of the Ounasjoki or in the plains of Parkkina? Why did I have to become a midwife by the grace of God? Why wouldn't the Lord afford me the one thing in this life that I wanted most? Sometimes, though I've ceased to trust in him, I imagine that the Lord has laid a curse upon me. For perhaps he was uncertain when he created me, just as the God of the Jews was uncertain about the love between Jacob and Isaac, perhaps my God decided to make my life hell because he knew that I wouldn't follow him after all or sacrifice to him my only son. That I wouldn't follow the path he had destined for me but would take a mortal as my lover, and that I would never fully understand my gift, my skill, my honor, any more than the average man understands his fearful herding dog or the currents understand a whirlpool in the creek.

"Have it your way," said the Jerker, fastening his buckle. "I'll be back soon, sure enough."

He began pulling on his coat; he hadn't taken off his boots. He scratched Hilma's neck as he walked past her.

"Cold winter coming," he mused. "You'd get good mittens out of that mutt."

The door rattled as he pulled it to. Just you try it, I thought. By then I'll have brewed a new tincture to flavor your tea. There might still be a drop of ricin oil in the bottle. I escorted the Jerker to the shore, watched as his boat glided into the mist and its colors disappeared. I took a long gulp of Captain Morgan and squinted my eyes so that the fisherman's body turned once again into your slender figure. All the while a sense of dread lurked in my mind: he'd promised to come back.

Oh, Johannes, how I've missed you and your benevolent gaze! Whereas you have soft black angel's wool growing on your chin, this fisherman's beard is a bitter, tangled gray. Whereas you smell of musk and the raw earth, this oaf stinks of cod, soiled bedstraw, and fear. You both have a big build, but whereas you are muscular, the Jerker is flabby and hunchbacked. His eyes are pitch-black, not smoldering embers but lumps of sodden coal.

I wanted to cry. With you I never needed to be dishonest. Without your eyes to behold me, my soul is black, my womanhood is lewd and beyond protection against the Devil's evil eye. I longed so much for you and your presence that I slumped to the ground and the Captain Morgan spilled into the bosom of the earth, and there I lay, alone in the tundra, beneath the stars, howling and hollering with agony to the heavens above.

DEAD MAN'S FJORD

October 1944

I feel ill. The Jerker's wife and their herd of children have arrived, all arms and legs, and are making a racket down by the shore. Earlier on his wife was pacing around, tidying the cliff edge. This is what war does to people. Back at the camp one of the prisoners used to wash herself night after night, and scrubbed the trusted prisoners' pricks because she'd been told to scour the dirt from them. They called her the Bird of Paradise. In the same way, the Jerker's wife is fretting around and sweeping the cliff with a broom. A frightful thought flashed through my mind: Could it be the same woman? No, surely the Lord wouldn't punish me so terribly?

At around midday the Jerker brought the whole brood for a visit. I recognized the woman instantly. I recognized her even though the women in Operation Cattlehouse always had their faces covered. Except toward the end, that is. Her husband and sons brought with them such a blinding, suffocating atmosphere that I'll have to air the cabin for days. I sat them at the table and started lighting a fire in the hearth, my hands trembling. Does she recognize me? No. She won't remember me.

The Bird of Paradise wandered around the cabin, pretending to admire what she saw, and I felt ill watching her red-nosed offspring tumbling over the armchairs. All the while I felt as though they could peer inside me, see the rot and the cankers. I could feel their gaze in my vertebrae as the Jerker's wife gawped at the layers of soot beneath the stove and counted up my empty rum bottles. She stared at me shamelessly. Me, the Fräulein Schwester of the Third Reich! If only you were here, Johannes! That woman wouldn't have been pottering around, swiping cobwebs from the corners as though she were inspecting a new home for herself.

"This place would suit us fine," the Bird of Paradise said with a sigh.

My heart was bolting in my chest. I had to sit down.

"I'm not going anywhere," I whispered.

"Thørgen says you'll be leaving soon," she quipped.

"Quiet, woman!"

I looked at the Bird of Paradise and wondered how it was possible that she hadn't recognized me. Because it *was* her. The bruises on her wrists weren't from just any kind of rough-and-tumble. It was a brutal hand that had gripped them, and most certainly not in defense of the fatherland. I handed her a cup. A dose of St John's wort, tobacco extract, and ricin oil half this size usually had the Hilfswilligers on the toilet for a week.

"You and me have got some unfinished business," the Jerker hissed.

I slurped tea from the saucer and felt the thigh of his dungarees pressing against my skirt. His flat-headed lads were staring out to sea.

"I've been thinking about you," he continued.

One of the boys crouched down and pulled Hilma's tail. Another blew in her ear.

"I'm not going anywhere," I whispered. "I can't."

"Your dog's been snatching fish from our outhouse."

Another of the boys raised his eyes and piped up.

"You can kill a loose animal if it comes back twice."

Silence. The scrape of Hilma's claws on the floorboards, the whimpering as she went from one guest to the next, placing her head in lap after lap in the hope of a glimmer of love.

"Aye, good dog for mittens."

"Stop it, Thørgen. We're leaving."

"What have I said? A mutt like that?"

At the door the Bird of Paradise turned and complained, "You should keep your dog tied up during wartime. It's the law."

Then she sniffed her armpit like a child and looked at her family.

"Thørgen is harsh to those boys. It's the war what's done it."

She came closer, and I was engulfed in a fug of wild cloudberries.

"I'll not turn you in, seeing as you're expecting."

Leaning against the door timber, I stood there, my heart thumping. So the Bird of Paradise remembers me after all. How long is she planning to hold her silence? I went back indoors and noticed that one of the Dead Man's diaries was missing.

Now I can feel the bonfire and hear the strains of an autumn-evening waltz on a mouth organ. It's out of tune. The Jerker is twirling his Bird of Paradise in the air; his imbecilic children are tripping into the sea and falling on top of one another in the long grass by the shore. I stopped to look at the sand and imagined I could see your footprints. Waves beat fiercely against rocks bearing the faces of children. The gulf stream carries junk from far away in the southern Caribbean, and anything shipwrecked along the Icelandic coast washes up on the Arctic shores. I hear the melodies again. He's got no ear for music. I suppose it's easy to see how such a big dick could produce two such defective offspring. As I look at the two-headed silhouette lilting against the sky, I can only hope that peeing is painful for the Jerker's wife too.

DEAD MAN'S FJORD

Johannes Angelhurst

July 25, 1944

We walk arm in arm along the shores of the fjord. The morning is soft and naked. I feel contented. I have swum, fucked, eaten, drunk, and slept. Above all, slept. In Wild-Eye's arms I never have nightmares, and Hermann Gödel's medicine makes my mind joyful and self-assured. But what if it runs out? Because of Wild-Eye, I might not need the medicine any longer.

We walk along the edge of the swirling turquoise sea and talk about the future. We work out where all the driftwood and the remnants of broken fish traps come from. But there are other things too: a tin bucket, the remains of some poor soul's shoe, a broken bottle of Belgian ale, and an enormous swimming cap in which a crab had carelessly made itself a home and suffocated. Wild-Eye says the sea doesn't give up all its gifts at once. It's as unpredictable as a Jewish business partner: it doesn't like obligation, and you can't force it to work for the common good. We mostly encounter rubbish from afar, from the Caribbean Sea or the Antarctic, and we turn it all into a history of our own. Wild-Eye is surprisingly good at it. An old propeller she claims must be from a seaplane belonging to Roald Amundsen, the explorer who disappeared. On seeing a washed-up scarf, I decide it must have belonged to Fridtjof Nansen. Without his scarf, the poor man had to ski across the frozen wastes of Greenland, fell ill with adult colic, and died. I don't know whether Nansen is dead or alive, but my father obtained a passport by that name for my mother when she accompanied him to Germany.

After the war we'll go to Berlin. You can taste Mother's cherry preserves, and we'll drink plum liquor from pristine glasses. We'll sit on the veranda and cycle to Grunewald to gather mushrooms. Mother can make a stew.

"Tell me about your mother," you asked.

So I told you. I told you that my father, Bomber Jaeger Fritz Angelhurst, and my mother, Annikki, met each other in the village of Alaluostari, Petsamo. My father was in the habit of lying on his back on Penitence Hill, as they called it, and counting the stars. The story goes that the hill was originally built by a monk who had been caught trying to smuggle a woman into his chambers. To repent for his sins, the monastery's hegumen ordered the monk to carry a sack of earth to the site every day. As a result of his life-long punishment, a hill had gradually formed, and a small chapel was built at the summit. Mother worked at the monastery, preparing ant-heap baths for travelers and eating raw fish and snow buntings. She had restless blood. One August night she climbed up Penitence Hill, where she met a mustachioed Bomber Jaeger who told her he was tired of the war and wanted to return home and write his memoirs. This impressed my mother. My father was impressed that Mother knew the name of every constellation in the sky. The Dog Star. The Rod of Moses, more commonly known as the Northern Star.

Wild-Eye pressed herself against me, held me.

"There's northern blood in you. You'll not come down with polar madness like the rest of them."

Again I was reminded of the task Eduard Dietl had assigned me. Why won't you believe me, my Wild-Eye? How I worry about returning to the camp.

"Why are you so frightened?"

Operation 1005, that's why. That and the fact that I'm meant to start digging a pit.

"Can't someone help you? Your uncle, perhaps?"

I've written my uncle twelve letters, begged him to have me transferred, to deliver me from evil. He won't answer. I'm afraid of my ugly dreams, afraid they might come true. I'm afraid of the part of me that can't remember what happened in the Ukraine.

On his last visit, Eduard Dietl told me what my task was to be. In the interests of national security, we must do the opposite of what we did at the outbreak of war. We must dig up that which was once buried, and bury it again. Dietl, the Arctic Fox, is dead now, killed in an aviation accident somewhere in Austria. But Hermann Gödel won't give up.

"What's so strange about that? Shovel it up, then shovel it back again. You'll be making a swimming pool for the prisoners."

"That's not how it works. The war hasn't touched you yet, Wild-Eye. You don't understand."

"Besides, we'll be at the same camp."

But what does she know about anything? She doesn't even know what goes on in Operation Cattlehouse.

"You think you're better than the rest of us. You're not. If we go back to the camp, the war will get to you eventually."

"When we go back to the camp, we'll make Masha a kite."

Masha, the little Skolt girl waiting for Wild-Eye back at the camp. And I decided straight away that we'd make her a kite. A fantastic kite, one spewing fire like the kites on a Peking night. A tail of fish ribs, ropes of lace, stripped stalks of water parsnip, seedless cones from the Siberian pine, Christmas-tree decorations, barricade tape, thistle blossoms that have survived the winter, a fairy's severed leg, a squirrel's tail. It will be the finest kite in all the world.

Wild-Eye said she was worried about the girl. I lied, saying nothing would happen to her. God would take care of that. And Gödel and the Resurrectionist. After all, the girl's a Finnish citizen.

"But don't let her into the Cattlehouse."

Everything that happens offers the hope of a better future. I believe in the Führer and the Third Reich. I'm not a traitor like my father.

My father lost his faith in National Socialism in 1933. I remember us watching a torch-lit procession of university students along Unter den Linden Boulevard from the safety of our high-ceilinged apartment, the home we would soon be forced to leave. Father was counting the torches and the books the students were carrying. Works by Thomas Mann, Stefan Zweig, Karl Marx, Sigmund Freud, Ernest Hemingway, V. I. Lenin, Albert Einstein, and Heinrich Heine. When they reached Opernplatz, they threw the books onto a great bonfire.

"Let's play chess, Son," my father had said wearily.

He strongly believed that if a man played chess, he could not be wholly evil. As the evening drew to an end, Father lay drunk in the rhubarb bushes, reciting his own poetry.

Now Wild-Eye pressed her nose against my chest, said she was listening to the beat of my good heart.

"Show me your pictures, of your father and everything."

Wild-Eye doesn't have a single photograph of her family.

"I want to learn about you. You're my family now."

I asked her whether she could prepare a bath for me, preferably one without any ants. Wild-Eye laughed and promised she would.

DEAD MAN'S FJORD

July 1944

All day I've been looking at that photograph. It was taken over there on the cliffs behind the cabin. It's not myself I'm looking at. I've got a silly, bovine expression on my face, and my arms are covered in freckles that not even frogspawn or parsley water will wash away. I'm looking at the shadow cast on my toes. It is your shadow. This is the only photograph I have of you. I have nothing else.

All things burn. All things return.

We lived as man and wife, in sin, but still I couldn't say whether I was cared for or abandoned, longed for or rejected. All the while, the words on my father's pipe hammered at the back of my mind: *Forgive Our Sins*. Until death do us part.

Possessiveness.

I'd never experienced anything like it before. Now I was jealous of every moment not spent in your company. Every time your eagle insignia disappeared among the cliffs. Every rock and field, every clump of moss that felt your steps before I could feel them, the depraved lapping of the receding tide beneath your feet, all this was too much for me.

"Let's get married," I began harping on. "This madness won't go on for long."

Soon we'd be in the finest hotel in Murmansk, and you could slurp champagne from the stiletto of a Russian lady of the night, and I'd wear the garland that you made me.

The boom of artillery fire came from behind the fell.

"My frilly hat," I kept repeating. "I'll wear my red frilly hat, and I'll be a lady. Don't you believe me?"

You didn't answer.

"Show me your photographs."

"No," you always said, time after time, always glancing fretfully at your camera bag, which lay on the chest.

All the while the air was light and smelled sensual, of whale skin and the sea, and my groin was constantly open with simmering lust. During those days pollen invaded my nostrils and raced straight to my heart, causing palpitations and battering my mind. Throughout that time I felt at one with the great unifying, purifying drama frothing and foaming in the fjord, something Hermann Gödel would have called a process of Darwinian natural selection. I could sense the salmon sniffing their way across the ocean to their spawning grounds, the ants mating by the cabin wall, their backsides attached to one another.

As for what happened next, perhaps it was inevitable. For what can be more sinful than a maiden constantly wracked with lust?

I opened the black cardboard folder by accident. I didn't intend to look inside, not even to peek. I was sweeping the floor with a broom of juniper branches. I'd already scoured the windows with wood-ash lye and rinsed them with elderflower and chamomile water. I thought about the compress I would prepare for your thumb: extract of wood sorrel and a plantain leaf. That day the straps on your bag weren't properly fastened. Later on I wondered whether they had been left like that on purpose. The cardboard box slipped to the floor by itself; the folder flew open, and photographs spilled from its velvet interior. I crouched down to gather them up. After all, someone had to gather them up.

At first I saw only newspaper photographs, shots taken at the officers' club in Kursunki. In one of them, Kriegskommandant Eduard Dietl was proposing a toast, a curious expression on his face. In another, Colonel Oiva Willamo and his adjutant were standing at attention outside the Rovaniemi Liaison headquarters. Albert Speer, the principal architect of the Third Reich, and the goggle-eyed Ferdinand Schörner. Photographs from a fraternity-of-nations sporting event at Rommel's stadium; an image of a guard hanging a rustic tablecloth on the barbed-wire fence around Little Berlin in Rovaniemi. But then my hand fell upon an envelope from which studio photographs printed on little cards began to slide out. I fumbled to open the envelope and emptied the pictures into my hand. There they were. Lots of them. Women. All kinds of women. Some with hats, some with their hair loose. Familiar and strange, shy and lewd, dark-haired, blondes, brunettes, their legs open, their lips pouting, the gray caps of the Lotta Brigade pressed down across their brows, Lappish girls with necklaces dangling crookedly across their breasts. They had all surrendered to the will of your camera. Lisbet Näkkälä with her back to the camera, the darkie bairn on her shoulder. Nothing but a sheet to cover her, and even that had slipped so that the folds of fat on her back and the curve of her fulsome breasts were there for all to see. I couldn't help myself imagining things. How you'd thought of taking these women, thought of thrusting inside them, these harlots, these whores of Babylon, how you looked them in the eye just as you had looked at me, whispered about how fruitful they smelled, how primal, like a dog's groin in heat. Different, each and every one of them. I of all people know what a woman's vagina smells like, and I know that every nipple is different when I take it in my mouth to suck for milk.

But more than anything I was plagued by the idea of how much those women had enjoyed you. How they had clenched their twotches around your prick. And as the Lord Almighty knows only too well, these women had experienced plenty before. Large and small, short and stumpy, thick and veiny, smooth ones, some curving slightly to the left. These they had tested while I toiled through the drudgery of a world of torn gooches, frightened of the sight of Big Lamberg's boots beside my bed. These women had experienced everything: a German SS officer's sturdy rod, sweat from the brow of Finnish country lads, and the makhorka spittle of the Russian prisoners. Harlots. Shameless. Many of them had dreamed of what was being thrust inside them, longed for it. Jewish stumps, snipped and veiny, Arabian sabers parched in the desert and quivering with passion after Ramadan, six-foot Negroes and their night-blue torches, mulattos the color of soft, milky cocoa. Bitter, marsh-tasting Asiatic men, Russian men, angular and reeking of ink, their members so preserved in vodka that they would not even rot in the grave. But they had never experienced the same sensations as I had with you, *God help me . . .*

Another photograph slipped from beneath the velvet lining and fell to the floor. At first I thought it depicted women lying in bed, their limbs wrapped around one another. The edge of a wrist, eyes raised to the sky, empty stares. Then I noticed the battered temples, the twisted ankles, the bruised stomachs, the bayonet gashes on their hips.

These women were dead. I turned the photograph over and read: *Babi Yar, Sept. 29, 1941. 6 x 6 cm, 80 mm, objective f11, exposure time 1/125s. Good depth and contrast.*

Fire will cleanse us. So says the Word of God.

I slid the photograph into my apron pocket and packed the others back into their folder.

A succubus riding naked on a hound of Satan must have charged through the fjord that afternoon. For otherwise I cannot to this day explain what came over me. I had lit a bonfire outside to roast the eider ducks caught in the trap. I picked up your black folder—how light it felt as I carried it out into the garden. Without the slightest hesitation

I opened the soft straps, turned the folder upside down in all its handsome beauty, and emptied its contents into the glowing embers.

If God had been merciful, the ground would have shifted beneath my feet. If God had been merciful, I would have been unable to light the kindle. But the Lord is fickle with those he has created for his own amusement. The peaty wood flickered happily into life. Fire will cleanse us, scorch the poison away.

Naturally, you arrived just as the flames were turning green. Your face shone with a hunter's pride. Oh, how you arrived, one hand holding your hares aloft, the other strands of sedge. You'd finally learned how to gather bilberries on a blade of hay and collect unripened cloudberries in the hat with the eagle insignia. I let you come up close, let you take me by the shoulders, kiss my ear.

"Wild-Eye. The fire is burning."

The joy drained from your face when you understood what was feeding the flames. As for me, I could no longer hold back my rage.

"Where did you get those pictures?"

As if I didn't know.

"That's my work, *meine Arbeit.*"

"Tell me this isn't real, this here!"

I handed him the one photograph I'd spared, the one with the pallid women staring at the sky, their limbs wrapped around one another.

"This is war."

This is war. So everything is permissible. We live like there's no tomorrow, for the Day of Judgment could come at any time.

At that moment your eyes looked old.

I finally came to my senses.

I began poking at the fire, at your work, but the magnesium surface of the photographs melted before my eyes, Lisbet's white thigh curled and turned to ash, a shoulder blade belonging to some blonde Berliner, a well-formed earlobe, its bud pierced with an earring shaped like a bolt of lightning. The smoking arc of painted toenails and bared shoulder blades.

This was all that was left.

"Why did you do this?"

"I don't know. Because."

Because I love you, because I can't live with the thought that someone else has touched you.

You pushed me away, shook your shoulders so that the body of the hare slapped against your hips. It was still twitching. Your officer's coat gave a crunch as you turned. I can floor a reindeer buck if need be. Flooring you presented no trouble at all. I am strong and agile by nature; you should have learned that by now. I took you by the hips and turned you over. Through your soft mountain-army trousers, I felt my nails digging into that most precious of regions, instinctively, as though I were carrying out a daily duty. You let out a squeal, probably more from surprise than pain. We wrestled there for a sweaty, heather-scented moment. The air shimmered; the earth caught us. I sat across you and sighed with passion and exhilaration. I waited to feel your hips, waited for you to plunge your SS body inside me, to grip my hair and pull my ear to your lips.

"Have you been eating fruit?"

"Why?" I'd ask.

"You smell fruitful."

Then I saw your expression. It was a look of shame. You were ashamed of me though there was nobody in sight, ashamed of this old dog's behavior, my rough play and reindeer-herder's manner. Just as you were ashamed of your mother and father, now you were ashamed of me too.

"Let me go."

I clambered off you. You staggered away down the hill. Rocks caressed by the Arctic currents rattled under your feet and, Lord, from that moment onward it was as though a deadly poison had entered my bloodstream. I wanted to run after you, succumb to you, fall at your feet, lick your every nook and sweaty cranny, to wail and whimper, anything at all for you to look at me and smile that slow smile that makes me float with elation in a burning sea of yellow barley.

I realized I'd done something terribly, terribly, terribly wrong. You didn't come back. Not that night, not the following night. I skinned the hare with a blunt Lappish knife, chopped up the meat, and pronged it on a skewer. I roasted it for you.

Forgive me, Johannes, for what I have done. I can't forgive myself, and God doesn't care. I stand here with the knife in my hand and amuse myself with the idea of cutting my toes out of the only photograph I have left of you. Your shadow falls on my feet, and I want to cut away the shadow. But then I would have to cut off my real toes, my flesh and blood. You see, I might still feel the softness of your shadow in them, so cunning and cruel is my body. It remembers the touch of your hands, the caress of your sun-kissed fingers. It remembers the weight of your body pressing down on top of me, the touch of your peat-smelling socks against my toes. The scar on my chin remembers the tip of your tongue, my nipples your smarting bites, my thighs the masculine hips pressing against them. Worst of all, of course, is my guileful twotch, which longs to be crammed full of you, for in all the years before, and from that moment onward, I have never encountered a cock that fitted me so perfectly.

DEAD MAN'S FJORD

Johannes Angelhurst

July 30, 1944

There is a hare in the trap. I am a hunter, a predator. I am Alaric, the savage king of the Visigoths. I keep my woman happy with fresh meat. My enemies fear me. I stride into the garden full of pride. I can smell the magnesium sulfate and see the edges of the photographs, curling and blue, the green-red flames, and her expression. Only then do I understand what I'm seeing. Wild-Eye is burning my photographs. Rolls of film, negatives, my ticket to a future, the images I'll use to apply to the Film Academy once the war is over. Wild-Eye holds out one of the photographs and asks what it is.

I want to hit her. My hand won't rise. Instead, I look at her through tears and try to focus. Good contrast, taken with a tripod. It was a sunny day; you can tell from the shadows on their cheeks. But I didn't take this. The women lying there were strange and lifeless, like a scene from one of my nightmares. Air catches in my gullet, and my throat gives a gurgle.

I snatch up my bag and storm off. I have to.

I head for the gorge and try to find the road. It must be here somewhere, the *riksvägen*, the highway to the west quarried by German troops. My ankle hurts after the wrestling match with Wild-Eye. I don't give a damn. I find a path trodden by the reindeer. I fall to the ground and lie there at the foot of a cliffside strip. This is supposed to be my second homeland, but it's foreign, cruel, and insatiable, just like she is. Up here time always seems to slip in the wrong direction; night shuns day, and shadows seep into the light. Everything happens too quickly, yet doesn't happen at all. Those photographs were the only things tethering me to reality. They showed me that there was a moment when the image was taken, a hundredth of a second, a fragment of a real, physical moment that time cannot smooth away.

Now Wild-Eye has burned these moments and conjured up a sliver of falsified reality, an event that never actually took place. That photograph quite simply does not exist.

I sit up and fumble in my belt for some tobacco. I must survive. I am not weak. My father was weak. Father fell to the ground, dead, the moment the war broke out. Word came over the wireless just as Father was changing the element in the stained green lampshade dangling about the stove. The Führer's voice suddenly filled the room. The voice said that the Polacks had attacked Germany. War had broken out. The oil burner flickered into life, the news filled the air, Mother and the servant girl raised their eyes and looked at Father in disbelief, the donkey in Helmut's field whinnied, and I had time to wonder where the prized bottle of plum schnapps might be hidden, a thought that brought on an instant bout of constipation, before Father let out a bewildered answer.

"Surely not," he blustered before toppling from the chair.

He was dead before he hit the ground.

Our army took care of the Polacks in only twenty-eight days. Though I grieved for my father, I was ashamed of his display of weakness at a moment of such significance for the German nation. But we were in for an even greater surprise at the old shoe workshop, where for years Father had been penning his memoirs. Mother said my uncle would help us out if the text was good enough for publication.

We broke down the door and stood in the light refracted in the colored shards of the broken window. I'd expected to see sheets of manuscript strewn across the floor. I had heard the clack of the old Remington for years. Father's divine voice when on Saturdays he crawled among the rhubarb bushes, reciting wordless strophes. Sheets of manuscript beneath the plum tree, dissolved by the rain.

Something.

Instead, every part of the room was filled with slivers of leather, awls, chisels, caustic soda, in the corner a tub of varnish and a barrel of linseed oil. On the floor there were shreds of newspaper, horsehair, and a pair of brown Jaeger standard-issue underwear that Father always called the breeches of faith. In the middle of the room, right next to the workbench, was a single wooden chest, newly decorated in the Kurbits style. It seemed to float there in the columns of light like a tombstone covered in flowers, descending to Earth to creak out some long-awaited happy news for humankind. We searched and searched, but after ten minutes it became clear that there was no manuscript. Only the charred corner of a sheet of paper with a crossed-out text: *All this will come to nothing.*

Inside the chest, Mother found a bundle of letters from an old acquaintance. When I asked her about them, she told me that Father had met a Finnish soldier during his time with the Bomber Jaegers.

My father, the man with the soul of stone.

Mother sat down on the floor and blew her nose on the underpants. The endless nonsense about Lapland and his great adventures there. About the Cause, the world, about us. None of that had been left to future generations. Only a wonky leather chest, which nonetheless stood up in comparison to other chests in how strongly the seams held together and how well the relief patterns on the surface repelled water. On the lid was a painting of a storm petrel, a bird that lives far out at sea, beyond our reach. It was a magnificent chest, but still, just a chest.

Father burned only his own manuscripts. Wild-Eye has destroyed my life's work.

The funeral was awful. My uncle was so ashamed that he couldn't bring himself to turn up. Some wretch had placed the chest on the veranda during the wake, covered it in lilacs. All evening I had the sense that if we lifted the wreathed lid, Father, cowering inside the chest, would squint his eyes and say, *Take a picture of this if you can, Son.*

I couldn't.

That chest was so strange. None of our relatives dared look at it, let alone touch it. That evening I wanted to sit next to Mother; I wanted her to tuck me under my blankets the way she'd done before. But Mother was sitting by the fire, slurping plum schnapps from a crystal glass.

"We'll have to ask your uncle for help."

The lantern and the horse chestnut tree cast slowly swaying patterns across the wall. Mother twiddled strands of her neck hair and bit her lips, humming that same Lappish lullaby that Wild-Eye is humming for me now.

I asked whether Mother ever longed for home.

"Home? Where's that?"

"Finland. Lapland."

Mother scoffed and said she'd only left behind a kid goat, and a constipated one at that. Life was grim. The archimandrite from the monastery at Alaluostari rode around on a three-wheeled contraption, one of many things he'd knocked together by himself. Her only relative was her sister, who always knew better than everyone else. A family of healers, a cult of blood-stoppers. Mother hadn't inherited any of those skills. There was nothing left in Lapland when Mother packed her bag, the one with the bone toggles, and set off.

"Aye, but it seems your father left something behind. He never really recovered from our return to Germany."

Then she sobbed and whimpered, told me to go and sleep in my own bed. Two weeks later my uncle visited us, and he hadn't brought his own sheets. A month after that, a strange Finnish man turned up at the doorstep, asking to collect Father's ashes. Mother handed him the urn without question and forced the man to take the Kurbits chest with him too.

"Take it as far as you can, Pietari. Take it to the ends of the earth where the poor man broke his heart."

I spent a long evening smoking the pipe I'd inherited, thinking hard. I didn't want to go back to the fjord. Wild-Eye would be waiting there with the remains of my photographs. But it wasn't about the photographs. The more I thought about it, the more insignificant their loss seemed to me. For what were they, after all? Surface, thighs, a barely perceptible lust. Besides, I have Wild-Eye now, a woman of flesh and blood. I would let go of those loose lassies if Wild-Eye asked me. At least I think I would, if not for her betrayal.

But there was more.

There was that other photograph, the one of lifeless women strewn about on the ground, their eyes staring into eternity. Such a photograph can't exist. It's not possible. Yet Wild-Eye managed to conjure it up before my eyes. I wondered whether this was some kind of conspiracy. Whether someone, Hermann Gödel perhaps, might have slipped that photograph into my folder. Whether he and Wild-Eye were plotting something that would send me to distraction. Whether the nightmares might come back and I'd start hearing women's laughter again from behind the fells.

Why would Wild-Eye wish me so ill? I still don't know.

But one thing is certain: I must get my hands on some medicine; otherwise the edges of the world will start to splinter again. Without Gödel's medicine, blackness will surge inside me as though my soul were sucking up the light and belching out nothing but darkness. I'll have to go back to the fjord.

DEAD MAN'S FJORD

July 1944

Every lost hour, every minute, every blink of an eye, every moment without you is futile. At any moment a German platoon could arrive and save us. At any moment Jouni might turn up, chewing on a piece of tree bark, and tell me to go with him. A troop of partisans, perhaps, or a resistance commando unit watching us through the crosshairs of their rifles. I wanted to tell you how finite everything is, and how I've been waiting for you all my life.

You could no longer bear having me near you. You returned as evening drew in and made to sleep beneath the upturned boat. The moment I approached you, your brow furrowed and you angrily turned your back to me.

Johannes, I loved this too; I loved the wall erected within you.

Every day you were furious with me, I felt pain and agony like never before. My mind ached, and I had to take plenty of valerian and moonshine just to keep myself together. I could no longer wade out into the turquoise sea with you, scrub your skin clean with seaweed, or walk side by side with you to the burn and fill the pail with water. You didn't hold my hips, didn't blow into my ear, didn't call me Wild-Eye like you had before. I couldn't join you when you went fishing for cod, couldn't lean against your side by the bonfire on the shore. What's more, you would no longer speak to me.

Your temper was stubborn. But you wouldn't be angry with me all summer because even you knew that the war wouldn't last forever, either that or there would be another war, one far worse than this. You'd have to relent before long. I might need you, though moreover you might need me out here in Dead Man's Fjord. I waited, collected driftwood, and moaned. My yearning for you made me grind my hips against the table and whine. At times I pulled from my apron pocket the photograph with the words *Babi Yar* on the back. I stared at it, wondering why it had made you so distraught. In looking for an answer, I turned your things upside down. I found socks, a bottle of mouthwash, a thin volume of *Mein Kampf*, a shaving brush, a mustache comb. Then I noticed a tiny phial of medicine in the side pocket of your bag. It worried me. At first I thought it must be Pervitin, a drug used to pep up the troops on marches and reconnaissance missions. I knew the stuff from my time with the Red Cross. The Fritz used to hand it out at field hospitals and told us to make a note of any side effects it caused. This was new, stronger stuff: Adolfin. I'd seen it among the medical supplies at Titovka, but I'd never used it on patients. I don't like the stuff, though it's far more effective than Pervitin and more scientifically tested than opiates like morphine or laudanum. It takes away pain and makes the patient feel light and happy, but that's where it ends. The effects don't wear off for quite a while. At harvesting time it makes a babbling moron of anyone who takes it. Time slips away as people yack and chat about nonsense when they should be doing real work. Not everyone returns to normal. I shook the phial of dimmed glass and wondered who had given it to you. Inside was a bluish, translucent liquid. The label on the bottle read *WPL, Hoecht 10820, Portion à 0.5 mg/d.* I walked outside and poured the substance into the thicket.

DEAD MAN'S FJORD

August 1944

The span of love is finite, and our moment was particularly so. It lasted only two weeks. Two weeks, five days, and fifteen minutes of fulfilment, anger, sorrow, forgiveness. In all that time we saw only one other person, the Jerker, but you drove him away too. Other than that, the landscape sighed, tranquil and secure. Ravens circled on the horizon, waiting for darkness to descend. Then the bombing would resume.

On Tuesday morning Jouni hobbled into the garden, and he wasn't alone. Not yet, not now, I cried to myself when I heard his voice at the door. But it was only once my eyes adjusted to the light and I saw whom he'd brought with him that I really took fright. At the end of a rope was the Russian prisoner who'd run away from the Titovka camp. My Russian lad. I remembered, for the first time in a while, that I was stuck in this fjord with an SS officer. I gave a start. Jouni had brought with him a fugitive from the camp, and that fugitive would recognize me. This didn't bode well. Thankfully the Russian lad didn't give the slightest indication that we'd met previously. Nonetheless, the war hound shackled to his ankle, the one that had eaten her own puppies, started to whimper and wag her tail and lurch toward me. A painful-looking fishhook had become stuck in her muzzle.

"Cur's taken a liking to you."

I shrugged my shoulders. Jouni yanked the war hound to the ground and told the Russian lad to look after her.

"But you know what they say, lunatics have a funny smell. Attracts animals like pox to a whore's loins."

Jouni said he'd found the malnourished Russian lad near Kirkenes. He'd been gnawing on a stolen potato in the barn where Jouni was planning to sleep; the boy's startled eyes had been gleaming from the hay. At first Jouni's reaction was to put a bullet in both of them, but the Russian turned out to be nothing but a boy and the dog came and licked his hand, and he'd started patting and stroking her so much that shooting them no longer seemed appropriate.

"What are we going to do with these two?" Jouni snapped, sitting down abruptly on the gnarled steps and throwing the prisoner's chain from his hands as if it were an adder. His gestures seemed exhausted, so I rushed inside to fetch water and boil some gruel.

"Jam too, mind," he shouted hopefully.

There was no jam, and Jouni continued complaining. He was carrying the old pipe from his combustion engine. Jouni and the Russian lad had managed to attach a new one after fiddling with the Ford for twelve hours. At first the soldering iron hadn't worked, and they were unable to seal the metal plates. Eventually the Russian lad scooped a handful of ashes from the burner and peed on them. He squeezed the stuff into a thick paste and stuffed it into the hole. It had worked, and now the Destroyer was waiting for us at the end of the road.

"Damned nuisance," Jouni muttered, the pipe carved from briar and its bone stem dangling beneath his mustache, and began investigating the cabin. "Fine place you've got here. All right for some."

Of course, you had to wander out of the shed at that very moment, my Johannes. I could see that my tar infusion hadn't stopped the midges feasting on your skin. Without looking at us, you washed your face in the barrel of rainwater. Still you refused to speak to me, though every morning I'd left a letter for you beside the boat and ointment rubbed from bog myrtle for your chilblains; though I'd lined the bottom of the boat with reindeer skins, washed the boots you'd left in the porch, and scrubbed them with varnish I'd found in the boatshed.

"Well, well, so that's what's going on! Who's going to cut the kid down if not the Fritz? I'll not do it, but we can't take him back to the camp neither. Don't kill him, eh. Take him under your wing instead! That's what it says in your Good Book, right?"

I couldn't remember whether there was anything in the Bible to that effect, but I didn't argue the point. The Russian lad was even scrawnier than before; it was a wonder he was still alive. Someone had given him a good beating, and the midges had ravaged him; one eye was swollen shut, and his feet were covered in sores. Someone needed to take care of him. But no. I'd already wallowed in the sleet-colored love of the fjord, and I'd lost you. I thought of Masha, the Skolt girl back at the camp waiting for her kite. I hadn't spared a thought for her either in all the days I'd been here waiting for your return. Besides, what would happen when you discovered that this was the prisoner that had escaped from Titovka? You'd shoot him.

"What's his name?" I asked.

Jouni turned to the Russian lad and interpreted.

The lad smiled and said, *"Menya zovut Alexei Ignatenko."*

Now the lad had a name.

"God knows what kind of creature he is. I found this on him."

Jouni fumbled in his rucksack and threw the old potato into the grass. Then he pulled out a wooden board with black-and-white squares drawn in chalk and coal. Jouni stared at the thing as though it were a spy's map drawn in secret code. But I knew instantly what it was, and so did you: a primitive chessboard, which explained why he'd been carving all those wooden towers and horses. The Russian lad gazed at his chessboard as though he thought it might disappear into the air like smoke.

"You know what that is?" asked Jouni.

"It's the game of the gods."

I looked over my shoulder, and there you stood, beautiful and stubborn, rainwater dripping from your cheeks. But surely the Russian lad couldn't possibly understand a game like that. The only people I knew with a grasp of chess were my father, Pietari, and you, Johannes, my master and sovereign. I've never learned the rules or the moves. A Russian misfit could hardly comprehend a game of this caliber.

"He needs killing."

I shook my head, though I didn't know what else we could do with him. If we took him back to Titovka, he'd be lashed and sent out to dig his own grave. After that, a bullet to the back of the head. Execution awaited anyone found fraternizing with fugitives or feeding them. You could get yourself killed for much less. I handed the lad a piece of dried meat.

You raised your Mauser and took aim.

I closed my eyes. It's for the best, you said. The boy was suffering from what Gödel called *seelische Belastung* (emotional distress), and, besides, he had been Judaized.

Just then a shot cracked through the air. The bullet tore off a piece of the wall timber. It came so suddenly that at first I didn't realize that the shooter was not in fact you but someone else, someone stalking us from behind the rocks, his gun propped upon a tussock. We all dove headfirst into the grass. The dog howled and cowered between my legs. You aimed your weapon somewhere into the skerry and took a haphazard shot.

"Time for us to go!" said Jouni, crawling behind the cabin, cursing. "This is exactly what I've been talking about!"

Once in safety behind the cabin, Jouni stood up and hobbled off sideways between the hills. I could feel you following behind us. The Rumrunner hopped over boulders and shouted commands into the air. First we had to get away from the open land, then head east; the terrain there was so rocky that following us would be hard. The clank of the Russian lad's chains echoed between the cliffs, and I wondered how the boy had managed to escape the camp in the first place.

About half an hour later, with the taste of iron in my mouth and the Russian lad following behind us on all fours, Jouni came to a halt.

"Who was that?" I panted, still in shock.

"Christ knows," Jouni snapped. "Best not think about things like that."

He lit his pipe and began assessing the situation. It turned out we weren't far from the road. Only a ten-hour hike, if that, then negotiate our way across the waterfall. After that the start of the road to Petsamo was a mere reindeer's bladder-break away, and from there it wasn't far to the red-white-yellow Miljoona Bridge. You climbed up toward the waterfalls to survey the landscape. You'd stopped talking about shooting the Russian lad. Jouni and I huddled together sulkily and watched you.

"So, what's going on with your strawberry sweetheart?"

"For the last time, woman, her name's Hedda. Don't you call her anything else."

"I'm sorry."

"What about you? Are you in love?"

"Don't know."

"You'll know fine well when it hits you."

"How can you tell?"

Jouni pointed toward the fjord. An ice floe was floating in the freezing turquoise water though it was the beginning of August.

"Would you swim out there if your Jerryman told you to?"

"Aye."

Jouni bit the stem of his pipe in the corner of his mouth and asked more abruptly, "Are you ready to be with him right to the bitter end?"

"Yes, I am."

"And you'll not disappear or die unless he gives you permission?"

"No."

Jouni tapped the remains of the tobacco against the heel of his boot. The aroma of sweet *latakia* and marsh tea wafted into the air. The Laplander fumbled with the collar of his blue driver's coat and cleared his throat.

"Times are changing, lass. Things at that camp are not going well. That Hermann Gödel, he's not a good man. There are plenty of fussers in this world, folk that'll trample you into the ground. He's one of them."

"Only the Lord Almighty, all-seeing and all-knowing, only he can reveal lies like that," I answered haughtily.

"Fine then. We'll pretend the kid's a trusted prisoner. I've got new badges for him."

Then Jouni did something strange. He took me by the shoulders and squeezed me in his arms.

"Don't you bother your head. It'll all turn out fine."

"What are you on about, man?"

"Lisbet's got news for you. She can tell you herself."

We set off. Jouni's Destroyer was about a day's trek away and started up like new. Alexei Ignatenko and his dog were told to lie down in the back beneath the tarpaulin. At the border you stuck your head out the window, and a soldier saluted us.

"Heil Hitler!"

The war seemed to descend heavily around us. In your cap with the eagle insignia you looked severe and distant. Throughout the journey my mind was a whirl of restless thoughts. You were silent too, though Jouni chattered on. We were on our way to Liinahamari, back to the camp at Titovka, and it felt like an unbearably harsh punishment. What was Lisbet's news? It seemed she'd recovered. Another terrifying thought crossed my mind: What if Uuno had turned up? What would happen then?

Before Miljoona Bridge you gripped my hand and held it tightly for the rest of the journey.

LIINAHAMARI

August 1944

We arrived in Liinahamari as the first stars lit up in the pale nighttime sky. Petromax lanterns twinkled in the distance like fireflies, and the oil tankers impounded by the Russians and the British cast whale-shaped shadows on the leathery surface of the sea. Somewhere behind the blackout curtains came the strains of Herms Niel's evergreen song "Erika."

Cannons boomed across Kalastajasaarento.

Jouni parked his Ford near the fish factory by the quayside, and we climbed out. The Party had sent a car to fetch us. The Alakunnas boy, Jaakkima, jumped out of a Tatra truck emblazoned with the eagle and sun cross, clacked his boots together, and raised his hand in a salute. I was glad I'd dressed myself up to the nines in my cretonne frock and frilly hat.

"Fr-fr-Fräulein Schwester. *Alles in Ordnung?*"

Still I squeezed your hand, and for a short, heavenly moment you responded to the squeeze. This is exactly how I'd wished to return to the camp. Triumphant, victorious, arriving on the arm of a handsome

German SS officer. Jaakkima would have to bow before me and kiss the back of my hand with his whiskers. We would eat plank steak with cranberry jelly, and everyone would stare at us and gossip among themselves. They would see that I was almost a wedded woman. They'd see you whisper to me all evening. *"Meine Ehefrau,"* you'd say, and give me meaningful looks before their very eyes.

And Jaakkima would bow and scrape. *"W-w-wunderbar! U-u-unglaublich!"* he'd cry out. And once we'd had enough of him, you'd give a Führer salute and send him into the corner of the room to serve as a coat stand. You'd bow before me, take off my frilly hat, and Jaakkima would hold it all evening, perhaps even all night. And you would look at me, only me and none of the canteen sweethearts, and none of them would dare look askance at me ever again.

As soon as we arrived in the canteen, I understood that none of this was going to happen. Lisbet all but jumped across the counter, flung her arms around you, and threw me an accusatory glare.

"Where've you been?"

"We were lost."

"Lord, Weird-Eye, you'll not believe what's happened to me. Thank you for bringing my Johannes back in one piece."

"Calm, now, lass," Jouni whispered to me.

Lisbet pressed her soft breasts against me and sighed with happiness. "Your ointment worked after all. I'm expecting!"

The world slipped from beneath me. I plunged into the infernal ravine at Kolosjoki and sank into a mire of snakes. From under her sweet-smelling armpit, I caught a glimpse of the whitewashed ceiling. I prayed to God to let the roof cave in. But when I looked up at the rafters, they seemed sturdy and didn't have the slightest intention of collapsing.

"I'm so happy. Better ask the Fritz for permission to marry."

"They'll not give you that," I heard myself say.

It was true. Germans weren't allowed to marry people with the wrong blood. What's more, they'd never give Lisbet permission to marry once they worked out why she was so familiar.

"They most certainly will when Johannes gives the order. Hickler doesn't check the paperwork anymore. Listen, we'll sort you out with a decent man too now that Uuno's gone and disappeared. What about Jaakkima? He might have fallen on his head, but he's a fine lad still. If we win the war, mind, he's on good terms with the Fritz."

And with that Lisbet started planning her wedding. She'd need a Lotta crown; no doubt they'd give her one seeing as she'd met Hickler himself. Of course, she'd also seen Albert Speer, architect of the Third Reich, and flounced around on the arms of Commandant Eduard Dietl, but this was different.

"Aye right, wh-wh-where'd you see the Führer?" Jaakkima piped up.

Lisbet eagerly assumed her starring role. It had all happened a few years ago at Mannerheim's seventy-fifth birthday celebration in a stationary saloon wagon in Immola. The student mannequins had curled their hair with tongs and handed out talcum powder to the Lottas so that the guests of honor wouldn't smell the girls' country ways. Of course, Mannerheim was an event all of his own.

"You could tell from the way his voice echoed down the corridor that it was a real warhorse coming."

Even so, it was the arrival of the Führer himself that stole the show. He was very polite, though he ate nothing but rabbit food. He even knew how to hold his cutlery properly, which was more than could be said for the Italian ambassador, who shoveled macaroni into his mouth with a fork and a spoon.

Again, Johannes, I couldn't help myself. Lisbet standing there behind the counter, her blouse primly buttoned up to the neck, her cotton collar and red cheeks. An air-raid badge had appeared on her uniform lapel, though she had no right to wear it. The airy purity of her made my cretonne frock seem like a rag tossed over a scarecrow.

"Didn't they send you back on the milk train?" I scoffed.

It was a blow below the belt, because the rest of the story was something Lisbet had told me in confidence while she was giving birth and made me swear to keep my mouth zipped. She'd been given the enviable task of bathing the Führer in the presence of one of his aides. There had been all kinds of rumors among the girls. People questioned the Führer's virility and wondered why he never winked at the ladies. Even in the bath he blethered tediously about Blondi, his Alsatian, and how she was going to bear him puppies in honor of the occupation of Stalingrad. There's something not right with a man like that, something wrong downstairs. Lisbet had been simply unable to resist the temptation: she gingerly lifted the cotton cloth covering his groin and slipped the bar of soap slightly farther down than she should have.

"Just to check whether he still had both balls. Well, he didn't."

A wee devil must have consumed me as I sat there, making me spill out her secret. Lisbet had been relieved of her duties in the Lotta Svärd Association and threatened with a spell in a penal colony. Adjutant Julius Schab and a couple of officers from the Rovaniemi Liaison headquarters had vowed that Lisbet's entire family, everyone from Aune to Jouni, would be hauled up before the court-martial and shot if they ever stepped foot below the Arctic Circle.

"Goodness me, what tosh," she said with a dismissive wave of the hand, and walked off to mix cream powder for the coffee.

She looked altogether sweet and innocent, but I knew those eyes. They were the eyes of the predatory female from whom I'd imagined your arms would protect me. Now you were sitting several benches away, politely listening to Lieutenant Holger Warva from the Rovaniemi headquarters as he slurred a toast to something or other. You wouldn't even look in my direction.

After the lingonberry pie it was time to repay the debt.

Lisbet had been especially attentive to me throughout the meal. Does Fräulein Schwester have enough pudding? Are you happy sitting there, or is the draft messing up your hair? She poured me moonshine and kept offering me more salmon, though she knew I thought it a coarse fish. The scent of pine snag hung in the air, and the lace curtains gently fluttered in the windows. Then Lisbet came up close and started furtively showing me the front of her Lotta uniform. As if by accident, a gap had appeared between the buttons to reveal her swollen, buxom tits. Her camisole was sugary and wet.

"Look, I'll soon be giving milk. Being in my third month, you know."

There seemed no stopping the flow of milk, she complained. When she went into the barn to fetch hay for the cows, the mice in the rafters went berserk. I asked whether she'd tried to pump some of it into a bowl with her bare hands. The seeping would stop with time. Lisbet cocked her head to one side. Her opportunity had come.

"Aye well, you'll not understand this, seeing as you can't have bairns yourself. Everybody knows why that is. You never hit a branch coming off a toboggan. You seduced your own stepfather, so you did."

I looked over at you, and you stared back at me with empty eyes. Silly, silly Lisbet. She shouldn't have said that, not while you were within earshot. It was a lie. A lie! I wanted to shout out loud that you were my first, you, Johannes! I wasn't ashamed of it, the memory of your prick inside me. I wanted to shout out, exalt the innermost quivering that I couldn't explain, caused as you slid in and out of my tightness. Back and forth. Back and forth. Take me now. Screw me from the front and from behind, screw me with conviction, look me in the eyes. The smell of your dick on my skirt, my breasts, my lips. How our sap combined and trickled down my thighs, how you came inside me with a little cry. That cry promised me more than anything in this world before. It promised me that there would come a time when you would set up your camera and your cable-release self-timer, and you'd stand beside me, and on my knee there would be a little girl with a lace collar and next to her a boy with thick spectacles. Could there be a joy, a happiness in all the world purer than this? Now Lisbet had taken that from me too.

She was humming, her head to one side, wiping the tables and occasionally dabbing her nipples, and once again that dark fire within me flared up, the force that makes me carry out the Devil's work. That same fire had burned your photographs. Now it whispered to me to give Lisbet a brew of deadly yew berries and puppy's blood, to scrape the fetus from her womb, just for you, because the hounds of hell command me. I tried to resist the voice in my head. Lord, hold me back! I looked at you and followed your eyes to Lisbet as she leaned over the checkered tablecloths, fulsome and fecund. And I understood. Of course you wanted a woman who could bear you a son.

After the meal you and Lisbet disappeared out to the veranda, and I trudged back to the loneliness of the officers' barracks. I pressed the sackcloth blanket over my ears so as not to hear what the Devil was trying to tell me. I pressed my eyes shut and bit my tongue until blood flooded my mouth. And at that moment I was more afraid than at any time in my life.

LIINAHAMARI

Johannes Angelhurst

August 10, 1944

Wild-Eye has a new pair of fish-skin boots. I bought a pair for both of them, Wild-Eye and the Rumrunner's sister. A peddler touted them, saying they were excellent for dressing up and for attracting attention. The boots' surface looks like snakeskin but is in fact made of cod. Wild-Eye accepted the gift as though I'd handed her a dead crow. She slipped them on her feet and wept.

She holds my hand as we press through the strafed land toward the camp at Titovka. On arrival we are to meet Hermann Gödel. I have been instructed to start digging as part of Operation 1005. My head hurts. I need more medicine. The Rumrunner's car jolts ahead, and the red brim of Wild-Eye's frilly hat taps against my temple. A sign has been put up at the intersection of Russenstraße: MURMANSK (30 MILES), COLOGNE (2,050 MILES), BERLIN (1,708 MILES). It's strange that I only notice this sign of longing and homesickness now that I have a desire to return home.

I steal glances at Wild-Eye as she stares out of the window at the broken, creaking service cables above, tears in her eyes. There's something about her that reminds me of the Norns in Wagner's *The Ring of the Nibelung*. She weaves together the threads of human destinies. I'm still unsure which of the Three Fates she is: Urd, the past, Verdandi, the present, or Skuld, the future. Our fates have crossed; there is nothing we can do about it now. I feel her cold fingers in my hand. She always has such cold fingers. Her pinky is crooked, an injury sustained while assisting in a complicated birth. The lines on her palms point straight toward me. If that hand holds me tight, I'll come to no harm.

"Lisbet Näkkälä is pregnant, apparently," Wild-Eye says, matter-of-factly but not accusingly.

She squeezes my hand and stares at the service cables running across the streams, cliffs, and marshes, as inexorable as the war itself. The Russian lad and his dog give off an unwashed stink, which mixes with the aroma of pipe tobacco and naphthalene. The wind sweeps the smell of gunpowder and burned flesh over the fells.

I am a bad man. Weak. I don't deserve Wild-Eye's love. I went with the Rumrunner's sister because she forced me to; I had no option. She's carrying my child. But there's an ounce of decency about me still. I didn't take her back to the officers' barracks, though she nagged and pleaded with me, because I knew Wild-Eye would be sleeping there. We went in among the air-raid cannons, and the Rumrunner's sister started hurriedly unbuckling my belt.

"Why have you taken such a fancy to Weird-Eye?"

I couldn't answer. Had something happened at the fjord? I vowed and assured her that nothing had happened. The Rumrunner's sister smirked and said she hadn't thought so. Surely I wouldn't take to lying with an old spinster like that. Then she lifted her skirt and told me to come inside her. I couldn't do it, though you'd think the girl's readiness would have been a relief after Wild-Eye's ecstatic whale song. But no, I couldn't concentrate. It felt as though the sky were pressing down on my neck. All the while I could hear the Lotta girls whispering by the acoustic location mirrors on the hillside. Silver-sounding planes have been hovering in the sky all day, flying low, looking for something. How do these silly lasses know whether they are our Stuks or Russian or Allied aircraft? They don't. An amateur would be unable to identify them in the dark, and the locals only turn on the searchlights once they're sure the plane is directly overhead. There came more wailing from the sky. I could feel my member withdrawing into my groin like a small, frightened creature.

"*Entschuldigung.* This is pointless."

I began to hoist up my trousers.

"You're not feared, are you, Johannes? Frightened of a bunch of tea drinkers and makhorka men?"

I know. They won't beat us. We have the best cannons and anti-tank devices to protect us. Soon the Führer will deploy the *Wunderwaffe*, blow Murmansk to smithereens, and replace it with a new, finer city called Dietlstad. But if the air-raid sirens go off, Wild-Eye is out there somewhere, alone. She is alone, she'll panic and come looking for me. I buttoned up my jacket and walked down toward the shore. The Rumrunner's sister's voice was tight with tears when she caught up with me.

"Johannes, listen to me. She'll never give you a bairn."

"Who?"

"Weird-Eye. Who else?"

I stopped by the gas station and lit my pipe. I wanted to explain. How Wild-Eye was at once crazed and innocent, strong and frightening, how I yearned for her. But I couldn't utter a word.

"It's not that," was all I could say.

"Promise you'll go away with me."

"I don't think we can get away. You'll soon be needing a midwife."

I told her I was worried about how Wild-Eye would fare at the camp. It'll be cold soon. She hasn't even got a decent pair of gloves.

Her fingers are always so cold, they'll freeze and she'll end up with frostbite. How will she bring my child into the world if we have to cut off her hands? This was a language the Rumrunner's sister understood, especially now that her mother was once again lying in the woodshed, moaning about her chest pains.

"She'll calm down sure enough, once you take me to the altar."

The Rumrunner's sister gripped my collar like a ticket to the future. The scent of her warm little muff. She promised to knit Wild-Eye a pair of gloves.

"You make sure that Weird-Eye doesn't freeze her fingers off. I need her. You're responsible for us now, mind."

The Rumrunner's sister tapped her stomach and leaned against the roughcast wall of the gas station. The church bells greeted us, and I noticed that the swastika flag above the hospital was flying at half-mast. A drunken Alpine Jaeger had died down at the shore that morning; he'd been fumbling under the quayside for souvenirs when he was stung on the finger by a weever fish. I stood staring out across mist-shrouded Liinahamari and waited for the knelling to end.

Now Wild-Eye's cold hand grips my own. Let her hold me tight, though I don't forgive her. Let her hold me as the world falls apart. She doesn't seem to understand what happens in war. The Russian lad gawps at her in awe. Now they're flicking through a copy of *Finnlands Lebensraum* and planning the future. The book promises Finland swathes of Russian territory ready to be covered in proper saunas for as far as the eye can see. The Russian lad seems enthusiastic, excitedly telling her he is a Mari, a people distantly related to the Finns. Wild-Eye promises him that his territory will become part of Finland, and the Rumrunner quickly adds the whole of Finnmark too. Do they have any idea what's going to happen here? My heart gives a twinge as I look at her. An animal's love is unconditional, and in that respect Wild-Eye is like an animal. Her love is torturous, burning, so manic that it's almost like a form of nervous disorder. *Polarkoller*, they call it. Darkness hysteria. I look at the blackened land and recall how we lay in the singing grass at Dead Man's Fjord. Wild-Eye is as tight as a ptarmigan's burrow in the snow. She's a good person. Is that why she wouldn't let me shoot the Russian lad?

Thinking makes my head ache. I need to get more medicine.

TITOVKA

August 1944

"Parmuska!" shrieks the Skolt girl as she runs up to me.

Her scrawny arms squeeze me so tightly that I have to catch my breath. We pull up in the forecourt just as the canteen bell gives a clang. Hermann Gödel and Montya, the trusted prisoner, give you a salute. From the doors of Operation Cattlehouse, the Resurrectionist stares at us as if we were a walking plague. The midges sing at the corner of the canteen and in the soldiers' overcoats. Beneath the flagpole is a tangled pile of barbed wire. I try not to think that we are entering a trap as Montya closes the gates behind us.

"Can you forgive me?" I whisper as we jump down from the truck's cab.

"I expect so. Now I've got work to do."

"What work?"

I try to grip your hand, but it's trembling too much. Your neck is covered in red marks from all the scratching. Beads of sweat trickle down your forehead.

"Digging work. I need more medicine."

"What if I run you a bath with valerian and marjoram first? You can wash."

"No! Medicine. Now!"

As I wandered through the camp, I noticed that something had changed. The trampled grass was dotted with old scraps of trousers, shards of glass, half-smoked cigarettes, crushed matchboxes, tin cans, ammunition shells, and darkened bundles of twigs. New plywood cabins and temporary barracks seemed to rise straight out of the bare earth. The Resurrectionist hadn't bathed the prisoners, and the bodies of tuberculosis patients lay in a stinking heap behind Operation Cattlehouse. Even the medicine storeroom was a shock. Bandages and syringes were missing. For blood transfusions, all that was left was an old-fashioned hand pump with a tube that looked as brittle as a Russian peddler's promise. Instead, the shelves were filled with boxes of sulfonamide, Dextrosin, strychnine, and Pervitin. It would take me days to sort out something approaching an inventory. There was some Adolfin in a corner where the smell of belladonna and some unfamiliar herb was so pungent that I sneezed. I picked up the 5 mg phial and took it to you. You tore off the mouth of the glass bottle with your teeth and downed the stuff, blood trickling from the corner of your mouth.

"Now will you help me make Masha a kite?"

You looked at me as though I were an imbecile.

"There's no time. I have a pit to dig."

Poor man of peace. As if nobody else could dig the pit instead. You trudged off to fetch a shovel, and I remained on the forecourt with Masha and Alexei Ignatenko. They were chatting in Russian and giggling. Bairns.

"What's that dog's name?" asked Masha.

I told her the dog doesn't have a name. She's just a war hound.

"We'll call her Hilma."

Both kids seemed to think this was a good name. There had been a Lotta in the canteen called Hilma; she'd handed out sugary caramels to the children, told them to lick any chocolate from round their mouths before quickly sneaking in a spoonful of cod liver oil. She'd boiled up turnips and rye flour to make broth for the sick. I decided there and then that I would be a similar guardian angel for these two little pups.

"Aye, that's the same Russian that ran off a while back."

The Resurrectionist had snuck up behind us. Her breath stank of moonshine.

"It is not," I snapped. "They all look the same."

"Aye, it is. I recognize them ears."

I glanced at Alexei Ignatenko's big ears and regretted that I hadn't thought to put a cap on the boy's head.

"Leave him alone. He's a Mari. They're a Finnish people. They live near the bend in the Volga."

The Resurrectionist muttered that they weren't Finnish as far as she was concerned.

"He's only a lad."

I promised to bring the Resurrectionist as much moonshine as she could possibly drink.

"Very well, while we're still blood brothers. But the lass needs to be put to work in Operation Cattlehouse," the Resurrectionist snapped. The girl had been running around the camp, causing a commotion. "Two weeks she's been lying idle in her bunk and weeping. The Cattlehouse will learn her."

Operation Cattlehouse. Again that strange place where women were taken and where the Resurrectionist wouldn't let me past the door. I remembered at the fjord you'd made me promise I wouldn't let the girl anywhere near the place. I stepped up to the door of the Cabinet and knocked. Hermann Gödel was standing there, examining maps covered in smudges of reindeer blood. The commander gave a start when he saw me, snatched his false teeth from the table, and clunked them into his mouth.

"Why, it's our little Fräulein Schwester. What a pleasure to see you're still alive."

I caught sight of the words *Operation Birke* and *Schutzstellung* before the maps disappeared into the desk drawer. Gödel poured some schnapps and placed the gramophone's needle on the clay disc. The needle jumped back and forth across the opening bars of a Wagner opera. Gödel cussed and began cleaning it. As I stood there, I looked at the photographs displayed on the mantelpiece and the table. It seemed that there were now more of them. One of them featured a familiar family portrait. A boy with thick spectacles and a girl with a lace collar. I didn't have time to give the matter any more thought as Gödel finally got the record playing.

"Fräulein Schwester, let us drink a toast in your honor."

We raised our glasses. Gödel downed his schnapps in a single gulp. His chin was covered in several days' stubble. The record crackled quietly as it spun.

"Decent music and theater, that's what we need here."

The commander tilted his glass and began pouring more schnapps. Everything beautiful was disappearing. The Moscow Philharmonic had contracted food poisoning and died. Tuberculosis and spotted fever were rife. Camp maintenance had slipped, and now even the Hilfswilligers did as they pleased. The eldest of the guards, Holger Heider, had spontaneously caught fire and run into the Titovka River like a human torch.

"I've come to speak about Operation Cattlehouse and the Skolt girl."

"You'll have to speak with Brigadeführer Angelhurst about that."

The clay record began to moan and wail.

"Johannes and I are childhood friends, you know."

I did know. Your mothers used to fetch pork liver from the same butcher shop.

Gödel placed the palm of his hand on my thigh and started caressing me.

"You see, Johannes is not quite right."

There couldn't possibly be anything wrong with you, I told him. At that point Gödel clacked his teeth and told me they were made from whale bones.

"Do you know how I lost the real ones?"

In the Ukraine. Babi Yar, that's the name of the place. You and the other soldiers had been amusing yourselves in a gravel pit by killing fledgling swallows, using the handles of your rifles like baseball bats and hitting them in the head, crushing their little skulls. Gödel had tried to stop you. You flew into a rage and knocked his teeth out with your Mauser.

I couldn't believe it.

"It's not true," I said.

The clay record gave one final squall and fell silent.

"It's not for nothing one gets the name the Butcher of Babi Yar."

Hermann Gödel gripped my chin with his delicate fingers and pressed a light kiss against my lips.

"Fräulein Schwester, you can always come to me. At any hour."

I sat there, my back rigid, and stared at the family portraits, in particular at the dacha-smelling photograph of the boy with the thick spectacles and the girl with the lace collar scowling piously at the camera. I recognized the man in the photograph too, but it wasn't Gödel. It was the Belarusian prisoner whose leg I had sawn off.

I marched through the prisoners' barracks to the northern end of the camp. On the way I pondered how well we can ever truly know someone. You had wanted to execute Alexei Ignatenko. And you had held my hand, and only then disappeared into Liinahamari with Lisbet, leaving me to bite down on my eiderdown quilt, and you slipped back inside at night, stinking of liquor and a strange twotch, another woman's saliva glistening on your lips.

I found you down at the quarry. Your boots were covered in mud and dirt, boots that you used to care for so meticulously.

"Why do they call you the Butcher of Babi Yar?"

"They're just fooling around."

"Johannes, at least look at me. Tell me you won't send Masha to the Cattlehouse."

"I don't make the decisions."

"But you are the commander of this camp! Now you're telling me things are different," I screamed.

Surely a man that filled his Cabinet with the family portraits of dead prisoners wasn't fit to run a camp? We need order round here. You shrugged your shoulders. The Finns were about to renege on the treaty agreement.

"Promise me."

"Not before she starts bleeding."

"I'll do anything to keep that girl safe."

You raised your hand to silence me.

"Can you hear that laughter?"

I couldn't hear anything. Ravens flew above our heads; other than that it was quiet. Even the midges had stopped buzzing.

"The crows are cawing, that's all."

"They're tormenting me. All day and all night."

"Who's tormenting you?"

"The little devils. The women in the pit. They're laughing at me now."

At that you raised your Mauser and fired into the air. There was a squawk, and a raven came crashing to the ground. It whimpered like a child.

"You see? Even this thing is mocking me."

"It's a raven. Killing the devil bird brings bad luck."

You raised your foot and pressed your boot against the bird's head. There came a crack. A beautiful red tear oozed from the bird's nostril.

"Quiet!"

"It's dead already."

But you weren't listening. You trampled the bird's head to a pulp. *"Halt's Maul!"* you shouted. "Quiet, quiet, quiet!"

Another shipment of prisoners arrived at the camp, and it was my job to weigh these scarecrows, these skeletons, to listen to their rattling lungs. Again I checked the men's foreskins and filed reports about any suspected Jewish prisoners. Gödel sent them with the Einsatzgruppe to a special camp countless days' travel away.

You didn't crawl in beside me that night or the following night. Masha and Hilma lay down on the bed next to me. How I missed your soft, whispering snores, now even more acutely than at Dead Man's Fjord. In the barracks I woke up during the night, and for a moment I thought you were next to me. Then I smelled the Skolt girl and the moist whiff of dog. I recalled how I used to calm you when you had nightmares. Your limbs trembled helplessly as nocturnal demons tormented your soul, but I sucked them out through your nostrils and hummed you into tranquil pastures of sleep. By my side you were safe. All night I lay vigilant, fending off the little trolls and devils trying to climb up the bedposts to attack you. I wouldn't let them slip into the shadows beneath your eyelids. But this time you didn't come. I would have torn out one eye just to lie on the same bunk as you and look at my beloved

Johannes with the other, to stare at the two-dimensional silhouette of your profile, to wait in the pale morning light long enough that my remaining eye slips out of its socket, and then I would touch you again, run my finger along the gentle veins in your temple, the fine cobwebs growing from the corner of your eye, the smooth contour of your nose, the ridge traversing your forehead.

Now I see you lying on the roof of the barracks. I know what you're doing. You're counting the stars.

Masha appears next to me on the forecourt.

"*Parmuska*, my golden bird, will you make me a kite now?" she asked in a sleepy voice.

TITOVKA

August 1944

If it hadn't been for Masha's kite, everything might have worked out differently. I would still have my teeth and a full head of hair. I never would have been sent to work in Operation Cattlehouse. But now I'm lying.

The real reason is that the Resurrectionist went and died, and there was nobody else in the camp to carry out the midwife duties. It all happened when they brought in the body of a dead woman in a jute sack. At the time, Masha and I were out in the gorge gathering thistles, saxifrage, wild ginger, and yarrow. I'd told Alexei Ignatenko to fetch twigs for the kite's frame down at the riverbank where the willows grew in a virulent, impenetrable jungle.

"Halt!"

At the gates the one-eared guard stopped me and asked what business I was on. It was the first time since arriving at the camp that I'd been asked to show documentation.

"Don't you start, One-Ear," I hollered into his remaining ear, barging past him. "And don't forget to rinse that hole in your head!"

I'd been forced to amputate his left ear the week before. Where it had once been, there was now a gaping wound; you could almost hear the cogs turning in his brain. He stood there gobsmacked, examining the structure of the watchtower.

The yarrow and angelica were fragrant. On the tussocks of grass we'd found clusters of lingonberries and wild cloudberries. We slowly filled our baskets, the cool berries rolling between our fingers, and Masha told me about her village back home, which Russian defensive lines had split down the middle. I'd always thought that this side of the Titovka River was like an old woman's groin, bare and rarely touched, but as Masha and I wandered the hillside, it seemed like a lush, leafy paradise. Masha pointed out streams where brown trout came leaping out of the water as soon as you opened your mouth. In the spring the globeflowers bloomed there, and the banks seethed with translucent amoebas brought up in the floods and trampled under countless hooves. In June they fried reindeer heart in their summer tents, and the river whispered its way back into its channel, green and almost apologetic for its springtime boisterousness. Masha's mother worked as a telegrapher for the Russians, and this is how Masha had learned to read, though she had never gone to school. She showed me how she still couldn't raise her left arm over her head to touch her right ear. This was apparently a test to establish which Skolts were accepted to the local boarding school. Then she began to curse and scratch herself again.

That told me I'd have to send her back to the louse sauna. Otherwise Masha seemed in good spirits. She chitchatted, hopped across the swamp from one tussock to the next, chasing the bumblebees.

"Tell me again about how the Negroes make kites."

I told her everything I'd heard from you, that in Africa they flew kites with fireflies and bumblebees tied up by their legs. I told her about the Berbers and their terrific fire-spouting wooden crosses. And every time I mentioned another place, Masha asked me, "Is there a war there too?"

"No."

Alexei Ignatenko arrived with Hilma, and together we made a kite. Our beady-eyed, red-and-yellow toy was the only splash of color in that ashen world.

The kite flew fantastically high, free and proud. Looking at it felt like a relief. Masha and Alexei galloped, whooping across the sedge. The kite hung in the air, pulling Masha's brittle body along behind it. The earth's gravity barely touched them. It was the wildest and most beautiful scene I'd ever witnessed. Even the prisoners of war raised their heads and took a moment's rest from the ditches they were digging. The SS officers forgot where they were, stopped shouting, and stood scratching the hairs on the back of their necks. Only two people in the camp had better things to do: you and the Resurrectionist. Your eyes were firmly fixed on the ground, on what was still to be buried there.

I sat down on a tussock. I'd been feeling dizzy quite often, and smoking a pipe only made me feel worse.

Masha's voice came from farther down the hillside.

"*Parmuska*, can I let go?"

"What do you want to do that for?"

Masha's cries echoed across the fell. The kite would fly far above the Arctic Ocean where it would prop open the gates of heaven. Then Masha's *Babushka* would be able to look down on her whenever she pleased.

I waved my hand, as if to say the children could do as they pleased. A warm sensation flared in my stomach. I scooped a handful of clay from the ground and began munching. I often longed for clay these days, clay and ash. I looked at the path trampled into the ground and wondered how far it was from here to Parkkina. Would I have the strength to walk there, to get safely over the fell if . . . Well, if what, indeed? I hadn't yet finished the thought when Hilma, the war hound, began running amok. She'd found something at the side of the road and was eagerly pawing the ground and wagging her tail.

I ran over to look, to make sure she wasn't eating an Arctic fox poisoned by the Lapps or some other cadaver.

It wasn't a fox that had been killed.

First I saw a leg. Then another. A bare, skeletal shin, its heel shaped like a hammer.

I knew it at once. There they lay, the Jewish soldiers cut down with a shot to the back of the head, the ones that the Einsatzgruppe had been instructed to move to another camp. They were all circumcised. I never wanted to remember their faces, and these ones no longer had any eyes.

I glanced up at Masha and Alexei. They were running around in the meadow, hanging at the end of the kite's string as though they were ready to be lifted up and set into orbit around the world. I placed my basket in the crook of my arm and headed straight for the camp.

"Time to get back. This minute!"

I looked for you at the camp and almost sobbed as I told you what I'd found. I was relieved at how pale you turned. I asked what they'd give as the cause of death in the report.

"Haven't you learned anything, *Finnenlümmel*?" you shouted.

Deaths at the camp were logged in only two ways: 14 F 1, *Natürliche Todesfälle*, and 14 F 2, *Freitod oder Tod durch Unglücksfall*. But neither of these would appear in the report, because these soldiers had died outside the camp. Montya and the one-eared soldier were sent to the location at once, a sack of quicklime, a shovel, and a canister of petrol over their shoulders. I didn't have time to catch the stench of burning flesh hanging above the tundra. Montya had another task for me.

"Fräulein Vaataja has died."

The circumstances of the Resurrectionist's death were the same as those that had originally earned her the name. A corpse had suddenly woken up halfway through her treatment. Once before, she'd saved a Red Guardist who'd skied all the way to Petsamo; this time, a woman brought into the camp had sprung back to life. The Resurrectionist had already started putting the dead woman into a body bag, because she had found a border pass in the woman's pocket, which proved that the woman had Finnish blood. There was an order that any deceased with Finnish blood were to be taken to Parkkina for burial. This time the corpse sat bolt upright and started shouting.

"Thørgen! Don't hit me!"

This was the second cadaver to wake up on her gurney, and the Resurrectionist's heart stopped right there and then. Thin, lichenous black hair and skin that smelled of wild cloudberries. If only the patient had died, instead. It was the Jerker's wife who had come back to life, though save for the smell she was barely recognizable.

DEAD MAN'S FJORD

October 1944

The Dead Man keeps up a racket. I still haven't seen Masha, but what I feared most of all has finally happened: the Jerker's wife has come to visit the cabin. Alone. I'd rather have received her lecherous husband with all his lewd propositions. You could survive a man like that with ricin oil, but not his wife. I wouldn't have opened the door, but she strode in without knocking, carrying a freshly baked husk loaf. The beguiling aroma of the bread slithered up my sleeve and caressed my wrist. Why is she barging in here like this? Worn, ragged boots far too big for her. A threadbare Lappish jacket, the hairs on her arms standing on end from the wind. She looked tired and was covered in bruises, just like last time. Against my better judgment, I moved to one side.

"Come in," I stammered.

"I'm Hedda."

The woman reached out her hand. I gripped it and she shook back, her grip warm and strong. She removed the scarf from her head. Her hair was cropped like mine.

"I don't know what's the matter. Why won't my hair grow?"

"Why did you come here?" I whispered.

"I came to tell you I'll not hand you over to them. I'll keep my mouth shut if you don't tell Thørgen where we met, if you don't let on I was at the camp."

Not this, my Lord, not this.

There she stood, sniffing her armpits, and I remembered how the previous summer she'd smelled of the sun, just like Masha. That was before she was sent to Operation Cattlehouse, before I did to her what I'd done to all the women who were sent there. Firm breasts, almost untouched by motherhood, and beautiful shoulders. Wispy hair between her legs and a gooch that healed by itself after giving birth. Every inch of her body probably tasted of wild cloudberries—before she ended up in the Cattlehouse, that is.

"Thørgen'll kill me if he finds out."

Hedda told me she was half-Kven and came from the village of Bugøynes. Her great-grandfather had moved to Varanger Fjord during the Russian occupation in the early eighteenth century, and had subsequently sired children the length and breadth of the fjord. Her mother had made her solemnly promise to marry an outsider. Someone like Thørgen.

"What's he so interested in this cabin for anyway? Always running about here with his binoculars."

"I don't know him."

Hedda gave me a look of pity.

"For sure, I understand," she said, and brushed her hand over my shorn head.

"Why is it they always want to cut the hair off?"

Hedda wiped crumbs from the table and sighed.

"I saw your girl up in the fjord a while back, the one that was always running around after you at the camp."

A warm, oat-porridge glow spread through my stomach. So Masha was alive. Where on earth was she sleeping?

"There's an old peat hut up there for the fishermen," Hedda said, answering my thoughts. "I took her some dried meat and a head of cod the other day."

"Thank you."

"Aye, I know fine well why she doesn't want to come anywhere near you now."

My eyes began to cloud over. But I refused to be weak in front of that woman! Hedda handed me a jar of ointment mixed from birch ashes and blue clay.

"For when you feel queasy, seeing your condition."

"Thank you. Again."

Hedda sniffed her armpit.

"Thørgen's away," she said. "You know, I'm almost relieved. He's got some sweetheart in Tromsø. Some slut."

I poured two mugs of Captain Morgan. Hedda drank and sniffed her armpit again.

"It's a queer thing, how fear smells just like sorrow. Can you smell it?"

I didn't dare try. All I could smell was my own shabby stench and the soft aroma of wild cloudberries hanging in the air next to me. We took another gulp of Captain Morgan. Hedda hiccupped, and her expression turned serious.

"Can I ask?"

"What?"

"I don't mean no harm, but you look like a sensible woman. How could you do it?"

How could I do what I did in Operation Cattlehouse? Because I am weak. Because I love you, Johannes. Because I'm carrying your child. Once I realized that, everything changed. After that I was prepared to do whatever it took to stay alive.

TITOVKA

Late August 1944

I was sent to work in Operation Cattlehouse before the Resurrectionist's moonshine-steeped body had been piled up with the other cadavers behind the barracks and covered with sawdust.

One of the prisoners was pregnant. The text on the patient's medical card read:

> *Prisoner Number 1322. Malnourished. Anemia from lack of iron. Premature delivery, fetus in sixth month. Complications. Fetus deceased during delivery. F12. Mother fit for work.*

A few days later I was summoned back to the Cattlehouse. The prisoner I'd sent there had died from a pulmonary hemorrhage. And then I saw it for the first time, there behind a stolen lace curtain carelessly pulled in front of the bed. Behind the curtain two bodies were jerking against each other. Montya's quivering buttocks, rocking back and forth. A faint moaning, hidden beneath the slap of flesh and the grunts coming from the trusted prisoner. On my side of the torn curtain, two drunkards waited their turn.

This was Operation Cattlehouse; this was what you had tried to hide from me.

"The boys need some form of entertainment, don't you think?"

Finally I understood the meaty sense of excitement among the guards and the trusted prisoners whenever a new consignment of prisoners arrived. New arrivals were immediately split into two categories outside the camp: those suitable for the needs of Operation Todt and those who would receive a sentence in one of our transit camps. The jury consisted of me and Montya, who made sure that a few female soldiers always found their way to the camp. A parachutist, a sweet-smelling telegrapher snatched from behind enemy lines, a Skolt who hadn't been evacuated, or a Norwegian fishwife charged with agitation.

A week later I was working in Operation Cattlehouse around the clock. There were often four women in there at a time, sometimes six, and on one occasion even twelve before the Einsatzgruppe took some of them to another camp nearer the Norwegian border. Hermann Gödel gave me a variety of medicines to be injected into the women's backs, hips, and buttocks. I was led to believe that they were testing different vaccinations to assess their suitability for the Nordic climate. To combat warble flies, which plagued the reindeer, they tried liquid penicillin laced with sulfate. Sometimes I wondered whether these injections actually contained cholera or some other infectious disease, so quickly the prisoners seemed to die after they'd been administered. Gödel preserved any aborted fetuses and placed them on a shelf for all to see. Sometimes he would come and observe my work the way you'd watch a fascinating theater performance.

I prayed that you would do something.

"Don't worry, Fräulein, all normal practice during warfare. Civilization will benefit from these experiments."

And so it was: the Devil only rarely gets his comeuppance in this world; he is allowed to have his way for too long. Far too long, because the weak and those inebriated by war never realize when it's time to take a stand. People like me.

"You know what they say, don't kill a cow with milk," said Gödel. "The same goes for prisoners of war."

Cows, prisoners, Russian women, soldiers. They were no better than vermin. Why should I care if the guards and trusted prisoners wanted to take them?

Aune and Lisbet Näkkälä arrived at the camp in Jouni's car on the day that the cuckoos again started to gather in an unnatural flock along the barbed-wire perimeter fence. I talked to Aune as soon as the opportunity arose.

"What the hell's going on here?"

Aune had crouched down to scratch Hilma's neck. She was blethering to herself.

"Aye. Did you think you could just stay here for free? Think the war wouldn't touch you? Is that it?"

I told Aune everything, told her that the female prisoners were put to work night after night in Operation Cattlehouse and that Gödel took all the aborted fetuses for himself; that the women were injected with reindeer blood and warble-fly vaccinations; that everything was written down and documented.

"I can't do this," I said.

"Poor, silly wee lass."

The old woman ran her hand across my cheek. It was a cold healer's hand, soft with age and smooth at the fingertips.

"You wanted to come here, and don't you forget it. You're a stubborn girl. Always got to do things your own way, just like your father."

"My father's dead now. I'm going to talk to the constable."

"You'll do no such thing," Aune said weakly. "You think you're better than everybody else."

"I don't think that."

"Aye, you do."

Aune gently stroked the hairs on my neck in a way that calmed me through and through. But there are some sentences that you simply can't say out loud without the body stiffening and the mind struggling against you.

I remember meeting Aune for the first time during a delivery. It was with Henriikka Autti; I was bringing her some tincture and a pile of Laestadius's sermons. Henriikka ran a large farmstead; her husband was away in the Karelian Isthmus, and the problem was that Vassily, the farm's trusted Russian, had made the mistake of sleeping at the wrong end of the bed. It irked me that Henriikka didn't seem to take any joy in bearing God's gift. She was lying on the sauna boards having contractions and did nothing to make her situation more comfortable. When I arrived, Aune was already there.

"Go away, Weird-Eye. There's nothing here for you."

Aune's eyes were blurred from the smoke in the fireplace, and she was holding a dirty sheet in her arms. My toes slipped on the floorboards, slimy with blood and birch leaves. In the light of the fire, I saw Aune's huddled back, her hobbling gait.

"I have to see it."

The child. It was more like a misshapen collection of limbs that had grown inside Henriikka. Nothing but a crumpled reindeer heart. Wing stumps protruded from its shoulders, and forty-four tiny little bone teeth lined its jaw. Nobody would believe it was human if there hadn't been eight tiny fingers on its hands, each with its very own shiny white chitin nail. Aune handed me the bundle.

"We'll need to burn it, before the constable gets wind of this. It would never make a man."

Without another word, Aune grabbed the bundle and hurled it into the fire. Holding her nose, she began poking the embers with a glowing pothook.

She reached into her breast pocket and stuffed a medical card into my hand.

"Fill that out however you please."

The upper edge of the card was tattered, and ink was smudged over the box for the child's weight.

> *Life-threatening bleeding, patient unconscious for 4 hrs. Horsehair to prevent womb slipping out. Mother in danger of dying from severe blood loss during delivery.*

"You've seen for yourself what happens when the womb falls at your feet on the way to the sauna."

It looks like the peeled flesh of a fruit, dripping with blood and hanging between a woman's legs.

"You know, lass, d'you really think God only cares for his own, that he doesn't want to share his own with other folks? You think he doesn't care for us, but for you it's different? Is that it?"

Oh, Johannes, how much I thought I knew about God's ideas back then. Sometimes, in a moment of weakness, I wondered whether my whole life had been God's punishment for harboring such proud ideas. How could I deem it acceptable to condemn others yet elevate myself?

I cried out, "The things happening at this camp are wrong!"

"That's the way it is."

"But we can't accept it!"

Aune lit her meerschaum pipe and stood on the steps outside Operation Cattlehouse.

"You might be right, and you might be wrong," she said. "It's our job to look after these women."

"You don't even help your own daughter."

Aune stood up straight and shook her rheumatic fingers.

"My Lisbet, that's different. She's going to be something one day. She's going to be the new Greta Garbo. I'll not let anything get in the way of that. The Fritz'll not let her marry that Johannes. They'll throw her overboard if she tries to go with him. All because we're not Aryan. We're just filth!"

We looked at your figure as you lay on the roof of the barracks.

"Is that the one you're after?"

Aune asked if I was sure. Do I really want to go away with him when the war ends, when a new war breaks out and I end up once again on the wrong side of the border?

"I do."

"Then let me help you."

Aune told me that Lisbet would be back in a week to ask for help. And then I'd have to do what had to be done.

"You know he's not right in the head? Folks get themselves into a fair state sometimes. It's as though they change when they reach a certain place. Something snaps in their head."

That's how you changed at the camp. You have a fragile, mushroom picker's soul, and you should never have been born in this age, in the middle of this conflict. You have a healer's fingers, a thirst for me, the ability to come so close to people. All I wanted was to take you with me to the barracks, but I couldn't. I knew nothing of the future, of the war that Aune predicted would soon follow. All I knew was that I would do anything at all to weigh your furry apples in my hand once again, to lick them slowly in the midnight light at Dead Man's Fjord. Anything at all to sniff your heavenly scent and to fall asleep next to you, damp with sweat.

"Aye well, be that as it may," Aune said with a sigh. "I'm off to eat something while I've still a chance. I've got cabbage bake and potato bread in the canteen oven, and I'll not trust my Lisbet to keep an eye on them."

PART FOUR

DEAD MAN'S DIARY

Scarface to Whale Catcher (SOE), September 22, 1943:
Operation Source successfully completed. Tirpitz *rendered unfit for combat. Turbines loosened from frames, repair possible only in shipyard. 6 dead, all 3 X-class miniature submarines lost. New code: Are the mice squealing yet? Response code: Only in Siberia.*

PS: *Permission to relocate following successful completion of assignment.*

Whale Catcher to Scarface:
You should be so lucky. Permission denied.

September 25, 1943

My dear daughter,

I recognized you the minute I saw you at the Petsamo infirmary in 1939, when this all began. That's when I became a henchman both for the Allies and the Gestapo, as I am today. A traitor and a straw man.

Until 1939 I had been undertaking small-scale reconnaissance operations for the Soviet NKVD. Nothing big. A package here, a package there. Then I was summoned to Berlin. As I've said before, I have had only one true friend in my life, Fritz Angelhurst, who died at the outbreak of this new war and who asked me to scatter his ashes in the Titovka River. It was early in the summer when Annikki asked me to collect the urn. I traveled to Germany on forged documents and collected the urn and the wooden chest with the Kurbits decorations. Fritz's polite brother was there too. He handed me a package in brown wrapping and a bundle of banknotes. Against my better judgment, and out of sheer greed, I accepted them. The German Reichsmark had risen in value again. Annikki smelled soft in her unwashed silken tunic. She was an exceptional creature, Aune's sister, and she had a beautiful voice.

I returned only to discover that there was an espionage trial going on in Petsamo. Our operation for the NKVD had been uncovered. In the south, people thought the war was going on in France and Poland. It was only on the eve of the Winter War that the Finnish Security Services finally woke up to the fact that the war in Petsamo had been going on for a long time using maps, cameras, and magnifying glasses. The Germans, the Swedes, and the Tommies were traipsing through the woods like tourists with measuring equipment under their arms and without any proper woolen socks.

The package that Fritz Angelhurst had given me was received by a red-haired, plainclothes Gestapo officer. He welcomed me to the employ of the Third Reich. Apparently they had been looking for an intelligence officer just like me. At this I felt dizzy. I never planned to become a spy. After all, it was only by accident that I'd ended up working for the NKVD. I was assigned to intelligence-gathering duties after playing chess with a one-legged commissioner and having the good sense to lose the game. I was given high recommendation: "Quick with telegraph key. Previous experience as wireless operator on a trawler." This was my salvation, because most members of the old Murmansk Legion had been executed in Northern Karelia in 1937.

That autumn they started rounding up anyone suspected of spying. One night a fire broke out in our hostel.

Arson, most likely. In the morning they arrested the others and interrogated them, stubbing cigars out on their bodies in the process. They filled a bus with people to be taken to Kemi. I only managed to get to the infirmary in Parkkina because nobody could recognize me; my face was so badly burned that the boys from the Security Services felt nauseated. You were on night shift and you were told to take care of us, because no one else wanted to look after Russian straw men.

I took you by the hand and asked, "Germany or Russia?"

You pulled your hand away with an air of routine. "No groping, unless you want a bismuth injection in the wrong hole."

My life was transformed there and then. On the next bed lay Aune Näkkälä's son. He'd shot himself in the foot to make sure he didn't get called up.

"There's a war coming, and I've no mind to stick around and watch it," said Jouni. Then he whispered to me, "For sure, I know who you are, Pietari. And someone else'll recognize you soon enough. You're in for trouble if you don't listen to me."

It was hard to concentrate. Right opposite me, a moron from Turku was holding you by the hand and simpering his love for you. A con man, that's what he was, a grifter, reindeer farmer, peat distiller.

The Näkkäläs are good at planning, and Jouni explained his plan to me.

"We'll dispose of two men injured in the arson attack. Not kill them, mind; we'll just let them languish without their bandages until morning, then switch our name tags

for theirs. We'll let the idiot from Turku live. They'll take me to the shores of the Arctic Ocean, where I can have some peace and quiet and a wireless of my own. There my mind can wander freely."

It plagued me having to cooperate with the Turku tosspot.

"Why can't we just shoot him?"

"Because he's working for the Allies, that's why. He can help you get started too."

Traveling with him was an unpleasant experience. He spoke in a terrible Turku accent and claimed to be some kind of biologist. Close-cropped, thinning hair. But at least this way I could keep him away from you, my dearest daughter.

Jouni whispered to me, "Seems they've killed half of our lot. County Governor Hillilä is here, and the folks with reindeer skins at the door will soon be extinct."

A reindeer skin hanging over the doorway was a sign to the NKVD that, when an attack commenced, that house was to be left in peace. Many people living in those houses died of lead poisoning that autumn.

Then Hillilä's right-hand man turned up, a local commissioner called Uuno; I can't mind his surname. A repulsive man with beady, goat-assed eyes. You could smell the crooked faith on him. Even brought Big Lamberg with him to tell you what to do. My own daughter. It enraged me.

I know what I did was cruel. He's related to your mother and uncle, but when I learned that you'd had to live at their house, my mind was made up. They both sported leather-soled shoes. I lay in bed and decided that your father, Pietari, would mend them no more. I kept the name in mind, and I doubt things went all that well for little Uuno in his final days.

But things were different back then. I couldn't let Big Lamberg see me. Jouni and I came up with a plan. We switched the name tags and hauled the dead men from their gurneys. We had no option but to take Jaarikki Peltonen with us. The imbecile from Turku was intent on leaving you his reindeer genotype and a lock of his cropped hair as his last will and testament.

"Jaarikki Peltonen, now there's a name."

"From now on he'll be your closest comrade."

"Can I say something to the lass before we leave?"

"Not if you want to live past tomorrow."

More often than not that's precisely what folks want, to glide through the following day and beyond, far across the horizon, far into the distance where the sky creaks on its hinges. Besides, I thought I might have managed to shake the ginger Gestapo officer from my tail. But not even three months had passed when this redhead stood rattling the door, demanding that I work for him.

TITOVKA

September 1944

Things started to go wrong on September 4. I was just examining a new convoy of inmates, categorizing them, deciding which were fit for work, and logging any potential illnesses. The only medicine in good supply was a tincture used to treat croup. The label on the bottle read *Sol. chlor, ferrio, spir.* I still don't know what it contained, save for Aune's moonshine. There were countless bottles of Adolfin too; all the Pervitin had been handed out to reconnaissance patrols.

Around midday, the camp's telegrapher ran in to tell us he'd just heard the president's speech on the wireless; Alexei Ignatenko had interpreted for them. Finland had agreed to a cease-fire with the Soviet Union. It was as though the wind suddenly changed course and began blowing backward, bringing in the salty Arctic Ocean air to choke us.

Hermann Gödel paced back and forth across the forecourt and bellowed at the telegrapher to contact the Liaison headquarters. I approached him with my medicine bag and asked what was happening.

"Things are changing, Fräulein Schwester. I suggest you reconsider my offer of joining the Cabinet."

Fräulein Schwester. Why didn't those words carry the same respect as before?

Just then I noticed a commotion outside. Masha was sitting on the ground, doubled over, leaning against the trunk of a large pine tree in the yard. Her voice sank into the earth, then rose again, whirling between the boots of the SS officers gathered around her and rising up toward their groins. At first I thought she and the dog were playing.

Then I saw it. Masha was sitting on the ground, her legs splayed open, and Hilma, the dog, was licking her attentively. My heart almost stopped.

I walked over to her, my arms flailing, but the damage had already been done.

"What are you doing?"

"I don't know, *Parmuska*. Hilma's eating me!"

"Pull your breeches up!"

"But I'm bleeding, *Parmuska*."

I wanted to let the tears come. The girl was bleeding, though I'd given her parsley to put in her underwear, fed her snapdragon and spotted orchids, made her promise to keep her legs crossed at all times, and to hide straight away if she started bleeding.

"Don't cry, *Parmuska*."

Masha was almost calm now and somewhat startled at her own wave of inebriation. I shooed Hilma to one side, pulled the lass to her feet, and waved the soldiers out of the way. Then I noticed you. You were standing in the shadows at the corner, watching the situation unfold, your cap gripped between your hands, your head tilted slightly to the side. I had the strange sensation that at that very moment you sucked the air and space from the forecourt, pulled the surrounding matter toward you so forcefully that I felt the yard shrink there in front of me and felt us hurtling toward the gaping jaws of nothingness, and there was nothing I could do to stop it.

"Johannes says he'll make me a new kite."

I slapped the girl across the cheek with the flat of my hand. The blow was hard, and I truly didn't intend it like that, but hard it was all the same. The sound of the slap cracked the air, and the girl's face swung to one side.

"Bring the girl to the Cattlehouse tomorrow."

Gödel's voice was soft and beautiful.

"Unless you'd care to discuss the matter with me this evening in the Cabinet."

That evening I swallowed a few camphor tablets to still my mind. I lay awake, my skin prickling, and wondered what the future held. I no longer cared for Big Lamberg; that much was clear. If only it had been just about me and Masha. But a miracle had occurred. At first I couldn't believe it was true, though the signs were obvious. I'd started to vomit in the mornings at the corner of the barracks. I felt faint and dizzy, and though initially I put this down to the water and rotten meat, it wasn't that. I'd started to crave clay.

Growing inside me was now the very thing I snatched from the other women in Operation Cattlehouse.

For a short moment I hesitated.

If the child had been conceived at the camp, the decision would have been easier. Whenever I saw you carrying your shovel and trudging off to your endless digging, or when I watched you lying on the roof of the barracks as the Northern Lights scratched at your temples, it would have been easy to run down to the shore, dig up a bone just the right size and shape, slip it inside me, and rinse everything away with vinegar, gone and unnoticed. But this child had not been conceived in a moment of madness. It was conceived in the light filament of a fragrant dell where heather grows and bearberries ripen, where dragonflies buzzed and bilberries, brambles, and cloudberry blossoms were crushed beneath our bodies as you entered me, claimed me for yourself, moved within me back and forth, back and forth we rocked, locked in a pleasure I had never known before. Did all women experience this? Did the universe explode and contract like this between two people anywhere other than in that fjord? No, I could not kill this child. There it was, your trace within me, proof that once I had been yours. This fetus was imbued with love, with a potent will to live, and I sensed that it was clinging to my womb so tightly that I would never get it out without bleeding to death myself. Some fetuses would rather kill their bearer than loosen their grip on life, and I knew straight away that this was one such child. I've seen for myself the way a termination using quicksilver, acetic acid, and knitting needles leaves young girls looking like nothing but rancid lingonberry porridge on the inside.

No. I will bear this child. After that they can wolf down my roasted flesh to their heart's content and pick their teeth with my forearm for all I care. This is both a parasite sent by the Devil and a gift from God to me, a woman who was never supposed to know the joy and the burden of motherhood. This child has resolved to come into the world, and it will be our child, dead or alive, whether its father has lost his mind or not. But for this child's sake I have a duty to survive and to live, to eat white clay from the riverbanks and kelp from the sea, to lick the ancient, egg-shaped rocks at Dead Man's Fjord, to vomit by the corner of the cabin, and to wake to the disconcerting feeling that I have almost wet myself.

Because of this child, I have been forced to surrender and humble myself, to kill and to flee. The rest is a blur.

TITOVKA

Johannes Angelhurst

September 5, 1944

As I dug that morning, I was struck by a strange sound. It took a long while before I understood what it was. A cry carried in from Hell's Gorge at Kolosjoki? A radio transmitter fitted inside my head, the enemy's whispering that stops me from thinking straight? A new message from the ravens pecking at the bodies of the dead? I lowered my shovel to the ground and paced through the camp. Then I understood.

Everything was quiet.

In Litsa the Russian cannons had fallen silent. The murmur of the trucks had gone, and the Russian girls in Maatti Fjord were no longer cackling with laughter. The prisoners in the forecourt were unguarded and stood holding their breath. I headed for the Cabinet and hammered on the door.

Hermann Gödel opened, his shirt unbuttoned. I asked what was going on. A cease-fire. An armistice between Finland and the Soviet Union.

And at that moment I saw Wild-Eye sitting in the green armchair, her petticoat hoisted up to her thighs and a look of shock on her face.

"Johannes, help me!"

I fled back to my digging.

I bitterly regretted ever having trusted Wild-Eye. How she had begged me and pleaded with me, then blamed me for something to do with the Skolt girl. She doesn't understand. Seeing the girl in the forecourt reminded me of a terrible dream I'd once had. She was sitting there with her legs open, letting the dog lick her groin. Gödel, a gravel pit in the Ukraine. And now Wild-Eye is sitting in the Cabinet, letting Gödel grope her. She's a slut. How stupid I've been, trying to help get the girl away from the camp and send her to Parkkina where the social services can take care of her.

"Johannes Angelhurst, you really are a bore," Gödel commented as usual.

The Skolt girl is the epitome of degeneration. Unworthy of humankind, just like Wild-Eye.

I returned to the pit and closed my eyes. I can still remember when it struck me for the first time that I love that woman. How I lay on the cliffs after Wild-Eye had burned my photographs.

The sea heaves in a bright turquoise mass at low tide and my back is burning, but in the shadows a chill creeps into my stomach. Wild-Eye roams the landscape like an animal. Again there's something in her step that reminds me of the figures in the legend of the Nibelung. She weaves together the threads of human destiny. I used to think she was Urd, the past. Now I've begun to suspect that she is Verdandi, the present.

My Wild-Eye, I whisper. You are not educated. You've probably never read anything beyond the Catechism, and even that with your lips moving silently. But the way you carry yourself, as though there's a potent life force pulsing through your body that even you cannot control or comprehend. You walk down to the seaweed-littered shore. When we first arrived at Dead Man's Fjord, I admired the way your heels and toes skipped across the rocks as though guided by a third eye.

Now, without glancing around, you start to undress, and the movements of your body are not calculated at all, only innocent and arousing. I almost take the Leica from my bag, prop it on its tripod, and let the film roll. The light is favorable. No, I decide to leave it after all. I've photographed hundreds of women, short-lipped, naked, fulsome, honey-heavy, thin, freckle-fannied, ugly, skinny, cloudberry-scented, and I've been aroused by all of them, because there was always a camera between us. The lens was my protective wall, my peephole into the outside world. I don't want to build such walls between us. I have no desire to photograph you. I want to enter your state, your spirit, for the wind to creep beneath our skin and for us to be one.

My Wild-Eye. You absentmindedly undo your stockings and release the silky fabric from its clips, and without losing your balance, you slip the stockings from your legs and place them on the rocks. A lace petticoat falls upon them, weighing them down, then your cotton dress, and I can feel the touch of the cloth on my hip. You stand there, not even shivering, the breeze teases locks of your hair, and even from a distance I can see that you're not afraid, not afraid of the cold or the beasts lurking on the seafloor, of the loss of Maatti Fjord or the fact that we will all soon be submerged by the clamor of Stalin's Organs.

Without hesitation you step into the Arctic Ocean. Your body glides straight into the sun. The sea sucks you into her fold, first your heels, then your thighs, the slender hips of a maiden who has not yet borne a child. You are beautiful though you don't know it, or perhaps for that very reason. Now your figure slips into the water; your breasts, neck, and face sink beneath the surface. Your mouth has time to take a deep breath, to fill the lungs, before it too disappears. I give a start.

What if you wish to drown yourself? What if you wish to die because you have incinerated my photographs and I haven't forgiven you? When I arrived back at the Dead Man's cabin to fetch more medicine, how you crawled and groveled until your knees were bruised and battered, how you pressed your head into my cold lap and blew warmth and laughter into me because I had returned. You sucked my toes until they were burning hot, just as you had once before.

But there was no medicine in the bag. I asked you where the bottle was. You wouldn't answer me, and at that moment I knew you were conspiring against me and that the photograph of the dead women was nothing but a lie, an attempt to trash my mind.

Now I see you disappear beneath the surface, and I take fright.

I can't swim.

What would my uncle do now? What would Horst Wessel do?

Then I see your rising head, your hair spilling out around it like seaweed. I sigh. Of course my Wild-Eye can swim.

I roll onto my side the better to observe you. A valerian shoot stings my bare wrist; it smells of marsh tea and malt. I calmly unbutton my trousers, grip myself at that tender spot at the base of the scrotum, pull back my foreskin. The sun catches the tip of my penis; I know without looking that it is sparkling. I begin pulling back and forth. I'm not thinking of the Rumrunner's sister or her unborn child, of the women at the camp or of Operation Cattlehouse. I'm thinking of Wild-Eye's tight, smooth hole, at first so tight that I couldn't enter her at all. Eventually it began to moisten; before long, sap was dripping down her thighs. Her nectar twotch. Its scent is wild as the Tunguska night. I imagine myself pushing inside and come almost instantly. She starts laughing, and so do I.

"How good this feels."

She offers me her backside like a dog, and yet not quite. She does it instinctively, without the slightest sense of shame. How her angular spine bends and curves, her thighs begin to tremble, how I press harder and harder into her tightness. Sparkles dazzle my eyes, my heart is thumping, I know I can't hold out much longer. Can I come inside you? Sow a child inside you? Yes, yes, come, come. I ejaculate with a moan. Lord, what a charge that woman gives me. I should marry her and not the Rumrunner's sister.

All at once, there and then, I knew I was in love with this woman. She offers something that nobody else can give, neither the Rumrunner's sister nor the girls from the Hitler Jugend, neither the inky-eyed girls from the Party office nor the tight-skirted students from the Ahnenerbe lectures, girls whose lips moved in time with Himmler's sermons on the glory of the ancient German people and the tomb of Alaric. Wild-Eye has faith, but not empty faith in a deity that so many primitive peoples use to explain the spirit of the world, a spirit that modern science distinguishes as radio waves and electric impulses. No, this woman's faith is different; it is so great and so powerful that it's hard to grasp. And she doesn't believe in God. She believes in me.

But what now? Now I understand. I must have this woman. It's as though they've installed sensors in my head. The ants at the corner of the cabin carry radio transmitters. I have to find more medicine. I have to know the truth.

TITOVKA

September 1944

"Let's go into my barracks."

You stopped in the doorway. I was lighting a fire in the stove cobbled together from a collection of stones and a couple of tin cans. The tinder lay smoldering on the coals.

"Say it isn't true, Wild-Eye."

"The armistice?"

You stubbornly scratched your ear and stood swaying in the door. You held the wind in your left hand like a gift, and in your right hand a half-empty bottle of moonshine. For the first time you looked strange and dangerous.

I followed you into the barracks.

"Strip."

I stripped, couldn't look at you. I stood naked in front of you and stared at the maps, the growth rings, and the watery varicose veins that the furniture beetles had burrowed into the wall.

"Are you sleeping with Gödel?"

I was so relieved, I started to snigger. Was that what all this was about? You pushed the bottle of moonshine against my lips and I drank.

"On your knees."

I pressed my head into your cold, dick-smelling groin.

"I'm yours alone. Will you believe me? He wants me right enough, but it's only to get at you."

"Drink, *meine Liebe*. I'm not the kind of man you think I am."

How I'd longed to hear your awkward accent. How I'd sniffed the wind for your scent and invoked you to my side, prayed to God that I might yet fill my mouth with your flesh, that I could taste you, suck you, bite you, how I wanted to debase our bodies all night, upside down and roundabout, to do you wrong, to right those wrongs, and to wake up next to you in the morning. How many nights I'd spent in the barracks without you, how I'd felt the heart yearn, the blood cry out, the body howl.

"Drink."

I took another sip of the moonshine, though it left a strange aftertaste.

"What's in that?"

Droplets glinted in the hairs at the corner of your mouth. You took a long, deep gulp.

"It's a serum to stop you lying to me."

I drank some more.

Reality fled along the barracks walls as lightning flashed. I sank into a strange, fantastical fusion of pain and pleasure as the substance mixed with the moonshine invaded my mind. I slipped into a deep sleep, a dream in which emaciated women rose from the Titovka River, their skin turned inside out; bow-legged soldiers stood dancing, silhouetted against the light; at the swamp a black scoter carried a dead puppy in its beak; and a great burning eye flickered above Pelastusvuori. I saw images that I have never seen since, and I saw images that came straight from the future, though I didn't yet know this. How it is possible, I cannot explain. I saw myself looking for you at the harbor in Parkkina while angels played trumpets above the fell. I saw a black-speckled snake crawling out of the side of a frozen mule. Female midges quietly rose from the bosom of the earth at Lake Iivantiira, the lemmings at Ruijanketo howled, you grew a pair of translucent leather wings, brimstone rained down on the Siberian Tunguska, and a birch in the yard was illuminated by streaks of lightning as my mother gave birth to me, looked at me, smiled, and died. After that I sank deeper into the realm of delusion. The world fractured. Big Lamberg's boots next to my bed, blood that had never before flowed pressed its way into my veins. On the quayside at the Fisheries Association, a thrashing bluefish brought up from a depth of a hundred fathoms, small stinging lights flowing from its gills, and I saw my father, Pietari, Saint Peter, changing the wick in the petroleum lamp at the shore of the Arctic Ocean moments before a rifle's bullet shattered the back of his head. The cabin's closing door caused a gust of wind that his lifeless body could no longer feel. The dying man's final thought, swaying cinnamon trees somewhere in the south, water flowing backward, but above all, the image, seared into the retina, of a pair of reindeer-hide boots careering down Pelastusvuori, snow swirling into the air, the glint of the sun. A cry: "Never leave me!"

We lay on the foldout bed, moist with sweat. Consciousness gradually returned to the recesses of my brain. The camp's towers rose around us, the barbed wire wrapped us in its embrace once again.

"Will you . . . ? After the war?"

"What?"

"Will you marry me?"

"Aye."

"Do you swear on Hitler's body and on the blood of John the Baptist?"

"Aye," you swore. "But I want something that'll leave a permanent mark. Something even your God will recognize. Something that says you're mine."

You stood up from the bunk, opened the stove hatch, and held the rounded end of the iron poker inside. You held it there until the metal gleamed red-hot. I am yours and you are mine. You took me by the arm.

"Willst du?"

"Ich will," I said, and started to giggle.

Then you branded me. You pressed the glowing metallic ring against my skin and held it there until the flesh around it began to bubble. But I felt no pain. I didn't feel the metal singeing my arm and didn't care that the stink of seared flesh filled my nostrils. The smell conjoined with a primordial fire of birth and strength.

"I'm marked for you now."

Pain seeped slowly into my brain. I started sobbing in fits, a delayed state of shock.

"Do you love me?"

"Aye, I do. How could I not?"

I handed you the poker. Without saying anything, you seared a mark on your own arm.

"Dead Man's Fjord."

"If we're ever forced apart, you'll wait for me there?"

"It would be a good life there. We'd be hidden from the war and the world. We could live under our very own magical spell."

We had been branded in God's eyes and joined to each other forever. I took the cradle-ball pendant that I'd inherited from my mother and placed it around your neck. It would protect you if, for some reason, I could not.

"Stolzes Mädchen," you whispered in my ear. "My proud lass."

DEAD MAN'S FJORD

October 1944

The sea lies in the fjord like an ashen, milky soup. The thermometer shows it's around freezing, and I don't know when I'll next be able to get out. The scar on my arm hurts. But nothing can dampen my happiness. Masha has returned! I was outside fetching water just in case the wind picked up, when I saw movement behind the boulders. Two heads appeared, and an arm waved a white handkerchief as a sign of peace. Bjørne and Jaarikki approached, rifles slung over their shoulders; they crept out as though they had been spying on something. On me?

In front of them they poked a pallid little creature, thin as a rake.

"Just checking everything's all right."

I looked at the girl and she looked at me.

"Shouldn't let your lass run loose around the gorge," Bjørne quipped, and walked inside.

Masha remained in the doorway, rubbing her shin and sniffing at the air in the cabin, her nostrils wide. I gave a sob. I wanted to run up to the girl, throttle her, and shake her. I let it pass so she wouldn't head for the fells again, ingrate that she is. She's an ingrate and a wild soul. Still, a tear trickled down my cheek, and I had to turn away to wipe it on my apron.

Masha is alive. Forgive me, Masha.

Making himself at home, Bjørne walked up to the Russian chest and began rummaging through its contents.

"There's some missing. Where's the rest?" he bellowed.

"Don't know."

"You seen anybody skulking around here?"

I watched Jaarikki's hands in his fingerless gloves as he eagerly leafed through my jotters. For some reason I decided not to mention the Jerker or his family.

"No, I've not."

"Seems these books are written in some kind of code."

Scarface gave a start and began scratching the whiskers growing beneath his nose with a blackened nail, eyeing the ceiling and the stove as though he expected a corpse to spring from behind it with a face stern and bloodied.

"Let me give you a piece of advice, lass: don't you be getting too pally with folks lurking around here," said Bjørne. "And you're going to give us that chest."

Your Russian chest. The one that reminded you of your father and the lilacs laid on his coffin.

"I can't let you take it."

Bjørne sighed and looked at me with that sad expression of his, and I knew what was coming.

"No point waiting here for your man. Go to Tromsø. We'll take you. You can go dancing in Tromsø."

A gust of wind that promised an autumn storm rattled the cabin. Scarface flinched.

"Aye, best get the women away from this place."

Bjørne stood up with a cough.

"But not tonight. Another time. We'd better be off. Don't want to get caught in a storm, eh?"

The men quickly unpacked the food they'd brought and left.

Once they had gone, I slumped at the table, confused. Who exactly were Bjørne and Jaarikki? They were more than just fishermen and peddlers. As I lit the fire, I'd noticed something familiar on Jaarikki's hands. The dark green fingerless gloves that Lisbet had knitted, pulled tight over his bony paws, the same gloves the Hilfswilligers had stolen when they'd left us for dead on the skerry. It seemed like an eternity since then.

But now I know where Bjørne's wealth comes from. It's coastal piracy, every penny. And with that, it dawns on me that the Hilfswilligers never made it back to the ship. I won't miss Montya.

Besides, now I remember where I've come across Jaarikki's name before. Jaarikki Peltonen. It was at the Parkkina infirmary in the autumn of 1939. I'd written his death certificate myself. In September that year, a consignment of men from the Security Service had arrived from the south. The guards shot a couple of Skolts and accused everyone else of espionage. A hundred men were taken to Kemi for questioning. A few officers passed through Parkkina, and that's when I first saw Jaarikki. Or at least someone by that name. He smelled of talcum powder, had cropped hair, and a reputation as something of a grifter. He wanted to marry me and left me some kind of reindeer prototype in his will. Mad as a hatter. How he hollered when Uuno tried to interrogate him.

"They'll kill us, they'll kill the lot of us!"

But this new Jaarikki was something altogether different. First, he was alive. Second, his face was so badly charred that his own bairns would barely recognize him. There was something oddly familiar about him. I struggled to remember who had fetched the bodies from the infirmary on that occasion. Out here at the edge of the world, it sometimes seems that nobody is who they claim to be, that everyone is lying and folks believe their lies.

Still, all this seemed insignificant given that Masha had returned. I put the girl to bed and rubbed her little feet. I baked some flatbread for her supper, just as you taught me, Johannes. I tried not to cry. I nattered away to the lass, my words smoothing the hairs on her neck, calming her. This flour is as fine as powder. All you need is a drop of honey and the dough is ready. Sprinkle with a few lovage leaves, and serve with a glass of warm, creamy sheep's milk mixed with clover and crushed Brazilian cocoa beans. Things are good for you here, Masha. Don't run off into the fells again.

Masha looked restful; her deep, marshy eyes were calm as they followed the movement of my hands. Knead. Smooth, calm movements, the dough gives lightly to the touch. Don't let your fingers tremble.

"*Parmuska*, what does it feel like?"

I gave a start. What does what feel like? Will she start blaming me for everything? Stop talking and run away again?

"What?"

"Now there's something growing inside you."

Hilma turned and rubbed her flank against my leg. I wiped my floury hands and took the girl by the jaw.

"It's a gift from God."

I could say nothing else, and there's nothing else I could say to a girl that age. For what else is it but hope, boundless trust, and a sense of sheer terror? It feels frightening, often so frightening that the cabin floor seems to gasp, the walls wheeze, the floorboards push frozen earth beneath my skirt, and I can't breathe. To bring a child into a world like this, a place where you don't know whether the sky will still be hanging on its hinges in the morning. It feels frightening, wild, demanding. It's as though you'd jumped into the sea after a burning star. At the same time it feels like, standing on the cliff edge, you jump, fly through the air, smash into the water beneath, watch the air bubbles swirling around your body. As though you filled your lungs with water and with nothing at all.

Masha reached her little hand toward my stomach, where the belly button had started to swell like a raisin on a giant wheat loaf. She felt my belly, a look of seriousness on her face.

"You're brave," she said.

If only she knew.

Then something happened, something that, for a brief moment, knocked the world off kilter. The bairn kicked for the first time. I don't know whether it was because of Masha's little hand or because it wanted to convince us that it was there and on its way—I'm coming, don't you doubt it! Within me there flared a sun so bright that my eyes twinkled with light. There it grew, your seed sown in the barren earth. Johannes, my dearest, your own child. Our child. It was all still so unfathomable that I couldn't bring myself to believe it was really true, until then. My womb existed just in case, just in case, like a spinster's nipples. And now you had thrust life inside me, and that life was petulant and resilient and didn't intend to give up lightly.

"I'll be its aunt."

"Of course you will."

Hilma barked; Masha pressed her head against my belly and listened.

"It's a good person, I think."

"How do you know that?" I asked.

The hormones inside me must have awoken as I took the girl in my arms and caressed her. The cur at my feet fidgeted happily.

"I can hear it."

"How can you hear it?"

"The bairn's singing in there," said Masha, pressing her small bony chin against my shoulder. "I missed you so much, *Parmuska*."

I rested my head against her neck.

"Why didn't you obey me? Why did you have to go into the Cattlehouse?"

Then from somewhere else: "Forgive me, Masha."

DEAD MAN'S FJORD

October 1944

Hilma's coat smelled softly of sea salt and my toes of blueberry petals as we sniffed each other, tickled each other's paws, and felt a wave of relief, and all for the simple reason that Masha had returned and my faithful dog, Hilma, was back beside me, farting and licking between my toes. It both amused us and saddened us, because she was getting on. I'll shoo the old thing outside once the stink is so strong it's hard to breathe. Masha went out to fetch hay for the dog to munch on and settle her bowels. The autumn sun shone gentle warmth on my face, and I felt glad at the thought that there were so many of us here waiting for you. I no longer felt jealous of Masha, my dearest Johannes. The baby's kick had brought me to my senses.

Hedda arrived at around midday, just as we were starting to fry up milk powder and stale slices of sweet white cake into "poor knights" in a skillet. Masha was singing a version of the "Karelian March" that she'd learned from the soldiers.

"Enemies we'll plunder all, lest we ever hungry fall . . ."

Hedda leaned against the doorjamb and sniffed her armpit.

"I've come to ask for help."

"What is it?"

"Thørgen's dead. Fell out of a window at the Gestapo headquarters in Tromsø. God knows where they've taken the boys. Just thought I'd come and tell you . . . because . . . well, that's all."

She'd come in a panic. I sat her down at the table, told Masha to take over the cooking, and started making some tea. My hands were trembling faintly.

"I don't know where to go."

"Here, take this."

Instead of tea, I set a cup of Captain Morgan in front of her.

"And that dog of yours. The boys say it'll make a good pair of gloves."

I stared at Hedda's pupils in the dim of the cabin and tried to decide whether she was still in shock.

I told her I wouldn't give her the dog for gloves.

"I didn't mean that. Our Thørgen was so heavy-handed with those boys, he's turned them into animals."

I drank my tea. I kept topping up Hedda's cup with Captain Morgan.

"Am I a bad person? You see, I don't really miss him."

She'd originally been in love with another man altogether, but her mother had made her swear to find herself a man farther away, at least as far away as Tromsø. Her mother had married her own second cousin. In the olden days, people in the villages along the length of the fjord used to think nothing of cousins marrying one another, as long as any couples lying together had an age gap of at least five years. Folks thought this weakened the effects of inbreeding and prevented hereditary diseases.

"My brother ended up with a bleeding problem. That's why my mother took a disliking to the Rumrunner."

Hedda swore she would have lived in sin with Jouni until the end of her days. But then Thørgen came along and, shortsighted as she was, her mother took a shine to him.

"Amundsen's airship was stationed in Vadsø. You know, the explorer. It was my job to paint the cabins. That's where we met."

After that they moved to Varanger, and Thørgen started beating her so often that she was ashamed to show her face at the local market. He was away gallivanting when they came to fetch Hedda. The Fritz took at least twenty-four villagers, sixteen of whom they killed with their bare hands in a fit of rage by the edge of a mass grave. It was revenge for the death of a German commander, drowned on some sunken ship. The women were then taken back to the camp for entertainment.

"I know a bit of German. They kept talking about wild ducks and the midnight sun."

The boys stood looking out of the window as the granary was set alight and the family watchdog was axed in two.

"You know, I really tried to love him, but sometimes things just don't work out right."

Hedda raised her arm and started sniffing her armpit. I had to pour myself a cup of Captain Morgan.

"He had a floozy in Tromsø . . . I don't know, a damned whore, that's what she was. *Vittans håre.* It's her what got him into all that resistance nonsense in the first place. Gave him an excuse to go into town and stare at a bit of skirt."

Now Thørgen had fallen out a third-floor window in Tromsø.

"Bankgata Thirteen, it was," Hedda continued. "I can't for the life of me remember whether it was the Gestapo headquarters or the whorehouse."

"What happened?"

"Broke his neck. Dead in a flash."

Hedda stood up, knocking her chair backward, and hugged me, and all at once I felt a slimy, mushroomlike squelch and a warm glow glisten inside me. They combined around my stomach into a gentle muddy sludge, an indeterminate sensation that I didn't have time to explore. Hedda's arms were like salt-encrusted jute ropes around my neck. Tears rolled down inside the collar of my jacket and moistened my shoulder blades.

"I feel like howling. What will I do without my man and my boys?"

"You'll live like me."

"You'll not survive up here without a man."

Then, amid her sorrow, Hedda seemed to remember.

"I'm sorry. What am I saying? And you in that condition."

I didn't dare think about my condition at that moment. I walked Hedda outside, and we smoked the pipe together. After that we sat on the porch for a long while, staring out at the sea. The whales were nowhere to be seen.

"What can I do now? I don't dare even go to Bjørne's store. I'm not sure I know what side he's on."

"Come and live here."

"Have you room?"

"When a tree falls, it leans on its neighbors."

Hedda chuckled. Amid all the horror she could still let that lovely, tired voice out of her mouth.

"You don't get trees up here."

This thought amused us. Hedda wiped her face and sniffed at her armpit again. Everything was still. Gnats seemed to float in the air. Hilma was investigating something down in the fjord, frolicking with frozen pearl crabs, washed up on the shores in a bygone age, and long, shiny fossilized flagellates. In the sunshine the surface of the receding tide looked like moist whale skin. After two cups of Captain Morgan, Hedda taught me how to say "good day" in Sámi: *buorre beaivi*. She taught me how to say, "There's a louse biting my bum" too, but I'd forgotten that one long before my head hit my makeshift bed next to the stove.

With the last wisps of consciousness, I heard the door creaking open. Hedda was snoring on the foldout bed, wrapped in sheep's skins and with Masha in her arms. It was Jouni Näkkälä. The rugged figure stared at the pair in the bed, his lips white and a knife in his hand. I was startled and wondered whether he too had lost his mind. Was it me or the other woman he was planning on stabbing to death? I got up from my bed by the stove and tried to focus my eyes on the new arrival.

"What the hell are you doing here?"

"You're in a fine mood."

"How have you got yourself in that condition?"

"Aye, and you look skinny as a twig."

Hedda hiccupped.

Masha squealed as the knife dropped to the floor. The woman in the foldout bed turned and slowly opened her eyes.

"Is that my Jouni? You coming to lie next to me?"

DEAD MAN'S FJORD

October 1944

"I told you not to come here. But no, you had to stick your nose in."

Jouni stirs a juniper cone in his wooden mug and looks at Hedda, not at me. He stares at her like a long-lost love. I know they belong to each other, and have done for years, but I can't help my feeling of bitterness. This is the piece of skirt he's been chasing around the Arctic for years. And now they too can experience that same maddening, inebriating, pure primeval drive and attraction that I felt. That we felt. Hedda's nipples jut from beneath her nightgown sewn together from pieces of muslin cloth, and the scent of Näkkälä's nectar coming from her twotch could be smelled all the way down at the fjord. It's you and I that should be sitting here, not them.

When I woke the next morning, I'd forgotten that Jouni had arrived. Someone must have carried me to bed. The Skolt girl was jumping among the pillows, making the bed springs squeak like a carousel. Her heady aroma wound itself round my neck: sunflower oil, baby sweat, an inflammation calmed with valerian. Her little tummy bulged with fat-tailed sheep's milk, and her nails had started to grow again. She was as excited as an Arctic fox cub at the first signs of spring.

"Jouni and Hedda are lying on top of each other, huffing and puffing."

I got up and started boiling some gruel. If Jouni hadn't expected to see me here, what on earth was he doing at Dead Man's Cabin? Wasn't there a war going on? How had he managed to slip through the front and make his way up here? I asked him this when he finally got up, sweaty and content, and went out to the gnarled steps to smoke his pipe. He seemed uneasy.

He'd had some luck. What's more: "The Fritz haven't the slightest sense of direction."

A solitary soldier out in the tundra could slip through the Fritz lines anytime. They sure knew how to lay mines and blow up things, but that was as far as it went; their three-year field exercise in the best wilderness in the world hadn't reaped results.

"I needed to cool off a bit. They had me sweating like a pig back there."

Jouni explained that he'd gone as far south as Mäntsälä looking for Hedda. Plenty of Skolts and other northern folks had been evacuated down there, but there was some funny business going on too.

"The place was like a prison camp."

Unable to find Hedda at the camp, Jouni headed north to Oulu to take care of some business matters. Now that Hitler wasn't calling the shots in Finland anymore, the decree on Lisbet and her family was no longer valid, and it was safe to travel around south of the Arctic Circle. In the Toppila district of Oulu, the Fritz were hard at work packing away their equipment, giving a canny businessman the perfect opportunity to drum up new business opportunities. One

Saturday evening a courier brought word that any weapons in Finnish hands were not to be returned. A group of Jaegers and White Guard nationalists had started stockpiling rifles. At the time, Jouni had been on business in the town of Ii, where a couple of Jack-the-lads told him there was a food and ammunition depot nearby. The big shot's name was Kumpulainen, and it was because of him that Jouni eventually decided to head back to the Arctic coast to cool down. This Kumpulainen had been a reservist during the Continuation War and had taken part in the retreat across the Karelian Peninsula. Only a few days ago, shrapnel from a hand grenade had hit him and taken his joie de vivre. Now he suggested to Jouni that they take what he called an advance on their pension from the state. Everywhere you looked, people were crying out for basic provisions, like fuel and medicine. Coffee and sugar were as expensive as gold, and when you considered that even the authorities looked the other way at people looting the Fritz's supplies as they fled the country, the idea of sharing these treasures with the wider population seemed almost legitimate. For a fair price, that is.

"I'm a fair man at heart, but I'm not stupid enough to give away things for free, mind."

And so, under cover of darkness, Jouni, Kumpulainen, and a few others had gone to the depot to stock up on food and communications equipment. Stashed away they found as many radios and telegraph cables as the men could carry. They'd taken milk powder and army blankets too, but left the weapons and ammunition in the warehouse. Then everything came to a halt. Kumpulainen had been going around the Oulu taverns, bragging that he helped himself to the White Guardists' supplies as and when he pleased, hinting that he knew this and that about larger operations too. He was overheard by a long-nosed adjutant, an assistant to Major Siilasvuo, who promised to make life very difficult for Kumpulainen.

"Keep your trap shut, man, or we'll break your legs and throw you in the swamp."

Jouni had thought it best to get out of town, before things turned nasty.

"What are you going to do with that Masha of yours?" he asked, puffing from his pipe. "You might have taken my advice, lass, eh."

DEAD MAN'S FJORD

October 1944

"*Parmuska*, Hilma is gone."

Masha is carrying an empty basket on her arm. I'd told her to go out and collect any cranberries frozen in the hoarfrost. The sea was frothing and writhing like a rabid cat, but I felt warm. The copper bathtub had melted a patch in the snow. I mixed valerian, wild mint, and clover into the water, humming to myself. Everything would turn out for the best. I would scrub all the dirt and filth from the girl, and once her skin and mind were back in their rightful places, I too would find peace. Jouni and Hedda were sitting on the shore, talking about the future. Now Masha was standing there with that same marshy look in her eyes. I dismissed the idea with a flick of my hand; Hilma had probably run off to her favorite place on the ridge. She'll be up there scowling at the turquoise sea, lurking among the rocks while waiting for fish to jump out at her, giving her backside a ladylike lick, and barking at imaginary seabirds.

"She'w be bak soo ewough."

It had been so nice these last few days that I hadn't bothered putting in my teeth.

"*Nyet!* She's dead!"

I went indoors, pulled on Jouni's moleskin boots, and threw more peat into the stove. I slipped my teeth into place.

"Someone's killed her!"

"Don't be silly."

"Come, *Parmuska*. I'll show you."

Masha took me by the hand, and we walked beneath the reddening, gusting clouds toward the cove. Masha tripped over her own legs, her bare toes curled against the sharp rocks underfoot. I really ought to get her a new pair of shoes, I thought. Galoshes, perhaps, once the war ended, or a pair of Löfsko ankle boots that I'd seen advertised in *Tide of the Times*, the kind Lisbet wore. No fish-skin boots for her. Night-flowering clammy cockles, sundews, and tumbleweed, strands of dwarf cotton and blueberry sprigs, all crumpled beneath my leather brogues as our steps gobbled up the terrain. Just before the shore stood a Stallo stone, on top of which someone had placed an arrangement of rocks, either for the gods or for shipwrecked sailors. Then I saw her.

Masha was right. Hilma, the war hound, had been killed.

Still barely alive, but killed all the same.

Her paws were tied together as though she hadn't put up any resistance, as though she'd lain down to play a game she'd thought was safe. Her neck was craned backward in a sign of submission. Then, as the dog lay playing dead, someone had driven an iron bar right through her bony skull, hitting the back of the head so that the bar ran beneath the skull and sank into her already tortured mind.

"Get back," I ordered, rushing up to Masha and pushing her behind the Stallo stone. She'd already seen it, but all the same I didn't want her there. I wanted to be alone, for when we are alone we can be weak. I can't be weak in front of Masha. I don't want to frighten her.

In case I started to cry.

In case my hands started to tremble.

I stepped closer. The brazen breath of the sea filled my nostrils, its waters sighing and writhing in anguish and sorrow. Did the sea have to behave like a living, breathing creature?

I crouched down; something squelched in my stomach. Hilma was still breathing. The soft fur at the base of her ear was matted with blood. Again I found myself thinking I ought to trim that hair. She looked at me with trusting eyes, without a flicker of fear. Her contorted muzzle brushed the back of my hand; her tongue licked her open artery. Still an independent soul. Hilma, the war hound, the dog that had eaten her own puppy and that had allowed me to stitch up the corner of her mouth with a darning needle. I am an uneducated midwife. In this world I have felt only one true emotion, and that is love; anything more I cannot bear. I don't know how to cope with grief.

There she lies, on her side, in the wrong position, her paws splayed helplessly, her skull wide-open. Eventually the mice would come and eat away at her head.

An iron bar rammed through her skull.

Hilma, my war hound. This time I can't save you. I kneel down to touch her soft fur. Her paws twitch as though she is asleep, but it's just the wind playing tricks on us. She seems calm despite her unnatural position. So still and satisfied with her present state that I feel almost envious.

I lift a stone from among the seaweed, a false-brown, oval egg that turns gray when it dries.

I strike. And strike. And strike.

I strike until I'm sure.

Can I take this to confession? Or will I be charged?

I pound the stone again and again until her little skull is entirely crushed. I feel her chest. Unlike a pike's, a dog's heart no longer beats after death.

I should have taken Masha away from the camp when I had the chance. I could have done it.

"There'll soon be nothing left for us round here," said Jouni, rubbing his beard.

"What's that mean?"

"Our boys will be fighting the Fritz before long. Come away with me."

"I can't. They'll not let me."

I'd nodded toward the guards in skull-emblazed helmets at the gate. One-Ear was staring at us suspiciously. Masha came skipping across the field, sat down on my knee, and fidgeted. She had a reed between her fingers; she blew into it, making it trumpet, and cackled with laughter. Again I was surprised at how little the camp seemed to affect her. As though she were protected by gauze that stopped death and other ailments from touching her.

"We're not leaving the lass here."

Jouni beckoned the girl over, blew in her ear, and scratched her nose. She was painfully trusting as she let him tease her. Jouni asked whether she could be perfectly quiet, as quiet as can be. Masha nodded excitedly and bit her lips together to demonstrate that she could. The two of them started nattering away in their own language. I couldn't understand a word of it, but it seemed to lend them a sense of secrecy, of a shared conspiracy. Eventually I had to ask him.

"What are you up to now?"

Jouni winked at Masha and said to me, "I already told you. We're getting the lass out of here."

"Can't understand a thing with you two."

"I'll be back in two days."

Jouni explained that the Fritz's cable car across Maatti Fjord was down and that he'd been called upon to transport bodies from Murmansk to Parkkina for burial. He would stow Masha away with him.

"We'll put the lass in a body bag and take her to Parkkina."

"They'll not do anything to her. Don't you worry your head," I'd said.

If only I'd listened to Jouni then. But it seems there is no evil in the world from which I can protect that girl, and from myself I can protect her least of all.

TITOVKA

September 1944

I truly believed that nothing would happen, that they would leave Masha alone. Alexei Ignatenko was teaching me the rules of chess. He was becoming impatient that I couldn't seem to learn anything.

"*Medizinitsa*, concentrate!"

Then a shadow appeared in the doorway, and Alexei scoffed in frustration.

"It's time to bring the girl in."

For several days I'd been telling Hermann Gödel that Masha was sick, that she wasn't to be disturbed. Now Montya filled the doorway. He was having none of it. War had broken out between Finland and Germany.

"No matter. Get the girl ready. There are new rules now."

"Whose rules?"

"Ours, Fräulein Schwester."

Mine, ours. How was I supposed to know who had decided on these new rules? Whom could I ask? For if Finland and Germany really had become enemies, that made me a prisoner. All communication routes had broken down. I wasn't allowed out of the camp. A ten-foot barbed-wire fence ran around us, and beyond that a second one. The SS guards shot anyone who tried to leave the camp without authorization. Guard dogs mauled anyone who tried to escape across the barren tundra, which you had to cross before reaching the riverbed, and even then the dwarf birches would scratch your feet raw and the swamp would suck your boots into its hungry jaws.

I should at least have tried to stop them. But instead of taking the girl by the arm and marching toward the guards or trying to escape under cover of darkness, I began wondering how I could make Masha the Skolt girl understand that she had to remain quiet. If only I hadn't known about my condition, if I hadn't been carrying your child, my love. Our child, Johannes . . . I simply couldn't take the risk.

But is that reason enough? That I didn't harness the wolverine maternal instincts raging within me, because I thought I'd never have children? Was that why I was prepared to do whatever it took, however desperate? Perhaps what Gödel had said to me was true after all. Perhaps I really am the spawn of the curse of the book of Revelation, and everything that happens to me is punishment for the sins of the whore of Babylon and Lot's daughters when they lay with their fathers. Perhaps I am a hussy and a strawberry sweetheart, a wicked *rivgu*, as Montya taunted me in Gödel's Cabinet.

If Masha screamed and shrieked and kicked as they dragged her into Operation Cattlehouse, there would be nothing I could do for her. My only defense is that, had I tried to intervene, they would have brutalized her all the more. In that sense I tried to protect her, tried to shield her fragility until the very end. Of that let God be my witness.

I asked Masha to visit me at my barracks. In her hand she had one of the lucky birds Jouni had carved for her. I should have washed her hair with the louse comb, rubbed the bruises from her legs, scrubbed the innocent dirt from beneath her fingernails. There wasn't time for a thorough wash. I straightened out the worst of the tangles and plaited her hair in a birch-scented wreath. Then I took it apart again; it looked too much like a bridal crown.

I lit the stove. We lay down on the all-too-narrow bunk. I beckoned her close to me, so close that her head rested between my breasts, her cold little legs tucked against my thighs, as though I were about to tell her a bedtime story.

"I don't like that Montya one bit."

"Don't you worry about him."

I told her a story about a Stallo, a gnome princess, and a magic wolf-skin. When she wrapped herself in the wolf-skin, the princess was able to escape her whale-smelling assailant.

"Who smokes makhorka and whose armpits smell of muck?"

I nodded. An assailant whose bony teeth gleam from behind his tangled beard and whose body is covered in hair as though he were swaddled in a carpet woven from a bastard foal's wool. Masha giggled with excitement.

"Just like Montya!"

"Just like Montya."

I got up to make supper. One of the heifers had been fed a diet of clover and had started giving milk. In a porcelain mug decorated with cherry blossoms, I mixed sleeping powder, valerian, and a gray bromine tablet, and no matter how much the mug's flowers writhed in agony, I didn't care. At least this way the girl won't be hurt, I kept telling myself. What's more, she wouldn't shout, for if she shouted, someone might knock her out or cut her, or worse.

The girl turned up her nose as she sniffed the drink.

"No, *Parmuska*. This milk is sour."

"It is not. Come on, drink up. It'll do you good. You'll fall asleep and dream all night long."

"If I drink this, will you make me a new kite?"

"Of course I will."

"Tell me about the Oriental kites again."

And so I told her. Afterward I sang her a lullaby and rocked her on my knee. Her eyelids soon began to droop. Her brittle neck slumped against my chest, her soft little paws fumbled lazily at my chapped knuckles. Her index finger started to quiver the way it always did when sleep was close. I stroked the wolf-shaped scar on her arm. Sweet little wolf's paw. My own little wolf cub.

"I'm so sleepy, *Parmuska.*"

"You sleep now."

I stroked the girl's cheek. An eider feather had stuck to the fluffy hairs on her skin. I picked it up and blew toward the window. It floated, suspended in the air. I hugged the girl and rubbed her legs to keep them warm. It might be cold in Operation Cattlehouse, unless Montya's lackey had brought more wood for the fire. These days he often seemed to forget. And who would tuck in the girl afterward? Nobody.

"When you wake up in the morning, remember that it was all just a bad dream."

I didn't have time to say more. Montya was already standing in the doorway, breathing a guff of makhorka into the room. If only I had the kind of dog that might frighten the Serbian rotter, I thought. But I guessed Hilma was probably cowering somewhere beneath the barracks. She was petrified of deep male voices. We poor womenfolk had no one to help us.

I carried Masha in my arms to Operation Cattlehouse.

Which is greater, the gift or the altar that sanctifieth the gift?

How many different ways I had interpreted that verse as I gallivanted around the fjord that summer.

"It's my fault. It's all my fault."

No. It's not my fault. This is all Masha's fault. What was she thinking, spreading her legs in front of everyone, letting Hilma lick her clean? She'd been asking for this, right from the outset.

I left Masha lying on the bed, went outside, and sat on the steps. I started singing the same old lullaby I'd long used to put children to sleep:

The wind blows 'cross the hillside high, the dusky land sleeps calm,
The dappled fawns in field and dell repose to evening's psalm,
And lo the moon glides o'er the fell, clad in morning's misty balm.

I tried not to listen to the sounds coming from inside. The horizon had turned the color of raw flesh. Wind blew in from across the fell, bringing the smoldering aroma of gunpowder and valerian. Far away in space, the moon twisted free of its hinges.

Once he'd finished, Montya stopped on the steps to tighten his belt. He spat on the ground and informed me that the girl was in a bad way, bleeding heavily. Take her away. I went inside. Masha was lying on a foldout bed, her little legs splayed open.

I carried her into my whitewashed barracks, placed her on the bed, and wrapped her in a blanket just as I'd wrapped you up at Dead Man's Fjord. If the bed became soiled, I didn't care a jot. I stepped outside to fetch some warm water from the canteen. I saw you up on the roof, my Johannes. There you lay, counting the stars, and you didn't even hear me when I tried to call to you.

At the corner of the canteen, I ran into Alexei.

"Get word to Jouni. I'll go along with his plan."

"How am I supposed to get word to him?"

"Don't know, just make sure you do."

TITOVKA

Johannes Angelhurst

September 10, 1944

I was thrilled as Wild-Eye approached me. But she arrived in the wrong way, started crying and shouting about the Skolt girl, saying they'd taken her to the Cattlehouse. I couldn't defend myself, couldn't explain that it was all her fault. She was the one who'd insisted on keeping the girl at the camp.

"Let's go up to the roof. We can count the stars."

We climbed up.

I am not a monster, though Wild-Eye called me one.

"You smell different."

I knew what it was. Barbed wire and fear.

"Nothing but filth and dirt around here."

"I can clean up."

No, Wild-Eye, you can't. Nobody else can clean up but me.

"I forgive you. I love you so much that I forgive you. On one condition."

Wild-Eye pulled the photograph from her pocket.

"I want you to tell me where this was taken."

I sat up and examined the photograph. My mind instantly caught the time and lens. An F16, I imagined, exposure 1/125 sec. Good contrast, taken on a tripod in bright light. There's something unreal about it, though, as if it were taken on an infrared film. Emaciated women piled on top of one another. A young boy's gaunt cheek pressed against a woman's shriveled crab-apple breast. An oval wound in a woman's forehead, her trusting eyes gazing into the sky beneath her long lashes.

"Where did you find this?" I asked.

Again I thought, determined: This photograph doesn't really exist. Hermann Gödel has found it somewhere and planted it in my mind.

The image is straight out of my nightmares.

The same dream that recurs every night. Pits dug in the woods, 160 yards long. People in cattle trucks, calm and hopeful. Returning home. At the command post in the pine forest, the officers guzzle down liquor and the clerks make a note of names and numbers. Women and children are stripped naked while it's still light. Ripped pairs of stockings, little boys' patched trousers. A red floral head scarf is caught in the wind and flies off, catches in the bough of a tall aspen. A woman starts to sob. I ask someone if this is necessary. Won't they be cold? There could be sharp branches in the woods; the children might fall into a pit. There might be a dog lapping the pus seeping from between a dead child's legs.

"Were you there?"

"No."

I wasn't lying.

I'm not a killer.

I have never fired a shot at a living person. My task was to dig a pit and to take photographs. Or perhaps it was someone else who dug the pits, on my orders. I have always been a respected superior, an upstanding chap. I have never resorted to brutality. I engaged with my subordinates, turned a blind eye to their horseplay. In the evenings I greased my boots, alone.

I looked at the picture again.

Feet, vaginas wrinkled in the wind, sunken cheeks, and the mark of a medallion ripped from around the neck. These bodies are bodies from my dreams. With some kind of weird magic, Wild-Eye has turned my nightmares into that image. There is no other explanation for it. It is as though the sky has fallen upon us, the stars are shouting at the corner of the barracks, and the Northern Lights are scratching at our temples.

"Can you make that happen?" I asked, pointing to the flaring sky.

Just like the Rumrunner's mother does. *Vuohkuta, vuohkuta, lurkuta, kurkuta,* she chanted, and every time the aurora rose instantly and shimmered.

"The aurora is a fire of atonement. You shouldn't mock it."

I asked you to tell me about the stars. You wept and called them by the same names Mother had once used. The Dog Star. The Rod of Moses. It was my uncle who finally explained that falling stars weren't in fact burning, dying souls but cold clusters of rock hurtling through the empty universe toward our atmosphere.

"Wild-Eye. Is this our last night?"

"Maybe."

Falling stars showered above us. I flinched each time one flew across the firmament. We counted and counted the stars, again and again, if only to confirm that they were there in their millions and that we would never reach the same number. Another star lit an arc across the sky, and I sensed Wild-Eye quiver.

"The Rumrunner's sister is expecting my child."

"Don't you worry your head. I've taken care of it."

Somehow, I believed that she had indeed taken care of it.

"Can you still love me? Despite that photograph? Even if it's true after all?"

"Aye, what else can I do?"

She touched the pendant she'd given me, the cradle ball, and said, "Swear to me. Swear to me you'll keep that close to your heart, and you'll never lose your way. If we're ever separated, make your way to Dead Man's Fjord."

I promised I would.

Wild-Eye pressed herself against me.

"Let's stay here a while yet."

Wild-Eye sniffled and wiped her face on my sleeve. She cleared her throat.

"Has a big star ever fallen?"

I shook my head, but then sat upright and said, "Aye, maybe there's a big star that's fallen."

We counted and counted. Something warm trickled down inside my shirt collar, but I didn't have time to see what it was because we counted and counted, for in the universe constantly hanging above us there was always one star missing.

PART FIVE

DEAD MAN'S DIARY

Scarface to Whale Catcher (SOE),
September 4, 1944:
Permission to relocate due to changed military situation.

Whale Catcher to Scarface:
Permission denied. My friend, just carry on stuffing your pipe over there. We'll look after you.

September 4, 1944

My dearest daughter,

I am worried about you. I know that you have spent time at Titovka Zweiglager 322. Aune's boy told me. It's no place for a Finnish woman, not now there's been an armistice with the Soviets. Up there the ground shudders and writhes in the grip of the autumn frost like a feverous patient. I have just deciphered a message saying that a village near Moscow moved sixty miles to the southeast last night. The Germans must realize they have to surrender. The land here is spitting out Russians vaccinated against nickel allergy. We've been trying to tell them this from the start, trying to explain that the Arctic Ocean coast is an unpredictable place, a living organism that rejects anyone and anything that tries to conquer it by force. What on a map looks like a road is in fact only a telegraph cable. What looks like a footpath is nothing but a torrent of rushing, icy water. Heavy artillery cannot cross, and the mules will drown. During the first winter of this war, fifteen hundred of them froze to death out in the tundra. And we can't be sure that the tundra will remain where it is. Sometimes it turns out that what looks like a peat bog is in fact a Russian fortification.

I have just decoded a Mayday message from Titovka Zweiglager 322. Hermann Gödel, the commander with the Hitler mustache, he's a nasty, brutal man. You must be careful of him. False teeth. He holds a grudge against Fritz Angelhurst's boy, the one who served in the Ukraine with Einsatzgruppe C. Keeps family portraits of dead prisoners in his Cabinet. If truth be told, I think he's not the full shilling. I noticed this in 1942, the first time I visited the camp. We were snowed in there for a few weeks. H. G., who spent his time shaking his fists at the whitened windows and downing Pervitin pills with a gulp of schnapps, used to shout at the top of his voice:

"*The cold won't stop us!* Die Arktis ist nichts!"

I don't know whether you understand everything that goes on at the camp. I hope you don't understand. The prisoners are used to test the effects of cholera and warble-fly infections. Operation Cattlehouse works as a reward system for the guards and trusted prisoners. Women are routinely abused and used as research animals. Operation 1005 has been invoked: all mass graves dug at the outset of the war are to be opened up and the evidence burned away with quicklime.

My only hope is that Fritz Angelhurst's boy is there to protect you. I hope he has understood what his father wrote in his final letter to me, dated June 22, 1938: "The Russians are a plague, and the Third Reich was supposed to be our salvation, though I have begun to fear that it is but another disease to afflict this corner of the earth." *Angelhurst knew this before the annexation of Poland. He sensed this long before anyone had heard of the rout at Stalingrad and before anyone accepted that Leningrad would not be conquered after all.*

The Germans will lose this war. My dearest daughter, it's high time you too switched sides.

TITOVKA

September 1944

"This one won't stop bleeding. Give her a shot."

Right away I knew it was Masha, though her face and shoulders were smothered behind a mosquito hat cut from a fishnet. There was no mistaking the wolf-shaped scar on her forearm. The girl's body looked even younger without her oversized frock and reindeer-skin coat. Her toes, crushed and misshapen from shoes that were far too small, those toes that only a while ago I had rubbed between my palms, her whirl of hair bobbing in the wind. Against Hermann Gödel's orders I removed the mosquito hat. Her eyes scanned the world, bewildered, without understanding a thing. Her fingers inched down her hip, where her skin was chapped and rough as tree bark, a glowing parchment, like a fledgling seagull plucked alive. I took some lavender-scented rainwater from the barrel, squeezed it over the girl's forehead, and gave her a sedative injection. I can still see her feverish, baby cheek as it pressed against the sickly-smelling pillow. I remember the stench that came from Masha's little vagina when I leaned over it. And I knew it. Long before I stuck a finger inside her, I knew it. She had been mishandled, far too violently, her organs were ruptured, and the inflammation had spread beyond even my capabilities. With just the touch of a finger, I could tell that the wall of tissue between the vagina and the rectum had been torn, and now feces were passing into the cervix. I took out a needle, sewed up the tear. I thought of Hilma, the war hound, who had so calmly let me sew her up without any anesthetic. The girl lay there in the same way, my little Masha, my precious little nestling, and let me stitch her back together. I managed to seal the damaged tissue, but there was still a tear in the rectum. That was beyond me. It would require either shortening the intestine or patching it up with bitumen, which I didn't have to hand.

I washed Masha's whole body with Estonian disinfectant and tried to stem the bleeding. I sang to her all the while, cooled the girl's feverish temples with a cloth soaked in lavender water. At that moment, that was the best I could do.

And I spoke out loud the words that I knew were futile: "We'll have to call a doctor from the next camp."

"Nein!"

I sputtered a jumble of Finnish and German, standing there in that semen-stinking morgue where death seemed as mundane as a sodden pair of old-man's trousers. All the while I could hear the escalating din of the foghorn, the Flak cannons, grenades, and tank fire. War mocked us as it drew nearer.

"Kill her."

Gödel crossed his legs, took a decorative knife from his pocket, and began carving a waxlike crescent from his thumbnail. It became very clear: nothing I said had any value. In hindsight, I could have grabbed one of the scalpels and thrust it into Gödel's stomach. Instead, I sat down on the Dutch surgical trolley serving as an operating table and stroked the girl's greasy, raven-black hair. I knew that she had died, though she was still breathing, and that her cause of death would be logged as 14 F 1, *Natürliche Todesfälle*. The girl would die as soon as she went back into Operation Cattlehouse—for there she undoubtedly would go, and nothing could save her. Nobody. Nobody but you, my Johannes.

I found you at the northern end of the camp.

"Help me, Johannes. The Skolt lass will be dead soon. Do you hear?"

You shook your head disparagingly, as you would at inclement weather.

"What can we do?"

"Help us!"

"Why?"

"For my sake? For the girl's?"

"Leave me be."

I was immaterial to you. So right then I said the very words I had resolved never to say. The words spewed forth, shredded into a flurry of vapor, a mangled riddle from the mouth of a desperate woman. I poured out what I'd already known for weeks.

"I'm carrying your child."

But you simply stared at me, stared as if you were trying to remember who I was.

"I'm going to escape, and I'm taking that lass with me."

"There's a war going on," you said, as though you'd just noticed it. "Can you not hear it?"

Oh, how I heard it, heard it drawing closer day after day.

"That's the call of Hell's Gorge at Kolosjoki."

I shouted at you, demanded you come to your senses, screamed that I'd single-handedly kept this camp alive after the preserves had run out and the Skolts' reindeer had been slaughtered and gnawed clean, stripped of their flesh right down to the last claw. Starving old Skolt men sat smacking their scurvy-ridden chops behind the barbed-wire fences.

"*Rivgu!* You, lass! Throw us some fish guts. *Liebuska!* Bread!" they shouted.

"One more day and we'll line this pit with cement," you said. "Then the prisoners can swim there like swans on Lake Wannsee, you'll see."

I turned away, fled through the gates. I heard One-Ear shouting after me, the barking of the dogs, a warning shot. Without heeding them, I made for the hoary tundra, running without a care. I surely would have run all the way to Parkkina if they hadn't caught up with me. At some point my legs buckled beneath me, and with my face raised toward the sky, I sat up on my knees and howled with misery.

My Lord, why did you create Johannes Angelhurst, I wailed as the guards hauled me up and carried me back to the camp. You should have been taken to the swamp the minute you were born and drowned there, Johannes, trampled deep down, so much suffering you have caused womankind, caused me, me alone. Me in particular, a woman who fell in love with you, experienced you briefly. An abyss opened up in my soul when you abandoned me, Johannes, an abyss into which I still plunge headlong. Every morning when I wake, I pray to God that he might take this smarting cup of love from me. For it is true. You are a part of my humanity, of my coarse soul, of my life, all now rendered incomplete.

As the gates closed behind me, I realized that I was a prisoner at Titovka Zweiglager 322. You didn't wish to help me, and God didn't seem to care in the slightest.

TITOVKA

Johannes Angelhurst

September 12, 1944

Wild-Eye's Skolt girl has run away. I'm not a monster, not a bad person. Wild-Eye said I was, screamed vulgarities as they dragged her into Operation Cattlehouse. Her hair was wild and straggled, catching round the trusted prisoners' wooden truncheons and buttonholes. Besides, she was dressed against regulations, buttons open down to her stomach with her breasts lewdly on show. I turned and looked away. The woman I'd thought was pure and untouched now made me feel ill. They came to a halt in front of the barracks, and the trusted prisoners asked something; I've forgotten what. I think I nodded, though I can't remember the details of the conversation. Something about *jus ad bellum*, the laws of war. Ten prisoners for every escapee. It could have been fifteen, or an entire village, as had happened in the Ukraine. Back there they were rounded up in the church and the church door bolted shut; then a fire was lit at the gable, the flicker of a flutelike flame, the whistle of bone, a blaze of activity—what on earth made me think of that now? I must have dreamed about it. Surely nothing like that has ever taken place.

"Ten," I must have said.

She was so small, after all, the runaway.

I am not a bad man. I have never killed anyone in my life. Even in the Ukraine I was only digging a swimming pool, just like this one.

Wild-Eye was hollering. I could make out her words, though thinking back, it seems strange, as her mouth was covered in sticky muck, but still I understood, because now she sounded like Mother, and Mother had a bad set of teeth.

"How can you do this? *Persveivari!*"

I didn't understand what that meant, and the Russian lad wasn't around to interpret, but there was no mistaking her expression. I went through a few words in my head: *Biest*, *Monster*, *Ungeheuer*, *Scheusal.* Badly pronounced, of course, but it was one of those. Or something worse still. It offended me. I dismissed them with a wave of my shovel. Everything fell quiet, as though I were suddenly wrapped in a blizzard of cotton wool. I gazed at the swimming pool I had dug, and it looked up to scratch. My uncle always says that hard work makes men of us. Smooth edges, dug into the frozen earth. All it needed now was a dusting of chalk to make sure the slurry didn't dirty the feathers of all those pretty birds.

That photograph, the one Wild-Eye had shown me. Who had staged that?

A clump of fine hair lay on the ground. I picked it up. Doesn't anybody follow regulations anymore? Didn't Wild-Eye specifically ask us not to allow animals to make a mess in the barracks? I sniffed the hair, familiar with the fertile, fruitful smell. The hair had a woman's smell, wild and free, a smell that manifests itself only in a certain caliber of person. In a certain person. In you, Wild-Eye.

Where are you now?

I left the hair fluttering on the barbed-wire fence. I stood watching the greening sky, listening to the momentary stillness that seemed to emanate more from within the earth than from the outer reaches of space. And suddenly, for no good reason, I felt happy, for the first time since receiving my assignment here at the camp. Now I know what we have to do. It will soon be winter, but after that, spring will come again. I will take you to Berlin, Wild-Eye, when the holiday season starts at Lake Wannsee. We'll let our sailing boat sing until six in the evening, and we'll feed the swans, which, despite what people say, care less for one another than we do. Mother will lay the table with strudel and gooseberry jam, make up the guest room with the sheets she embroidered herself, and she'll even agree to speak Finnish with you. The chestnut trees will be in bloom. We'll sit down at the table, cherry-patterned porcelain bowls in front of us, and my uncle will be nowhere in sight. Father's photograph will stare at us from the mantelpiece above the hearth. Pale green jewel beetles will soon hatch from their cocoons, and dandelions will push through the cracks in the asphalt in front of the Brandenburg Gate.

I lay on the roof of the barracks for a long while, thinking about all this. How happy we will be. I took out my Mauser, lightly wiped the dewdrops from my hands, and warmed the metal, imagining it was your frozen, gentle finger. We'll lie in the grass along the shore, and you'll feed me raspberries pronged on a twig to stop me from cutting my lip on a thorn. You'll place brambles and wild strawberries on my tongue, anoint my throat with petals and pistils, and none of those flowers will be a snapdragon, one that stares right inside you and might sting you in anger. No, your rugged mildness sticks to my palate, and my breath flows with the movement of your fingers. You have a healer's hands and the power to steer my mind, Wild-Eye, if you so wish. Anything can happen if you stick your fingers in my mouth and let me inhale you.

I must have lain on the roof of the barracks for a long time, the barrel of the Mauser resting in my mouth.

Eventually I pulled the trigger.

The stars turned on their orbits, and at some point one or two of them fell through the sky.

I later climbed down from the roof and crawled into my bunk. I took a gulp of schnapps and a bromine tablet to keep the dead out of my dreams. My final thought before falling asleep was that I must remember to fetch more bullets for the Mauser.

TITOVKA

September 1944

What does it sound like when someone has her teeth rammed to the back of her throat? I should know, but I can't remember. Strange that you can forget a thing like that. I can't even remember whether it hurt or not. I'm sure it did. All I remember is the shame and the knowledge that I was no longer untouched. Someone who has not been touched cannot understand.

If there was one thing I was proud of as a young girl, it was my set of beautiful teeth. They were shiny white bone, strong enough to snap a wolf's spine. Many young people of my age had already lost a third of their teeth, but I had all of mine. Jouni had begged me to accompany him to Liinahamari. Alexei Ignatenko said he was planning to go underground and implored me to do the same.

"It's no good when they see *dyevushka* is gone."

"Don't talk nonsense. Nobody here would dare touch me."

Surely nobody could blame me for Masha running away.

I was wrong. I awoke to find Montya dragging me into the forecourt by the hair. My toes left hasty, jittery trails through the overnight rime frost. Out in the yard stood Hermann Gödel, dressed in full SS uniform. He ordered me to the court-martial for helping a prisoner escape. This was serious.

"Johannes, help me!" I yelled.

Needless to say, you didn't come. Gödel clacked the heels of his boots together and commented that the lieutenant was somewhere at the northern end of the camp, digging a swimming pool. I drew breath, tried to gather all the dignity I could muster.

"He's a senior lieutenant. Take me to Johannes!"

They dragged me by the hair and arms between the rows of barracks and past the prisoners' dugouts. All the way I raged, writhed, screamed, and kicked. You'll get what for! You don't treat an SS officer's woman like this and get away with it.

When I caught sight of you, all hope melted from around me. Your cheeks unshaven, your beautiful boots scuffed, your pupils so wide that a reindeer could have wandered around in them without feeling the least bit caged in. Your spade stood in the ground, and you were leaning against it. You hadn't slept for days.

"Don't let them take me!"

You covered your ears and pulled out a white handkerchief to shield your eyes, sensitivity to noise and light a side effect of the Adolfin.

"Johannes," I whispered, "I'm carrying your child."

Gödel stated that I was guilty of facilitating a prisoner's escape. He asked how many prisoners should be executed, ten or fifteen.

"Ten?" you asked as though you were surprised that someone would bother you and interrupt your digging with such a trivial question.

"What about this one? Do we execute her?"

For one terrible moment I thought you would give your consent. But you shook your head as though there were a midge in your ear. Gödel nodded. Then Montya and one of the other trusted prisoners dragged me back to the forecourt. The swastika flag sagged limp against the flagpole, abandoned by the wind, and there were no other nurses or prisoners in sight. At that moment I regretted not taking Jouni's advice and jumping in his Ford, regretted that I'd refused Gödel's offer of a trade-off, whereby I would only have had to open my legs once and allow him to thrust his way into SS-Gruppenführer Johannes Angelhurst's lover. Of course, Gödel was a bitter man, and he was using me as a way of getting to you, Johannes.

"This'll teach you."

"Not my stomach! Knock out my teeth if you must, but don't hit my stomach."

Montya shrugged his shoulders and raised his Luger. The butt hit me square in the mouth. I felt my teeth come loose; the warm taste of iron bubbled and frothed across my tongue. I breathed in through my nostrils and vomited immediately. Someone wrenched my head backward. I don't know whether the hand belonged to Gödel or one of the other guards. Montya struck me again and again. The sun's beady eye didn't stay to watch me slump to my knees on the frozen earth. Montya started shearing my hair. Blood spurted from my mouth, dribbling onto the frosty ground. I thought about how autumn was on its way, and the beauty of my blood's red hue, and I found myself wondering where Montya had suddenly found the shears. I even managed to remember how once you had complimented my teeth as being the very bones of God. You said you could see I was from good stock. Then everything went black.

When I came to, I was slumped on a bunk in Operation Cattlehouse. God alone knows how long I'd been unconscious. My last recollection was the pair of dirty boots beside the bed. I can't remember whom they belonged to. Uuno, Big Lamberg, maybe somebody else. The petroleum lamp lit the barracks as it had before. Someone had hung a straw mobile from the ceiling. It spun, slowly, slowly. I watched its movement. It was a beautiful mobile with twenty-four straw crosses.

I gingerly began touching and feeling my body. My arms ached. My skirt had been hoisted up over my hips, and there was something sticky on my thigh. But I had not miscarried; that much I could feel. I sat up in the half-light and ran my tongue over my gums. Rough and sensitive like a hare's severed leg. My front teeth and some of my back teeth were missing. I craned to the side to spit in the enamel bowl that I'd left at the side of the bed for situations like this, my logic being that I didn't scrub the floor with my own hands until the tiles gleamed white just to have them covered in spittle and all manner of Russian scum.

A lot of blood came from my throat. It's a miracle I hadn't choked while unconscious. Pain washed up and down my spine, one vertebra at a time. I slumped back in the bed, stared at the same rafter that so many women had stared at before me. It looked fragile. It reminded me of the last time I'd seen Lisbet.

She'd been in bed.

"You sure you're just checking the bairns are fine in there?" she'd asked trustingly.

Poor Lisbet. She turned up at the camp in Jouni's car, oozing maternal happiness. She shouldn't have come here, neither to ask for help and iron ointment nor to tell me she'd knitted me a pair of fingerless gloves so I'd be able to help her during the birth. She shouldn't have told me there'd been a miracle, and now there were two children in her belly.

"I guess I'm just so fruitful. But I swear they're both from Johannes. The first one must be from the bomb shelter and the second from Liinahamari."

Lisbet, my sister, my little heifer, you didn't know whom you were speaking to.

"I'm worried they'll start a scuffle in there."

Two fetuses, one old and one new. How was such a thing possible? I'd once delivered two bairns from the same woman, one red-haired and one raven-black. Clearly by different fathers. They came out covered in bruises, fists at the ready, and it looked as though the ginger one had tried to strangle the dark-haired one with the umbilical cord.

Lisbet's lips were chapped, and her stomach ached. I took her into the Cabinet and told her to lie down and rest. I asked what her groin smelled like in the mornings. That was almost always a sign that the vagina had begun to rot, that pieces of the placenta had been left inside the patient, or the womb was about to slip out and dangle between her legs.

"Cabbage stew."

Sunlight danced across her skin through the lace curtains, making her look brittle and ethereal. Her left flank looked painfully swollen. I dumped my midwife's bag on the floor, kicked the shoes from my feet only to notice that in my hurry I'd trampled them out of shape.

"I want you to check everything's as it should be."

"Why don't you ask your mother for help?" I asked.

"Because I trust you."

I fetched the iron forceps from the porch.

When I came back into the room, Lisbet had sat up on the pillows.

"Do you swear on God's angels you'll never tell a soul what I'm about to tell you?"

I didn't answer.

"Do you swear by Hickler's farts?" she asked, her lips attempting a smile despite her anguish.

"I suppose so," I said, though I don't know why.

"Johannes promised to marry me once the bairn's born."

Lisbet gripped my hand and pressed it against her soft breast. Beneath her skin I felt the soft, swollen flesh, the sweet blood bubbling in her veins, and I wanted to grab her, hard and fierce, sink my nails into the spot where I knew she'd feel it.

"This might hurt," I warned her, pushing a chunk of aspen wood between her jaws. "Bite that."

"So he's not got a cwooked hingey ahter all."

I gripped her thighs, their skin the color of soured milk. I prized open the cervix and slid the forceps inside.

What kind of satanic beast was snapping at my heels? What made me do what I did? You had been inside Lisbet, there in the bomb shelter, with Jouni only a few feet away.

I clamped the forceps around the fetus and yanked.

I've always been strong, and Lisbet's bairn was no match for me. She squealed with pain, her back arched like an English suspension bridge. It felt good. I instinctively pressed my tongue against my upper teeth, ran it along their pristine enamel surface. I remember thinking how much better I was than Lisbet or the Pöykkö woman or Henriikka Autti or anyone else. Better morals, better teeth. I had bravely staved off the Devil for thirty-five years, and the only thing to enter my twotch was one stupid branch at the foot of the hill at Pelastusvuori all those years ago; at least that's what Big Lamberg liked to tell folks. And even if it was Big Lamberg who had thrust inside me, it didn't matter; in the eyes of God, you were the only man to lie with me.

I remember Lisbet's smug, victorious expression as she said, "If I'd a bairn with that Johannes, I'd keep it."

Something snapped inside me; I don't know quite what. *He that hideth hatred with lying lips, he that uttereth a slander, he is a fool.* That's what it says in the Good Book. Lisbet lay silhouetted in the sun, and all her divine wisps of hair played in the shafts of light. Her chest glistened, and her skin, so spoiled with heifer's milk, gleamed hot, her hips trembled in the shimmering, horsefly heat emanating from the dry bedsheet. How beautiful she was there amid all that gore. And at that very moment, blessed by the Devil himself, my darkened soul swore that if anyone were to bear you a child, it would be me. I would do anything at all for you, and I would show no mercy. I tore out the second fetus. I had planned to give her witches' ointment for the pain and perhaps even a pale gray bromine pill rolled in catsfoot powder. Maybe when she wakes up. But so ferocious was the instinct within me that I didn't do it.

I stare at the rafter, and it looks just as weak as the rafters at the Näkkälä croft, a house that belongs to the other world. A world in which I was untouched and robust, in which the war hadn't got a grip on me. Above the bunk in Operation Cattlehouse, the straw mobile spins itself around, slowly, slowly. I wait for the scuffed boots to stop next to my bed.

If I can have that man, Lord, I'll wish for no other.

I got what I asked for. Now it's time to pay.

I can't help thinking that this is something the Lord has sent to test me, that there must be a meaning to all this. If not, I don't think I can comprehend it all. Why did this happen to me? I only did what was right. I was one of those women who always remembered to button her blouse right up to the top and who rolled her sleeves according to the regulations: only up to the elbow, and only on sweltering nights at the canteen. I'm nobody's hairy willowherb or marsh-petal pussy, I'm nobody's strawberry sweetheart, floozy or fancy bit, nobody's cock shiner, treacle twotch, or Jerryman's joy-hole. I'm not a butter bolete, a summer fling, a fireman's hose, a petticoat strumpet, a riding crop, a village bicycle, a corporal's plaything, or a jerker's spittoon. And I'm not a hand-job harlot, a threepenny tart, a midsummer slut, a visitor's pass, a calling card, or the gate to Lapland. I'm simply not.

So why did this happen to me?

Because I fell in love with you.

Where are you, my love? Is it evening already? Are you lying on the roof, counting the stars, or are you still digging your never-ending swimming pool? We both know fine well what was soon going to fill it.

I remember Aune Näkkälä's words of warning.

"Let me help you. I'll give the lass some ipecac root, and within a week she'll come to you and ask for help. But after that, God's no longer on your side, you understand? Then you're at the mercy of the war, just like the rest of us."

I didn't believe her. How could something so worldly ever touch me, a child of God?

"I'll help you if you want. But that'll be the end of it. You'll not get help from me again. Get rid of Lisbet's bairn and you can have your Johannes," Aune swore. "You can do it, and there's nobody will come after you once the war's ended."

I did as I was told and killed your children inside Lisbet.

I lie on the bunk and watch the mobile. If I can have that man, I'll wish for no other. I found lust; I found your love. I have been taken, right here, beneath this very sky, in every position, from all directions. I have moaned and howled with passion to the heavens above. I have taken my fill of you. But only now have I understood that it's not love that awaits me at the end of the prick; it is fatigue, aching, countless inflammations, the bright yearning of morning, and a sense of eternal shame.

The war has got a grip on me.

TITOVKA

September 1944

Hedda and Jouni are preparing the boat. We agree that Hedda should wait for us at the fjord, for security reasons. The killing of Hilma, the war hound, had made Jouni nervous.

"It's a warning. We should leave."

Masha is skipping around them and trying to help, yanking the floats when she shouldn't, poking at the wood burner, and eventually knocking Hedda's flatbreads into the sea, but nobody gets angry. In the midst of it all, Hedda comes up to me and whispers.

"I'll not tell them about you. If you don't tell them about me."

As if I could have told anyone. As if there were words for what took place in Operation Cattlehouse.

Hedda was the only person who cared about me.

I lay in Operation Cattlehouse with a hood pulled over my head, fretting about my unborn child. I didn't know what was happening in the outside world, and nobody else at the camp seemed to know either. All communications were down. It was as though Zweiglager 322 had turned into a world of its own, a world in which the only laws were the laws of beasts. The trusted prisoners did as they wished, beating their chests, beating their underlings with wooden truncheons, and bellowing in their shrill, fluty voices. In the evenings they turned up, asking for extra food rations and various other favors. Who was running this camp: Hermann Gödel or the Hilfswilligers?

I didn't know. What was clear, however, was that I'd become a prisoner. We were no longer comrades-in-arms; there was no more musky fire in the Cabinet's hearth, no more photographs of pretty young relatives. I couldn't believe it was really happening, but there was nobody I could ask. Besides, how could I have asked at all? It's hard to stammer words without any teeth. What is it that makes us human? Our language, our bodily integrity, being able to make ourselves understood, and not having to lie in a bunk with a bared twotch, petrified at the thought of another prick. Language and integrity. Both had been taken from me.

I couldn't see Alexei Ignatenko. I couldn't see you. Only the day before, Hilma, the war hound, pattering around without a care in her dog world, approached the bed and licked my hand. She'd dashed into hiding the moment she caught the scent of someone coming. I could always sense Montya; he smelled most strongly of moonshine. I imagined I could withstand the weight of the hefty bodies heaving on top of me. I could withstand the creaking of the bed, the antlike tingle of chest hair in my belly button, the weary moans of the other women prisoners. They sounded almost gleeful, relieved that they would no longer be repeatedly violated now that the Fritz and the trusted prisoners had a new sweetheart, none other than the honorable Fräulein Schwester. Everybody wanted to try her out now they had the chance. Every last one of them remembered how I'd bossed them around, told them to scrub the sauna boards, how I'd scorned their dirty shoes, blamed them for their own plight. Every last one of them wanted to return the favor, and this I felt between my legs as I squatted over the enamel bowl to pee after each successive violation.

What worried me most was the idea that one of them would be so brutal with me that the child would come out. But this bairn was gutsy and didn't want to give in. As morning broke and I was left alone, I felt two hearts beating within me. One old, one new. One broken, one still pure.

You didn't come. Alexei didn't come. Jouni didn't know what was going on, or whether anything was going on at all, for that matter. Aune had warned me: I was on my own. I couldn't see you, couldn't hear you, and I wondered whether Gödel had finally managed to do away with you. Adolfin is a dangerous substance. Dipped in that stuff, a piece of chicory no bigger than a fingernail would have you singing *"Edelweiß"* on the edge of a cloud.

I was still expected to carry out my duties as both a nurse and the Angel of Death, but I wasn't allowed to leave Operation Cattlehouse. I watched the emaciated women as they dragged themselves from their work back to our windowless barracks. The male prisoners' shift ended when they arrived back at the camp from their work building the road. They sat in the canteen, slurping their meager soup, which contained fewer pieces of meat with every night that passed. At least they were allowed to relax for a moment, to warm their feet against the stove flues improvised from tin cans. But the women's shift carried on through the night. There was one girl with a scar across her tummy; only a week and a half ago I'd had to deliver a fetus from her at four months. She had a beautiful singing voice. She sat on the edge of her bed, singing in the darkness once all the men had left. The cloudberry-smelling woman was the only one to show me even the faintest friendship. The others were openly hostile toward me—I was, after all, the feared and dreaded Fräulein Schwester, who snatched babies from women's bellies, who allowed all this evil to take place, who had brought her own foster girl into Operation Cattlehouse, drugged her, and sat on the steps, puffing at a pipe while the trusted prisoners shafted the girl one after the other.

But Masha had brought it on herself! It was Masha's fault.

Throughout my time as a prisoner, I vomited continuously and worried whether my growing child would get enough nourishment. My stomach couldn't cope with the watery rutabaga soup they called food. I'd secretly started eating the chalk used to disinfect the floors, and night and day I craved things like bitter cranberry sauce and almond potatoes. I longed for cloudberry ice cream, morel sauce, lumps of white clay from the shore. And blood. I had dreams about wolves galloping across the fells, beasts that I hunted with my bare hands and whose blood I lapped up under the moonlit sky in shoeless feet.

On one occasion the cloudberry-smelling prisoner caught me eating some orange lichen growing on the wall timbers. To myself I always called her the Bird of Paradise, because she was always so eager to clean her bunk. The skin around her stomach had never retracted after giving birth.

I was doubled over at the side of the barracks, trying to make myself vomit, when the Bird of Paradise appeared.

"How're you holding up?" she asked, pointing at my stomach. "Feeling bad?"

I nodded and showed her I was expecting.

"I've no grudge with you."

The following day the Bird of Paradise brought me a snake she'd found at the work site and showed me how to roast it in the stove. She told me there was such a lack of meat in these parts that I should try to get my hands on frogs, lizards, and cockroaches.

"All mollusks need to be skinned or peeled before eating, mind."

I started to sob.

"Can you sing me a song?" I asked.

I could no longer sing. Me, a woman who had lulled and rocked so many to sleep. I couldn't even hum to my own child. Hedda pressed her shaven head against my stomach and began singing a slow, sleepy melody. Her cheekbone against my stomach felt angular and brittle. Without my noticing, I began stroking the stubble on her head. I suddenly recalled that she'd had a full head of ginger curls when she'd arrived. Now they'd use my hair to darn the socks of submarine crews. Perhaps it too would be turned into blankets, mattress stuffing, insulation around the barracks. My hair would mix with Bulgarian hair, Jewish, Ukrainian, Lithuanian, Egyptian, Gypsy hair. If there was any justice, the hair of every woman in the world would be tied together and stretched out across deserts, forests, and villages in a single gray, accusatory web.

If I die, so be it, I thought. Johannes, I wanted to tell you that, through you, I have felt God's love, even out here at the edge of the earth, and that I have encountered the Devil twice. As for the things I haven't yet experienced with you, I have imagined them, dreamed about you even as the world around me was engulfed in filth and insanity.

I dream always of you, only you, because for me you are the only true man, and I miss you and ache for you, for your nature belongs to me, within me your soul strokes the rough world, and I love you, though you have wronged me so much, though you were a bad-tempered good-for-nothing with a taste for tits and moonshine, trussed up in a Fritz uniform, wretched in wrath and generous in love. I won't forget how you abandoned me. Yet still I love the kernel of goodness that resided inside you, that resides to this day. We were destined to look out on this world with two pairs of eyes, just the two of us, together, for without our love this world is nothing but a gaping hollow through which a cruel and rotten wind blows.

BJØRNE'S STORE

October 1944

My good mood evaporated as we arrived at Bjørne's store. I'd already said that I didn't want to set foot on the jetty. For safety reasons, we'd left Hedda at Dead Man's Fjord. Out at sea, I could see the figure of Bjørne following us, and he was waving so much, I was surprised his arm didn't fall off. I cursed to myself. That man probably has a third eye reserved for bad times.

"Aye, we've been expecting you."

It was best not to ask how Bjørne knew we would be visiting the store on this particular day. What's more, Jaarikki didn't make any attempt to keep the expression on his burned face neutral, gawping first at me and then at Jouni. It looked to me as if Jouni and Scarface knew each other. But how could that be possible? That was the bit I couldn't fathom.

"How you doing, lass?"

I tried to avoid the stink of cod and stood sideways between the shelves so that Scarface couldn't follow me, but still he somehow managed to slip between me and the boxes of oat flakes. I noted that his expression seemed unusually pointed.

"You planning on leaving now?" he whispered.

"What?"

"Get away from that fjord, lass. This minute."

There was genuine panic in his eyes. I snatched a packet of oats and moved to the rows of preserves. Smoked salmon from the Lofoten Isles and the coalfish that I tolerated from time to time were now available only in boxes and cans. The ancient, dried, blanched, tough crabmeat, the cod, the coalfish, whitefish, stockfish, halibut and flounder, the catfish meowing in their tins; it all nauseated me. I wanted some peace and quiet to choose the food that my child might abide for the next week, but no. Jaarikki's head bobbed between the shelves.

"The mice squealed for me last night. Made me swear I'd get you off that fjord. I want you to go with Aune's boy," he said, and with a blackened crescent of a fingernail pointed at Jouni, who stood at the back of the store, talking urgently with Bjørne.

I carried on examining the tins while Jaarikki stared at me from between the shelves.

"You've got to get out of here, lass."

Reluctantly I looked him in the eyes. The tin dropped from my hand. Now I finally was able to place that expression. It wasn't the polar madness causing a rush inside my head. It wasn't what I thought I'd seen in that poor, tortured soul. It was agony, the same kind of agony I'd seen in the Lappish folk at Petsamo when the Fritz dug up their ancestral burial grounds to build a grocery store. I'd seen that expression before on a gold digger who'd stared far too long at the Northern Lights, and it didn't bode well for a man looking at the world with eyes like that. For the first time I saw in Jaarikki an old, lonely man. And something distant and familiar. I made out the human where before I'd seen only something rugged and abhorrent, almost like vermin.

"You came into the world like a burning coal, so you did," he sputtered, tears caught in the folds of his skin. "You ripped your mother apart, and you survived."

"What in God's name?"

"Swear to me you'll get the hell out of here."

Then he handed me a pipe with the engraving *Forgive Our Sins.* I'd recognize that pipe from among a thousand others. It wasn't possible. No.

"Thief."

"I've not stolen this one."

No, but he was wearing the gloves Lisbet had knitted. My fingers were trembling.

"I want those back."

The old man slipped off the gloves and handed them to me.

"Fair enough, I looted them from a wreck. But the pipe's mine."

Forgive Our Sins.

"You'll have to believe me," he said.

I turned the pipe in my fingers, touched its smooth surface. I recalled how my father had smoked this in the moonshine taverns of Sahanperä. My handsome father, not this Scarface, not this wild brute of a man who turned up at Dead Man's Fjord whensoever he pleased and wouldn't tell me who he really was. This made no sense at all.

"Put it in your mouth," was all I could say.

Scarface gripped the pipe and placed it between his cracked lips.

"Like this?"

"I can't remember any longer."

One thing I did remember.

"What was it you always used to tell me? What was it my mother said, about the Communist Cause?"

"If the Communist Cause comes from the Lord himself, there's precious little we can do about his kingdom."

"And?"

"And if it's from the Devil, it'll die when the time comes."

"So which is it?"

"I don't rightly know."

"You abandoned me."

"Aye, lass, I'm sorry. How's life treated you?"

I didn't know how to respond. Oh yes, it's treated me fine. Nobody's ever called me a Red whore. And nobody ever mocked me because I was barren. Nobody spread gossip around the congregation; nobody ever accused me of having bad blood. I'd never held my breath as Big Lamberg's fish-skin boots came to a stop beside my bed.

"What's to tell?"

"You must get away."

"I'm not leaving."

"Promise me! I can't help you any longer."

All I could do was nod.

Suddenly I felt that I couldn't take it anymore. I ran out to the boat, leaving my groceries behind, and ordered Masha to follow me. Bjørne appeared and waved good-bye, not to help me carry things back to the boat but to talk to Jouni. I saw him slip Jouni three passports and a bunch of papers, which he quickly secured in the leather pouch hanging around his neck.

We sat down in the boat. My head filled with the buzzing of gadflies dying in the twinflowers. Jouni rattled the engine into action and we set off. The figure of Scarface remained standing on the shore, pointing us in the right direction. I stared at the shrinking creature on the shoreline and tried to comprehend what kind of trickery, what deceptive magic was at work here. It seemed that now, finally, I'd heard the truth.

"I've made arrangements to get you out of here."

Jouni handed me his bag, and I pulled out the documents Bjørne had slipped him. Three passports and emergency visas. That would get us into Sweden, and from there we could travel by sea to southern Finland. Masha's eyes gleamed like those of a cow in the moonlight.

But I couldn't concentrate on their excitement. I had recognized those eyes, there was no doubt about it, and they belonged to another time, another world. Boiled sweets pinched in honor of the seventy-five-day-old self-proclaimed People's Republic of Rovaniemi. My sticky lips, when in the spring I licked trickles of resin oozing from the walls of newly built houses. The rocks of Ounasvaara that warmed my toes.

Everything is clicking into place. Now I have a father again.

DEAD MAN'S FJORD

October 1944

We puttered through the fresh and yellowing autumn evening back to Dead Man's Fjord. Jouni steered the boat along the shore with a sense of routine, and from this I finally understood that he'd done all this before, that he and Jaarikki were working together and had known each other for a long time. I felt gutted.

"Why didn't you tell me sooner?"

"What's that?"

"About Jaarikki. That he's my . . ."

"Quiet! You know you're not to talk about such things out loud," Jouni snapped before showing me a bunch of letters. "You can read these once we're safe."

At one point I noticed a shipwrecked war vessel on the horizon, but it was so far away that I couldn't quite tell whether it was the SS *Donau*, which had brought me to Dead Man's Fjord in the first place. In another spot stood the ruins of a German prisoner-of-war camp, now nothing but a strip of land in the middle of the tundra, fenced off with barbed wire. Jouni seemed riled at the mess the Fritz had left behind. A mountain of empty tin cans on the shore, broken parts of an abandoned plywood shack, and the cadaver of what looked like a horse or a mule; it was hard to say which, because scavengers had gnawed it well and truly.

We set ashore, hidden behind the cliffs, in the spot where to the north there stood a skerry that looked like a shark's fin jutting from the water, and beyond that the snow-covered mountains. We unloaded the boat and climbed over the thicket-covered hillside back toward Dead Man's Cabin. Hedda came running up to us and hugged Jouni.

The two started simpering to each other. "If only the war would end. We could go back to Varanger Fjord, to Kirkenes," said Hedda. Back there the salmon swim up to the shore, sniffing and licking your toes like dogs. Masha would have a good life there.

"I knew you'd come back," Hedda whispered.

Jouni disappeared somewhere near the mouth of the river and returned after half an hour. Before long there was a bonfire of driftwood and pieces of bark outside the house, warming us and roasting the fish. Jouni proudly placed a fish dripping with fat in front of Hedda, and she duly praised him.

Jouni asked if we had anything against his swallowing his catch whole. We didn't. Nonetheless, watching this procedure almost made me throw up.

"She's expecting," Hedda explained.

That wasn't the reason. Every time I eat trout, I think of you. You were a freshwater lad, a pale Berlin boy. Back in the summer, you'd said Arctic fish made you sick, that you preferred freshwater fish, perch and whitefish, the kinds that, when you look at their skin, you can see and feel that they're not human. The Arctic salmon's skin is like that of a child that's just been swimming. Swallowing its soft flesh feels tantamount to cannibalism.

"You've got to eat," Hedda scolds me.

I swallow. The bones are so small that they melt and dissolve in my mouth. Jouni knocks the smaller salmon sprats down his gullet in long, gratifying gulps. Some folks get through life just like that.

After eating, Jouni pulls Hedda into his arms, and they roll around in the cooling sand. I take Masha to see where I buried Hilma. She's found a piece of bunting on the shore and wants to lay it on the grave.

"Where's Hilma now?"

"She's gone to heaven."

Masha seems content. "What about us? Are we safe now?"

I nod toward the darkness and tell her what's there. Nothing but turquoise lagoons surrounded by shores of silvery sand, and nobody lying there in wait for us. Only lagoons, the summertime kingdom of angry seagulls and razorbills. The shells pecked to pieces and littered across the sand and the mutilated starfish at the northern tip of the peninsula were evidence enough of that.

"There's nobody out after us."

Jouni lets out a tirade of timeless curses. I hear him slump to the ground and start gathering more twigs for the fire, and imagine the fire drying their sweaty skin, making it steam. Masha and I sit behind the knoll and stare at the stars flickering in the sky.

"Aye, mating with you feels fine enough."

Jouni grabs Hedda behind the knee as she tries to hike up her skirt. She falls into his arms and buries her nose in his smoky neck.

Let them mate. After all, that's what it is. A shared moment of twitching for those bereft of love, a moment of flesh against flesh to keep warm. John Thomas'll think it's Christmas, or whatever it was the Jerker had said. No. It's more than that. Jouni and Hedda have something I don't. They're going to be a family. Hedda will have a family, though she too has worked in Operation Cattlehouse, just like me, and lain staring at the straw mobile dangling from the ceiling, just like me. How did she get away from the camp? I don't know and I daren't ask.

I hear Jouni and Hedda whispering to each other.

"So, want to be my fishing buddy?"

"I could do. If you'll take a buddy like this."

"Aye, I will that."

It's a long time before either of them speaks again.

TITOVKA

Late September 1944

Our flight from the camp came just when I had almost given up hope of ever leaving. Before the morning roll call, a messenger appeared on a three-wheeled Husqvarna cobbled together from scrapped mopeds. He spoke to Hermann Gödel as you would an underling. I was standing behind Operation Cattlehouse, digging a pit for the aborted fetuses that Gödel didn't care to add to his collection.

Straight away I noticed something was afoot. Gödel's posture, for one. No longer as clear and confident. Volleys of shouting. Montya bellowing orders.

"Evacuate the camp. All prisoners in the infirmary to stay here."

A wave of hope and fear rippled through my womb, hope that we might finally get away from here. Yet all the while I knew that's not what would happen. The women from Operation Cattlehouse wouldn't be allowed out of the camp to tell all and sundry about what they had experienced.

Gödel came up behind me in his wolf-skin coat and said, "You know where everything is."

The documents and photographs. Everything had to be destroyed.

"But I don't want to help you."

He weighed the Luger in his hand.

"I won't ask you again. For Johannes Angelhurst's sake."

Johannes, for you I was prepared to do even that, to make sure you weren't shot. Gödel told me to take Alexei Ignatenko with me and to burn and destroy everything I could get my hands on. Montya followed after us. As I walked up the steps of the Cabinet, I wondered what powers were shifting now, and what would happen to us. I lit the stove.

Where were you all this time? Digging your pit, lying on the roof of the barracks, or had you finally been executed? The infirmary patients and the women from Operation Cattlehouse were rounded up at gunpoint.

"Line up, in order of height. All prisoners outside, in order of height," Montya yelled from the window of the Cabinet, as though it were of the utmost importance that the shortest prisoners met their death first.

I stuffed handfuls of documents and photographs into the green-and-orange flames as Montya prodded me in the back with the barrel of his rifle. In went the prisoners' documentation, their identities, evidence of the experiments carried out on them, the abortions, the death certificates, the number of injections. Even Gödel's twisted photograph album flew into the stove. Last of all I threw in the Belarusian prisoner's family portrait, the girl with curly locks and the boy in spectacles with the Bible under his arm.

"The Third Reich no longer requires your services," said Montya once everything was burned.

Alexei and I were marched outside and told to join the file of sick prisoners.

As the sun set, I stood and watched the line of prisoners fit for work winding its way toward the western entrance to the camp. The women and the infirmary patients trudged toward the northern end. First five, then ten at a time. Shots could be heard farther ahead. I knew instantly where the line ended—at the mass grave dug by you, my love, my Johannes. There was no swimming pool; the Fritz had been preparing for the eventuality that the camp might have to be evacuated and all undesirables eliminated. Had you known that all along, my love? Could you comprehend anything of this world any longer, or had the Adolfin already done its job and taken you over the edge for good?

A terrific chaos ensued as squadrons of Alpine Jaegers fleeing from the Russians began to hurtle past the camp. Some had been told to help evacuate the prisoners of war; others were frantically loading equipment onto the backs of black trucks. Medical and food reserves would have been destroyed too, if there had been anything to destroy. The merciless evening stank of petroleum, male sweat, hurry, and cheap pipe tobacco. A pale-faced commander with a green insignia on his cap had arrived and was now hollering instructions into a crackling megaphone. It was he who announced that all foreign workers, especially Finnish citizens, should be evacuated from the camp without delay.

My heart bolted in my chest. Salvation! Through the din I caught only snippets of his speech:

"Finnen . . . verlassen . . . unmittelbar . . ."

It's hard to explain, my love, exactly what happened at that moment. It was as though I had woken from a nightmare, as though in the crack of a whip I rejoined the land of the living. I was a Finnish nurse, not a prisoner of war. I had regained my dignity, my respect. In a daze I nudged Alexei.

"Shout out, tell them we're Finns!" he said.

"I cah . . . t."

We ran toward the Cattlehouse, where my bag of instruments and the Resurrectionist's Lotta uniform were still packed inside two cardboard suitcases. My eyes blurred with tears and I tripped on the steps. My tongue hit my gums where my front teeth had once been.

If only I could speak. I pulled the Lotta uniform from the box and began slipping off my prison gown so hurriedly that my thighs quivered and my breasts, now so heavy, seemed to yell.

"Fräulein Schwester," Gödel hissed from behind me, raising his Luger. "Surely there's no hurry?"

"I'w leawing," I mumbled through my toothless mouth.

I didn't sound convincing.

"Whores will be quiet when the SS-Hauptsturmführer is speaking."

It seemed like a joke rather than a command, and Gödel struck me more out of habit than for the joy of beating me. And you, Johannes? Where were you, and what rank did you have in the new order?

"Johawes wi make you pay for dis."

Gödel clacked his false teeth and said, "Johannes Angelhurst is a coward. Without his uncle's intervention, he would have been sent to Dachau to carry jute sacks, after the farce in the Ukraine."

Then something occurred to me. At the gravel pit in the Ukraine, at the place where they were killing swallows, the birds had been women, not swallows, and Gödel, not you, Johannes, had been beating them.

I mumbled the accusation at Gödel, but he didn't seem to remember what I was talking about. A look of boredom spread across his face. He raised his weapon again and cocked it. I noticed how close the commander's eyes were to each other.

Now I'm really in a jam, I thought. Lord, please don't let this child die!

Somewhere in the farthest corner of my consciousness, I noticed that a figure had appeared behind Gödel. I couldn't focus; it seemed that the world had suddenly become blurred and was spinning quicker and quicker. All I could see clearly was Gödel's face, the flared nostrils, the handsome cheekbones, the false teeth longing to grind my flesh.

"*Medizinitsa*, watch out!"

Alexei swung his arms. I saw he was holding a spade. There came a thud, and for a moment Gödel looked unusually confused. Then he fell face-first against the wooden floorboards, scuffed smooth by the boots of the soldiers and the trusted prisoners.

After that there was no time to think.

Alexei yanked off Gödel's boots and britches. His wolf-skin coat, his brown shirt and cap, his odd socks, and the stockings attached to them. Finally he took the leather gloves, one of which remained on the floor holding the gun while Alexei stripped off his own clothes. Alexei opened Gödel's jaws, stuck his fingers into the commander's mouth, and pulled out the set of false teeth. I was so taken aback that I was unable to help.

Alexei handed me the teeth and drily surmised that we would never get out of this camp if I couldn't speak.

I slipped the teeth into my mouth. They fitted me.

We stuffed Gödel's naked body into a sack of animal fodder. Alexei pulled on the commander's clothes, and I stepped into the Lotta uniform. Little Alexei almost drowned in Gödel's trousers, and I had to look for some string to stop them from falling down. The turned-up ends of his sleeves made me nervous. I laid out blankets to cover the blood on the floor; they instantly turned dark red and sticky. The strange teeth in my mouth made me want to vomit.

"This isn't going to work," I said.

So I could speak after all!

"*Davai!* Yes, it will."

"Right, let's go!"

Alexei shook his head.

"He's still alive."

I caught my breath and crouched down to check the pulse of the wrist jutting out from the sack. Something inside him was still beating.

"Kill him."

Alexei Ignatenko raised his spade, then hesitated. A look of disgust made him scowl. He handed me the spade. I shook my head. I was no killer, not really.

"Call for help."

I went to the door and shouted to an SS soldier with baby-fresh skin, ordered him to come and help. I was startled when I saw a familiar guard running toward us. Beneath his cap there was a neat, oval hole where his ear had been cut off.

"One of the prisoners is trying to escape!"

The words seemed to trip and stumble out of my mouth, but out they came.

Another soldier appeared and stood at attention when he saw Alexei's officer's uniform.

I looked at One-Ear; he looked back.

"What shall we do with this one?" One-Ear asked.

"Throw him in the Titovka River," I said for want of any better ideas.

"Jawohl!"

There was a taut note to One-Ear's voice, betraying that his voice had only just broken. There was sickness in his eyes. As I left I caught a glimpse of the boy's legs and noted that his trousers were ironed and pressed according to camp regulations and that his boots were shiny with whale blubber. He had them on the wrong feet. I realized I hadn't once seen those boots beside my bed in Operation Cattlehouse.

Alexei stood in his SS uniform and cracked Gödel's whip against his thigh. The guards began dragging the sack toward the northern end of the camp. Just as the gates closed behind them, Hilma, the war hound, crawled out from beneath my bed and gave a cheerful wag of the tail.

Alexei showed me the rucksack in which he'd stuffed Gödel's wolf-skin coat, his chessboard, and its pieces.

"Shall we go?"

My two cardboard suitcases were still standing by the guard's post outside Operation Cattlehouse. I fetched them.

"You have everything?" asked Alexei as we marched straight for the main gates without so much as glancing left or right.

He told me he'd been hiding out beneath the canteen floorboards for days, eating slurry and vegetable peels from the rubbish dump at night.

The ground moaned and crackled beneath our feet; darkness was falling. The last files of sick prisoners were making their way toward the mass grave. The soldiers had given up on an organized roll call.

"I am a Finnish *Schwester*, and this is Kommandant Hermann Gödel. We have orders to report to Parkkina."

We climbed aboard a truck. Hilma lay down at my feet and began licking my ankles between my socks and woolen trousers. Our muscles tense, we sat side by side throughout the journey, listening to the shots booming behind us.

As evening drew in, we finally saw the searchlights combing the clouds to the east of Parkkina. I quietly took Alexei's hand and squeezed it. The Russian lad's scrawny body quivered as I touched him, and I prayed that the driver hadn't seen. Regardless, I leaned into Alexei and whispered, my lips tight against his shell-shaped ear.

"*Spasiba*, Alexei. A thousand times, thank you."

DEAD MAN'S FJORD

October 1944

"I'm leaving in the morning, *Parmuska*."

The little fledgling was sitting by the stove, fidgeting and flapping.

That's right. Go then. Let her go and take her tiny, bony limbs and swollen joints, her habit of stretching her neck as though she were standing on the shore, wondering whether she dared go swimming. I take hold of the girl in all her gangly awkwardness and shake her, frightened that she still might not believe I care about her. I take her by her badly trimmed fringe, wisps of hair that someone will need to look after. I remind her that she must comb her hair every evening. At least fifty strokes with a whalebone comb, she must wash it with soft soap, pick flowers, and place them behind her ears. Masha asks why I'm not going with them.

"I'll join you later."

"Will you make me a kite then?"

"Of course I will," I lie, causing my throat to tighten. "You can't really understand these things yet."

Jouni witters on, repeating the same thing he's been saying for days: he won't help me if I stay here.

"Will you make me a pair of skis?"

Jouni agitatedly tugs his beard.

"No, I will not. You'll die all the same."

"It's all one. I'm staying."

"You're too good a woman to die out here, you know that? I could have told you long ago, but I'd not the heart. They'll kill you, lass."

Jouni's eyes linger in the no-man's-land between light and shadow. "He's not a good man for you."

"But I can't be without him either. From the very first second, I knew I couldn't."

"The whole fjord could have told you that, lass."

"You were never one for talking nonsense, not even to women."

I step close to him and run my fingers across his dark stubble. My hands smell of the same fish as his beard.

"Don't you worry your head. Things have worked out just fine for you."

"Aye, love sure tastes sweet," he says, his voice hoarse.

"You never had a beard before."

"And you've no hair," Jouni says, stroking my downy scalp. "Why didn't I get you out of that place when I'd the chance? I'd seen everything with my own eyes."

"You didn't see the half of it."

"You've always been a wild one. Wild and . . . brave."

"All the braver for running around with a coward like you."

Jouni hunches his shoulders and begins poking at the embers in the stove.

"I'll take you away by force if I have to."

"I'm not leaving. I promised Johannes."

"He's not the same man."

That much is true.

"That was then. Now is now," Jouni muses.

That was also true.

"No point holding on to the past. No point dwelling on it, eh?"

No, there was no point. Hedda touches my silken hair, ruffles it. I try to smile, but the uncomfortable false teeth make it nothing but a painful keening. My hair will grow soon enough; my teeth will not.

"Take Hedda away with you, and Masha too. I'm not coming."

Jouni fumbles in his pocket and drops something into my hand. The cradle ball. The pendant I'd given Johannes.

"Found this on the railings at Miljoona Bridge. Now do you believe me?"

"That he's alive? Aye, I believe he's alive."

"That's not what this means."

"Give Lisbet my best. Tell her I'm sorry."

Jouni pulls a bunch of papers from his bag.

"Your father gave me these, wanted you to read them when you're safe. But what can I do for you now? Take them. Do as you please."

Jouni crawls next to Hedda to sleep; at their feet, Masha is already snoring. I kick a spot free for myself next to the stove, then stand at the window for a long while, staring at the moonlight descending across the fjord. Two figures are riding through the mist on reindeer bucks, one tall and with a black beard, the other stumpy, both with lancets at the ready. I let the images come and go like the wisps of mist where currents of wind meet across the fells. Frost creeps across the shore, claiming one cloudberry leaf after another, but I don't feel the cold.

I lie down on the floor to sleep.

Hedda is curled up, safely asleep in Jouni's arms. There she lies, pulling his calloused thumbs so close to her that she can feel his heart-beat in his fingertips. Things are good for her there, good and safe. Still, it's a shame things don't work like that, I think as I eventually drift into sleep. For though that was then and now is now, as Jouni philosophized, it doesn't change anything. May the Devil take you, Johannes Angelhurst! You had to come here to the land of witches and sea monsters, didn't you! You had to barge in, tormenting us, tormenting me, a poor mortal wretch carrying your child. I grip Lisbet's gloves in my hands and throw the passport and visa into the stove.

I've no regrets, though some things I'd do well to regret. I will stay here. The others will leave. I have given my word, and I will keep my word. And with that I will atone for everything.

PARKKINA

September 1944

The last time I saw Lisbet Näkkälä was in Parkkina. They were shipping Finnish women to the safety of Kiruna in northern Sweden. A line of prisoners of war was shuffling from the quayside toward Tårnet and Neue Straße, the same street that many of those poor souls had built only a while ago. These survivors were nothing but skin and bones, bleary-eyed, trudging to their death. The officers from Operation Todt bellowed orders and struck with the butts of their rifles anyone who looked likely to keel over into the verge. Shapeless, lullaby-soft snowflakes fluttered to the ground. I've always loved the first snow, but now it terrified me because though there must have been thousands of men marching past us, I can't remember hearing the clack of their wooden shoes. Perhaps it was because the snow had fallen, or perhaps because they had become so thin and weightless.

The snowflakes cast shadows on the faces of the women sitting on the backs of the trucks. There they sat like cattle on their way to the slaughterhouse, their reddened eyes gawping at me in confusion as I strode past the Fritz with Masha in tow. I'd been worried about meeting Lisbet. But she took me in her arms, implored me to go with them, begged me to join the other womenfolk and be evacuated to northern Sweden and then back to Finland via the south. She handed me her soft package all the same.

"Here's something to warm your fingers. You'll not have a chance by yourself, Sister."

I almost believed her as I stood shivering at the harbor. Injured Alpine Jaegers limped and hobbled around us, provisions officials, Finnish SS men. Lisbet tilted her heart-shaped head, and light from one of the searchlights glinted against the specks of salt in her eyelashes.

"What did they do to you at that camp?"

I didn't answer.

"Can't you see we're done fighting this war now? Nobody is going to eat us alive out there. They'll give us funny looks at first, but they'll come around eventually."

I wanted to believe her.

"The Fritz lads promised Jouni they'll not torch our cabin if they have to retreat," I said.

I glanced at the women sitting in the truck, but none of them seemed to hear me. Most of them were gazing off toward the jetties and the breakwater. A few of them looked familiar. There was Laina Helppi, whimpering and scratching the edge of her shoe with her gnawed fingernails; over there was Henriikka Autti who had the gall to sing a hymn that would have landed her a good beating at the church: "Lord, may I walk on earth a stranger." She'd once had the authority to boss folks around. Now she sat there, crooning like an old milkmaid. Her betrothed had been given leave to come home and marry her, but he'd turfed her out when he learned she'd been fooling around with the trusted Russian. Her husband-to-be had dragged her into the sauna by the ears, scrubbed her groin with moonshine and castor oil, and made the Russian philanderer drink the twotch water before driving him out of the village at gunpoint. I looked Lisbet in the eyes, and there was no sense of accusation in them. They were soft with near-sightedness, open to the world. In those eyes I saw the reflections of future summer nights on the riverbank, midsummer bonfires, and yellow globeflowers. Houses rebuilt, coffee substitute, and a slowly heating smoke sauna. Crocheted housewife curtains in the windows welcoming guests with a ripple. Lisbet tickled my hand and leaned over to rest her cheek against my cropped scalp.

"Uuno'll soon be released from the prison camp at Tammisaari."

I didn't answer, and she wasn't expecting a response. I could certainly get work as a midwife at the hospital once it was rebuilt. People always need nurses, especially amid a worldwide conflict like this; you couldn't let an able woman like me go to waste for nothing. People would understand.

"Aye, we've all to survive one way or another," she whispered, staring at me with her bleary, film-star eyes.

Suddenly I felt a surge of longing for her. I wanted to lean into her, sniff her breasts, her milky neck, but something held me back. How I had betrayed her. The fetuses I'd hurled into the stove. Did she suspect anything? Her expression was as open and vacant as ever before, and buttoned away behind her reindeer-skin coat.

She eagerly began imagining the future. Uuno would take me to the altar, and Lisbet would find somebody too. A rich man from the Kemi Forestry Company, for instance. They'd build a house right next to Big Lamberg's cabin, and soon there would once again be logs to float downstream from Salla. They might even hook us a few logs too, farther upstream and under cover of night. We could all work together and celebrate when the house was ready.

"I hate his boots."

"Well, wash them," she said.

Soon the Rovaniemi fair will open again with the bearded woman, Sámi folk in sleds wrapped in animal skins, loggers, and at Midsummer a crocodile and two Negroes would arrive in a bus just as they did in 1929, do you remember? After Stalag Zweiglager 322, Lisbet's prattle seemed like a blissful daydream. I wanted to believe her. I wanted to sniff both of them closely, Lisbet and the lie. Why not, indeed? Where else could I go?

I approached the driver and asked what time he was leaving. He was smoking a hand-rolled cigarette and wiped the frost from beneath his nose on the back of his glove as though he hadn't heard me. I straightened the wolf-skin coat on my shoulders and repeated the question, louder this time, in the resonant voice I had used at the camp to give the prisoners orders. The driver flicked the cigarette butt into the wind with his thumb and middle finger.

"Wh-wh-whore," he stammered, and hacked a carefully considered glob of spit on my leather brogues.

"Excuse me?" I turned to look at the driver, and he met my stare. A familiar boy, Jaakkima Alakunnas. His pupils were like beads of nickel floating in slush as he repeated it, this time more clearly.

"Whorrre."

I glanced at Lisbet. By the look of her, you could tell there was soft, sugary hair growing in her nostrils and armpits. Lisbet gave us her film-star smile. Perhaps she would never hear such insults. I'd always had more sensitive ears.

I glimpsed at the other women. I couldn't bring myself to pity them. These weren't the Finnish nurses or Lotta girls from the canteen who had been sent away to work for the Alpine troops. These women probably had no more understanding of the occupiers than what they'd seen in Liinahamari or the Little Berlin district of Rovaniemi. I was a different breed from these sisters, girls as pure as fresh snow, girls who at best might have carried bottles of lemonade into the officers' club. I was the Fritz's whore, and life in a defeated Finland wouldn't be easy for a woman on the losing side of history. The Communists were already polishing their knives, ready to sharpen their teeth on the bones of German brides. On my return I'd have a bastard child in my arms. I could have picked up venereal diseases in Operation Cattlehouse, infections that even gray ointment mixed from mercury and reindeer fat wouldn't fix. But there was more, much more, for my wounds were in my soul, and that made them harder to treat. I returned to a decimated Lapland, the bloodstains of our former brothers-in-arms on my skirt, and for what? For a moment of lust, they'd say. For a pair of stockings ripped open at the crotch, some cheap French cognac, a few yellowed, shriveled raisins, an occasional farewell ejaculated on my thighs and rubbed against the fresh, resinous wood of the canteen wall. They wouldn't understand. They wouldn't understand that I had no choice. In all its cruelty, love does not care for age or race.

I turned on my heels and strode toward the customs office. I explained to the officer from the AOK 20 division that I was in the employ of the German army and that I'd been assigned to join the medical corps on the next ship to Narvik.

"*Jawohl,*" said the officer, paging through his gray-covered harbor inventory. "The medical officer on the SS *Donau* has come down with tuberculosis. But you'd have to be mad to go to sea now. The Russians are bombing the hell out of the fjord."

I shrugged my shoulders. The lieutenant glanced at my belongings and muttered that there was a medical warehouse in the harbor where I could pick up some equipment. We both knew that I would get nothing at the field hospital; they were more likely to take a Russian's head off than give me any bandages and penicillin. He stamped my papers. I tied my suitcase straps in the knots I'd picked up at a camp by the White Sea, slung them over my shoulders, and called for Masha. I turned to take a last look at the Liinahamari harbor. The Neitiniemi Peninsula was covered in lingering swathes of magical white mist. To the left stood the fish-powder factory and the Fisheries Association wharf. Terraced barracks rose farther up the hill. The customs office gleamed white. The monastery was just out of sight; so too were the hotel and the morgue behind it. Along the quayside people were hurriedly hammering, hauling, dragging, tying, and pulling all manner of war equipment into steel-hulled ships, men and sacks being hurled on board. The black loaders, the hydraulic lifts, the trawlers, and factory chimneys, even the submarine wharf that the English had cobbled together at the far end of the fjord—everything was as it had been when I'd left, and yet everything had changed. Behind Parkkina an army of sixteen thousand crosses had been raised in honor of the fallen Germans. Gone were the red frilly hat and the Skolt boy fishing on the jetty, the evening we'd spent drinking schnapps from glasses decorated with sun crosses.

I raised my eyes to the sky one final time and prayed that the Lord would give me a sign. And right then I had a revelation. A Russian rocket appeared from somewhere behind Kalastajasaarento. It flew straight up into the sky and hit a star, and no one saw the star falling but me. It was the Dog Star, the same star I'd shown you so many times. It burned bright and landed somewhere nearby. Three angels began playing their trumpets above Pelastusvuori, and I recalled the evening we'd lain on the roof of the barracks and I remembered what you'd said to me. The Lord had indeed sent me a sign. I turned on my heels. Lisbet remained on the back of the truck, radiant and weeping, as with dry eyes I walked toward the ramp leading up to the armored SS *Donau*, with Masha trailing behind me.

TITOVKA

Johannes Angelhurst

September 25, 1944

Everybody has gone. I woke up in the chill of the barracks, without my underpants. I had wet myself. The last time such a thing happened was when Father died and I saw the Kurbits chest. The chest, that pointless relic, proof that Father never achieved anything of substance. Now that same chest is up at Dead Man's Fjord. And it is the same chest, though I can't explain how it got there. How is Annikki, my mother? Is she happy with my uncle? How does Horst Wessel rest in his grave, the martyr of the Third Reich, the bully about whom we now sing songs? And why? Because he had the good sense to die in time and is no longer here to witness our shame.

I lie still. My skin has frozen fast to the mattress. I have no underpants. If there is one thing Father taught me, it is that a man should always have a decent pair of underpants. Not those army-issue gray ones, not underpants that other people have used before you. The kind that have a good Husqvarna double seam and that don't catch on the pleats of your khaki trousers. A pair that'll warm you so as not to put the family line at risk. Mother sent a pair like that to the Ukraine just before she married my uncle.

"Wild-Eye," I whisper. "Where are you?"

The swimming pool is ready. I want to tell her. The pool is ready and we can go now. I'd tried to send word to Parkkina, to see if someone would come and help with the pool. We'll have to decide where to siphon the water. We'll need one of the engineers from the new fortifications to explain how it's done. The Titovka River is too low-lying, but perhaps we could set up a pumping system. If nothing else, I'd like some recognition for the work I've done. *By the tomb of Alaric, Johannes, what a fine worker you've been. You put the aims of the Third Reich before your own needs. You are a hero like no other, a magnificent, unerring warrior.* Less acknowledgment than this would be enough. But, Wild-Eye, it is their utter indifference that offends me. Completing such a job in the frozen, godforsaken earth is no laughing matter. You have to understand the density of the soil and the fact that mining work at Kolosjoki is constantly shaking the ground beneath us. You have to make sure nothing ancient escapes the grip of the earth and flies into people's dreams.

Wild-Eye does not come and listen to me.

Instead, I lie in the empty Cabinet and stare out at the stream. A bird's wing has become caught in the turbine. It spins slowly, hypnotically, like an angel that has flown into a Ferris wheel. I can't catch its smell, though it must surely smell of flesh sliced in two, of a feather pillow and intoxicants, for that is what blood is. I need some medicine. Then I'll be able to think clearly.

I step outside. There is no one in sight. No trusted prisoners, no Holger Heider, whom if truth be told I haven't seen for some time. Where has he gone? Where are the Sonderkommandos? Hermann

Gödel isn't here. This means I have become the Hauptsturmführer, the camp's leader. But there is nobody for me to order around. The SS officers are nowhere to be seen, and the military police are gone.

The O wing of the barracks complex is on fire. The Hilfswilligers' D unit has collapsed; the basement is ablaze. The water tanks behind Operation Cattlehouse have been emptied and the ammunition warehouse blown up. This is a party to which nobody else has been invited.

But I am content. I have completed my work.

Approaching it wasn't easy. A covering of sleet. My footsteps crunching on the ground; I went to the swimming pool and swore I'd cordially inform the Party that next time they could find someone else to do these impossible tasks. Gravel covered in early-morning frost, frozen footprints. Bare feet. You can tell the level of the degeneration from the height of the plantar arch in a human foot. Many of those who have passed here seem to have a Greek-shaped sole. How is this possible? These degenerates, this human detritus from the bend in the Volga. The people of the ancient Minoan civilization were famous for their delicate plantar arch, and the foot of Alaric's beloved was set in gold and preserved in his tomb. I know this is true. Gödel once went off in search of the tomb of Alaric at the upper reaches of the Busento River. All they found was a footprint cast in gold. My beloved Wild-Eye has the most beautiful plantar arch in the world. Her heel is too big, but her toes are pretty.

There was a sudden pain in my big toe. Only now did I notice that I too was barefoot. I bend down to pull a shard of glass from my foot. It looks like a cracked lens from a little boy's round spectacles. I tug the glass free and fling it away.

I arrive at my swimming pool. There is no water inside it, only a thin layer of sleet.

I look at it. I look for a long time.

And I understand.

It is a grave, just as it was always destined to be.

"We'll dig up what we've already buried once," Eduard Dietl had said. Operation 1005.

The mass graves dug in the first years of the war were exhumed, the bodies incinerated, and gold teeth yanked from the mouths of the dead. Bodies that previously had been worthless were now unfortunate pieces of evidence. And I'm no better. I detested the Jews and the conspiracy of the Elders of Zion as much as anybody else. But there at the gravel pit in the Ukraine, they didn't look like they were planning a great conspiracy. They were terrified country folk, children, and grandmothers. That's why I couldn't give the order. And that's why I struck Gödel, for letting those children strip off and climb into the pit.

And that's why I hate Wild-Eye for bringing that Skolt girl of hers into the camp to remind me of it all.

The way a war hound licked the body of a girl lying in the pit.

I sense my memory trying to shield me from something.

There's nothing shielding me now.

Neither my memory nor the medicine.

I stare at the pile of corpses and try to comprehend the sight. The Adolfin has partially left my body. What have I done? I can hardly breathe. I want to rush behind a camera, to flee the aberration in front of me. I can cope with the world when it is upside down in the camera's viewfinder. I understand the world when I have to calculate exposure time, lenses, and shutter speeds. I don't want to see limbs, frosted eyelashes, death surrounded by more death.

Then, amid the myriad bodies, I see something familiar.

A slender, oval hand, a familiar eagle insignia on its middle finger.

Gödel. He is lying there, dead. Killed. Brutally, some might say. I knocked out his teeth at a gravel pit in Babi Yar in 1941, and since that very moment I have lived in fear of his revenge. You can't march the children outside stark naked, I'd said. But they continued to strip off the children's clothes, and I gave the order. I did something else too. I struck Gödel, and that's why he hated me. If it hadn't been for my uncle, I would have been executed. That stray bullet that made me lose my memory. I'm convinced that Gödel was standing just within sight and taking aim.

Suddenly I remember. Wild-Eye. I have to get away from this camp. Think straight now, Johannes!

It's just over twenty miles from here to Parkkina. I have a compass, and I know we're on the sixty-ninth parallel.

Russenstraße has doubtless been heavily mined, and I haven't received any instructions from Liaison headquarters.

I have to lead my troops now.

A temporary retreat to Kirkenes. Gödel explained it all long ago.

Operation Nordlicht, the scorched-earth tactics.

The sixth and second Alpine Jaeger divisions have bases on the banks of Vuoresjoki and Litsajoki. So-called *Stützpunktlinien*, bunkers strengthened with concrete and steel pipes, complete with trenches, cannons, command posts, in three rows one after the other. The Russians will never get past that. Or will they?

I remember something else. I remember what Wild-Eye told me.

My child, out there somewhere.

I must get to Dead Man's Fjord.

Wild-Eye will explain everything.

Once the war ends we'll go to Berlin, to the shores of Lake Wannsee, the call of dozens of cuckoos, the thick aroma of tree resin, the glint of the whitewashed veranda, the circus lanterns lighting up each night on the opposite shore in shades of red, yellow, and green. We'll sit in deck chairs beneath the Bavarian lilac bushes. I'll have the fool's-gold-plated lead chapel that we found in Kolttaköngäs brought back for you.

Wild-Eye can wash her hair in nightingale's milk. Everything I have, I will give her. For of the three Norns, it seems after all that Wild-Eye is Skuld, the future.

PART SIX

DEAD MAN'S DIARY

Scarface to Whale Catcher (SOE),
June 12, 1944:
Code name Hyyryläinen is an informant. Sends false information to Murmansk, has now lured the NKVD partisans to their death (as per Funkgegenspiel*).*

Whale Catcher to Scarface:
Mission: Hyyryläinen to be eliminated.

Scarface to Redhead (Gestapo),
September 30, 1944:
Funkgegenspiel *completed. Contact revealed. Report immediately to Gestapo headquarters in Tromsø.*

November 1, 1944

My dearest daughter,

I am an evil person. I have lied, informed on people, sent men to their death. I have betrayed the Soviet Union, the Allies, and the Third Reich. I've betrayed my fatherland too, though it betrayed me first. I don't regret informing on Redhead. I told him to go to Tromsø and report for duty. At the same time, I sent a message to Gestapo headquarters accusing him of having nationalist tendencies. I hope they throw him out of a window and feed his body to the crabs.

I don't want to lie any longer, not the way I lied back in the summer to save my skin. The Merchant paid me a visit. Apparently he'd been wondering how I'd ended up with the only transmitter the Fritz couldn't trace. When was the last time someone was killed out at Dead Man's Fjord, he asked me. Then he cocked his pistol and answered the question himself.

"I can tell you, and it'll be soon enough."

Fearing for my life, I told him about the notebooks and the information I'd been gathering. Those notebooks contained plans for Operations Midnight Sun and Birch Tree, for the burning of Lapland throughout Finland and Norway; they held details of operations in Vadsø and Varanger as well as information on all the barricades. Those notebooks contained the timetables, routes, and positions of important warships. That information and those coordinates would decide the fate of the North—in the Allies' favor. And I am the only man who can decipher it.

I made him an offer. The Merchant's mate, Hyyryläinen, has lost his mind, spends his time herding his reindeer around the fells and curling his hair all day long. We'll kill him. I've been responsible for the sinking of at least twenty ships and submarines since 1942. I'm an asset; I can be of use. All the while I was frantically calculating things in my head. Jaarikki Peltonen, our Gestapo go-between, would soon be taken out. By assuming his identity, I might finally be able to shake off the NKVD. I've asked for a transfer dozens of times. The answer is always the same: Comrades must remember the oath they have sworn. Should a Comrade fail to keep his word, the righteous hand of the Soviet Union will catch up with him in any corner of the world.

At that point I was ready to go back on my promise, on all the promises I'd ever made.

If I handed the notebooks over to the Allies, I'd finally be able to get out of this fjord.

The Merchant placed his gun on the table and scratched his beard.

"Very well then."

It was that simple.

Hyyryläinen was killed with a single shot to the back of the head. My life was spared. I tasted my new name: Jaarikki Peltonen. The police commissioner arrived and concluded that I had committed suicide. We informed the Allies of the information we'd uncovered, and we would have shipped out the Kurbits chest straight away, but the Tommies forbade us. Poor cowards. They were like that back at the time of the Murmansk Legion too, swilling their tea and sniggering at the logger lads' prattle. They wanted to wait for reinforcements from the Shetland Islands. Apparently they were worried about another catastrophe like the one at Lingen in 1941, when an entire battalion of volunteers was massacred in an instant. Instructions eventually came from above: we could fetch our pipes and the diaries in the spring once the fog over the Arctic Ocean finally lifted.

That day the moisture in the air clung to the bone toggles on the Merchant's coat, and the body of a drowned German soldier became tangled in our fishnet. We received the coordinates for the ship.

"Listen up, Pietari. Time to put bread on the table."

We set off and found ourselves a decent haul of loot on board a warship that had run aground at the skerry. Bjørne suggested we pick up the jotters left behind at Dead Man's Fjord right there and then. I agreed. Foggy weather is good weather: no bombing raids in fog.

Things got more complicated when I saw you on the cliffs. It fair pained my heart. You were so noble, so strong and untouched, a cloudberry petal just like your mother. My Weird-Eye, my one and only. Bjørne would have murdered you long ago. Perhaps you never realized quite how many times I managed to stop him just in time. I begged him: we can get the information another way. Still, by then he'd already killed the dog.

Thankfully Aune Näkkälä's boy turned up and promised to take you to Sweden. At that point I figured I might never see you again, and I'd had enough of the skulduggery. I wanted you to know that there was still someone in this world who cares about you. I couldn't help but reveal myself to you, though I'm not sure whether you believed me. I'll give these letters to Aune's boy. You can open them once you're far away.

The following day I stared out to sea as long as the light allowed. In the early evening I caught sight of Jouni's boat at the northern end of the fjord. To my relief I saw that there were three people in the boat: a man, a woman, and a girl. So you were on your way to safety after all. Because I can help you no longer, lass. I received a communication from Whale Catcher: "Directions from SOE to assume control of the resistance base at Dead Man's Fjord. If Gestapo officers arrive at the cabin, all occupants to be eliminated."

For the first time in my life, I pray to God. Whether it's the god of their crooked cross or not, it's all one. I pray that you'll soon be safe, because now Bjørne has resolved to shoot anyone who gets too close to the cabin.

DEAD MAN'S FJORD

January 1945

I've spent all day reading the letters Jouni left me, weeping. With joy or sadness, I don't know. The bairn will be born soon. The contractions are coming every five minutes now. I'm dilated two inches, but still I can't feel the child's head. For the first time in my life, I'm afraid. What if it's a breech birth? How will I turn it around? With forceps? Impossible. I try to measure my pulse—it's elevated, and I know my heart is racing. I'm worried about the bairn. Is the umbilical cord wound round the neck? I've done this a thousand times and still I'm terrified. I cry for help, first to God, then to you, Johannes. Neither of you answers me. I can see myself from above. Push! I can hear myself from above. Push! I grip the cradle ball my mother gave me. I squeeze so hard that blood seeps between my knuckles. I try to find that cool sense of calm and knowledge that I've always had. But it has gone, abandoned me. Now God no longer uses me as his instrument. Now he has no mercy. I cannot lie down; the position feels wrong.

I'm dilated three inches.

At times I have to crouch on all fours on the floor and shout.

Come to me, Johannes! Come right now!

My thighs stiff from the exertion, I lurch back and forth across the cabin and howl. The liquid glow of the Northern Lights cuts through the grainy windowpane; frozen wind claws inside through the window frames and at the corners of the cabin. I pick up the Dead Man's pipe lying on the floor. *Forgive Our Sins,* read the words delicately engraved along its side. How lonely must my father have been out here. And how tortured I must have been after my time in Operation Cattlehouse that I didn't notice the tenderness his battered old soul was showing me, in happiness, sadness, and pain. Far too many strands of sorrow have already been crammed into this vast world.

There is no way out now. It's the door's fault.

"Only the boastful let their doors open outward," Big Lamberg used to say, and for once he was right. Up here at the Arctic Ocean, you should never put hinges on the outside of the door. Now I understand why. The wind will soon whip the loose snow into a drift six-feet high. Red tallow drips through my mind, and a whispering fear resides in the roots of my hair. Silent sea spirits burrow into my inner ear, hauling themselves along the green tunnel between the ice and the shore beneath the receding tide, all the way to Dead's Man's Cabin. They have bare, concave heels and curved nails that could slice the frozen earth asunder. I've been thawing the snowdrift for water and burned the last of the peat to warm the water. My child will soon be born. Our child, Johannes. That's one thing you can't deny, Johannes, you damned beast, you monster-child, you tainted tosspot, twotch teaser, knob stump, backdoor buggerer, you tern tickler, barnacle shafter, honey cock, skew-eyed peeping tundra-tom, you cod-booted clown. The man who wasn't good enough to become a fighter pilot for the Third Reich. You didn't have it in you to swoop through the air into the enemy's camp. The only thing you shot was your load into young women, first Lisbet, then me, and you've taken responsibility for neither of us, content instead to dig your pit, to immortalize the annihilated, to photograph the dead, and to lie on the roof of the barracks, counting the stars. Let me tell you a thing or two about love.

I have killed for you. I have been humiliated, crawled through the world's mires for you. I have been abused. Strange members have been shoved into my toothless mouth, I have been forced to swallow lengths of Balkan-tasting sausage, and nearly choked on the Kyrgyz prisoners' rancid ejaculations. I have been ordered to kneel on all fours, stuck fingers into myself, spread my legs. Foreign objects have been thrust into my every orifice, one after the other. I have been beaten, spat upon, demeaned. I have betrayed, and others have betrayed me. I have abandoned my God, and he has abandoned me. I have found my father and lost him again. But for your sake I still dare to live, because your presence makes all these wrongs seem insignificant. For you, I am prepared to do anything and everything. For you, I am willing to die here and now.

DEAD MAN'S FJORD

January 1945

The child was born prematurely. I know precisely what I would have written on the patient's medical card:

> *Relatively old first-time mother, 36 years. Complications, placenta delivered normally. Sex: female.*

The card would say nothing of the child's translucent fingers and toes, twenty in total, each bearing a gleaming pearly nail. It would say nothing of the tiny fist that grips my nipple, nothing of the child's soft, lamb's-wool scent mixed with the smell of blood, pus, and excrement, of the milky liquid trickling from my breasts. It would say nothing of the shadows slithering across the walls, waiting for the petroleum lamp to die out so they can attack us. Nothing of the love that fills me.

My child. Our child.

I place the girl beneath my blouse to sleep; lying on my chest, she can reflect for a moment on the world into which she has arrived. She won't have long to admire it, for I shall soon lose consciousness. Who will look after her out here? Nobody. All at once I wish that my father would arrive, but no. Both Bjørne and Jaarikki think I have gone to Sweden with Jouni. *Now they'll shoot at anything that moves along the fjord.* I know what that means.

I call the girl Helena, though it won't matter. She'll die anyway, poor child, the silent creature, barely half the length of my forearm. We've run out of peat for the stove, and I haven't the energy to chop up the furniture. But the girl suckles at my nipples all the same, sucks as though she has every intention of living, of surviving. She puckers at my breasts, now expressing milk as they never had before, before you took me and held me there on the bed of hay. With one hand I squeeze the girl against my chest, and with the other I hold my father's pipe. *Forgive Our Sins.* It seems as though I have forgiven my father too, forgiven him for abandoning me and running off to the ends of the earth before turning up here at Dead Man's Fjord and defying death by assuming the identity of the Turku imposter and grifter. I forgive my father. I forgive you, Johannes Angelhurst. I won't forgive Hermann Gödel. His fate is now in the hands of a greater power.

DEAD MAN'S FJORD

Johannes Angelhurst

February 2, 1945

Arrived. Finally. It's a wonder, as my snowsuit is ripped between the legs and one of my skis snapped as it struck a branch jutting up from the ground. I took the skis from a Norwegian soldier who'd frozen to death in the snow. Before that, with snowshoes on my feet, I'd paced across the frozen surface of the raging glacial streams as they roared defiantly at death. When the ice cracked, I hopped across the slabs of ice in the northern gullies, with each step careful not to tread on one of the Wehrmacht's parting gifts. In every cove along the fjord, houses were smoldering, reduced to piles of ash, and the gnawed, rotting carcasses of slaughtered farm animals littered the ground. Once I thought I saw the devil painting a solitary wall with his tail, but it was just the wind playing with the shadows. Another time I wandered too far inland and found myself at the end of a road. Out of sheer exhaustion I began walking along the road, when suddenly I noticed movement down by the stream. An Arctic fox was nibbling something, but darted into its snowy burrow as soon as it heard me. In the frozen stream I saw a boot, and what's more, another boot next to it. What a stroke of luck, I thought. My own moleskin boots were worn through at the heels, so I approached the boots carelessly and full of joy. Only then did I see the stump of a leg protruding from one of the boots and saw what had happened to its former owner. Gingerly retracing my own footsteps, I walked back to the tundra and continued my journey, far away from the mines left behind by my compatriots. Aside from that boot and the section of bone jutting from inside it, I saw no signs of other humans. Three fjords farther along I came to a torched cluster of barracks, nothing but a single signpost swaying in the wind on the main street: *Zum Friseur.* To the barbers.

Dead Man's Fjord. Moonlight whitens the dull shadows of loneliness. For a moment I am a feather; I float across the moonlit fjord, through a landscape devoid of waterbirds. My own laughter startles me, a laughter that no one is there to greet. For the cabin is nothing but a silent scab on the Lord's skin. Why is there no smoke coming from the chimney?

DEAD MAN'S FJORD

Late January 1945

I shall write a few more lines before the last candle burns out. The bairn is quiet and won't eat. I've made her a crib from an old fish crate lined with cotton wool and reindeer hide, and placed it next to the stove. Puffs of chilled breath rise from her nose. The corners of the room have frosted over, but I'm not worried. I can feel you getting closer, Johannes! I sit here in the bluish dusk of the winter darkness, still bleeding, still listening. I leap to my feet every time I think I hear your voice out in the gorge and run outside to greet you, for I've no intention of punishing myself a moment longer. And if I die now, I'll die knowing that you are on your way. I've been waiting so long, and now you are finally coming to my side.

I already know precisely how you will arrive, how the sound of a puttering outboard motor will wind its way around the fell, and I'll sense it immediately. It's you, Johannes, you and nobody else. My heart will start thumping in my chest, and my breath will gallop beside your boat, just like Hilma, all the way to the fjord. I'll hear the boat crunch against the shore, and the wood burner will stop chattering. I almost wish Hilma would start barking and frolicking, because that would give me an excuse to run up to you, headlong, but of course the old dog would sense straight away that this is an expected guest and start writhing at your feet, just as I would like to do. But I don't step into the yard. Instead, I listen, listen to the way the Norwegian hiking boot on your left foot creaks with every step. How right you were, Johannes, when you said that if anyone fully understood the Fritz's flat feet, it was the Norwegians.

Your breath. The inexplicable, comfortless yearning that suddenly grips my throat, and for a blinding moment I feel how I have longed for that breath for many months, for those murmuring snores in the nighttime silence, your leisurely pottering during the day, your breathless ardor in my ear in the evenings. How close you are, yet how much I fear that something might happen right now, that you might suddenly think that your life should have taken another direction, elsewhere, that you have another woman in Aachen and that your fourth son, colorblind, needs a new set of red-and-green crayons. I fear you'll remember that there are places in this world other than Dead Man's Fjord, that you'll suddenly choose another reality, sweet evenings at the Berlin Tiergarten, nights filled with Negro music and green glass beer bottles at the ladies' lips. That you'll simply change your mind, turn on your heels, and leave. That something will occur to you at the last minute, strike you on the head, a burning ember or a dead smew, a comet the size of a tern, wrenched from its orbit, the claw of a saber-toothed tiger carried in the talons of an eagle. All of a sudden the door is open and you're standing on the threshold, without knocking, without asking a thing or greeting me. You pull off your boots; they're stained with motor oil, and you explain you had to change the oil in the boat's motor for the first time in your life. That's why you took so long. I stand up; the chair creaks. Now I'm walking across the floor, a floor that's six feet across and an eternity long. I've decided to greet you calmly, take your coat like a true hostess, and show you to your chair to wait while I fetch a mattress from the attic, explaining that I wasn't expecting a guest so soon, look at the clock, lean nonchalantly against the chimney stack, and let the full wonder of you sink in. But I can't. I come to you, and you pull me to your chest. I kiss you and smell you, and I know that you are here and that you don't long to be elsewhere after all. We speak into each other's mouths at the same time, the way lovers do after an interminable absence, and I press myself against you and take a step back again, self-assured, as though I'd never been able to step away, to let go of anyone before. I show you the bairn. I take her in my arms and huddle beneath the blankets, waiting for you to follow me, for once without having to be asked.

And you come to me, I make room for you, make us a downy nest all of our own, and we lie in each other's arms in the foldout bed at Dead Man's Cabin, there among the lambskins and the lemming shit. You sniff the bairn, sniff my hair, kiss me on the forehead.

"Have you been eating fruit?" you ask me just as you'd asked before.

I answer just as I've answered every time before: "Why so?"

"You smell fruitful."

"I've already given you one bairn."

"My wee girl."

"You took your time."

"Sorry."

That evening I'll not be sad, I'll shed only a few tears, and you'll wipe them away the way only a chosen few know how, erasing them for good and leaving the skin dry, not just December-damp and leaving me to weep some more. Good tear-wipers don't grow on trees, and in that respect too, my bird's-milk boy, you are blessed. You burrow down my stomach and blow a raspberry into my navel, and when I try to resist, you suck the brand mark on my left arm.

"Why did you do that?"

"I don't know. Because I want to be yours."

"Who are you, Johannes?"

"Don't know. A killer. You've no idea what I've had to do."

"No, but I can guess right enough."

"Do you really want to love a man like this?"

"I don't want to," I reply. "But I do."

Because I cannot not love you, and we can't choose things like this. For now I know that you are the man the Lord has sent to test me, the one who will reveal to him the goodness within me. You've a good, dear soul, Johannes. No matter what flames this war has scorched you in, they cannot burn that soul away. You have the most beautiful balls in the world and the unhurried soul of a mushroom picker, and for that reason alone I could never turn my back on you. Where once there was nothing but my own loneliness, now we are a trinity beneath the reindeer skin. You light the calabash I inherited from my father, and the tobacco aroma wafts through a hole in the tarpaulins and out into the frigid air, and I tell you about my father and show you the diaries, and explain that I believe he would have been happy for us. *Forgive Our Sins.*

You tell me that Hedda, Masha, and Jouni send their greetings. Lisbet is pregnant again, this time by an officer of the Control Commission. Apparently she now lives at the grandiose Hotel Torni in Helsinki and makes sure her family has everything it needs and is once again allowed to travel freely around the south of Finland.

Then there's the bairn. You take her in your arms and babble to her. A girl is better than a boy, you say, she'll never be ordered to kill another person. To that, I say nothing. Perhaps the water for the tea is ready. I hand you a cup, you drink your tea, and then the whales arrive. For they haven't yet bid us farewell but return that evening to greet us. In perfect silence we watch the fountains of water from their blowholes, and even Hilma knows not to bolt around the cabin now because there's no rush. We're not hurrying anywhere any longer, for she's alive after all; how could I possibly have thought any differently? I rest my head on your shoulder, blow on your nipple, and pinch it beneath your thick woolen jacket.

And even in the midst of my daydream, I know that I must ask, ask no matter how much I fight against it: "When are you off again?"

And you answer me, your eyes squinted, your voice full of the laughter of happier times, a sound I enjoy so much, that I've longed for, and everything is forgiven, now and evermore, my Lord, thank you, amen, and as smoke billows from the corner of your mouth, you take a final glance at the whales as they flip their tails against the boulder jutting out in the fjord.

"I'm not going anywhere. I'm staying put."

DEAD MAN'S FJORD

February 1945

When I finally awoke, there you were. For some reason it didn't surprise me at all. You lay there, staring at me, half-covered in strange hair, there in the light of the petroleum lamp by the bed. It was the most beautiful sight I'd ever beheld. It felt as though I'd woken from the dead. You leaned over and took my toe in your mouth, sucked the life back into it. I felt the warmth returning. It crept back along my fingertips and the soles of my feet, painful and excruciating, rushed through my limbs with such force that I thought my veins would burst. Then the pain subsided, and I knew I was truly alive. I could hear the wind rattling in the stove. That and the sound of the tiny heart beating against my chest. The bairn hadn't died after all. We are together once again.

I have nothing left to tell.

EPILOGUE

In summary, the deceased were found on an iron foldout bed, lying next to each other. The murder of the woman and my grandfather, Johannes Angelhurst, seems to have taken place while they were asleep. The bodies were picked up by the Norwegian police, who had received an anonymous tip. The deaths were registered at Kirkenes, and the post-mortem report mentioned the cause of death only in vague terms; the official documentation was drawn up by an outsider. At the time there were around twenty thousand prisoners of war in Norway and fifty thousand German soldiers attempting to leave the country. An isolated double homicide did not therefore spark particular interest, even though one of the deceased was an officer of the Third Reich.

Dead Man's Fjord has a special place in local folklore: the area was thought to be cursed. Due to particularly strong magnetic fields, compasses do not function normally, but point to a location at least twelve degrees to the east. The precise location of the fjord is not known. Legend has it that when the area was charted in the eighteenth century under the direction of Friedrich Georg Wilhelm Struve, local cartographers left a blank spot at the site. According to local lore, a cabin stood there at the time of Struve's exploration, and the cabin's original owner had met with a similarly violent death. The identity of his murderer is still unknown, though rumors suggested it had something to do with local piracy and animal abuse.

The identity of the murderer of my grandmother and Johannes Angelhurst remained unknown until as late as 2008, when one Bjørne Asbjørn, a local merchant and veteran of the Norwegian resistance movement, finally admitted to the crime on his deathbed. He confessed to the murders in writing at his home in Lakselv and wished this new information to be entered into the official case file. The culprit felt great remorse for his acts and stressed that everything had occurred as the result of a misunderstanding. Asbjørn claimed that the agent operating under the code name Scarface played no role in the murders; on the contrary, Scarface had assured him that the female victim had already left the fjord in the company of Jouni Näkkälä. Asbjørn, however, was aware that the deceased was still residing at the cabin in Dead Man's Fjord, and claimed that eliminating her was a matter of necessity. Asbjørn had already noted the deceased's connection with one Thørgen Knepps, alias Redhead, who had served as an informant and a provocateur for the Gestapo.

The background to the case is as follows: Bjørne Asbjørn and Jaarikki Peltonen had been using the cabin inhabited by my grandmother as a base from early 1940 onward. At that time, a telegrapher who had been enlisted to serve with international troops had moved into the cabin. The role of Scarface was to intercept messages from passing German vessels and to report on these both to the British intelligence services and to the joint Norwegian and Swedish resistance movements. Due to its remote location, the fjord was ideally suited for undercover radio communication with the British.

Scarface was known to have held both Finnish and Soviet citizenship, and during the war he worked as a double, and perhaps even a triple, agent. During his final months at the cabin, his sympathies shifted strongly toward the Finnish and Norwegian resistance movements. It appears that Scarface was of some significance in intercepting radio signals. The sinking of the German warship the Tirpitz *signaled a dramatic power shift during the period 1942–1943. Ultimately the damage to the warship was of largely psychological significance.*

The role of the Gestapo agent operating under the code name Scarface was revealed to the resistance movement in early summer 1944, and a warrant was released for his assassination. At this point Scarface, whose real name was Pietari Kutilainen, revealed his archive of intercepted communications to Bjørne Asbjørn, whom he convinced that he possessed information that could be of vital importance to the Allies. Moreover, he suggested that he switch identities with Jaarikki Peltonen. Thus Peltonen was murdered, and Pietari Kutilainen, alias Scarface, assumed his identity. After this, Asbjørn and Scarface agreed to hand over their archives to the resistance movement. Their plan derailed when the female victim moved into the cabin. When war broke out between Finland and Germany on September 15, 1944, retrieving the so-called Russian chest, where the archived information had been stashed, became a necessity. Despite repeated attempts and warnings, the female victim refused either to vacate her new abode or relinquish the chest containing the vital information. When a German SS officer arrived at the fjord in early 1945, Asbjørn decided to act. My grandmother is the only known female to have been eliminated by the resistance movement in northern Norway. Between 1940 and 1945 the resistance movement executed a total of sixty-five informants with German sympathies.

Nothing is known of the movements of Pietari Kutilainen, alias Scarface, after 1944. Bjørne Asbjørn claims that Kutilainen set off for northern Sweden in search of his daughter and refused to continue working for the resistance.

A few words should be said about the life of my grandmother and Johannes Angelhurst. They lived together in sin for nine months. They had a child, my mother, Helena Angelhurst, whom Bjørne Asbjørn handed into the care of Jouni and Hedda Näkkälä in the spring of 1945. It seems the Näkkäläs also had an adopted daughter called Masha, as well as two sons from Hedda's previous marriage. Hedda Näkkälä, formerly Knepps, was one of the few women to survive the Germans' revenge operations against local civilians in 1943. As part of Operation Midnight Sun and Operation Wild Duck, German troops torched entire villages and murdered around three hundred civilians in northern Norway. Hedda married Jouni Näkkälä in 1945. Of Masha Näkkälä, we know the following: her name appears on a medical matriculation register. According to this document, she studied at the medical faculty of the University of Tampere and later worked as a general practitioner in the municipalities of Ivalo and Rovaniemi.

Other observations: judging by his diary entries, Johannes Angelhurst, my grandfather, suffered from acute post-traumatic stress disorder, presumably triggered after taking part in the massacre at Babi Yar, Ukraine, September 29–30, 1941, when over thirty-seven thousand Jews, Gypsies, Communists, and other undesirables were summarily executed and buried in mass graves. My grandfather's precise role in these events is unclear; however, as a lieutenant and commander with Einsatzgruppe C, he likely gave the orders as opposed to merely carrying them out. Nazi Party documentation reveals that the majority of the officers involved in the bloodbath were later transferred to low-level assignments away from the front line. While at the Titovka camp, however, Johannes Angelhurst was forced to take part in Operation 1005, which involved destroying evidence of previous atrocities. It is assumed that well over a thousand such operations took place across the European continent. Bodies were exhumed, their bones crushed, and valuable items, such as gold teeth and rings, were collected. After this, the remaining evidence was covered with earth.

With regard to the deceased's account of events at the Titovka camp, a number of matters should be considered. Around three hundred Jews fought in the Finnish army, defending their homeland. There was no Jewish civilian population in the areas of northern Finland occupied by the Germans. However, there is evidence to suggest that captured Russian soldiers were checked to establish whether they were circumcised, and that a small number of Jewish prisoners were executed when transferring them to a separate camp was impractical. The Finnish army also handed over a number of Jewish prisoners to the Germans. There were no so-called extermination camps in German-occupied areas of Finland and Norway, though the death rate at some prison camps in these areas was equivalent to that at the death camps in Eastern Europe.

There is no concrete evidence of the existence of Operation Cattlehouse. We know, however, that the Soviet Army enlisted female soldiers too, and that when captured, these women were subjected to brutal sexual violence at the hands of soldiers and other prisoners. It is also true that Nazi Germany maintained a "reward system" by which women were forced into sexual relations with guards and prisoners. All documentation from the Titovka camp was destroyed during the German retreat.

A few other facts about the deceased, my grandfather Johannes Angelhurst's beloved, and the protagonist of this story, are worthy of note. The Rovaniemi parish registers of 1908, the assumed year of her birth, show no record of a girl of that name, and there is no mention of a nurse meeting her description in the archives of the Petsamo field hospital during the years of the Winter War of 1939–1940. Neither is there any mention of her in the records of the Red Cross or the Lotta Svärd auxiliary organization for women.

Helena Angelhurst
Sammatti, Finland
October 20, 2011

ACKNOWLEDGMENTS

The Finnish National Council for Literature, the Finnish Cultural Foundation, the Jenny and Antti Wihuri Foundation, the Alfred Kordelin Foundation, the WSOY Literature Foundation, the Arts Center Finland Board of Library Grants, the Finnish National Archive.

Special thanks to the following experts and other individuals who influenced and assisted in the preparation of this book:

Jussi Kyrö, Ville Laurila, Marjut Aikio, Lars Westerlund, Markku Pääskynen, Lasse Klemm, Antti Meriläinen, Antti Kasper, Jan Forsström, Ville Vuorjoki, Alexandra Stang, and Ville Piirainen.

ABOUT THE AUTHOR

Photo © WSOY / Ofer Amir

Katja Kettu is an award-winning Finnish writer. Born in Rovaniemi, Finnish Lapland, in 1978, Kettu works not only as a novelist but also as a columnist and director of animated films. Her books are suffused with traditional Finnish nature mysticism and the richness of northern Finnish dialects. Kettu is also known for startling plots and original, poetic language. After her 2005 debut, *Surujenkerääjä* (*The Sorrow Collector*), Kettu released several books that portray lives on the margins of history. *Hitsaaja* (*The Welder*) combines the fate of the cruise ship *Estonia* with the story of the Far North. *Kätilö* (*The Midwife*) depicts a passionate love story set against the severe backdrop of World War II's Arctic front in Lapland. This Runeberg Prize–winning book became the year's most widely read title in Finland, and translation rights have been sold to nineteen countries. A feature film adaptation premiered in September 2015. Her collection of short stories, *Piippuhylly* (*The Pipe Collector*), followed, featuring many similar themes to *The Midwife*. Kettu's novel *Yöperhonen* (*Hawk Moth*) is a tale of tenacity and survival spanning to the bare landscapes of northern Europe and the fringes of central Asia. Translation rights have been sold to nine countries. *The Midwife* is her English debut.

ABOUT THE TRANSLATOR

David Hackston is a British translator of Finnish and Swedish literature and drama. He graduated from University College London in 1999 with a degree in Scandinavian Studies and now lives in Helsinki where he works as a freelance translator.

Notable publications include *The Dedalus Book of Finnish Fantasy*, Maria Peura's coming-of-age novel *At the Edge of Light*, Johanna Sinisalo's eco-thriller *Birdbrain*, and two crime novels by the late Matti Joensuu. David has recently completed translations of Riku Korhonen's latest novel, *Sleep Close to Me*, and the first two crime novels by Kati Hiekkapelto. His drama translations to date include three plays by Heini Junkkaala, most recently *Play it, Billy!* (2012) about the life and times of jazz pianist Billy Tipton. David was a regular contributor to *Books from Finland* until its discontinuation in 2015. In 2007 he was awarded the Finnish State Prize for Translation.

David is also a professional countertenor and has studied early music and performance practice at Helsinki Metropolia University. He is a founding member of the English Vocal Consort of Helsinki.

Made in the USA
Monee, IL
03 July 2022

99034966R00225